KIZMIC'S JOURNEY

A NOVEL

ODESSA ROSE

COOL WATER
PUBLISHING HOUSE LLC

Baltimore

KIZMIC'S JOURNEY

Odessa Rose begins *Kizmic's Journey* like her earlier works, delving deep into the sounds, smells, and sights of the character's world. As she introduces Kizmic and her supporting characters, you are transcended back in time when the simple joy of shooting marbles in the park could fill a child's whole day. Rose captures the unique worldview of a child whose world (and body) is changing around her, keenly identifying the significance of the smallest details. It's a story we can all see ourselves in, no matter when or how we grew up. It's a game-changing work of literature that is sure to take its place among the classics. Read *Kizmic's Journey* as a gift to your inner child. You won't regret it.
—Jamelle Thomas, filmmaker

Kizmic's Journey by Odessa Rose introduces readers to a young rambunctious girl on the verge of coming of age. Kizmic, a professed tomboy, enjoys playing marbles, spending time with her two best friends, and tormenting her older sister, Kalaya. Rose's writing pulls the reader into Kizmic's world with detailed descriptions that puts the reader right there with the characters. Once you start reading, you will not look forward to putting it down. Kudos to Rose.
—Priscilla C. Johnson, Cilla's Book Maniacs

What an awesome read. Nostalgia. The clothes, the candy, and the neighborhood alone made me revisit my childhood. *Kizmic's Journey* took me to a Judy Blume novel, an episode of "Good Times," and the movie Eve's Bayou. *Kizmic's Journey* is a phenomenal read, sure to peak all ages curiosity. Odessa Rose has surely risen to the occasion on this one!!!
—Teresa Davis, author of *Hysterectomy of the Hood*

"*Kizmic's Journey* takes place in Baltimore, Maryland, though it brings back fond memories of my childhood in Bronx, New York. I say kudos and thank you Mrs. Odessa Rose, for sharing your childhood and letting me recall mine."
—Cheryl Beebe, The Page Turners Book Club

WATER IN A BROKEN GLASS

"Rose's meditative insights into family closeness and loyalty and her exquisite sense of detail make this a promising debut and a strikingly unusual romance."
—Whitney Scott, *Booklist*

"Odessa's writing is the kind that makes literary agents, editors, and publishers salivate. She's a brilliant wordsmith, a master of metaphor, and a wonderful storyteller. Wondering what decision [Tonya] would make had me swiping my phone like a crazy woman, that along with Odessa's beautiful, imaginative writing that swept me into a whirlwind of suspense, anger, frustration, and laughter."
     –Alretha Thomas, Actress

"The manner in which Rose writes this novel is just as vivid and colorful as a newly painted portrait..."
     –Tee C. Royal, The RAWSISTAZ Review

"Mrs. Rose has created real people—flawed, strong, hopeful people—and allowed us to watch their lives unfold and share their struggle, growth and emergence."
     –Talibah Chikwendu, *The AFRO American Newspaper*

"Odessa Rose makes the reader comfortable with the characters, as well as their surroundings and graciously helps the reader to truly understand Tonya's confusion!"
     –Cheryl Robinson, Just About Books Internet Radio Talk Show

"From beginning to end I found myself so engrossed with Tonya that I just couldn't put it down. A definite classic for any lesbian or African American ..."
     –Sistahs on the Shelf

"Boldly and masterfully, the author demonstrates her unique take on a world full of challenges and idiosyncrasies, and blends this understanding with local Baltimore flavor ... this novel fearlessly speaks to an often invisible culture with the hope that the reader will walk away a little more human, a tad more tolerant, and a heck of a lot smarter."
     –Doni Glover, Journalist and On-air Talent

"This is the first novel I've read where homosexuality played a theme with the main character(s), and Rose did an excellent job in writing the scenes and feelings of the characters in a tasteful and realistic manner."
     –Shonell Bacon, Author of *Draw Me With Your Love*

"[This] sensuous story twists and turns . . . It's a joyous journey through eroticism and art alike . . . A major triumph of African-American lesbian literature."
     –Accredited Online Colleges.org

"A fantastic Book!" –Delegate Barbara Robinson

"... Rose's work is a beautifully written love story of personal growth and self-acceptance."
     –Eternity Philops, Author of *Visions of a Cryptic Mystery: Volume One*

"It's about time someone explored or ventured out and wrote about us African American lesbians...as I was beginning to think we didn't exist."
    –Readers Paradise

"[Rose] amazingly portrayed the struggle of coming to terms with the fact that you are something other than straight and doing that while still in a straight relationship."
    –First Draft Publishing

"Rose has written a powerful novel rivaling James Baldwin's *Giovanni's Room* in the intensity of issues that it brings before the reader."
    –Rosa L. Griffin, Author of *Attraction Sexy Tales of Good, Bad, and Ugly Relationships*

"*Water In A Broken Glass* is the most deliciously written book I've read in quite some time."
    –J. Dulcet, AUniQue Publishing Company

"... *Water In A Broken Glass* echoes other memorable works in the canon. Tonya Mimms can be added to the likes of Zora Neale Hurston's Janie in *Their Eyes Were Watching God*. [Rose's] gift for creating characters of depth and settings that carry the taste of reality make this book a real delight for those who prize vivid characters and realistic settings in their fiction."
    –Ed Doyle-Gillespie, *Word House*

"In her first novel, Rose demonstrates that she is a highly capable writer who can confront complex issues and the ripple effect they cause with down to earth language and humor. She blends music, color, and a range of characters and human emotion, thus creating a wonderful field of texture upon which the reader can play."
    –Ann Cobb, Assistant Professor, Coppin State University

"... intensely lyrical and profoundly bittersweet. Rose's voice is unique."
    –Vincent Williams, Author of *Temples*

"Intriguing. Once you encounter the mix of characters you can't put it down."
    –B.J. DeGraff, Black Writers' Guild of Maryland

"The story creates an awareness and a sort of sensitivity towards those who are struggling to learn who they are."
    –Flavor Book Club

"Odessa Rose makes the reader comfortable with the characters, as well as their surroundings, and graciously helps the reader to truly understand Tonya's confusion!"
    –Cheryl Holloway, Author of *The Bane Bath Salts*

IN THE MIRROR

"... intense ... had me on the edge of my seat . . . the entire book."
    -Talibah Chikwendu, *AFRO American Newspaper*

"...very well written...many surprises throughout...The storyline is just amazing."
    -BOOST Book Club

"Characters are Rose's bread and butter, and she does them well, making you feel as if they are your friends and sometimes your enemy, wondering what makes them tick and what will tick them off. In the end, reality bleeds true... The closet will never be the same again after reading *In The Mirror*."
    -Anondra "Kat" Williams, author of *Sista Girl*

"This novel encompasses all the markings of an interesting read— passion, lust, romance, heartbreak, shocking truths, and paralyzing self-discovery."
    -Minister Shinelle Davis Oglesby

"Odessa Rose is the ultimate storyteller and does not disappoint with *Mirror*. This novel promises to open your eyes to infidelity like you've never experienced before ..."
    -Lady Brunchers Book Club

"... a very intense story."
    -APOOO Bookclub

"In the Mirror evokes emotion. The story stays with you."
    -Classy Image Bookclub

"Take a look at *In the Mirror*. You just might see yourself."
    -Dahni McPhail, author of *My Girl Is Your Girlfriend*

Dedicated To

DANA PRYOR

1968-2017

I miss you soooo much, girl.

"Never doubt the gift you have. Your writing touches the soul."

—Uncle Douglas

ACKNOWLEDGMENTS

Kizmic's Journey is not autobiographical, but I was able to draw from the beautiful relationships I have with the great people in my life to write this book as authentically as possible.

Daddy and Mama, you made sure your children were loved, safe, and happy. From Christmas, Thanksgiving, and Easter dinners, Sundays in church, Birthday and New Year's Eve parties, trips to Hershey Park, the beach, picnics in Druid Hill Park, Memorial, July 4, and Labor Day cookouts, to family night at the movies in our living room, you gave us a childhood full of wonderful memories.

Michael, I often look back on the day we met in Craig and Anthony's back yard playing basketball when we were twelve years old. We had no idea that we would get married one day and have a beautiful family. Thank you for being such a great friend way back then and for being the best husband and father now.

Brian, Marcus, and Nina, by the time y'all came along, a lot of the joy that made growing up in our northwest Baltimore neighborhood fun was gone. You guys brought much of that joy back for your father and me as we taught y'all the games we played and watched y'all have fun mastering them.

Rachel, you are the greatest little sister a big sister could ever ask for. Linda, it's been a wonderful journey going from childhood to womanhood with you as my best friend. David and Vicky, y'all are the sweetest brother and sister to Michael and me, and the sweetest uncle and aunt to Brian, Marcus, and Nina. Mama Ann, thank you for being such an awesome godmother. Calvin, you are such a cool kid. I am so proud to be your godmother. Yvonne and Elizabeth, thank you for playing four square and hopscotch with me and the kids and reliving our childhood. Rev. Leona, thank you for telling me the amazing stories about your parents and sisters. Dr. Patricia Fitzhugh, thanks for helping me keep a level head. Tina Arthur, thank you for pushing and challenging me as a writer. Kevin Green, thank you for playing church hymns for my research. Mark and Ieisha, I am loving watching you two rear Nyasia, Jaden, London, Lyric, and Aubrie to be such beautiful, smart, and kind people. Clinton, you will always be my baby. Uncle Douglas, thank you for insisting that Michael and I become disciples of Koinonia before dedicating our children. Because of you, they know God the way Mama and Daddy made sure we know God. Aunt Anna, I've watched you in church since I was a little girl, and I've always thought you were one of the most beautiful, intelligent women of God there could be. Pastor Dante K. Miles, you are a great, loving, and extremely supportive pastor and cousin. Mr. Henry Patrick, thank you for telling me your story. Tash, Paul, and Claudette, thanks so much for always supporting me. Jamelle Thomas, you will forever have a place in my heart. Lawrence Banks, thank you for drawing football plays for me so I could get it right. Marlena Neal, thanks for taking such a wonderful author photo. Etosha Bakari, thank you for hooking up my hair for my photo shoot. Jo and Melodie, keep shining, ladies. Canaan, Gabrielle, Gregory, and Mark, your mama and I are so proud of you.

Salute to these Extraordinary People
for their Love, Faith, Courage, Beauty, Strength, and Perseverance

Victoria Rose
Nicole Scruggs
Rachel Brown
Jennifer Houk
Catherine Cody
Jenny Wall
Sam Cook
Deacon Emmanuel Montgomery
Carroll Sonny Smith
Darlene Giles
Valerie Logan
David English Rose
Brandon Geoffrey
Allyne Montgomery
Joseph Montgomery
David Montgomery
Tanya Brown
Sandra Fields
Mildred Ivery
William Miles, Sr.
Reverend John Miles
Reverend Claudia Miles
Michael Mitchell
Linda Bussink
Shirley Richmond
Edith Bernadette Garrett
Karla Brown
Reggie Smith
Genell Collins (Gigi)
Ernest Mathews

CHAPTER

1

"IT'S A HOT, HOT, H-O-T NINETY-EIGHT DEGREES out there, Baltimore!" the disc jockey chimed over the last thirty seconds of the Average White Band's "Pick Up The Pieces."

"I'm talkin' burnin' up! And I'ma heat things up for ya a little bit more." His vinyl voice trumpeted from the speakers of Old Man Graves' new, 1975, Hawaiian blue Chevrolet pickup as he parked in front of Johnston Square Elementary.

Dressed in a pair of gray, motor oil stained coveralls, Old Man Graves got out of the truck, took off his black baseball cap, and wiped the sweat from his brown forehead with the back of his wrinkled hand. Returning the cap to his gray-haired head, he walked stiffly around to the rear and folded down the tailgate. A medium-sized, metal cage with ten black and white Rolling Pigeons was strapped to the bed floor. The pigeons cooed excitedly as Old Man Graves unstrapped the cage then pulled it onto the tailgate.

"I'm Melvin the Supa Dupa Thrilla DJ Spellman," the disc jockey bellowed. "And I want you to keep your radios tuned to 1360 WEBB, baby, on your AM dial while we boogie on down to the smokin' sounds of this little diddy that's burnin' up the charts!"

Fire truck sirens and bells wailed and clanged as the Ohio Players' hot song "Fire" lit up the airwaves. Old Man Graves moistened his thick, dry lips with a few quick licks of his tongue, opened the cage, then blew three short whistles. The pigeons flapped their wings and took flight up and over to Johnston Square Park.

Surrounded by Homewood Avenue, East Biddle, Valley, and East Chase streets, the park sat like an island in the middle of the east side neighborhood.

Under the July sun blazing high in a hazy blue sky, sweaty, teenaged, black boys faced off in a heated five-on-five game of basketball. Neat Afros absorbed the sun's brilliant rays as the boys, some shirtless, others wearing white tank tops, cut off dungarees, blue, green, or black gym shorts, and red or green striped tube socks pulled up to their knees, soared through the air and dunked the ball, just like Kareem. Worn, low and high-cut Chucks, Pro-keds, and Bata tennis shoes squeaked on the weathered black top as the boys dribbled, crossed the ball over in front and behind their backs, and passed it from this guy's hands to that guy's hands in a skillful game of keep away and shoot.

"Shoot!" shouted some guys standing outside the high, chain link fence in a crowd of ballplayers who had next after next after next.

The lanky, walnut brown-skinned boy dribbling the ball pulled up at the top of the key and shot a jumper over the long, twiggy arms of his opponent. The ball went *Sswiissh!* in the rusty, orange hoop that had just a piece of net hanging on one side.

"That's some Docta J shootin' right there, son," he bragged as they hustled to the other end of the court, all the while cutting their eyes at the group of bronze, cocoa, and mahogany girls gathered outside the fenced in court, hoping those cuties had seen the spectacular show they had in part put on for them.

Standing in their flat and platformed sandals, the girls "Ooohed!" at every dunk, layup, and airball, and "Ahhhed!" at every brick, fadeaway, and gooseneck as they ogled the guys' sun-kissed, muscular physiques and put on a show of their own. Their bright pink, orange, and yellow tube and halter tops displayed the smooth flow from their long necks down and across their broad shoulders, down to their flat and top-heavy chests, and finally down to their navels. The shorts, gauchos, and thigh high dresses they wore showed off their slender, curvy, and chunky hips, thin and fleshy thighs, round behinds, and fetching legs. Man, if they weren't built like Thelma on "Good Times," they didn't know who was.

The girls smiled and winked and blinked and rooted for the players they liked, and when the boys took their heads out of the game for a second to smile or wink back, the girls ran their hands through their pressed or *Ultra Sheen* relaxed hair to make sure the hot sun hadn't straightened their curls or beaded up their kitchens. The ones with naturals patted their hairdos, checking to see if the heat had frizzed up their cornrows or soaked up the *Afro Sheen* and flattened their fros or taken the puff out of their Afro puffs.

A few yards away, on the open, grassy field, some younger boys engaged in a fierce championship game of football, dove for touchdowns that would make Mean Joe Greene stand up and cheer. On the other half of the field, a hard-fought baseball game on par with game six of the Reds vs. Red Sox World

Series was in its last inning, and the players, another group of young boys, were crowded around home plate, arguing over whether the batter tipped the ball or struck out.

On the Biddle Street side of the park that faced the old, spooky cemetery, Kizmic Waters was thoroughly enjoying the tail end of this alluring, blistering summer day by indulging in her favorite pastime—lying between two old but still young-looking oak trees in the cool, leafy shade with Cyrus Jackson, better known as CJ, and Theodore Wigfall, better known as Sleepy-eyed Ted. The trunk of the first tree had names and notches carved into it. Kizmic's name had one hundred and one notches and counting under it. More than any girl around her way. Actually, hers was the only girl's name on the tree because none of the other girls her age fooled around with boys the way she did— building and racing go-carts, riding bikes and skateboards, playing football, baseball, stepball, basketball, and Kizmic's first love, marbles. Getting down on her hands and boney knees or stretching out on her belly in the dirt to knuckle her shiny Dragonfly shooter marble was a joy Kizmic had relished since the age of four, when she first discovered a netted bag of them in the toy section inside Montgomery Ward. The brilliant black, amber, cobalt blue, and light blue ribbons that swirled around and throughout those small balls of glass so dazzled her that she opened the package while standing in the aisle. She loved the smooth, hard feel of them in her hand and the clacking sound they made when she poured them out of one palm into the other. But that sound was nothing compared to the clack of her shooter hitting an opponent's marble out of the ring or the clacking noise of her dropping marbles she'd won inside her purple Crown Royal cloth sack *or* the marvelous clacking sound of her dropping her winnings into the thirty-odd cardboard pencil and shoe boxes in which she stored her Blackies, Alley Swirls, Wasps, Corkscrews, Yellow Jackets, Blue Ladies, Tiger Eyes, Popeyes, Grasshoppers, Onion Skins, and Bumblebees. Kizmic thought it was so cool the way the beautiful swirls, swooshes, patches, twirls, coils, spindles, and waves of color resembled the things the marbles were named for. Now at age nine, Kizmic's love for those tiny, round works of art had her lying on the edge of the circle drawn in dirt with her brown-eyed sights set on winning her sixth straight game.

Two long, thick, black plaits, decorated with light blue, twin bead bubble pigtail holders, dangled from either side of Kizmic's head and lie in the dirt with her. Right eye squeezed closed, left trained on the lone, orange cat's eye marble across from her, barely sitting in the ring, Kizmic started to flick her Dragonfly shooter at the dead duck when CJ went, "Meow." Only once. Not loud. Not long. He didn't take the bite out of it by giggling before or behind it. Just let that one soft "Meow" pounce on the air around them, trying to make Kizmic flinch.

On the surface, it seemed like a ridiculous thing to do, but CJ knew what everybody in the neighborhood knew, which was Kizmic had this thing about cats. Where this thing came from, her mother and father couldn't even say. She had never so much as been scratched by a kitten, still nobody could tell Kizmic that cats weren't creeping around waiting for the chance to leap on her and dig their sharp claws into her flesh and scratch and scratch and scratch until the white meat showed. So, whenever she spied one of those flea-bitten, fur-balls, Kizmic didn't fall to her knees and call, *Here, kitty, kitty, kitty!* like other kids who loved stroking a cat's soft, furry body and listening to the sweet sound of its meow and the ticklish rumble of its purr. Instead, Kizmic, who itched at the sight of a cat's nasty, furry body and couldn't stand the menacing sound of its meow or the chilling rumble of its purr, would yell, scream, stomp, kick, and throw things to shoo the mangy beast away.

Even with her thing about cats, CJ should have known that crap wasn't going to work. First of all, when was the last time they saw a cat roaming in the park? Never. Dogs ran around all the time, but not cats. Second of all, they were always meowing, trying to psych her out, especially when they were losing, which they had been doing all week long. Shoot, between the two of them, they only had about thirty marbles left to their names. That's why CJ bought a bunch of cat's eye marbles from the corner store and threw them in the ring, thinking that would at least stop her from playing for keepsies. The only problem with CJ's thinking was Kizmic had learned the hard way that if she didn't play for keepsies when it came to cat's eye marbles, they would always haul out cat's eye marbles, and *she* wouldn't have a marble to *her* name.

So, yeah, she got the whole let's-mess-Kizmic-up-'cause-we-ain't-got-no-more-marbles thing, but meowing...

"Psshhh!" Kizmic said as she cut her eyes up at CJ.

CJ stood bent over top of his marble, hands resting on his kneecaps, legs spread apart so that the soles of his blue and white, low-cut Pro-Keds tennis shoes almost touched the rim on either side of the circle. He was a small boy with high yellow skin a suntan darker than his father's white skin and thick lips that spoke boldly of his mother's blackness. A large, blond, bushy Afro covered his flat head. His blue eyes were full of fun and, at times, full of fight, for every so often he had to say with his fists that his light skin didn't make him a punk.

"What?" CJ asked, hunching his shoulders, his voice squealing feigned innocence.

Holding a Chick-O-Stick, Sleepy-eyed Ted stretched out on the ground next to Kizmic and propped himself up on his elbows. Staring at her with his heavy-lidded eyes, Sleepy-eyed Ted took a bite of the orange, peanut butter candy and between munches asked, "What's the matter?" *Crunch, Crunch, Crunch.*

"Cat got your shot?"

With his long, lean body and legs, big, black, Beta-sneaker-clad feet, close hair cut outlining his pointy ears, and two big front teeth dominating his mouth, Sleepy-eyed Ted looked to Kizmic like a dark brown-skinned Bugs Bunny, snacking on a Chick-O-Stick instead of a carrot. Of the three of them, Sleepy-eyed Ted had the biggest marble collection, which included clay and stone marbles his uncle had given him. He kept them in jars and cataloged them in black-and-white composition notebooks by drawing them, putting the names beside the drawings, the date he got them, and where. In another notebook, he drew designs for marbles and gave them cool names like Ice Cream and Cake, Comb Your Hair, Boogaloo, and Ouch! Sleepy-eyed Ted even drew shooters that he named after CJ and Kizmic. CJ's shooter was red with yellow and green bands. Kizmic's was purple with orange and blue swirls. Sleepy-eyed Ted also had a bunch of marbles he made using different colored pieces of Play Doh and clay he'd gotten from art class in school. He said that when he grew up, he was going to be a master marble maker.

"'Cat got your shot?'" CJ repeated, laughing like it was the funniest thing he'd ever heard.

Sleepy-eyed Ted got up on his knees and held out his palm.

CJ reached over and slapped him five. "That's a good one, man."

"Good one nothin'," Kizmic said, twisting her full lips. "Ain't no cat got my shot."

"Well, come on and shoot then," CJ said.

"Yeah." *Crunch, Crunch, Crunch.* "My mama'll be callin' me for dinner in a minute and you takin' all day," Sleepy-eyed Ted complained.

"Ain't nobody takin' all day." Kizmic lined up her shot again.

Sleepy-eyed Ted joined CJ in meowing to throw Kizmic off her game.

See, I wasn't even gonna play for keepsies this time, Kizmic thought. But now I'ma take all his marbles.

She slanted her right hand, planted the knuckle of her index finger on the ground, and zoned in on that cat's eye marble and that cat's eye marble alone. Suddenly, she couldn't hear one meow. It was as if she'd stuck her fingers in her ears and started singing, *La, la la, la! I can't hear you! I can't hear you!*

Kizmic flicked her thumb and put a backspin on her marble that sent that bad boy flying across the dirt. *Clack!* CJ's marble ricocheted out the ring while Kizmic's marble spun to a stop inside the circle.

Kizmic jumped to her feet. "Meow that, suckers!"

"Awww, shoot!" CJ pouted.

"Told you ain't no cat have my shot. But I got y'all's marbles." Kizmic scooped up her winnings and put them in her sack, now so packed with marbles it bulged at the seams. "Carve it up," she gloated.

"Aiight, aiight," Sleepy-eyed Ted huffed. Chomping on the last of his Chick-O-Stick, he dug inside the back pocket of his blue jeans and pulled out his red, Victorinox Swiss Army knife. Eyes narrowed in concentration, he pushed the spearpoint, metal blade into the tree bark, and with one hard stroke carved line one hundred and two under her name.

Kizmic looked at her blue Teeter Totter wristwatch. Above the little, gold boy and girl going up and down on the seesaw, the big hand was on the ten and the little hand was on the six. Dinner time.

The three of them hopped on their skateboards and headed home in a single file, with Sleepy-eyed Ted out in front. The hard, rubber wheels spun smoothly as they cruised uphill on the asphalt, past the playground, where the smaller children squealed and yelled and laughed and screeched as they slid down the hot, metal sliding board and landed in a pool of baking sand, hung upside down on the monkey bars, climbed over, walked across, ran, or crawled through the concrete tunnels, and swung on the swings, seemingly high enough to stick their feet in the clouds. CJ, Sleepy-eyed Ted, and Kizmic should have leaned left on their skateboards and rounded the bend that ran along the outfield of the baseball diamond, but they took their usual detour, veering off to the right and rolling over to the cement hill that surrounded the park.

Since its inception, the park, maintaining a relatively flat terrain, gradually rose above the streets and sidewalks, creating a hill that reached the third-floor window sills of the red brick rowhouses on Homewood Avenue and East Chase Street. Covered in lush, green grass, the hill's gentle slopes dropped to a second smaller tier, then dipped down to the sidewalk, like the last two humps on the giant yellow slide at the Baltimore City Fair. During the day, the hill belonged to the little kids, who delighted in the dizzy rush they got rolling their bodies down it or riding their homemade cardboard sleds down the slopes when it snowed. In the later hours, before the street lights came on, teenagers claimed the hill and got high off the freedom they had up there that was forbidden in their houses below. And late at night, when the kids and teenagers were asleep, grownups grabbed a couple beers, gathered at the top of the grassy hill, and relaxed in the moonlight's crook.

Everyone claimed that hill for their own except the city. It was a public park, which seemed to mean to city officials that the public needed to tend to it. The public in this case being the men in the neighborhood, who once a month got together and used their lawn mowers to cut the grass. And even though the White House claimed that the energy crisis was over, gas was still too expensive for them to be using their hard-earned money filling up the tanks of their mowers, especially when their tax dollars were supposed to cover the upkeep of local parks. For years, on a monthly basis, the grownups complained about this in letters and phone calls to their city council representatives, who always promised to "take care of it." Well, last April, after an article ran in the *Afro-American* newspaper talking about how officials had not taken care of it, they finally made good on their promise. Around ten o'clock one morning, a yellow city truck rumbled into the neighborhood and poured concrete over the whole lot.

Man! The grownups had a fit that day! They jumped on the phone and cussed people out, marched down to City Hall and cussed some more people out. Kizmic came home from school one day and her mother was in the kitchen on the phone laying somebody out, telling whomever, "It's a *Got*damn shame that y'all would dump some *Got*damn concrete on the *Got*damn hill rather than just cut the *Got*damn grass! And y'all have the nerve to run around the *Got*damn world calling *us* lazy and ignorant!"

Every month since, the grownups argued with city officials about the concrete-covered hill being not only an eyesore but a safety hazard, for when they buried it in concrete, they buried the gentle slopes, leaving sharp inclines that lured children to it with promises of thrills and rushes, the likes of which they could only experience riding a roller coaster at Hershey Park. All they had to do was gather at its peak with their bikes, wagons, homemade go-carts, Big Wheels, skates, skateboards, refrigerator doors and ride it like a wave. Only this concrete wave did not end on the sandy shores of Gunpowder Beach. The two steepest slopes ended in the middle of busy East Chase Street and Homewood Avenue and East Chase and Valley Streets. Either side meant constant anxiety for grownups, because no matter how much they forbid, threatened with punishment, or a good behind whuppin', their hard-headed, had-to-stick-their-hands-in-the-fire children pressed their luck and went careening down that hill and right out into the street, some narrowly escaping being hit by a car. Some not.

CJ and Sleepy-eyed Ted surveyed the hill, mapping out their path. Kizmic watched cars vroom along Chase and Homewood. Spotting a yellow Volkswagen Beetle, she whirled around, hit Sleepy-eyed Ted square on the arm as hard as she could, and shouted, "Punch buggy!"

"Wow," he laughed, downplaying the pain from her punch. To further take the delight out of Kizmic's victory, he added, "You hit like a girl."

"Your mama," Kizmic cracked back, hitting him where it really hurt. He couldn't stand it when people made fun of his mother.

"Don't be talkin' 'bout my mama!" Sleepy-eyed Ted warned.

"Your daddy too," she grinned.

Sleepy-eyed Ted shook his head in annoyance, then put his foot on the red, double nosed deck of his skateboard. "See ya later, alligator."

"After while, crocodile," Kizmic said.

He pushed off just once. The hill was so steep that's all he needed and *Zoom!* Long, skinny arms out, knees bent, tall body leaned back, t-shirt flapping against the hot air, Sleepy-eyed Ted looked like a sail on a schooner as he rode the concrete wave, hollering, "Woooooo! Woooooo! Woooooo!"

CJ turned to Kizmic. "Well, gotta pee."

"Bumble bee," she said.

CJ hopped on his green, fiberglass board and was gone. His blond Afro was blowing this way and that way as he zoomed down the hill, flinging his *Wooooooo's!* back to Kizmic, taunting her, double daring her to follow them, and they would show her a real good time. But Kizmic just stood there with the front wheels of her blue, fiberglass skateboard hanging over the edge, like she did every day of the week.

Man, I bet I'm the only kid around here that ain't been down this hill, Kizmic thought.

But everybody else's mama wasn't like her Mama. When her Mama said, "If I catch you walking down that hill, I'ma tear your behind up," she meant it.

So Kizmic had to settle for riding down that hill vicariously through CJ and Sleepy-eyed Ted, while at the same time acting like she wasn't missing nothing by throwing her head to the sky as soon as they hit the sidewalk.

"Hey, Kizmic! You see how fast we were goin'?" CJ would gloat.

"Naw," she'd answer. "I was lookin' at that snow cloud comin'."

"Man, did you see me almost flip over!" Sleepy-eyed Ted bragged the day his wheel hit a dandelion sticking up through a crack in the concrete.

"Huh? Naw. I was lookin' at that rainbow over the church steeple," she fibbed.

But today, the thrill-seeking appetite that hungered for her to ride alongside CJ and Sleepy-eyed Ted was as hot and unrelenting as the sun beaming down on the white, steel, pyramid roof and its four turrets on the Maryland Penitentiary, making the whole thing shine like a castle. So when they neared the bottom and started zigzagging, then spun around to a stop inches before the sidewalk ended and Homewood Street began, Kizmic couldn't pretend to have her head up in the clouds. Eyes sparkling with envy, she let CJ and Sleepy-eyed Ted see that she hadn't missed not one spin of their wheels since the first time they said forget their mothers and sailed down that hill, leaving her stranded like a castaway. But not anymore.

"That's it!" Kizmic ripped opened her overstuffed bag. "I don't care what Mama said." She grabbed a handful of marbles and stuffed them in the right pocket of her denim shorts. "I'm goin' down this sucka today!"

She grabbed another handful and packed them in her left pocket. Some fell out and clattered like hailstones as they hit the concrete and rolled down the hill. CJ and Sleepy-eyed Ted scrambled around, pocketing her marbles.

"Finders keepers!" CJ yelled.

"Losers weepers!" Sleepy-eyed Ted shouted.

"Shoot! I'ont care." Kizmic pulled the gold drawstring, securing the rest of the marbles inside, then wrapped it tightly around the bag, which was now about the size of a softball and easier for her to grip.

Sleepy-eyed Ted's eyes widened. "What you gettin' ready to do?"

CJ stopped grabbing marbles. "She gettin' ready to ride down."

"Ahhhh, no she ain't," Sleepy-eyed Ted said.

Wanna bet! Kizmic thought.

She couldn't remember ever being so pumped to do something she had no business doing. The excitement of finally being able to feel the wind on her face as she shot down that hill rolled over the fear of getting caught. Still, she had to take precautions so she *wouldn't* get caught.

She started pushing her skateboard back and forth, back and forth, back and forth, kind of nonchalantly like . . . *Go down this hill? Naw, uh-uh. I ain't 'bout to go down this hill. My Mama said I can't go down this hill. I'm just standin' up here lookin' at Old Man Graves' pigeons.*

Kizmic wasn't entirely faking it. She actually was watching them dive and tumble and roll in the air, wondering if this would be the day that they would finally fly the coop. They were birds, free to fly anywhere in this whole wide world, but every single day they flew back to Old Man Graves' yard and walked inside the red, wooden coop he built that looked exactly like the rowhouses, except for the roof, which was slanted instead of flat so that the rain drained off. But while that coop was a penthouse the way Old Man Graves had it all decked out with fans, electricity, perches, and nesting boxes, it was still a cage.

Leaning on the chain linked fence that separated his yard from Uncle Monty and Aunt Beana's, she asked Old Man Graves once, "Why don't they fly away?"

"They got fresh food, water, a clean, safe place to sleep, breed, lay eggs," he said, sitting on his stoop watching the pigeons return to the coop. "They're warm in the winter, cool in the summer." He hunched his shoulders. "It's home."

The pigeons glided south and performed backward somersaults above the rowhouses on East Chase Street, giving Kizmic the perfect opportunity to inconspicuously scope out the three white, wooden frame windows on the third and second floors and the two on the first floor beside the front doors. Fixed on the park, those windows served as vigilant eyes for mothers, aunts, and grandmothers, but there were some that couldn't be as watchful as others. Like the ones that had air conditioners propped in them, blocking their view, or white shades pulled all the way down, essentially blinding them. Kizmic didn't have to worry about those. The windows she had to concern herself with had shades pulled all the way up, giving a wide-eyed view, or shades that were pulled halfway down, making the windows look drowsy but awake nonetheless. The same was true for the windows that had curtains tied into knots that hung in the center of their sightlines. Kizmic also had to be mindful of the windows that had box fans sitting on their sills, as well as windows that had a potted plant or supported full-fledged gardens on their ledges, for best believe, whether lying in their sickbeds, pacing from room to room cradling a teething baby, mopping the hallway floor, watching the soaps on TV, or peeling potatoes at the kitchen table, those women could still see what was happening in that park.

For Kizmic, the windows were like the eyes of the people in those old portraits hanging on museum walls looking dead at her no matter which way she went, especially the windows of the Highway Christian Church on the corner across the street. Shaped like the headstones in the cemetery, the arch windows in the face of the stone church had nothing blocking their view. Even with their colorful stained glass, those windows were wide awake, giving credence to her mother's saying, "God is always watching."

Keeping up her cover, Kizmic followed the flock, appearing to be totally mesmerized by their stunning aerial acrobatics. She whistled, making up musical notes as her eyes swooped down and, as though looking through binoculars, zeroed in on Miss Barbara leaning on the sill of a second-floor window, looking up the street. Next door, Miss Ann was in the first-floor window watching her grandchildren make a Slinky walk down the marble steps. Three houses up, Miss Fannie was in the third-floor window yelling down to some people standing in front of her house. Next door, Miss Darlene's black cat was sprawled out on the sill of the middle second-floor window.

Ugh! Kizmic shivered.

Relatively sure that no one who would tell on her was paying any attention or had more important juvenile exploits to thwart, Kizmic got set to launch.

CJ stood with his mouth hanging open, his blue eyes sparkling, waiting for her to come flying down that hill. Sleepy-eyed Ted, still not buying that Kizmic had it in her to disobey her mother, stared hard at her with his low-hanging eyelids now triple dog daring her to do it.

Oh, you don't think I'm gonna do it? Kizmic tightly tied the laces of her black, high top Converse tennis shoes. Shooot! I'ma do it.

She snatched her blue striped tube socks up to her knobby knees.

One for the money!

She stomped her right foot on the deck of her skateboard.

Two for the show!

She did a quick sweep of the houses on Homewood.

Three to get ready!

She lifted her left foot to push off.
And four to —
SKEERRT!

CHAPTER

2

"KⅡⅡZMⅠC!"

CJ had his small hands cupped around his mouth, screaming her name like she was a mile away. She wasn't. She was still standing at the top of the hill, motionless as a chameleon trying to evade the eyes of a predator by blending in with the grass and dirt of the baseball field.

"KiiizMic!"

From what she could tell, they hadn't seen her.

"KⅡⅠzMic!"

But it would only be a matter of time before the whole neighborhood saw her with CJ squalling her name.

"What's wrong with her, man?"

Sleepy-eyed Ted laughed, "She scared."

Yeah, scared CJ's big mouth is gonna get me caught, Kizmic thought. So before he could yell out her name again, she threw a finger to her lips to shush him, then jabbed it alarmingly across the street. *Uh-oh!* rounded their lips and ballooned their eyes as they whipped around to see how much trouble Kizmic was in based on whom she was pointing at. They saw Kizmic's older sister, Kalaya, and her cousin, Plum, in front of the Highway Christian Church talking to Angelo and Craig. They turned back to Kizmic, frowning with confusion.

"What?" CJ asked.

Kizmic pointed again. They looked again then turned back to her.

CJ hunched his shoulders and said louder, "What?!"

Ahhh! That's right, she sighed. They don't know.

If Kizmic had gotten up the nerve to do this a week ago and Kalaya and Plum had showed up, she would have shot down that hill three or four times and wouldn't have thought twice about it. She and Kalaya had this I-won't-tell-on-you-you-don't-tell-on-me unspoken agreement. But the last few days, Kalaya had been carrying on like a nut, fussing about everything, crying about nothing, making Kizmic question whether or not she would honor their code of silence.

Erring on the side of her sister's sudden craziness, Kizmic decided, "I ain't lettin' Kalaya see me do nothin' I ain't 'posed to do." She just forgot to tell CJ and Sleepy-eyed Ted.

"Teeed!" Miss Wigfall's dinner time call traveled a block and a half from her front steps.

"Shoot, y'all, I gotta go," Sleepy-eyed Ted said.

"You comin' down or what?" CJ shouted.

She hated to do it, but Kizmic took her foot off her skateboard and shook her head, *Naw. Uh-uh.*

"See, man, told you she wasn't gonna do it," Sleepy-eyed Ted said.

"Later, scaredy-cat," CJ said.

"She ain't no scaredy-cat," Sleepy-eyed Ted said. "She a chicken." He bent his elbows and started flapping his arms like chicken wings. "Bawwwk! Bawk Bawk Bawk Bawwwk!"

CJ and Sleepy-eyed Ted rode away on their skateboards, bawking all the way home.

Kizmic thought, They can call me chicken all they want. I ain't gettin' in trouble foolin' around with them. I'll ride down the hill tomorrow.

The *KRACK!* of a bat sent a boy running to first base as Kizmic zig-zagged by the baseball field on the flat, no thrills pavement. At the end of the path, she hopped off her skateboard and picked it up, all in one smooth motion, then bounced down the concrete steps that led out of the park. Once on the sidewalk, she jumped back on her board. Its spinning wheels clacked as they hit the gaps between the concrete squares. Halfway up the block, a peculiar sight stopped Kizmic in her tracks.

Kalaya, who hadn't cracked her lips to smile all week, was grinning up in Angelo's face, as if she were having the time of her life hanging out with the handsome, star high school running back. And Plum, who hardly ever smiled for anything or anybody except Kalaya, was shyly yukking it up with Craig, as if she were having the time of her life hanging out with the cute, star high school point guard. But they were with 13-year-old, picklehead, beanpole, slowpoke Angelo Parker and 13-year-old, countrified, short, non-dribbling Craig Hall. The same Angelo and Craig who teased them about their hair, clothes, called them bubble gum head, pie face, skinny legs, bombed them up with snowballs, chased after them with bugs or mud-covered worms dangling on sticks, snatched away their jump rope or the heel for their hopscotch, stole the ball while they were playing jacks. The same Angelo and Craig who were forever doing something to make Kalaya and Plum squeal, scream, *grrrrrrh!* or go *ewwwww!* The same Angelo and Craig that Kalaya and Plum swore up and down were the ugliest, stupidest, most simple acting, pain-in-the-behind boys God had ever created.

Kizmic shook her head. Man, I swear to beans, those two are gettin' stranger by the minute.

Angelo passed Kalaya a note then he and Craig coolly bopped over to the park. Kalaya and Plum walked up Homewood then cut down Biddle Street, heading home.

They lived on a little alley street named Proctor that had a bunch of red brick rowhouses all hugged up together like family. There was nothing spectacular about those rowhouses. They were cramped boxes with small living rooms, little kitchens with narrow flights of stairs that climbed up to second floors that had two tiny bedrooms and bathrooms with barely knee and elbow room. Between the living room and kitchen was a corridor no wider than the basement door that was in it. So, as Kizmic had often heard her mother say, these houses had no chance of landing on the pages of *Better Homes & Gardens* magazine. Still, some families fussed over those tiny, five room boxes, because they symbolized their step up and out of projects like Lafayette Courts, Flag House, and Murphy Homes. For Kizmic's parents, uncle, and aunt those rowhouses symbolized their step out of the small, wooden shacks they lived in down south. And for every last one of those families nothing represented their steps up and out more than the front stoops, which were three fine slabs of white marble that added a touch of class to some otherwise humdrum houses.

For the children of Proctor Street those marble steps were simply the bases in games of tag, it, or hide-n-seek, the places parents ordered them to be when the street lights came on, and they were one of their many loathsome chores. Every Saturday morning, unless it was raining, snowing, or freezing cold, children filed out of their houses carrying scrub brushes, cans of Ajax or Bon Ami Powder, and buckets of hot water and scrubbed those marble steps until they were gleaming. No mother would have been caught dead with a dirty stoop. Kizmic's mother said that that was "triflin'" and tantamount to letting her husband and children run around wearing dirty underwear.

Kalaya and Plum sat on their marble steps, heads together, no doubt sharing juicy secrets. The sidewalks on either side of Proctor Street were crowded with girlie-girls having a bat-n-ball contest, hula-hooping, playing hopscotch, four square, dodge ball, and double-dutch. So Kizmic rode to her house on the bumpy concrete street.

"Hey, Kalaya. Hey, Plum," Kizmic said.

Plum acknowledged Kizmic's presence with a polite but uninterested glance then immediately returned her attention to Kalaya, whose thoughts were sharply concentrated on a scrap of paper she was clutching in her hand like it had the day's winning lottery number printed on it. It wasn't a lottery number, but it was a number. Angelo's phone number.

"What you got his number for?" Kizmic asked.

Noticing her little sister for the first time, Kalaya snatched the paper away from Kizmic's prying eyes. The tight, bitter, annoyed look that for the last week had been blinking on and off her face like a broken neon sign was on again, glaring harshly at Kizmic.

"Stop signifyin'," Kalaya barked.

"I thought you didn't like him?"

With an extra hard suck of her teeth Kalaya said, "Well, you thought wrong."

"Nuh-uh. You said you hated his guts," Kizmic reminded Kalaya.

"Just leave her alone," the always calm, always wise Plum advised.

Plum was a dainty, henna-skinned girl with thick hair combed into a big bush ball on top of her head, and private eyes the size and color of chocolate blowpops. She spent most of her time bent over her Corona portable typewriter making up stories or scribbling in black and white marble composition notebooks, which she used as diaries and carried everywhere she went. Although, the one Plum had with her that day she used as a shield. With her slender arms poking out of the short sleeves of her rainbow striped shirt, Plum hugged the book in front of her acorn-sized breasts.

"I ain't botherin' her," Kizmic said. Then, despite Kalaya's demand for privacy, she told her sister, "Mama said you can't have no boyfriend."

"He's not my boyfriend," Kalaya insisted, staring off into space, like Angelo being her boyfriend was all she'd ever dreamed about when he was pushing her down or yanking her hair.

See there? See right there? Something wasn't right about her sister. Kizmic couldn't put her finger on it, but Kalaya was not Kalaya. If that made any sense. Which, of course, it did not, because who was Kalaya if she wasn't Kalaya?

Kizmic looked her sister over with the intense eye of a doctor, examining a patient for a rare, fatal disease. In her white, short-sleeved Polo shirt and red overall shorts, Kalaya's body was long and lean, athletic but soft and feminine, even more so with her newly developed breasts, which were about the size of plums. Her thick, medium-length, permed hair was gathered into a sleek ponytail and held together by a pretty, yellow barrette. She had full, cupid-shaped lips and sweet coconut brown skin, silky and smooth. Her eyes were large, brown, bold, and seeking, like they wanted to know everything there was to know about life. This girl looked exactly like her sister, but she wasn't acting like her. Her sister wouldn't have dreamed about calling Angelo Parker.

Kizmic glanced at Plum's diary. On one of its pages Plum had literally marked the day her sister started liking Angelo.

"You ain't 'posed to be callin' no boys," Kizmic told Kalaya.

"Will you mind your own business?"

"This is my own business."

"Shut up!" Kalaya yelled.

Not the least bit intimidated, Kizmic said, "Make me."

Kalaya tossed a looked at Plum that asked, *Should I even bother?*

Plum shook her head.

"Forget you," Kalaya said with a dismissive wave of her hand.

"Forget you, forgot you, never thought about you," Kizmic sang and stuck out her tongue.

Kalaya made a fist, stomped her foot on the step, jerked her shoulders, and faked like she was going to knock Kizmic into the middle of next week. Kizmic tripped over her skateboard evading a blow Kalaya had no real intentions of throwing.

"Ha-ha! Made you look stupid," Kalaya laughed.

Plum moved her notebook up to hide the chuckles on her face.

"Wench," Kizmic said, trying not to feel as stupid as Kalaya's laugh and Plum's chuckles made her feel.

"Your mama," Kalaya cackled.

Her comeback made absolutely no sense to Kizmic. "We got the same mother, stupid."

"I know what we got. Stupid."

"So you callin' Mama a wench?"

Kalaya rolled her eyes.

"I know you ain't callin' my mother no wench."

"When are you gonna call him?" Plum asked.

As quickly as changing a channel, Kalaya's mind switched from the argument she was having with her baby sister to more mature activities. She looked at the slip of paper again. "Tonight. When Mama and Daddy go to sleep."

"I hope Mama and Daddy don't never go to sleep," Kizmic said then tried to walk up the steps between them, but Kalaya blocked her way.

"Don't you tell Mama," Kalaya said.

"Tell Mama what? That you out here callin' her a bunch of names or that you plannin' to call some stupid boy?"

"You better not tell her neither one," Kalaya said.

"I ain't gonna tell Mama nothin'," Kizmic said.

Kalaya scooted out of her way. Kizmic stomped by, then reached down and plucked Angelo's number out of Kalaya's hand.

"I'ma show her!"

Kizmic wasn't really going to show their mother the number. She was just fooling around, paying Kalaya back for being so mean to her.

"Grrrr!" She heard Kalaya growl. *Growl*, like some she-creature off the "Night Stalker" television show.

Sheesh! She actin' like I'm sho'nuff gonna tattle, Kizmic thought.

Kizmic turned to haul tail in the house, then *BALOOMP!* She hit the waxed hardwood floor in the living room, which was lit only by the early evening sunlight filtering in through the two windows above the floor model television. Marbles spilled out of her bag and pockets and scattered into the shadows under the couch and coffee table. Thinking she had tripped up the step, Kizmic hurried to get back on her feet, but she couldn't because the step didn't cause her fall. Kalaya, who was on her like white on rice, as the saying went, had tackled her from behind.

Stretched out on her belly in the rectangular shape of sunlight now standing in the doorway, Kizmic squirmed under Kalaya.

"Give it here!" Kalaya said through clenched teeth, grabbing at Angelo's number.

"Get off me!" Kizmic yelled, wildly waving the number out of her sister's reach.

Kalaya caught a corner of the paper between her fingers, but it tore off. Kizmic balled up the paper and switched it from fist to fist, like the guessing hand game they played in which some kids sat on the bottom front step while another kid stood in front of them holding out his fists, where he had hidden a button, marble, penny, or piece of paper. Those who picked the correct fist moved up a step. The first to make it to the top step won. Kalaya wasn't in the guessing mood.

In her ear, Kizmic heard and felt Kalaya's hot breath blasting through her nostrils like a bull seeing a room full of red.

"I'm not playin' with you." She seized the hand that clutched the number and tried to pry Kizmic's fingers open.

Kizmic wriggled until Kalaya's grip slipped. Then she came up with the brilliant idea to tuck Angelo's number under her stomach.

Kalaya straddled her. "Give it here!"

"Give you what?" Kizmic taunted.

Kalaya reached under her.

"Mama!" Kizmic shouted.

As if she had gotten too close to something on fire, Kalaya drew back her hand. Kizmic stared at the kitchen doorway, hoping their mother would come investigate her cry for help.

"Don't call me unless you're bleeding or dead," their mother yelled from the kitchen.

I'ma 'bout to be both, Kizmic thought.

"And stop running through my house," she added.

Assured that their mother was not coming to Kizmic's rescue, Kalaya started pulling on her again. Everything inside Kizmic screamed, *Just give her the daggone number!* But the pesky little sister in her that enjoyed making her older sister sweat wouldn't turn it over.

"Leave me alone!" Kizmic cried out.

"Gimme!" Kalaya yelled.

"Ow! Ow! Ow!" Kizmic whined then hollered, "Stop it!" as if Kalaya were brutalizing her.

"I know one thing," their mother said. "Y'all better quit wrestling around in here!"

Suddenly, Kalaya stopped. Kizmic peeked at her out of the corner of her eye.

Kalaya's eyes became little slits of cunning anger. "That's all right. Go on and show it to Mama," she said in a whisper.

Yeah right, Kizmic scoffed, feeling the cool threat coming on Kalaya's hot breath.

"'Cause I'ma tell Mama I saw you getting ready to ride your skateboard down the hill."

Kizmic's eyes ballooned. She assumed Kalaya was too busy flirting with Angelo to see anything, let alone notice her up on the hill. Still, Kizmic laid on the number.

With what Kizmic called Kalaya's Medusa stare, her sister looked at her with piercing, treacherous eyes, trying, it seemed, to turn her into stone. What Kalaya was actually doing was far worse. She was searching her memory of dirt on her little sister for the one thing that would make Kizmic give up that number. When she found it, Kalaya leaned in again with a conniving, Grinch smile. "Or I can tell Mama you were over on Greenmount yesterday playing marbles with some boy older than me."

"Aaallllll!" Kizmic said, totally in shock.

Kalaya got off her and stood with her arms folded. Kizmic clutched the number in her hand and got on her feet as well. Her eyes narrowed with confusion. Kizmic had taken extraordinary precautions to make sure no one saw her. She walked around the block four times, then scanned the crowd for ten whole minutes. And I ain't see no doggone Kalaya or no doggone Plum, Kizmic thought, retracing her steps in her mind. Anyway, I only did it 'cause CJ and Sleepy-eyed Ted was up there braggin' to this boy named Leon about how they knew a girl who could beat him at marbles. I told them I wasn't gonna get in trouble playin' against him, but then Leon said, "Y'all think this pea-head girl gonna beat me?"

Sleepy-eyed Ted said, "I bet my Doomsday Defense TOPS football cards that she gonna beat you."

"Bob Lilly, Larry Cole, Jethro Pugh?" Leon asked.

"And George Andrie," Sleepy-eyed Ted said.

So I had to kick his butt, Kizmic reasoned. Now would her mother agree? No.

A shrewd snarl curled Kalaya's lips. *What's it gonna be, little sister?* her stare asked.

Kizmic fixed her own evil eye on Kalaya. "You ain't gonna tell," she whispered.

"Wanna bet?" Kalaya whispered back. Her Grinch smile peeled her lips apart, exposing her sharp teeth. "Hey Mama," she called, her composed voice hanging menacingly over Kizmic's head.

"What?" their mother asked.

Kalaya held out her hand. When Kizmic didn't put Angelo's number in it, she started walking toward the kitchen.

Awww, man! She gonna tell, Kizmic thought, puckering her lips. She had some other stuff on Kalaya, but nothing that would get her off the hook for playing marbles against Leon.

"Here!" Reluctantly, Kizmic threw Angelo's number at Kalaya's sandals.

"You play too daggone much," Kalaya said, snatching up the crumpled piece of paper. She stomped toward the front door. "Heifer."

"You," Kizmic spat.

Brushing off their minor skirmish, she got down on her hands and knees and picked up her marbles. She then plopped her bulging sack of marbles on the TV Guide laying on the coffee table and diddy bopped into the kitchen.

Although located in the back, the sunflower colored kitchen was the center of the house, partly because the stairs leading to the second floor were in there, tucked in the corner beside the refrigerator and facing the side of the sink. But just as the marble steps were more than a way in and out of the house, the red oak stairs were more than a pathway to the bathroom and bedrooms.

Kizmic used them as a chair and desk, where she sat and learned her 123's, ABC's, spelling words, and multiplication facts from her mother, who quizzed her on them as she coated lake trout with flour or washed dishes. Every day Kalaya sat on those steps and whined about all the annoying things Angelo and Craig did to her and Plum while her mother dried and stacked plates, bowls, and glasses in neat rows inside the white, metal cabinets and offered advice on how they could ignore Angelo and Craig. From those steps Kizmic gave a shot-by-shot account on how she beat CJ and Sleepy-eyed Ted at marbles or horse as her mother put Swanson fried chicken TV dinners in the oven or shook crumbs out of the toaster. Kalaya sat on them and presented her and Plum's side of some he said/she said stuff they had going on with some girls while her mother filled the ice trays and told her how to stay out of that kind of nonsense. With the Sears Catalog or *Ebony* magazine on her lap, Kalaya talked about hair and clothes as her mother did laundry in the small washing machine on the other side of the sink and helped Kalaya choose hairstyles and outfits that weren't too grown. So basically, the kitchen was the hub of the house because the heart of the Waters family was always in there doing something.

Magdalene Waters stood at the kitchen sink, stirring a large pitcher of grape Kool-Aid.

She was a tall woman, long and fit, like an athlete. Not one who worked out daily. Her body was more like a former athlete whose heyday left muscular markings on her biceps, thighs, and calves. She had pretty, soft skin the color of ginger, mild, focused, brown eyes that turned into slits when she laughed, and full, delightful lips. Unless she was going to work, in which case she wore her white nursing assistant uniform and white Lady Red Wings shoes, or going to church, in which case she wore one of her elegant dresses or skirts and high heels, or going out for a night on the town with Turk Waters, in which case she wore a form-fitting, jaw-dropping dress and heels, Magdalene always had on jeans or sweatpants, t-shirt or sweatshirt, and tennis shoes. That evening she was dressed in blue jeans, navy blue Deck tennis shoes, and a white "Free Angela Davis" t-shirt, and her long, black hair was pulled back into the ponytail she also usually wore at home.

Plum's mother, Beana Davis, sat in the high-back chair closest to the opened back door, soaking in the sunlight that leaned on the two window sills over the round, oak table. A lit Pall Mall cigarette was between her thin fingers and her large, brown, poppy eyes were knee-deep in Peter Benchley's novel, *Jaws*. Her full lips moved slightly, like a ventriloquist just learning her craft, as she mouthed the words of the story. She as well had gotten out of her nursing assistant uniform and had put on a yellow and white sundress with laces that crisscrossed and tied at her small bosom and a pair of yellow flip-flops. This, along with the sunshine highlighting her smooth, toasted brown skin and short, kinky curly hair, made Aunt Beana look like a school girl relaxing in a lounge chair on the beach instead of a thirty-year-old woman.

"Hey Mama. Hey Aunt Beana," Kizmic said.

"Hey yourself," Magdalene said.

"How you doing, Kizmic?" Aunt Beana asked, taking a moment to look up from her book.

"Good." Kizmic went over to the stove. They were having a family favorite for dinner — white rice, string beans, and fried liver smothered in onions and brown gravy.

"What were you and Kalaya out there tearing up my house about?" Magdalene asked.

"Nothin'," Kizmic said.

"'Nothin'," she marked, turning around. "Kizmic Alexandria Waters!" She set the pitcher on the table. "You are absolutely filthy!"

Kizmic rubbed the dirt off her elbows and knees, but she couldn't get it off her shirt, shorts, and socks.

"What were you doing out there? Just rolling around in the dirt?"

"I was playin' marbles," she said, wondering why her mother was making such a big deal about dirt being on her clothes. Dirt was always on her clothes, because despite Magdalene's wishes and efforts to the contrary, Kizmic managed to be the quintessential tomboy. Her body was boyishly trim, straight up and down, just the way it would stay if Kizmic had any say about the way things went in this world. In Magdalene's eyes, Kizmic, with her sweet, heart-shaped face and pretty, brown hair, was girlhood in its wondrous prime, but the only time she got to see Kizmic really look like a girl was on Sundays. That's when she forced Kizmic to dress up in frilly, lacy, girlie-girl dresses, stockings, and shiny, patent leather Mary Jane shoes. Kizmic hated those ugly dresses, itchy stockings, and those God-forsaken, uncomfortable shoes. And she loathed having to come in early on Saturday nights to sit in front of the stove and get her hair pressed and her ears and neck burned by the hot straightening comb, although Magdalene always swore up and down that the heat from the comb, not the comb itself, burned her skin.

"Do I have any sons?" Magdalene directed the question to Aunt Beana, who laughed as she shook her head.

"Well, then tell me why my little girl is out playing marbles."

"Awww, Mama," Kizmic moaned at the age-old complaint.

"Kizmic, it's time you stop hanging around all those boys."

"Why?"

"Why? Because you're a girl, Kizmic. You're a lady. A flower."

Kizmic looked at her mother and laughed. A flower! Man, Mama sure can come up with some stuff to say.

"She doesn't smell like a flower," Kalaya said, sauntering into the kitchen. "She smells like a dirty boy."

"You mean like Angelo?" Kizmic smirked.

Kalaya gave her that Medusa stare again. "Wench."

"You," Kizmic said.

"Kalaya, leave your sister alone," Magdalene said.

"She started it."

"No, I didn't," Kizmic denied.

"Well, I'm ending it," Magdalene said.

Kalaya rolled her eyes.

Plum quietly entered with her head held low, like she was trying not to be seen. She handed Kizmic her skateboard and a few marbles, then sat down at the table, opened her notebook, and began writing.

Aunt Beana took a deep drag off her cigarette. The ash glowed orange then grayed. After exhaling what little smoke didn't get trapped in her lungs, she asked, "You just gonna come in here and not speak?"

Poppy eyes still on the sentence she was writing, Plum muttered, "Hello."

"Where have you been all day?" Magdalene asked Kalaya.

"Outside," she answered.

"Outside where?"

Kalaya hunched her shoulders. "I don't know."

"What you mean you don't know?"

"Around the neighborhood, that's all."

"Uh-huh. Well, I told you to come home and check in."

"What are you talkin' about, Mama?" Kalaya asked in a tone that wasn't exactly disrespectful, but was only an inflection or two below it.

Aunt Beana blew smoke out of the left corner of her mouth. She looked Kalaya up and down and up and down, then settled her eyes on her goddaughter, hard and deliberate, warning Kalaya to cool it. Plum's pen came to a stop in the middle of her scribing. Lifting only her eyes from her journal, she stared at her best friend the way she would if Kalaya had decided to step in front of a moving car. Kizmic watched her mother, trying to gage if she was going to let Kalaya slide or slide Kalaya right on out that kitchen. It took a lot to make Magdalene mad, but once someone plucked her last nerve, which Kalaya was suicidally close to doing, ooh, boy, look out!

Gravy boiling rapidly enough to bubble and splatter on the stove demanded Magdalene's attention. She turned off the burner and stirred the liver, onions, and gravy around to keep the food from sticking to the pan and to give herself a moment so she could cut Kalaya some slack, for at least the tenth time that week.

"I haven't seen you since I left for work this morning," she said in a forgiving manner.

Instead of taking Magdalene's response as the benevolent pardon it was, Kalaya took it as another chance to show off her preteenaged behind. "Just 'cause you didn't see me doesn't mean I didn't come in."

Kizmic shot her sister an angry, distressful look that screamed, *What's wrong with you?!*

Plum's poppy eyes remained on Kalaya's head, amazed to see it still on her neck and not rolling across the white and burgundy checkered tile floor.

Aunt Beana took another long drag on her cigarette and didn't stop until the ash burned up to the filter. She squinted at Kalaya through the cloud of smoke that billowed out of her mouth. "Enough is enough," she said. "And too much is good for nothin'." She smashed and twisted the cigarette butt in the ashtray until it was extinguished.

"Kalaya, you got one more time to talk to me like I'm one of your little friends in the street," Magdalene said. "Now, I don't know what your problem is, but you better get yourself together."

"I don't have a problem. Is dinner ready?" Kalaya asked, in a tone that said she was fed up with her mother always having something to say.

That's when Kizmic knew her sister had lost her marbles. They must have rolled under the living room couch when Kalaya tackled her. Maybe Kizmic picked them up and dropped them in the purple sack with her marbles.

Magdalene whacked the spoon on the lip of the pan. *BAM! BAM! BAM!*

Kizmic and Plum jumped. Aunt Beana just sat there like, *I tried to tell you to stop runnin' off at the mouth.*

Magdalene slammed the spoon down on the counter and stomped over to Kalaya, who stood tall and stuck out her barely budding breasts, as if she were woman enough to handle whatever punishment Magdalene could dish out.

Magdalene pointed her finger in Kalaya's face and opened her mouth to lay that child of hers out, but Al Green stepped in from the living room singing "Let's Stay Together." That could only mean one thing—Turk Waters was home.

Turk had crates full of 45s, 33s, 78s, and 8 tracks that took up one whole side of the living room. He played them on the Steepletone record player he'd had since he was a teenager and on his prized Grand Prix, 8 track, AM/FM record player. With these two glorious machines Turk made The Supremes, The Drifters, The Temptations, Ray Charles, Marvin Gaye, Smokey Robinson and the Miracles, Gladys Knight and the Pips, Archie Bell and the Drells, Patti LaBelle and the Bluebelles seem like members of the Waters family.

Wearing a black t-shirt, tan work pants and boots, smelling of sweat, dirt, concrete, and sun, Turk two-stepped into the kitchen and cut in between Magdalene and Kalaya. Tall and muscular, Turk had grown up on his family's farm laboring under the sweltering rays of the sun, planting, cutting, dragging, and hanging tobacco, which explained how he got his handsome, reddish-brown skin. He now worked at Decon Industries making precast brick, clay, and concrete building components. The job was just the way he liked it—dirty and physically demanding. And when he came home, he rinsed the dirt and aches off his body with the same thing he shook his tiring workday off as a boy—a dance.

"Scuse me, scuse me, scuse me," he said to Kalaya, waving her out of his way with his hand. Two-stepping in front of Magdalene, Turk lip-synched the song.

Still teed off, Magdalene glared at Kalaya around his dancing shoulder.

Refusing to be upstaged by a funky attitude, Turk got directly in Magdalene's face and began moving his neck back and forth to the beat of the music, looking smooth. Smooth as a turkey.

Turk broke down his clean-shaven mug. "My name is Big Willie and I'm here to give you a big thrillie." He then started doing his signature flickeded dance move, in which he bounced at the knees, rocked side to side, and rotated his shoulders backward. "What's your name, girl?"

His corny lines and comical dance moves wilted Magdalene's anger and a sweet smile bloomed in its place, for with all the banging of the spoon and the pointing of her finger and the anger marring her face, Kalaya had not plucked Magdalene's last nerve.

"Puddintane," Magdalene answered. "Ask me again I'll say the same."

"Ummm! I like puddin', 'specially chocolate." Turk wrapped Magdalene up in his arms and tried to make her slow dance with him.

"Get off me, man." Magdalene pushed him away. "You're all stinky and sweaty."

"Stinky?" He grabbed Kalaya. "Am I stinky?"

"Ewwww! Get off me, Daddy," Kalaya laughed.

"Plum, am I stinky?" Turk hugged her.

Plum laughed and wriggled out of his arms.

"Don't come over here messin' with me, Turk," Aunt Beana said.

"Am I stinky?" He gave Aunt Beana a bear hug that lifted her up from the chair.

"Put me down, Turk," she said as her flip-flops slipped off her feet.

"Kizmic don't think I'm stinky. Do you?"

"No," she said, hugging all up on her father, breathing in his funk as if it smelled as appealing as Old Spice cologne.

Magdalene, Aunt Beana, Kalaya, Plum, and Kizmic were all laughing now. The heat must have gotten to them for a minute and Turk came in like a summer rain shower and cooled things off.

"Now that's more like it," Turk said with a high jingle in his deep voice.

"Yeah, it is," Magdalene smiled.

"Monty back yet?" he asked Aunt Beana.

Plum paused her pencil at the mention of her father's name. As a trucker, he spent a lot of time away from home hauling furniture, food, chemicals, or whatever around the country in his green, long-nosed, 1972 Peterbilt 359 semi truck. Aunt Beana and Plum were used to him being gone, but they hated it just the same.

"He's supposed to get in about two in the morning, thank the Lord. You know them truckers have gone crazy with that Hoffa missing."

"Them truckers was crazy long before Hoffa went missin'," Uncle Monty said.

Delmont Davis stood at the back door, his thin lips grinning at them through his scruffy beard and mustache. He was a dark-complexioned man, tall, heavy-set. Not giant tall, not overweight, just naturally big, big hands, big feet, and a slight beer belly. The way he tromped about, he reminded Kizmic of a playful, cuddly grizzly bear. His eyes gave him a sad, boyish face. They were small and sloped down at the outer corners, his right eye more so than his left. Some people said he had a dead eye, but that eye was far from dead.

Uncle Monty said, "This here eye lives off people's stares. The more people stare at it, the more I can see out of it. It ain't never gonna die, 'cause people ain't never gonna stop starin' at it." Then he laughed and that dead eye smiled.

Aunt Beana said it was the other way around. That Uncle Monty's dead eye gave life to other people. "I wasn't thinking about Monty," she said. "Not until I looked at that eye. It made me feel so pretty and alive inside. Shoot, all I thought about was Monty. It hooked me."

"What you doing sneakin' in town?" Aunt Beana asked.

"Now, is that any kind of way to greet a man you ain't seen in two and a half weeks?" Uncle Monty asked. He leaned over and gave Aunt Beana a kiss that was as fresh and passionate as the day he left for California with his load of sugar.

Plum watched them with a faint smile on her face.

"I thought you weren't coming in until late," Aunt Beana said.

"Why you so worried about me comin' home early?" Uncle Monty asked. "You got a boyfriend you plannin' on seein' tonight?"

"No, not tonight. Tomorrow maybe," she joked.

"You hurtin' me to my heart, woman," Uncle Monty said, shaking his head, on top of which sat a floppy, blue fisherman's hat. He collected them the way Kizmic collected football cards. The only time he didn't wear one was when he went to church.

Uncle Monty walked over to Plum. "Hey, Little Girl," he smiled, then hugged and kissed her on the cheek.

"Hey, Old Man," she smiled, hugging him back.

"If you had let me know you were getting in so early, I would have been home cooking you something to eat instead of sittin' 'round here readin' and runnin' my mouth with Magdalene," Aunt Beana complained.

"I called Little Girl on the CB and told her I was a 10-76, and she said 10-4," Uncle Monty said.

He bought Plum a CB radio so he could say goodbye before he got out of range and hello when he was close to home.

Aunt Beana cut her eyes at Plum.

"I forgot," Plum said.

"You forgot?" Aunt Beana asked. "How about I forget to buy ribbon for that typewriter of yours? You copy that?"

"Awww, leave the girl alone. She's got a lot on her mind," Uncle Monty said, and winked his droopy, hooded eye at Plum. "Besides, what Magdalene's got cookin' smells good. You got enough for one more starvin' soul, don't ya?" He removed his hat, held it against his chest, and looked down at her with pitiful, begging eyes.

"Always enough for a starving soul," Magdalene laughed.

"How'd you get in so early anyway?" Aunt Beana asked.

He gave Kalaya a loving squeeze then placed his hat on Kizmic's head. It was damp with sweat and a little smelly, but Kizmic didn't mind. She liked Uncle Monty's hats because they seemed like they were part of him.

"There weren't any Kojaks with Kodaks, so I put the hammer down, baby, and here I be," Uncle Monty laughed.

"You better stop driving like you're crazy. I'm too young to be a widow."

"And I'm too young to be dead," Uncle Monty said.

"Sometimes I wish you'd give up truckin', at least long haul truckin'."

"Can't, woman. It's in my blood."

"Speakin' of blood," Turk said. "Who got cut?"

"Huh?" Magdalene looked up from the plate she was putting rice on.

"When I came in I saw some blood on the steps."

They all walked to the front door. A round, bright red spot of blood sullied Magdalene's spick-and-span stoop.

Immediately, she accused Kizmic. "Girl, did you get cut fooling with those boys?"

Kizmic frowned, shaking her head. "Uh-uh," she said. Her mother stayed on the lookout for an excuse to make Kizmic stop playing with CJ and Sleepy-eyed Ted.

"Magdalene," Aunt Beana called. Her voice had an ominous tinge to it. "What does that look like to you?"

Magdalene stared at the spot. "What do you mean ..." she began.

Kizmic watched her mother's face as whatever the spot of blood looked like dawned all over it.

"What is it?" Turk and Uncle Monty asked at the same time.

Magdalene pressed her eyes on them. Aunt Beana lit another cigarette and took a quick, nervous puff.

"No," Turk said, catching their drift.

"Already?" Uncle Monty asked.

No and already what? Kizmic thought.

"Who was sitting here?" Magdalene asked, her voice shaky with fear, as if the question were a bullet loaded inside the cylinder of a gun used in a game of Russian roulette.

Kalaya spoke up. "I was."

Turk and Magdalene looked grimly at each other. Plum looked at the back of Kalaya's red shorts, and her blowpop-sized eyes filled with shock and envy.

Aunt Beana said. "Well, at least now we know what the hell's wrong with her."

CHAPTER
3

How can Kalaya bleed without being cut somewhere? Kizmic went from her mother to her father to her uncle to her aunt to Plum asking, "What's goin' on? Why is Kalaya bleedin'? Where is she bleedin' from? Is Kalaya gonna die?" Although the fact that their father didn't throw Kalaya in the car and rush her to Provident Hospital told Kizmic that her sister wasn't dying.

So what's happenin' to her?

No one would say. All of them just pushed Kizmic and her questions aside as if they didn't have time to explain it. But surely Aunt Beana could have told her something while she washed down the stoop, puffing on cigarettes. Her father and Uncle Monty could have said, *Well, this is what's going on* before they drove off in Uncle Monty's blue Econoline custom van to get a six-pack from the bar. Her mother could have said, *Okay, baby, it's like this* before she shut herself up in the bathroom with Kalaya.

Curiosity and worry sent Kizmic searching for answers in her room, which in reality was Kalaya's room. With there only being two bedrooms in the house, Kizmic and Kalaya had to share a room. But Kalaya had lived in that room a full three years before Kizmic was born, and she had decorated it with all the things she loved — pinks, yellows, purples. Fingernail polish, jewelry, and flowers cluttered the dresser. Her bed was covered with dolls, stuffed animals, and, of course, Plum.

Kalaya and Plum, a.k.a. Annette Davis, were destined to be best friends since before the day they were born, way back in 1962, when Turk Waters and Magdalene Johnson joined the horde of Blacks leaving the Jim Crow South, migrating north hoping to escape poverty, unemployment, lynchings, and for some the Civil Rights Movement. On a Greyhound bus going from Lynchburg to Baltimore, Turk and Magdalene shared their bag of greasy fried chicken and cornbread with Delmont Davis and Beana Cruise. So, Kalaya and Plum had been talking to each other since they could babble, walking together since they could crawl, and loving each other even before they knew it was love they were feeling. No wonder Kizmic at five years old looked around that room and understood that she didn't *share* a room with Kalaya; she slept in Kalaya's room.

Plum was out front with Aunt Beana, watching her scrub the stoop. Her diary was laying right there in the open on Kalaya's bed, giving anyone access to her private thoughts. Kizmic could have read every last word in Plum's diaries if she wanted to, for Plum always left them laying around. But she hadn't been all that interested in Plum's secret thoughts until that day.

Kizmic stood beside Kalaya's bed. She glanced down at Plum's diary then looked up at the door. Her fingers crawled across the pink bedsheet and on top of Plum's diary. Keeping her eyes on the door, Kizmic opened the book and flipped to the last entry.

I thought Craig was going to ask me to the party, Plum wrote, *but he didn't. I guess he doesn't like me. Angelo asked Kalaya. I guess I'll still go. Kalaya started her period today!!! I wonder when I'll get mine.*

"Hey!" Plum yelled.

Kizmic jerked her head up.

Plum marched into the room and slammed her diary closed. "That's private!"

"I'm sorry, Plum."

"You shouldn't read people's private stuff."

"I know. I didn't mean to, but nobody'll tell me what's goin' on," Kizmic said in her defense.

"That's 'cause you're a kid," she said, snatching up the book.

"So are you."

"No, I'm not. I'll be thirteen next month."

"Is that when you'll get your period?" Kizmic asked.

Plum stared out of the room at the closed bathroom door. "I hope so," she said, talking to herself.

"Why?"

"Because you're supposed to get it."

"Why?"

"Because," Plum said, like that explained everything.

"What is it? What does it do? What's it for?"

Plum looked down at Kizmic, whose eyes were full of wonder and fear of the unknown.

"Please tell me, Plum," she said.

Taking pity on her, Plum sighed. "All right. Look. It's something that—"

Just when Plum was about to let Kizmic in on the big mystery, Kalaya strutted into her room like she carried something inside her that would change the world as they knew it. Her eyes were wide and gleaming with this magnificent thing. The awesome power of this thing was twitching in the big, wild grin on her mouth. To be honest, it scared Kizmic. Anything that incredible, that impregnable should not be in the hands of a child, certainly not in the hands of her older sister. Whatever it was Kalaya had their mother needed to take it away from her right then and there and bury it in an unmarked grave in the cemetery or there was going to be trouble. Kizmic could feel it, could hear it in Kalaya and Plum's voices as the two girls huddled together on Kalaya's bed and whispered about some "friend" named Mary and how Plum couldn't wait until her "friend" came.

Kizmic didn't find out what was wrong with Kalaya that night or the night after that or even the night after that. In fact, six whole nights passed before she learned what had happened to Kalaya.

Sitting up, Kizmic stared at Kalaya's empty bed. For the past three nights, Kalaya stayed in Plum's room.

"More privacy," she told Magdalene, who questioned why she was spending so much time away from home.

"Kalaya doesn't like me anymore," Kizmic said to her mother when she came to tuck her in.

"It's not that, baby girl," Magdalene said, propping the tan box fan in the window.

Summer nights on Proctor Street could be unbearable. Those tiny houses breathed in great gulps of hot air and humidity and held them inside their walls the way children held their breath inside their cheeks to keep from eating vegetables or taking medicine. Magdalene turned on the fan and a hum entered the room as the spinning plastic blades chopped the oppressive, hot night air up into a warm breeze.

"What is it, then?" Kizmic pressed.

Magdalene sat on the side of her bed. "She's just going through some stuff right now."

"What stuff?"

"Just stuff," she said. "Stop worrying so much. You're like a little old woman sometimes, the way you worry." She kissed Kizmic on the forehead. "Go to sleep."

Kizmic couldn't do either, so she was staring out the window when she heard Magdalene go downstairs around eleven-thirty and Turk go looking for her a few minutes later. With a quietness she had used a thousand times to sneak downstairs and watch television long after the public service announcement aired asking parents if they knew the whereabouts of their children, Kizmic tiptoed out of her room to the top of the stairs. Turk was sitting wide-legged on the fourth step and Magdalene was on the third step, Kalaya's step, nestled between his legs with her arms draped over his thighs and her head resting on his chest.

"Alright, woman," he said, stroking her hair. "I just laid some of my best moves on you."

"Yes, you did," Magdalene sighed in an easy, melted voice. "Yes, you did indeed."

"And you had what, four, five ..."

"Two," Magdalene yawned softly. "Only two."

"What you mean 'only,'?" he asked, a little insulted.

"Nothing. I'm just setting the record straight."

"Well, you're settin' it crooked as crooked can be, 'cause I counted at least four screams."

"Then you must be counting the two times I made you scream."

"Scream? Two times? Me? By you?" he asked, making it sound like she would see a two-headed dinosaur before anything like that would happen.

"Yes," she answered in a matter-of-fact tone.

"Woman, you must be crazy," he scoffed.

"Oh, now don't sit there and try to pretend I ain't never put it on you like that," she warned.

Kizmic stood in the unlit hallway totally in the dark about what her parents were discussing. She tried to decode their playful banter, but she got dizzy on the parameters of the circles they talked in and got lost in the bushes they beat around.

Everybody's got secrets, she griped.

"Gettin' back to my original question," Turk said. "If I put it on you the way you know I put it on ya, why you still lookin' like you lost your best friend? And for the record, you ain't *never* put it on me like that. Never!"

"For the record, I did. For your question ... I feel like I *am* losing my best friend."

"Somethin' goin' on with you and Beana?"

"No. Kalaya."

"Oh," Turk said.

Kizmic had to strain to hear because her mother had suddenly lowered her voice, like she had something she didn't want to say to herself.

"This is it, Turk. It all goes down hill from here."

"I can't believe she started already," he said.

"Shoot. Kalaya's late for the women in this family. I started when I was ten." Magdalene giggled. "Mama didn't say anything to us about it because she wasn't expecting any of us to start that early. So when I woke up with my monthly, I ran around the house like Carrie in that Stephen King novel, screaming like crazy. 'Get Mama! I'm dyin'! Oh, Lord! Jesus, help me! I'm dyin'!'"

Her parents' heavy laughter climbed the stairs.

"We still crack up about that to this day, but back then, we were scared to death. The good thing about it, though, was when it happened to Ella when she was eleven and Katherine when she was twelve, we knew what it was."

"What'd Kalaya say when y'all was in the bathroom?" Turk asked.

"Nothing. Just wanted to know when we were going to the store to get some Kotex."

What are Kotex? And what's a monthly? Kizmic's head was reeling with questions.

"Well, I guess it's time for you to have that talk with her," Turk said.

"Me! What about you?" Magdalene asked.

"What am I gonna say to her about that? I don't even know what to say to you every month when you come in here yellin' and actin' all crazy."

"I do not act crazy," she denied.

Ha! Kizmic almost said aloud. This was the first thing her parents had talked about that Kizmic completely understood. Most of the time her mother was really content and happy with her life and her family, but then there were times when she seemed fed up with everything and everybody. She would let them have it about unmade beds, dirty dishes, dirty clothes, unswept floors, fussed about not being a maid, but when they tried to help clean, she yelled for everyone to get out of her way.

"I do not act like that," Magdalene laughed.

"You do, too, and you know it. That's why you laughin'. But I tell you what. Next month, I'ma do you like they used to do women in the olden days and put your behind in a tent over in the park, and when Kalaya and Kizmic ask where you at, I'ma say, 'Your mother's got that evil spirit in her, so she gonna stay out there 'til it's gone.'"

Magdalene playfully slap Turk's leg. Kizmic loved the way her parents kidded and played with each other. Some kids' parents never laughed. They fought all the time. And not just with their mouths; they fought with their fists, feet, bottles, bricks, lye, bats, bed slats, knives, guns. Not that her parents didn't argue. They did. Sometimes loudly and for days. There were times when they'd gone a whole week without speaking and her father slept on the couch. But they didn't call each other ugly names, neither one left home, and they never put their hands on each other in anger.

"Seriously, though, Turk. We need to talk to Kalaya. My mother didn't talk to us and we were told all kinds of stupid things by our friends about it."

"Magdalene, what am I gonna say about a period, for real?"

"I've already talked to her about her period. You have to talk to her about boys."

"Oh, well, that'll be easy. Don't talk to 'em, don't touch 'em, don't let 'em touch you, don't bring 'em home, don't talk to 'em on the phone, don't even look at 'em."

"Turk ..."

"I'm not playing, Magdalene. If I catch Kalaya with a boy, I'ma kill him *and* her."

"Turk—"

"Don't 'Turk' me. That's all there is to it."

"No, it's not. You know daggone well that ain't gonna work."

"Magdalene. What about Kizmic?"

What about Kizmic! Kizmic asked with a sudden intake of breath.

"She's already nine. Do you think—"

"Don't say it, Turk! Don't even think it!" she said. "If we don't claim it, it won't happen."

A deep, fearful hush collapsed on them. Turk kissed the top of her head. "Come on. Let's go to bed.'"

Kizmic scurried back to her room.

As her parents walked up the steps, Turk said, "And you never put it on me like that."

"Did too."

"Did not."

"Did."

"Didn't."

"Did."

"Didn't."

Magdalene switched into their room and said, "I'm getting ready to put it on you again right now."

Turk laughed as he closed the door.

Whew! Kizmic thought as she got back in bed. I'm safe from whatever Kalaya's got. Mama and Daddy ain't never gonna haveta worry about things goin' down hill with me 'cause I ain't claimin' none of that stuff, not no period, not no monthly, not no friend, and not no boyfriends. All I'ma do is ride my bike and my skateboard, play basketball, football, baseball, and marbles with CJ and Sleepy-eyed Ted.

That was Kizmic's resolve, even more so when things started going down hill with Kalaya just as her mother had feared, as if the very breath she used to speak her worries had been drawn from a witch's vial. But it wasn't Magdalene's words that brought her fears to life.

Before Kalaya bled on their stoop, she, Magdalene, Aunt Beana, and Plum were best friends. They hung out together all the time doing their hair, painting their fingernails and toenails, having cooking parties, and shopping. Man, they shopped like nobody's business. They went shoe shopping, dress shopping, pants shopping, shorts shopping, underwear shopping, stocking shopping, sock shopping, skirt shopping, shirt and blouse shopping, belt shopping, earring shopping, watch shopping, ring shopping, necklace shopping, book shopping, bed shopping, table shopping, linen shopping, pots, pans, and dishes shopping. Why, those shopaholics even went window shopping. They ran from Mondawmin Mall to Security Square Mall to Westview Mall. When they came home, high off their shopping spree, they got out of the car laughing loudly, like a bunch of drunks coming in from happy hour.

Then Kalaya bled on their front stoop and two months later, Plum bled in her bed, and the bond between them, which was strong to begin with, seemed to grow even stronger, and soon the two girls preferred each other's company over anybody's, especially their mothers. So, it was with each other that Kalaya and Plum went shopping, saw triple features at the Hippodrome, the Town, the Howard, the New, and the Mayfair. They tied up the telephone talking about nothing, did each other's hair, and shut themselves up in their rooms and sang and danced to the latest Earth, Wind and Fire, Kool and the Gang, Rufus, Parliament-Funkadelic, or Donna Summer albums. They complained about their parents, their mothers in particular, whose sole mission in life, they believed, was to stop them from enjoying all the things the world had to offer teenage girls, the most extraordinary of which were boys.

As far as Kizmic was concerned, Kalaya and Plum were going crazy. Magdalene and Aunt Beana said they were "smellin' themselves." Kizmic had no clue what they meant by that because she never caught Kalaya or Plum smelling herself. She did catch Kalaya lying naked on the bed with a mirror looking at herself. What she was looking at or for only God knew. Kizmic eased the door closed and thought if "smellin' herself" meant Kalaya was doing nasty, disgusting things, Kizmic could shake her head, yeah. But if it also meant Kalaya was doing some plain old weird things, well, Kizmic could whole heartedly agree with that, too.

Kalaya and Plum used to be so much fun, especially in the summertime. Even with the box fan propped in the window blowing directly on them, Kizmic, Kalaya, and Plum couldn't sleep. Man, on those hot, sleepless nights they would sing Christmas carols, or sit on the floor like girl scouts around a campfire scaring themselves silly reading one of Aunt Beana's horror books, or playing Truth Or Consequences, Double Dare, Repeat, which Kizmic vowed never to play with them again after Kalaya dared her to knock on their parents' bedroom door. The challenge for Kizmic came not from knocking on the door, but from knocking on the door while all these strange moaning and squealing sounds were coming from the other side.

"What are they doin'?" Kizmic asked after those sounds chased her back to Kalaya's room without completing the dare.

"It," Kalaya said.

"'*It*'?" Kizmic frowned. "What's 'It'."

Kalaya and Plum dissolved into prankish girlie-girl giggles, just as they did when Kizmic asked if they were going to buy underwear for their fathers because they sat up half the night whispering and giggling as they looked through the men's underwear section of the *Sears* catalog.

Kizmic wanted to ask Kalaya and Plum what they found so fascinating about men standing around smiling in their drawers, but she knew what their answer would be. Before they started "smellin' themselves," Kalaya and Plum would answer all of Kizmic's questions.

"Hey Kalaya. What's that?"

"A praying mantis."

"Hey Plum. Where does the sun go when it gets dark?"

"The other side of the world."

"Really! Where's that?"

"China."

"Hey Kalaya. Is it true that stars are really angels that have gotten their wings?"

"Yeah."

"Hey Plum. Why you always writin' in that book?"

"It helps me get out things that bother me."

"Y'all wanna go outside and play?"

"Sure."

After the marble step thing, Kizmic's questions changed because Kalaya and Plum changed, and they only had two answers for anything she asked.

"Hey Kalaya. Who's Mary?"

"Get out!"

"Hey Plum. Who's Mary?"

"None-a-ya."

"Hey Kalaya. Who you talkin' to?"

"Get out!"

"Hey Plum. Why you keep writin' Tony in your book?"

"None-a-ya."

"Hey Kalaya ..."

"Get out!"

Kalaya and Plum did dangerous things too, like toyed with truckers on Plum's CB radio. Uncle Monty specifically warned them against that. "Some of those dudes ain't wrapped too tight," he said. That didn't stop Kalaya and Plum from getting on the channels calling themselves Peaches and Cotton

Candy. The hot, rough, static sound of the men's voices crackling out of that little box scared Kizmic more than the ghosts, vampires, and monsters in Aunt Beana's horror books. But what scared Kizmic more than anything was the way Kalaya and Plum began getting smart with Magdalene and Aunt Beana. Kalaya more so than Plum. Plum wasn't mouthy. Aunt Beana said, "Plum operates like a boy. She doesn't stand in my face tellin' me what she ain't gonna do. She just flat out don't do what I tell her to do. And when I lay into her little behind, she stands there all respectful, like she's really listenin' to me, you know. Then she'll turn right around and do exactly what I told her *not* to do."

Kalaya, on the other hand, was always trying to tell Magdalene what she wasn't going to do. Magdalene was reared by a mother who did not believe in explaining herself to her children. Whatever her mother said went. That was that. Geneva law. And there was a high price to pay for any of her three daughters who dared to question her about anything.

"Me and my sisters weren't allowed to even have questions in our eyes," Magdalene said. "And I promised myself that whenever I had children, I would at least give them the right to ask why."

And she did. She let Kizmic and Kalaya ask her all kinds of things.

"Mama, why can't I sleep with you and Daddy?"

"Mama, why can't you and I stay home together?"

"Mama, why can't I stay up with you and Daddy?"

"Mama, why can't I help you clean up?"

"Mama, why can't I help you cook?"

"Mama, why can't I wear my sandals in the winter time?"

At nine, Kizmic was still asking some of these cute, sweet, funny, innocent things, but after this "friend" business, Kalaya's whys stopped being cute, sweet, funny, and innocent and became annoying and sometimes down right disrespectful, nasty, and spiteful.

"Why do I have to go to bed at ten? That's too early."

"Why can't I stay home by myself? I'm old enough."

"Why do I have to go to the store with you? I don't feel like it."

"Why do I have to clean up? I didn't make the mess."

"Why do I have to help cook? I don't even like chitlins."

"Why do I have to go to the mall with you? I want to go with Plum."

"Why can't I have a boyfriend? I'm not a baby anymore."

"Why can't I go over his house? His mother is home."

"Why do I have to get off the phone? I'm in the house."

"Why can't I see that movie? All my friends have."

"Why can't I wear makeup? You wear it."

"Why do I have to come in at nine? Everybody else goes in at ten."

"Why can't I have a boyfriend?"

"Why can't I wear that dress? It ain't that short."

"Why can't I get a gold tooth? Everybody else has one."

"Why can't I go to the party? All my friends are going."

"Why are you always trying to stop me from having fun?"

"Why don't you leave me alone?"

"Why can't I have a boyfriend?"

"Now you see why I never let y'all question me," Grandma Geneva said when she came for a visit and heard Kalaya asking Magdalene a million and one questions, as if she were the mother instead of the child. "Ya'll wasn't gonna stay little forever and when you got older, your whys was gonna change 'cause the things you was gonna wanna do was gonna change, and no answer to y'all's questions was ever gonna be good enough. And I didn't wanna haveta hurt none of ya."

Grandma Geneva was right because the only answer that satisfied Kalaya's whys was the answer that allowed her to do exactly as she pleased. Magdalene found herself going back and forth with Kalaya and fussing to walls, ceilings, floors, and slammed doors about why she started that why business in the first place, and how she was going to stop Kalaya from going word for word with her before she had a real mess on her hands.

Like she didn't already, Kizmic thought.

CHAPTER

4

PING!

"GO! GO! GO!"

Kizmic's fingers clutched the chain link fence behind the batter's box as she watched Sleepy-eyed Ted drop the aluminum bat and run toward first base with his head down, turning left and right. A fly ball to center field sent Herman back peddling, glove up, eyes to the blue, cloudless sky. Easy out. Except he lost sight of the ball in the glaring June sun and it dropped—*Blump!* — right behind him.

"GO! GO! GO!"

Arms pumping like mad, Sleepy-eyed Ted tagged first base then booked to second. Herman snatched up the ball and hummed it to second base.

"STAAAY! STAAAY!" CJ and the rest of his teammates shouted when they saw Sleepy-eyed Ted getting ready to take off for third base.

Kizmic was supposed to be in the game, not riding the bench. But she had to stay home and pack up everything she owned, because today they were moving.

Movin'! Man ...

Kizmic still couldn't believe it. Two giant U-Haul trucks were parked in front of her house as well as Uncle Monty and Aunt Beana's, taking up almost the whole block. Every room had been stripped, boxed up, and loaded into the low decks and Mom's Attics of those trucks. Still, their moving was as unreal to Kizmic as it was when her parents first announced it during dinner this past April.

Turk and Magdalene sat at the table passing silly grins back and forth between them. Kizmic didn't think much of it. Her parents were always grinning at each other, especially if they had done *it* the night before, which Kizmic knew for a fact they had because she heard them when she got up to use the bathroom. Little did she know that them doing *it* the night before was in celebration of the horrible secret they were about to spring on their unsuspecting daughters.

Right before he took a bite of his barbecued chicken, Turk grinned at Magdalene then said, "Your mother and I bought a new house today."

He said it so nonchalantly, like he was telling them they bought a new couch or refrigerator. Nothing as life shattering or life ending as ...

"We're moving at the end of the school year," Magdalene grinned back.

How they went from eating dinner to moving was simple. The tiny houses her parents, uncle and aunt rented on Proctor Street were beyond one or two of their dreams, but with the projects to the left of them, the city jail to the right of them, the cemetery behind them, the abandoned buildings all around them, and that accident-waiting-to-happen concrete hill, those houses were nowhere near the castles in the air that their wildest dreams were constructed of. And for the longest time, Kizmic had been overhearing them talk and pray about getting as close to their wildest dreams as possible. The professions life's circumstances landed them in were not going to allow them to realize their wildest dreams, but they would allow them to do better than the little houses on Proctor Street. Especially after affirmative action slowly squeezed its foot then head through the racially barricaded doors at Decon Industries last year, forcing its owners to grudgingly promote two of the twenty-odd black employees to supervisory positions. Turk, who had more knowledge, skills, and experience than most of his white supervisors, was one of the two. Although, if it had been up to his boss, he would have turned down the job.

Imitating his boss' bitter tone, disparaging words, and resentful grimace, Turk recalled the conversation he had with him. "'You know, this affirmative action thing is gonna help you people take over.'"

It was the last really warm evening in October. The street lights were on and the oval globes on top of the iron poles standing tall and erect endlessly up and down the block looked down on the neighborhood, their spotlights crisscrossing so there appeared to be one wide continuous bright light that illuminated the streets, sidewalks, and alleyways. On Turk's turntable, Fred Wesley and the JB's "Damn Right, I Am Somebody!" played and the groovy horns trumpeted confidence and defiance out the open living room window. Turk, Magdalene, Aunt Beana, and Uncle Monty were sitting on the grasshopper green, metal porch chairs, which were on the sidewalk to the left of the marble steps, where Kizmic, Kalaya, and Plum sat. Kalaya sat tall and erect on the top step in the same spot as she had on the day those steps came to mean more than just a base, a chore, or a gathering place to her and came to represent her step out of girlhood and her giant Mother, May I? step into adolescence. Not that Kalaya asked her mother. With the rhythm and long-legged stride of a marching band leader, Kalaya gleefully high-stepped into it.

"What's affirmative action?" Kizmic asked from the bottom step.

"A law that makes whites hire a certain number of blacks," Magdalene explained. "Not enough to take over, though."

Uncle Monty guzzled down a few swigs from his can of Pabst Blue Ribbon beer, then said, "You got that right"

"I asked him, 'Us take over?'" Turk said. "'I don't see how. There's ten of y'all and only two of us.'" He chuckled, took a sip of beer, then once again in his boss' condescending voice, said, "'Yeah. Still. If I was you, I wouldn't take it 'cause they only givin' it to ya to fill some damn black quota.'"

"The nerve!" Aunt Beana said.

"What did you say?" Magdalene asked. "'Cause I know you said something."

"I said, 'You know what, John. When y'all start turnin' down jobs that y'all get just 'cause y'all white, I'll still take this one 'cause I worked my ass off to get it.'"

A month later, Kizmic was sitting cross-legged on the living room floor in front of the television eating a bowl of Corn Flakes and watching Fred Flintstone try to stop Barney Rubble from repossessing his television set.

Magdalene walked in and said, "Kizmic, hurry up and eat that before you're late for school. It's already seven forty-five."

Holding the bowl up to her face, Kizmic shoveled two spoonfuls of cereal into her mouth, then turned away from the screen and to her surprise saw that Magdalene wasn't wearing her uniform or headwrap. For work, Magdalene always wrapped her hair in one of her colorful, cotton headscarves. Sometimes she tied the scarf into a big bow, wrapping her hair up like a Christmas present, or she'd bundle it into a high bun or giant Afro puff and wrap the scarf around it like a headband. That morning, Magdalene was dressed in a pretty black, half sleeve, high waist dress and black heels, and her hair was pressed and styled in a tight bun.

"You got the papers?" Turk asked as he walked into the living room, decked out in one of his church-going blue suits on a Wednesday morning.

"Where y'all goin'?" Kizmic asked, frowning with curiosity.

Turk held his freshly clean-shaven chin up while Magdalene straightened his tie. "To see a man about a horse," he replied, which was what he said when he didn't want to tell her where he was going.

Kizmic ran on to school and didn't think anymore about it, not even at dinner when her parents started passing those silly grins across the table at each other. What Kizmic didn't know was Turk's promotion came with a slight increase in salary, not higher than his white coworkers, of course, but slight enough for them to afford a new house. Magdalene and Aunt Beana left Holy Cross and took positions and pay raises at Blue Crystal Fountain Nursing Home in northwest Baltimore, one block up from Pimlico Race Track and not far from their new neighborhood. Uncle Monty was bringing in good money as well, and because the neighborhood was in transition, he and Aunt Beana were able to buy a house right around the corner from them.

Turk told this to Kizmic and Kalaya as if he expected them to jump up and ecstatically throw hugs around his neck, and Magdalene smiled as if she expected them to be happy about leaving their friends, their school, and the only neighborhood they had ever known or cared to know, for that matter. Kizmic and Kalaya stared at their parents with angry looks that claimed shock and surprise. But their claims were as false as their parents' expectations were unrealistic.

"Hey, Kizmic!" CJ called.

The baseball game was over and he and Sleepy-eyed Ted ran from the other side of the fence.

"See. I told you they weren't gone yet," CJ said.

"Awww, shut up. You ain't tell nobody nothin'," Sleepy-eyed Ted said.

"I don't shut up. I spit up and then you go around the corner and lick it up."

Sleepy-eyed Ted laughed at his weak comeback then said, "Here," to Kizmic.

From the pocket of his shorts, he pulled out a marble. Not just any marble. The purple shooter with orange and blue swirls he'd drawn in his notebook and had named Kizmic. It was made of clay and was the most beautiful marble she'd ever seen. Amazed, Kizmic turned the marble around and around on the tips of her fingers and practiced holding it between her thumb and forefinger.

Sleepy-eyed Ted shoved CJ with his elbow. "Give her the other thing."

"Aiight, man. Quit pushin' me."

From the pocket of his glove, CJ pulled out their baseball and handed it to Kizmic. A couple months ago, the three of them chipped in a nickel and bought it from the thrift store after their old one rolled down the sewer. So it wasn't anything special. It wasn't autographed by Jim Palmer, Brooks Robinson, Reggie Jackson, or Ken Singleton, but it was signed. CJ and Sleepy-eyed Ted had scribbled their names and phone numbers in blue ink over the scuff marks, dirt, and grass stains on the cowhide. She never knew their numbers until that day. Never had a reason to. When she wanted to talk to them, she just knocked on their front doors. Not anymore. Their phone numbers on that baseball hit home. She was moving away.

Today, she thought, eyes tearing up.

"Kizmic!" Magdalene yelled from their back door.

Her stomach dipped at the sound of her mother calling her home. Only she wasn't going home. She was going to some strange, new house far away from there, far away from her friends.

"Awww, come on, Kizmic, don't cry," CJ said, smiling at her with his gentle, blue eyes. "It ain't like you ain't never gonna see us again."

Patting her on the shoulder, Sleepy-eyed Ted said, "Yeah, man. We friends forever. Don't be cryin' like some old girl."

"I ain't ... cryin'," Kizmic lied, lowering her head and closing her eyes so tears wouldn't roll down her cheeks.

"KIZMIC!" Magdalene called again.

"Come on. We'll walk home with you," CJ said and picked up his skateboard.

Kizmic turned and looked at the hill. Man, I didn't even get a chance to go down it, she thought.

She could have ridden her skateboard down it plenty of times, but with Kalaya acting a fool, she didn't want to give her mother anything else to worry about. Besides, she had all her life to go down that hill. Now she was moving and she just had that moment.

"Lemme hold your skateboard," Kizmic said and snatched CJ's board out of his hand.

Sleepy-eyed Ted grabbed her by the arm. "Your mama gonna kill you." His sleepy brown eyes peered at her with the protective look of a friend or brother looking out for his buddy or sister.

"My Mama ain't here, and I won't be either in a few minutes."

"Aiight then," he said and turned her loose. "This is what you gotta do. Don't zig-zag when you first start. Just go straight down. Then when you get half way, start to zig-zag, but not too hard. And when the wheels hit the sidewalk, turn and you won't even go into the street. Cool?"

"Cool," Kizmic said.

Sleepy-eyed Ted held out the palm of his hand and Kizmic slapped him five.

"Ride down with her," he ordered, shoving his skateboard at CJ. He ran down the hill to show Kizmic the path then stood at the bottom and waved them on.

Kizmic took a few deep breaths and pushed to the back of her mind her parents' threats of whipping her behind if they ever caught her riding her skateboard down that hill. She put her right foot on the deck of the skateboard, pushed off on the ground with her left —

WHOOSH!

"WHOA!"

Kizmic dropped. No kidding. There was no little dip, no gradual descent.

Kizmic essentially rolled off a cliff, because that hill was ten—Naw *Twenty* times steeper than it looked standing on the sidelines watching everyone else go down. The plunge was heart stopping. A second ago, Kizmic could feel hers pounding anxiously in her chest. Now she couldn't feel it beating at all. She shot down that hill so fast that it probably came right out of her body and was hanging in the air where she took off.

I shoulda stayed back there with it, Kizmic thought, clutching the baseball hard enough to crush it with her bare hand.

But more than likely her heart was still in her chest, frozen with fear. Fear that her mother was right. Fear that she was either going to fall off that skateboard and break her doggone neck or go careening out into the middle of Homewood Street and get hit by a car. Either way, her mother was going to kill her, because she was not making it down that steep hill in one piece.

ZOOOOM!

The wheels spun so fast that sometimes they lifted off the ground, which was good and bad. Good, because the concrete wasn't smooth. It was bumpy as all get out, and it made the skateboard vibrate and the wheels shake like they were about to fall off. Bad, because when the board went airborne, she had trouble controlling it when it landed. She lost her balance more than once and almost fell off. Maybe she wouldn't have had such a hard time if she were on her board. She wasn't used to CJ's. Regardless, Kizmic wanted off this ride.

What if I put my foot down? She glanced at the ground whizzing by. No, I'm goin' too fast. I'ma fall, she thought, envisioning that ill-fated skier crashing down the slope on the intro of *ABC's Wide World of Sports*.

Kizmic looked at the street below. Cars were zooming all over the place.

I can't stop! she thought, panicking, wanting to scream for her Mama, like she did when she got stuck on a ride at the amusement park that went too high and too fast.

Man, Mama's gonna kill me if I get hit by a car!

Alarm was blaring in her ears, but somehow she heard Sleepy-eyed Ted's voice.

"Kizmic! Zig-zag!" he yelled. "You gotta start zig-zaggin'!"

"Yeah," CJ said.

She had forgotten he was riding beside her. Remembering she was not alone, Kizmic watched CJ zig-zag, then mirrored his movements.

"That's it!" Sleepy-eyed Ted shouted.

The zig-zagging slowed her roll and helped her gain control of the skateboard. She and CJ moved left, right, left, right in sync gracefully, like figure skaters in the Olympics. She was no longer plummeting down that forbidden hill; she was gliding. The hot summer air rushed over her body. She didn't feel the bumps in the concrete. The ride was smooth and every bit of the thrill kids who had ridden down claimed it was.

CJ hollered, "Woooooo!"

Sleepy-eyed Ted hollered, "Wooooooo!"

Kizmic hollered, "Woooooo!"

"Now turn!" Sleepy-eyed Ted yelled as they neared the sidewalk.

Kizmic turned and with a scraping skid, the skateboard stopped right at the edge of the curb with CJ and right in front of Sleepy-eyed Ted.

She looked back up the hill. Old Man Graves' pigeons circled overhead. Kizmic watched them and listened to life in the park go on under the hot June sun as usual. And she wondered how life there could go on without missing a bounce, a swing, a throw, a hit, a catch, a slide, a tackle when her life was coming to an end. At least her life on Proctor Street.

Turk led their four-vehicle caravan from the east side to the west side, dancing in his seat behind the wheel of the U-HAUL truck, yelling, "Ahhhh! That's my song!" whenever any song came on the radio.

Sitting next to him, holding the Kizmic shooter in one hand and the baseball in the other, Kizmic looked out the window, watching them get farther and farther away from Proctor Street, and trying to ignore her father so she could stay good and mad about it. But he was so doggone happy and he wouldn't leave her alone. He kept tugging on her plaits, poking her on the arm, covering her face with his big-ole hands, tickling her side! Kizmic hated to be tickled.

"Stop! Daaady!" Kizmic whined, hunching her shoulder to get him to quit sticking his finger in her ear. *I shoulda rode with Mama and Kalaya.*

Ordinarily, Kizmic would have raced or argued with Kalaya for the privilege of riding shotgun, to no avail nine times out of ten. Kalaya always left Kizmic in the dust during their foot races to the car and when she wasn't in the mood to run, she won their arguments by claiming that as the eldest the front seat was her birthright. Even when Kalaya had copped an attitude with Magdalene about something, she never forfeited a race or relinquished her birthright. She plopped her angry behind in the front seat and gave Magdalene the silent treatment just as loud as she could, like that was going to make their mother give her whatever she wanted. It never did. Most of the time Magdalene ignored her. Kizmic knew her mother was ignoring the heck out of Kalaya as she tailed them in Turk's 1970, green Plymouth Scamp, because Kalaya had a serious 'tude with Turk *and* Magdalene. Not about the move. It didn't cause her to leave her best friend behind. Kalaya's anger stemmed from something inside the new house she felt she was entitled to, like the front passenger side seat.

Kizmic planned to ride in the back seat, not giving their mother the evil eye like Kalaya, but pouting in silent protest of the move. Her sit-in, however, was derailed by Turk, who said, "Uh-uh. Y'all ain't gonna gang up on my baby with your funky, little attitudes." He scooped Kizmic up off the side walk. "You ridin' with me."

Turk beat the drums on the dashboard and played the electric keyboard on the steering wheel for Eddie Kendricks' song "Keep On Truckin'." Kizmic's body rocked to the motion of the van as they traveled up Belvedere Avenue.

"That's where your mama and Beana will be workin'," Turk said, slowing down and pointing with a jerk of his head to Blue Crystal Fountain Nursing Home.

Kizmic stopped turning the baseball, leaned forward, looked out the driver's side window, and saw a squat, red brick building with a tall, sky blue wall enclosing a courtyard.

"Daddy, why we gotta move?" she asked, flopping back against the seat, her face reflecting the sadness in her voice.

Turk glanced at Kizmic then back at the road. "Well, 'cause me and your mama want y'all to grow up in a nice house."

"I like our house," she said. Her throat ached as tears built up in her eyes.

"You like being cramped up in that tiny room with Kalaya?" he asked.

Heck no, Kizmic thought, especially not now with Kalaya acting crazy all the time.

But ... "I'on't wanna live 'round here either."

"How you know you don't wanna live around here when you ain't never lived around here before?"

"I'on't know." She went back to rolling the baseball around in her hand and stared out the window. Through the high chain link fence surrounding Pimlico Race Track, Kizmic saw trainers feeding or hosing down horses in the stables and riding thoroughbreds on the elevated track. The horses' hooves kicked up clumps of dirt as they trotted and galloped around their grand stage.

At the red light on the corner of Belvedere and Park Heights Avenue, Turk looked at Kizmic with shiny, sympathetic eyes. "Come on now, Kizmic, you actin' like you 'bout to die."

"It feels like it."

"No it don't. You just gettin' started livin', baby girl. Give it a chance. You might be surprised."

"I've Got To Use My Imagination" came on the radio.

"Ahhhh!" Turk shouted. "That's my — "

"Song," Kizmic said, puckering her lips, and thinking, Gladys Knight and the Pips were singing her song too, because she was going to have to use all her imagination to get over not being able to play with CJ and Sleepy-eyed Ted.

The light turned green. Turk steered the truck with his knees and continued clapping and dancing. Driving down Belvedere, they passed Mr. Baker hair salon and Little Tavern on the right, and on the left a big, stone church with *GOD IS LOVE* written in giant light bulbs on the roof of the building. On the same side, directly across from the church, was a multipurpose center. Then came the rowhouses on both sides of the avenue's long blocks, big, pretty, two-story houses, all different colors—white, green, blue, gray, red, yellow, pink. And even though they were connected, they weren't scrunched up. They had room and large front porches. Black kids were everywhere, playing on the big porches, running up and down the wide sidewalks, walking around eating snowballs and frozen cups, or just hanging out on the corners talking. Each block ended or began with a corner store, and kids ran in and out of them with candy, cookies, ice cream. A boy riding an orange ten-speed bike up the street yanked on the handlebars and popped a wheelie. He pedaled, turning the handlebars back and forth to help keep his balance. He reminded Kizmic of a cowboy whose stallion was standing on its hind legs. She half expected the boy to whip off his baseball cap, hold it in the air, and yell, *Hi O, Silva!*

Wow! Kizmic thought, then quickly reined in her excitement when she noticed Turk looking at her with a *See, what'd I tell you* smile on his face.

Shoot. That don't mean nothin', Kizmic told him with a frown. I still don't see no place to play ball around here.

There was no park in the center of the neighborhood. Just islands running down the middle of Belvedere, covered in splendid green grass and lined with small, attractive green trees.

Turk turned right onto Beaufort Avenue. Magdalene followed. Uncle Monty honked the horn of his U-HAUL and kept straight on Spaulding, heading to their house at the corner of Spaulding and Litchfield. Aunt Beana and Plum tailed him in his van.

The brakes of the truck squealed sharply as Turk whipped it into a parking space in front of a red brick, two-story, semi-detached house. Magdalene pulled up behind him, leaving enough room to extend the loading ramp.

Turk shifted the truck in park, shut off the engine, looked at Kizmic, and smiled, "We're here, baby girl."

He leaned over, pressed his soft, full lips on Kizmic's forehead — "MmmmmMuah!" —then hopped out. In the side view mirror, Kizmic watched her father walk toward her mother, swinging his arms wildly behind his back and bopping hard, imitating George Jefferson's smooth walk. Magdalene got out of the car clapping and singing the Jefferson's "Movin' On Up" theme song. Then they kissed on the lips out in the middle of the street.

Shaking her head as if she could shake off her embarrassment, Kizmic scooted to the edge of the seat and checked out the block.

Up the street was a red brick building that had a corner store on the first level and an apartment above it. In addition to the house next to theirs, across the street were two other two-story, semi-detached, red brick houses, except they had been turned into two-unit apartments. On the right side of the alley near the apartment directly across the street from their house, sat a forest green, three-unit apartment building. Framed in the windows, seemingly closed off from the world outside, were children and grownups. One, two, or three lily-white faces hung in the windows, like drabby curtains. None of them smiling, none of them waving, none of them shouting, "Hello! Welcome to the neighborhood."

It echoed scenes from the nightly news that broadcasted white men, women, boys, and girls fighting against school desegregation, their eyes nothing more than angry black slits and their mouths nothing but gritted white teeth or deep black holes that yelled and cursed and threatened. Some smiled brightly for the cameras while proudly holding up handwritten signs that shouted for them, "KEEP CITY SCHOOLS WHITE," "INTERGRATION IS UNCHRISTIAN," "SEGREGATION FOREVER."

While the whites in the windows didn't yell or look hostile, Kizmic read on their opossum-still faces, *KEEP OUR NEIGHBORHOOD WHITE*. Or rather Jewish, because that's who lived in that apartment building. With flat blue, hazel, green, and brown eyes, they stared at Turk and Magdalene, who stood in front of their new home with his arm draped over her shoulder, and her arm wrapped around his waist.

Turk escorted Magdalene up seven stately, dark slate gray and white, wood steps that had white, wood railings on either side. The wood porch was broad and dark slate gray as well. White, wood railings wrapped around it and two black, iron columns held up a flat roof.

Turk turned around and waved his hand. "Come on, girls!" Anticipation rang like Christmas bells in his heavy voice.

Kalaya slowly got out of the Plymouth. On her face was a mug so flawless that it appeared as if her anger had been sewn on by a high fashion seamstress. Bothered by the unfriendly stares of her neighbors, Kizmic sat back in her seat.

Turk came to get her. "What's the hold up, baby girl?"

"Them," Kizmic said, cutting her eyes in the direction of the frozen, bleak, closed faces.

Turk looked at the people next door, glanced over his shoulder at the people across the street, then turned back to Kizmic and asked, "Is that all?" like

Pssshh! He opened the door and laid on her his large, loving smile, which always made her feel like nothing could get through him to do her harm.

"Baby girl, we grew up in Lynchburg, South Carolina, so we used to white folks doin' a heck of a lot more than just lookin' at us hard," he chuckled.

Hearing her father laugh confirmed his invincibility for Kizmic. That being the case, well, Pssshh!

Kizmic hopped out of the truck. Squinting from the sun's boastful glare, she looked around at all the sun claimed this neighborhood to be and doubted that it would live up to even one shiny ray of hype.

From the pocket of his jeans, Turk pulled out a silver key. Grinning, he turned it back and forth the way a magician would to show his audience that his prop was really what it appeared to be. He stuck the key in the gold lock of the big, white door and opened it like—abracadabra—magic!

A large, bright hallway, cream colored with beautiful chestnut hickory wood flooring and staircase welcomed them inside. To the right was a spacious yet cozy living room with beige walls, white woodwork, and tall windows. Painted soft antique white, the dining room had an elegant, gold, five-light chandelier hanging from the ceiling and two windows that provided a tall, wide view of the back yard and also brought in a stream of shaded sunlight. The kitchen was three sizes bigger than the kitchen on Proctor. It had a bunch of wood cabinets, *and* a pantry, yellow, laminate countertops, a double bowl sink, three windows, and honey-yellow vinyl flooring that matched the bright yellow walls. The back yard was enormous with tall trees and carpet-like green grass. Upstairs were *four* big bedrooms. The bathroom was large, powder blue, with a dome-shaped skylight in the center of the ceiling that brought in so much sun that the light didn't have to be on. And it had a shower! That house truly was something straight out of *Better Homes and Gardens Magazine.*

Kizmic walked into her medium-sized, bright, airy blue bedroom. Standing in the middle of the floor, she thought that having her own room was a poor consolation for making her move away from her friends, but at least now she wouldn't have to listen to Kalaya and Plum talk and giggle about boys and wouldn't have to deal with Kalaya rolling her eyes every time she came into the room. She'd no longer have to keep her marble collection under the bed, and she'd be able to put stuff she loved on the walls, like the tiny, plastic basketball hoop her father bought her. She had no place to hang it in Kalaya's room, but in *her* room, Kizmic found the perfect spot, right over the door that led out to the infamous upstairs back porch. Kalaya's birthright.

It seemed the developers had placed the design of the homes in the hands of an architect that most parents believed had to have either been high on marijuana or living in some fantasy world because the houses had two back porches—one off the kitchen, as usual, and one attached to an upstairs back bedroom.

"Now tell me. What fool would build a porch off a child's room?" Aunt Beana asked. "Puttin' a child—"

"Puttin' *our child*," Uncle Monty emphasized.

"in that room is like sayin', 'Go on, Plum. Run the streets all hours of the night while we're asleep. We don't give a damn,'" Aunt Beana said.

Parents concluded that the pothead or crazed architect didn't have any children, because any parent with just a bit of common sense would have known that even the most obedient, straight-laced, chicken-hearted children would find it difficult to resist the draw of the wild, unsupervised fun they would hear the cutest and coolest children brag about having after midnight when all the square, uncool kids were at home tucked in bed like good little mama's boys and girls. Turk, Magdalene, Uncle Monty, and Aunt Beana had more than a little sense about them, so they knew that sooner or later curiosity would grab hold of Kalaya and Plum's good, common sense and shove it into a closet. Desire would take their caution and stuff it into a drawer. Raging hormones would overpower their fear and kick it into a corner. And the next thing they would know, Kalaya and Plum, who were far from the most obedient, level-headed, straight-laced, chicken-hearted teenagers in the world, would be standing on the edge of that upstairs back porch, ready to jump in on all the fun.

So it was that in the Waters' household, like every other in the neighborhood, the youngest child was awarded that back bedroom. Uncle Monty and Aunt Beana planned to turn theirs into a library for all of Aunt Beana's books and put a deadbolt lock on the door to the back porch.

"What if there's a fire and that's the only way out?" Plum asked.

"Your father and I have keys," Aunt Beana told her. "The door will get opened."

"Or the window," Plum said, as a smile sneaked across her face.

"Climb out that window if you want to, hear?" Uncle Monty said. "You won't climb out nare 'nother one."

Pretending her baseball was a basketball, Kizmic went up for a jumper and made an imaginary three-pointer. In the middle of her celebration dance, Kalaya walked in, her eyes pressed hard against the door, her mouth open in awe of it. She didn't even look around, because to Kalaya the room was not the draw, but a nonessential accessory. If she were a realtor, her sales pitch would have been, "And this wonderful back porch also comes with a room. It ain't much, but it's a good place to take a catnap."

With the delicate fingers of a safecracker, Kalaya slowly turned the lock until she heard the bolt slide open. Savoring the excitement inside her, Kalaya hesitated before putting her hand on the knob. Finally, she opened the door and a soft white light jumped on Kalaya like a puppy welcoming her owner home. Then it ran wildly into the room. Kizmic had not realized how dark the room was until the sunlight rushed in and illuminated every corner, every crack. Drawn like moths to the beckoning daylight, Kalaya and Kizmic walked out onto the porch. And it was like walking into another room inside the house.

The previous owners had freshly painted the wooden porch a dark, forest green, which blended well with the two tall, leafy green, ripe berry trees that flanked it. There wasn't a loose plank or beam anywhere. It had a slanted roof that shielded them from the brunt of the sun's heat.

As Kalaya stood on that upstairs back porch, her brown eyes glittered with the prospect of all the dirt she could get away with if that room were hers. She let out a deep, long sigh that curled her full lips into an unruly smile.

Kizmic watched as Kalaya's mind filled with intoxicating, mischievous thoughts. She became so inebriated by them that she actually swayed and had to hold on to the railing to keep from falling over. Magdalene's sudden presence on the porch didn't even sober up Kalaya.

She stood between Kizmic and Kalaya, folded her arms, and looked up toward the sky. For a few quiet moments they admired the view. It was nice being together like that. It felt to Kizmic like old times, when they were back on Proctor Street, standing on the hill, looking over the city. If the house could bring peace between her mother and sister, then the move was worth it.

Kizmic looked at her mother then at Kalaya and saw that her sister wasn't with them. She was admiring a whole different view. Her eyes were cast downward at the alley, for Kalaya thought of the view in the same way she thought of the room, as an okay accessory.

"Well," Magdalene said. "We'd better start unloading."

She turned to go inside, but Kalaya asked in a voice that seemed far away, "Why can't I have this room?"

Magdalene paused and frowned a bit. "What?"

Awww man! Kizmic thought with dread.

"Why can't I have this room?" Kalaya asked again. Asking why when her mother and father had told this girl how it was going to be and that should have been the end of it. But it never was with Kalaya.

Magdalene flatly refused to go over it again. So the two of them stood there, glaring at each other. Kizmic looked from mother to daughter, from daughter to mother. Both were tall, both had the same intense, insistent brown eyes that held impossible expectations for the other. Both had the same full lips that twisted, bent, turned down, and curved up as her mother swore that when she was Kalaya's age, she was nothing like Kalaya and as Kalaya swore that when she grew up, she would be nothing like her mother. Both swears were utterly ridiculous to Kizmic because whether they wanted to acknowledge it or not, they looked alike, talked alike, walked alike, dressed alike, danced alike, sang alike, smiled alike, frowned alike. They even slept alike.

Y'all would see that if y'all would stop fightin' long enough, Kizmic thought.

"How you gonna give this room to Kizmic?" Kalaya pushed, sounding like Kizmic didn't deserve the room because she couldn't possibly appreciate the gift that it was.

Magdalene's face darkened, her eyes narrowed, and her lips flattened across her face in a straight line. "You want to know how?" she asked in a voice much calmer than the teed off expression on her face.

The calm in Magdalene's voice made Kalaya leery, so she shut her mouth. Kalaya always did that. Kept on and kept on until her mother was pissed. Then she would stand there with this dumb look on her face, like she didn't know why her mother wanted to kill her.

"You really want to know how?" Magdalene asked. "I'll show you how."

With nervous curiosity, Kizmic waited to see what her mother was going to do, not expecting Magdalene to seize her arm then drag her into the house. The grip Magdalene had on Kizmic's arm left indentations on her soft skin.

"Mama," Kizmic cried in alarm, dropping her baseball.

It rolled out onto the porch. Kizmic feared it would go under the railing and fall down into the yard, but it came to a rest against Kalaya's feet as she stood with the same *what-are-you-doin'?* look on her face that Kizmic had on hers.

When Magdalene reached the middle of the room, she stopped. "This is how."

Kizmic was so mad at her mother for dragging her into the middle of their argument. She wanted to tell Magdalene and Kalaya, Y'all can have this room! Y'all can come in here every day and scream and holler at each other all day long. I don't care! Y'all make me sick, fightin' 'bout nothin', messin' up everythin' all the doggone time.

"Mama!" Kalaya yelled as she stomped inside.

"First of all, don't you *ever* yell at me! Second of all, 'Mama,' nothin'." Magdalene turned her head slightly to the side and her voice went up a little higher as she asked, "Kalaya, do you really think your father and I are stupid?"

Kalaya looked at her mother as if she had no idea why she would ask such an absurd question. Of course she thought they were stupid.

"You're not getting this room and that's all there is to it."

Kalaya stomped her foot and yelled, "That ain't fair!"

"Life ain't fair!"

"I want this room!"

"And people in hell want ice water!"

Kalaya had a smart mouth, but the person she inherited it from was more than time enough for hers. Magdalene was forever coming back at Kalaya with stuff she could only dream of saying to her mother, and she dreamed out loud about saying stuff all the time. Sleeping in Kalaya's room made Kizmic subjected to it all. Every other day, Kalaya slammed her door and with that scornful, powerless glare bloating her face, she told their mother off. So even as Kalaya stood silent in front of their mother, Kizmic heard the rant going on inside her head. *Just 'cause you're all old and can't have any fun ... Oooh, you make me sick! I can't stand you! I can't wait until I'm old enough to move outta here! You get on my nerves!*

Magdalene was not without her own particular rants and accompanied threatening glare. Every other day, Kizmic watched her mother's angry face as she waited for Kalaya to play like she had lost her mind, and when she did, she would whup her behind.

"Go on. Say something," Magdalene begged Kalaya. "I dare you. Say anything and I'll beat the livin' daylights outta you."

Kizmic prayed Kalaya wouldn't say another word. One second. Two seconds. Three seconds passed. Right before the fourth second, Kalaya pressed her arms against her sides, balled her hands into fists, closed her eyes, threw her head toward the ceiling, and just screamed. Screamed like a crazy person.

Oh, my God! Kizmic said to herself.

She was used to Kalaya yelling. Used to her crying, stomping, jumping up and down. But wailing like a banshee? She wasn't used to that. Worried that her mother had finally succeeded in driving Kalaya insane, Kizmic rushed to comfort her. She threw her arms around her big sister, but they were too small to pull Kalaya back from the edge her mother had shoved her over. Kizmic looked to her mother for help. Magdalene didn't move. She stood there with the disgusted look of a woman watching her thirteen-year-old daughter go through the terrible twos.

Turk rushed in. "What the hell's goin' on?"

"Nothing," Magdalene said.

"Nothin'? Well, what she screamin' like that for?"

"Ask her," Magdalene said, pursing her lips.

"Kalaya?" he asked.

"She won't let me have this room," Kalaya cried.

Turk stood there for a moment, blinking in disbelief. "Are you serious?" he asked.

"Yes, she is," Magdalene laughed humorlessly.

"Kalaya, you are too old to be screamin' and hollerin' like you're two."

"But, Daddy, I want this room!"

That was it. The last straw. The straw that broke the camel's back. Whatever you want to call it, Kalaya broke it in half. All of them saw it when it broke. Magdalene's entire face shut down. Turk reached for his wife's arm, but she yanked loose before he got a good grip. She tramped toward Kalaya, who backed up and out onto her prized back porch. Magdalene kept coming until Kalaya's back was pressed against the railing.

Kizmic stood frozen, afraid that her mother might actually pick Kalaya up and throw her off that porch. Kalaya must have been afraid of the same thing because she grabbed the railing and held onto it for dear life. From behind, Turk got a hold of Magdalene's arms.

Magdalene was straining to keep from sounding like her own mother, but she couldn't help it. Her mother was in her blood. So she ended up sounding the exact same way her mother sounded every time she gave an order and expected her daughters to follow it without question. Standing almost nose to nose with Kalaya, she asked, "You want to know why you can't have this room?"

Kalaya was too afraid to even nod her head.

Gritting her teeth, Magdalene said, "Because I said so!"

Tears that Kalaya didn't seem to know she was crying ran down her face. And that, as they say, was the end of that.

CHAPTER

6

ALL NIGHT LONG, KIZMIC DREAMED that she was in the park playing marbles
with CJ and Sleepy-eyed Ted and, as usual, kicking their behindases. One of
her shots with her clay Kizmic shooter netted ten of their marbles, which she
added to the pitcher's mound of marbles beside her. And check it out. There
wasn't a cat's eye glaring at her in the whole bunch. Oh, Kizmic was dreaming
like a mug!

Then right after CJ used his pocketknife to note Kizmic's eight thousand
five hundred and thirty-seventh win on the tree trunk, morning came and with
it, reality, spelled out in black magic marker on the cardboard boxes stacked
against the wall on the opposite side of the door to the back porch. *KIZMIC'S
ROOM, KIZMIC'S ROOM, KIZMIC'S ROOM, KIZMIC'S ROOM, KIZMIC'S
ROOM, KIZMIC'S ROOM*

Kizmic lie in bed, staring at the words her mother had carefully written on
the boxes with the purpose of not simply identifying which room to put them
in, but to drill in Kizmic's head that they no longer lived on Proctor Street.

Kizmic sat up and looked straight out into the bright day through the
opened door. The air was filled with different tweets, cheeps, and chirps from
brown, black, and red birds that flew in and out of the trees, chasing one another like kids engaged in a game of tag. The birds came so close to the doorway at times that Kizmic thought they would fly right into her room, but they
always swooped up to the roof at the last minute. Squirrels squeaked as they
scurried across the porch railing. White and black winged butterflies fluttered
about. Yellowjackets, honeybees, and bumblebees buzzed around. Dogs arfed
and bow-wowed. Woodpeckers drummed holes into trees.

"It's like Wild Kingdom out there," she said.

Kizmic got out of bed, pulling down the top of her Scooby Doo and the Gang yellow pajamas. She grabbed the baseball off her nightstand and walked onto the porch. The raised growth rings on the wood planks felt rough and cool on her bare feet. An easy breeze was blowing, rustling the leaves in the trees and scenting the air with the sweet smell of grass, dirt, and flowers. When they moved, Kizmic believed she would never again be as close to the sky as when she stood at the crest of concrete hill, but on the upstairs back porch, she could look out over the rooftops of her new neighborhood. They were lined up nice and neat, except for the chimneys, which were off an inch or so to the left or right on each house. Some were made of red bricks, others were made of concrete. The ones made of brick had triangular tops; the ones made of concrete were simply square. They were rather hideous and the way they perched on the rooftops reminded Kizmic of gargoyles, dead still during the day, then coming to life at night to protect them from evil.

A flock of pigeons cooed. Homesickness played tricks with Kizmic's mind and got her believing that Old Man Graves' pigeons had followed her there. Eager to see some familiar faces, Kizmic lifted her brown eyes to the sky with a cheerful smile that dropped when all she saw above her head were white clouds drifting over a sea of blue. She realized then that the coos were coming from below.

"Somebody's got a coop around here," she said.

Kizmic leaned over the railing and looked up the alley, but the full, green trees in the yards blocked her view. When she stood upright again, she caught sight of a man across the alley standing on the upstairs porch of the pink house on Belvedere. He was high yellow, a little shorter than average height, lean, with a huge, round Afro, finely edged around his high forehead. His eyelids were droopy, like Sleepy-eyed Ted's, but his eyes were nowhere near as friendly. He had a gaze. Not an unwelcoming stare, like the white people in the windows of the green apartment building. A gaze that was hard to look at, because it was ...

"Creepy," Kizmic mumbled, trying not to frown from the willies the man's gaze stirred up in her.

She also found his gaze to be rude.

He shouldn't be starin' at people all hard without speakin', Kizmic thought.

That's what her mother told her. Then again, she was staring at him, too, and hadn't parted her lips to say boo.

But I ain't lookin' at him all creepy, Kizmic thought. And *anyway*, I'm only lookin' at him 'cause he lookin' at me. Plus Mama and Daddy told me not to speak to strangers.

The man's coal-black eyes sat on his long, oval face, not twitching, not blinking, not jumping. Just sat there, lifeless, gazing at her.

Why 'on't he stop lookin' at me like that? she complained. Then, sucking her teeth and dismissively waving the hand holding the baseball at him, said, "I'm goin' in the house."

Before she could turn away to go inside, the man smiled the creepiest smile Kizmic had ever seen awake or when she was asleep having a nightmare. The smile didn't spread across his face. That thing crawled and slithered on its belly like two thin, pink snakes lying on top of each other. His smile was crooked and jagged, as if someone had carved it into his face with a butcher knife, the way you carved a smile on a jack-o'-lantern.

Realizing he'd presented his creepy, crawly smile in response to her wave, Kizmic thought, I wasn't sayin' hi; I was sayin' poot you.

Suddenly, the man's eyes sprung to life, like opossums that had been playing dead.

"Whoah!" Kizmic nearly jumped out of her skin.

The man's coal-black eyes moved fitfully inside their sockets as he peeked through the gaps in the wood spindles, trying to get a whole look at her.

Men looked at Kizmic all the time. The ice cream man, the mailman, the arabber man, the oil man, the trashman, CJ and Sleepy-eyed Ted's fathers. But none of their eyes ever made her feel the way this man's eyes made her feel. Kizmic couldn't put her finger on how or why, but in this man's gaze she felt as if her pajamas were laying in a heap at her feet. She actually looked down at herself to make sure she hadn't jumped out of her clothes instead of her skin when his eyes startled her. Uncle Monty's good or dead eye didn't make her feel buck naked. Her father looked at her every day of her life with his brown eyes, and all Kizmic ever felt was loved, special, smart, and pretty, tall as him sometimes, small as a helpless baby other times, safe all the time. That's how she knew something wasn't right, not just with his eyes, or the way he looked at her, but ...

Somethin' ain't right with *him*, Kizmic thought.

As she squinted at the man trying to see exactly what wasn't right, the static, male voices that pawed at her, Kalaya, and Plum from inside the CB radio clicked on in her mind, and she got the eerie feeling that he might be one of those truckers Uncle Monty said wasn't wrapped too tight. She imagined the man driving his big rig cross-country, going without sleep, food, and water because he couldn't wait to lick the sweet, syrupy taste of Peaches on his fingertips and suck the sticky Cotton Candy on the roof of his mouth until it melted into pure sugar on his tongue. While picturing this, the loud, rapid tapping of Popsicle sticks hitting the spinning spokes of bicycle wheels drowned out the roaring horse-powered engine of the eighteen-wheeler in Kizmic's mind.

She followed the tapping down to the alley and in a flurry — "One, two, three, four, five, six, seven, eight — Eight!" Kizmic counted — young, black boys soared through the alley.

They moved past the large gap in the overhanging trees near her yard so fast that she saw only glimpses of them and thought they too were figments of her homesickness. Then she heard them talking.

"Last one there is a rotten egg!" one of them shouted.

"That ain't fair. You just called it," another boy complained.

"Awww, stop cryin', man, and come on," said another.

Kizmic was struck with wide-eyed, opened-mouth excitement by the fact that they were real as real could be, and at the moment she only wanted to know two things: who those boys were and where they were going so she could meet them there.

Sprinting through her bedroom, Kizmic joined their race, hoping to get to her front door before they reached the street. In the hallway, she hit the stairs two at a time. Downstairs, she pushed open the screen door, ran onto the front porch, and —

"HISSSSSS!" A cat leaped into its attack stance, back arched, tail bristled, and claws out.

Petrified as a defenseless bird, Kizmic flew back in the house, slamming and locking the front door then backing away from it, as if the cat might pick the lock with a claw.

"Kizmic, what in the world are you doing?" Magdalene called from the kitchen.

Shaking and breathing hard and fast, she yelled, "There's a cat on the porch!"

"I don't care. You better stop slamming my door."

On tiptoe, Kizmic approached the door, praying she had scared the cat as much as it had scared her, and it had gone on about its business. Nope. The beast was still sitting on her porch, licking itself. It was a slender, short-haired, blue point colored cat with large ears, big almond-shaped, sapphire blue eyes, and a long, skinny tail. Of all the cats Kizmic was afraid of, she was deathly afraid of *that* cat because it was Siamese, and she had heard that those cats were particularly mean. Why, they would turn on their owners if they were pissed off enough.

"Get off my porch," Kizmic demanded, staying safely behind the screen door.

The cat didn't lift one paw to leave. Kizmic leaned as far forward as the wire mesh of the screen door would allow, but with the door closed, she could only see a little ways past the alley.

"Go away!" she barked, motioning as if she were going to throw the baseball and hit it upside the head.

The cat rolled its eyes at her and sat there calmly wagging its tail back and forth.

Once again, Popsicle sticks flapping against the spokes of the boys' bicycles tickled Kizmic's ear. A mahogany-skinned boy riding a black Schwinn Sting-Ray and a peanut-head boy on a yellow Huffy slingshot stood as they rode, their bikes rocking left, right, left, right, left, right as fast as they pedaled. On the banana seat of a red Slingshot sat a high-yellow boy with his back resting against a high chrome Sissybar. An orange flag attached to the rear axil of a black Huffy fluttered a few inches above the head of the pointy-eared boy riding the bike with his hands cooly stuffed in the pockets of his shorts. Beside him, a heavy-set boy smoothly zig-zagged along on a Schwinn with an orange frame and yellow handlebars. A frog-eyed boy on a blue Schwinn and a red-boned boy riding a silver Huffy had popped wheelies. The red-boned boy held up his wheelie with just his right hand because his left hand had a cast on it almost up to his elbow! And there was this big-headed boy on a green, 3-speed Raleigh Robin Hood, or "truck" as most kids called those big, clunky bikes, but he was riding it as if he were on a 10-speed.

Kizmic watched the parade of boys until they disappeared around the corner. That's when the cat yawned, stretched, then sauntered off the porch, letting Kizmic know it was only leaving because she had ruined its nap.

See, that's why I 'on't like no old cats.

Within twenty minutes, Kizmic had showered, rummaged through a large, green trash bag of clothes, grabbed out an orange t-shirt, a pair of blue shorts, and threw them on. After lacing up her black Jack Purcell tennis shoes and putting on her watch, Kizmic once again bolted down the stairs but had to slow her roll because that stupid cat was still camped out on their front porch. Behind the security of the screen door, she stomped and shoo-shoo-shooed until the cat got tired of her making so much noise and left. Kizmic then swung open the door and had one foot on the porch when ...

"Kizmic!" Magdalene called.

"Awwww!" she groaned, throwing her head toward the roof of the porch. *What does she want?* Kizmic thought.

Although, from the sound of her mother's *Where-do-you-think-you're-going?* voice, she had a sinking feeling that whatever she wanted was going to throw a serious monkey wrench in her plans.

Unless I pretend like I ain't hear her.

"You can act like you didn't hear me if you want to," Magdalene said.

Kizmic sighed heavily as the screen door closed. With the hesitancy of a person expecting bad news, she peeked into the living room. Dressed in a purple t-shirt, dark blue sweatpants, and tennis shoes, Magdalene stood over a cardboard box, pushing the sharp, silver blade of a box cutter through its taped flaps.

"Huh?" Kizmic asked.

"Where do you think you're going?" she asked.

Shoot! "Outside," she answered.

"Oh no you're not," Magdalene chuckled sarcastically, as she used the thumb slide to retract the blade into its metal casing.

"Why not?"

"Because we have work to do, Kizmic," Magdalene said with one hand on her hip and the other waving the boxcutter at the hundreds of boxes and bags and just stuff piled all over the living room, the hallway, the dining room. Not to mention the kitchen, the upstairs hallway, *and* their bedrooms. The way it looked, she could literally be stuck in there for hours, days, weeks.

The whole dag-on summer! Kizmic fretted.

She cut a pleading, whiny *Daaad!* pout at Turk, who was also in the living room, over by the windows, preoccupied with the most crucial part of the move — hooking up his stereo. Unlike Magdalene, who could work in complete silence, Turk couldn't change a lightbulb without at least humming. So, nothing was going to get done until his music was good to go.

She called on her father because he knew exactly where she was coming from. Kizmic couldn't count the number of times Turk had had his mind all set to watch a football game, sit on the couch and enjoy his music, or hang out in the back yard with Uncle Monty drinking beer and eating raw oysters doused in hot sauce and her mother had shot his plans all to heck by making him paint, replace the toilet, patch a hole in the ceiling, or some other nonsense. When it came to housework, her mother didn't have an off switch.

Kizmic used to lay the blame for her mother's obsession with cleaning at her grandmother's feet. With all the speed a Greyhound could muster, Grandma Geneva made her way up from Lynchburg about four or five times a year, without so much as a letter or phone call, because writing or telephoning would defeat her purpose, which was to keep Magdalene on her toes. It could be blazing hot, freezing cold, raining cats and dogs, or ten feet of snow on the ground, Grandma Geneva would walk through their front door with her hand on the trigger of her index finger ready to point at stacks of dirty dishes in the kitchen sink, a grimy ring in the bathtub, messy bedrooms, piles of dirty laundry, an empty refrigerator, filthy windows, mice, roaches, unkempt or undisciplined grandchildren, and a neglected or abusive husband. She never found what she came looking for, because, one, she reared her daughters to take extraordinary care of their households, and two, as determined as she was to point her finger and say, "Ah-hah! See I told you so," Magdalene was just as determined to point her finger back at her mother and say, "Ah! Hah! No, see *I* told *YOU* so!"

But Grandma Geneva was only part of the reason Magdalene cleaned like it was a religion. The truth of the matter was Magdalene loved to clean. It relaxed her in some crazy way Kizmic couldn't understand. The more she had to clean, the more she kicked back when she got done. She would sit on the living room couch, at the kitchen table, or on her bed and, as if she were inhaling the beautiful scent of spring flowers, she'd breathe in the Lemon Pledge she used to polish the furniture, the Pine Sol she used to mop the floors, the Cheer she used to wash their laundry. Magdalene revered her work in the same way an artist admired her paintings, drawings, or sculptures. And she was trying to pass her insanity down to Kizmic and Kalaya.

"Daaady!" Kizmic cried.

Turk stopped fiddling with the speakers long enough to give her a *my-name-is-Bennett-and-I-ain't-in-it* hunch of his broad shoulders.

Slack-jawed, Kizmic stared at them, totally bewildered.

"Ooooh!" Magdalene said. "I get it." She turned around to Turk. "Baby, you and I are supposed to unpack everything and clean while Kizmic goes outside and plays marbles and Kalaya sleeps all day."

How am I gonna go outside and play marbles? I ain't even unpack them yet.

"You know what, babe?" Turk said, shaking the speaker cables in his hand, "You're right. I don't know why I was thinkin' they were gonna help."

I thought you wasn't in it, Bennett, Kizmic frowned.

Magdalene opened the flaps of the box and began pulling out items that were wrapped in newspaper. "Little girl, go upstairs, tell your sister to get up, and y'all come on down here and help us get this house straight."

Eyebrows furrowed, Kizmic whined, "Well, when am I gonna get to go outside?"

"When we get done," Magdalene said.

"Awwww!" She spun around and started stomping up the steps.

"Stomp up one more step and you'll be in here all day," Magdalene warned.

Kizmic soft-shoed it up the rest of the stairs, which she now hated.

What they doin' in the hall *anyway?* If they was in the kitchen like at the old house, I coulda snuck outside and she wouldn't've even known I was gone. Shoot! She make me sick.

If Magdalene made Kizmic sick that day, she made her want to *die* in the three days that followed. From the moment the sun rose until the moon took its place in the sky, Kizmic and Kalaya worked, like hard labor worked. They had had to help clean the house before, but there was more of this house. More rooms, more floors, more doors, more steps, more walls, more windows, more closets, more cabinets, more yard. Not that Kizmic got to set foot out in it. To the tune of Magdalene's drill sergeant voice and whatever song came on Turk's radio, Kizmic and Kalaya swept, scrubbed, mopped, wiped, organized, reorganized, unpacked boxes, shuffled this, reshuffled that, put this in the basement, put that in the hallway, put such-and-such-thing in the dining room, picked that up, put that down, pushed this over there, shoved that in the corner.

Two hours into that first day, Kalaya said, "Umph! She's not working me to death."

Magdalene was in the dining room, rolling out a beige rug in the center of the floor. Kalaya was in the living room and had voiced her protest into the box she was unpacking and not just under her breath but also under Elton John singing "Bennie and the Jets." Still, Magdalene heard her. She always heard them. No matter where they were in the house, Magdalene, with her Bionic Woman hearing, picked up their groans, mumbles, grumbles, and gripes as if they were stupid enough to express them out loud to her face.

"What did you say?" Magdalene asked, tugging on the rug to straighten it.

"Nothing," Kalaya lied.

"Well, don't let me hear you say *nothing* again," Magdalene threatened.

Kalaya patted the bun on top of her head and the bangs covering her forehead. "I just did my hair. I'm not sweating it out fooling around with her."

"Kalaya, you got something to say?"

"No," she said, then muttered, "Ain't nobody scared of you."

"What?" Magdalene asked.

"Nothing."

Of course, Kizmic was doing her share of talking back to her mother as well. With her hands on her skinny hips, she whined, *Everybody else is outside playin' and I gotta stay in here and clean. That ain't fair!* Moving her head from side to side, she grumbled, *I don't even like this old, stinky house. You and Daddy the ones wanted to move here, so y'all should clean it.* Lightly stomping her foot, she bemoaned, *You moved me away from my friends and now you won't even let me go outside to make some new ones. That ain't right!*

Yeah, Kizmic told her mother *off!* In her mind. Behind the wall that was behind Magdalene's back. Way, way, *way* under her breath and while Turk was blasting Martha and the Vandellas' "Dancing in the Street."

As aggravated as Kizmic was with her mother, she was more annoyed with Kalaya. Kizmic had a strategy: Do whatever Magdalene told her to do as fast as she could do it. That was the key to getting out the door. But Kalaya, with her simple-minded, pain-in-the-butt-self, stood flatfooted in the way of Kizmic's freedom by taking forever and a day to do the littlest thing and plucking Magdalene's nerves every chance she got, which caused them to argue, and when they argued, they stopped working, so something that should have taken ten minutes to do took an hour. That's why Kizmic had no sympathy whatsoever for her sister when, shortly before noon on the third day, Magdalene *herself* opened the door and set Kizmic free, ironically, because of the very thing Kalaya was doing that kept Kizmic from going outside in the first place.

A bag of Kalaya's clothes sitting in the hallway two days after Magdalene told Kalaya to take it up to her room sparked yet another argument, during which Kalaya claimed, "I didn't know those were my clothes."

"How are you not going to know they're yours when the tag on the bag says *Kalaya's Room*?" Magdalene asked, walking toward the stairs carrying one of her large, woven baskets of headwraps.

"I didn't see the tag," she said in her defense.

"That's beside the point, Kalaya. I asked you to take it upstairs two days ago. Now had you done as you were told, you would have known they were yours and the bag wouldn't still be down here."

"But—"

"'But' nothing, Kalaya!" Magdalene dropped the basket on the hardwood floor with a thud. "You always have something to say. You need to stop running your mouth all the time."

Oh! My! God! Kizmic exclaimed. I'm never gettin' outta here.

Down in the dumps, she trudged up to her bedroom and flopped on the bed. Picking up the baseball, she looked at CJ and Sleepy-eyed Ted's phone numbers, which were a little smudged, but she could still make them out. In a box marked *School,* she found a blue ink pen and traced over the numbers to keep them legible. She then went into her parents' room, sat on Magdalene's side of the bed, picked up the green Trimline push button telephone on the nightstand, and started dialing.

"I'm sorry, Kizmic, but he just left out," CJ's mother said.

"I'll tell him you called," said Sleepy-eyed Ted's mother.

Of course they wouldn't be in the house on a sunny summer day.

"They probably in the park playin' marbles," Kizmic sighed wearily. "Playin' baseball, ridin' their skateboards down the concrete hill."

She placed the phone back on the hook and chucked the ball across the room. She didn't realize how hard she had thrown the ball until it hit the wall near the window. *Blump!* Then hit the floor. *Blomp!* Kizmic fell back on the bed. She felt like crying she wanted to go outside so bad.

"Are you playing ball in my house?" Magdalene walked into the room and plopped down her basket.

Kizmic flung her arm over her eyes. "No," she sighed.

"It certainly sounded like you were," she said, picking up the evidence.

"It fell out my hand," Kizmic said.

"Fell out your hand, huh?"

Magdalene looked at the ball then sat down beside her daughter, smiling adoringly at Kizmic the way she often did before she kissed her good night. But Kizmic didn't want her mother to adore her; she wanted her to let her go outside.

"So, how are CJ and Ted doing?" Magdalene asked.

"Fine, I guess."

"What do you mean, you guess?"

"I didn't get to talk to them."

"Why?"

Kizmic lifted her arm, turned her sad eyes to her mother, and said, "They outside."

Like every other kid in the world, she didn't say.

"Oh." Magdalene lowered her head.

Kizmic put her arm over her eyes again.

Magdalene sat there for a few minutes looking at the baseball. Then, out the blue, she nudged Kizmic. "Go on outside."

Surprised, Kizmic peered up at her mother. "Huh?"

She placed the baseball in Kizmic's hand. "Go on now before I change my mind."

Kalaya had a natural born fit when she learned Kizmic had been sprung.

"How come she gets to go outside?" she huffed, as if one, she was going to do something other than sit up in her room, and two, as if Kizmic had been the one mouthing off to their mother and dragging her feet on everything she was told to do.

"If you want to act like you don't know the answer to that question, be my guest," Magdalene said.

Kalaya said something back, of course. Kizmic didn't hear it, because the unmistakable sounds of a basketball game being played bounced in through the back door. Kizmic stepped out onto the porch.

"You ain't got nothin'," a boy taunted.

"Go on, man! Shoot!" shouted another boy.

It was the boys who had ridden through the alley on their bikes.

"There it go, right there," another one of them said.

BAM! The basketball hitting the backboard rebounded up and down the alley.

"BRICK!"

"Ha-Ha!"

"Told y'all he ain't have nothin'."

"Yep! That's them!" Kizmic said, excitedly.

Five houses up the alley, she stood outside the fence to a long, rectangular back yard that had a two-story rowhouse at the top of it that looked like a red brick wall with a door, windows, and what amounted to be a small, brown landing instead of a grand porch off the kitchen. Short, green grass covered the half of the yard closest to the house. The grass at the back of the yard had been bounced and trampled down to dust, for nailed to the thick bark of a tall tree was a basketball hoop, made from a square piece of plywood and a gray, plastic Clover Milk crate. As crude as that makeshift basketball court was, Kizmic couldn't wait to get on it.

The boys' high top and low cut Chuck Taylors, Pro-Keds, Adidas, and Fish-heads tennis shoes kicked up light brown dirt as they played ball. Kizmic couldn't put names to the faces she'd seen the first time she saw them riding their bikes because, of course, she didn't know their names. So she put what she did know to the faces now running around the yard.

The high yellow boy Kizmic had seen riding the red Schwinn with the sissybar went up for a jumper. All of their eyes were on the ball, watching it go toward the basket.

"BOING!" laughed the big-headed boy when the ball hit the square rim and bounced over the fence and into the alley.

He was ridin' the truck, Kizmic recalled.

"Dang, Onion!" his teammates yelled.

The high yellow boy spun around. "It ain't my fault. Steebo was 'posed to be stickin' him!"

"Stickin' who?" Steebo laughed. "Wasn't nobody over there with you. You was wide open."

Looking at Steebo's pointy ears, Kizmic remembered, Oh, yeah. He's one of the boys that was ridin' a black Huffy.

"Nuh-uh! Fatboy had his hands all up in my face," Onion swore.

"How I have my hands in your face from all the way over here?" Fatboy argued, standing at least four feet away from Onion, waving his chubby hands in the air.

Fatboy, Kizmic smiled to herself. He was ridin' the orange bike.

"Face it, Onion, man. You can't shoot," Steebo said.

"Your mama can't shoot," Onion said.

"Onion, man, don't be talkin' 'bout my mother," Steebo warned.

Steebo reminded Kizmic of Sleepy-eyed Ted, the way he got upset about people talking about his mother.

We gonna get along real good, she thought.

She picked up the ball and started dribbling, behind her back, between her legs, the way her father taught her when her mother wasn't looking.

Kizmic balanced the ball on her forefinger and spun it like Curly from the Globe Trotters. She looked at the boys and grinned, Check me out!

They checked her out all right. Fatboy's pudgy, chestnut brown face was twisted like, *Yeah, yeah. Now give us back the ball.* The frog-eyed boy that had the blue Schwinn chewed on a strawberry Twizzler, eyelids half closed, totally bored to death. The kid with the gigantic head opened his mouth wide, as if he were about to shout something like, *Hey! That's cool!* Then, in a classic psych-up-boy move, he let out a loud, fake "AHHCHOOO!" and punctuated it with "Ha-ha." Onion just stared at her with big green eyes. The puny boy picked dirt out of his fingernails. The boy with the broken arm put the hand in the cast to his mouth and yawned. Kizmic noted that the dingy white plaster had names scribbled on it: Steebo, Man, Meatball, Babyfrog, Onion, Peanut, Fatboy.

The mahogany-complexed boy that rode the other black Huffy sucked something out from between his big front teeth. He was tall and had a high butt to go along with his wide hips. Kizmic bet he knew how to use that behind and those hips to box somebody out without being called for a foul.

"Ball," he grunted, sounding like a caveman that only knew three words.

Kizmic passed it with a quick, hard shove. The boy's arms extended well past the gate. The palms of his hands were huge; his fingers long as chopsticks. He grabbed the ball, then held it by his side, palming it with one hand.

Sweet, Kizmic thought, approaching him.

He dropped his gumball-sized eyes to her feet, as if to make sure the blue smiles on her Jack Purcell tennis shoes didn't cross the line that separated the yard from the alley.

"I got next," Kizmic said.

"In your dreams," spat the puny boy.

He walked to the gate, chewing a wad of gum. He had copper brown skin and a widow's peak that accentuated his peanut head.

"Why you say that?" Kizmic asked.

Staring at her with close-set, beady eyes, he blew a pink bubble almost as large as his little, mean face, sucked it back into his mouth, then said, "'Cause you ain't playin' with us."

"Why not?" Kizmic asked.

"'Cause we don't play with girls, that's why," Onion said. His green eyes were soft despite the harsh glare coming from them.

Kizmic folded her arms and cocked her head to the side. "Why? Y'all scared ya gonna lose?"

Steebo jerked his head back and looked at his friends, surprised and confused by Kizmic's accusation. His eyes were squinted, even though the sun wasn't beaming in his face. "Is she serious?" he asked.

"Yeah," Kizmic said.

The boy with the giant head looked Kizmic up and down and snorted, "Naw, we ain't scared."

The redboned boy grabbed the ball, turned around, and with his cast-clad hand shot it from where he stood. It dropped through the square hoop with ease. Nothing but crate.

"'Cause girls can't play ball," the puny boy proclaimed.

The eight of them laughed, slapped one another five, and bopped away.

"All bottoms, just like The Iceman, Redtop!" Fatboy said.

They resumed their game and Kizmic watched them, awe gleaming in her eyes, putting faces to the names written on the boy's cast. She already knew who Steebo, Onion, and Fatboy were, and now she knew which one was Redtop.

So the big meatball head boy with all the jokes must be Meatball, she thought. Somethin's tellin' me that little, mouthy one is Peanut. The kid with the poppy eyes has gotta be Babyfrog, and I bet the tall boy is Man.

Man 'n 'Em Kizmic instantly took to calling the boys in her mind.

CHAPTER
7

ONE MINUTE LEFT IN THE GAME. Kizmic had the ball. She dribbled up the left side of Man's back yard, over to the three metal trashcans. Man rushed up to her and tried to hip check her. Kizmic dribbled around him and ran straight into a double team. Steebo and Babyfrog came at her from both sides, but they were slow-footed, so Kizmic drove down the line, right through them. She dribbled over to the grill, where Fatboy stood. She didn't have to worry about him, though. Man 'n 'Em usually used him to set up picks. She blew by Fatboy like he wasn't even there. Onion jumped in front of her. Kizmic did a head fake up and he fell for it, leaping wide-legged in the air. She bounced the ball under him and continued her journey toward the basket. Meatball headed her off, swiping at the ball. Kizmic did a spin move to her right and was gone. Redtop dropped out of the tree, it seemed, in front of her. She dribbled the ball low. Left, right, left. Redtop reached in on the right. Kizmic left him flat-footed as she took off dribbling to her left. Now the only person standing between her and the winning shot was Peanut. He stared her down. Kizmic went full steam ahead. Peanut crouched, ready for her. She dribbled, pulled up, and shot a jumper right over top of his peanut head.

"SWISSH!" Kizmic said.

"KIZMIC!" Magdalene yelled, yanking Kizmic out of her imagination and plopping her back in her bedroom, where she had been playing basketball with the miniature hoop she had tacked above the door to the upstairs back porch.

She opened her bedroom door. "Yeah, Ma?"

"Don't 'Yeah, Ma' me," Magdalene said, from the bottom of the stairs. "Stop bouncing that ball in this house and take that stuff out of those boxes like I told you to do an hour ago."

"Okay," Kizmic said.

She closed her door, tossed the mini basketball through the hoop one last time, and looked at the boxes, which she had started to unpack, beginning with her marbles, of course. But when she came across her basketball hoop, Kizmic decided to practice so she would be ready the next time Man 'n 'Em were out there talking junk.

She went onto the porch to see if she could hear Man 'n 'Em in the yard, and who did she run into? That guy with the creepy eyes and jack-o-lantern smile.

Not him again, Kizmic frowned.

He was on his porch, staring at her.

What'd he do? Stay there the whole night waitin' for me to come outside? Jeez!

He had on a bright yellow, short sleeve dress shirt, black slacks, and polished black shoes. Kizmic remembered him being all dressed up the other day, like he was going to work.

I wish he'd go on somewhere. Shoot! I 'on't want him lookin' at me every time I come out here.

Instead of the man going in the house, to work, to the store, or wherever else he could go so long as he wasn't standing over there staring at her, he slowly lifted his hand, and started waving hello to her. That friendly gesture irritated the heck out of Kizmic.

For the past two days, she didn't feel obligated to speak and felt completely justified in her rudeness. He was a stranger and her parents forbid her to talk to strangers. His waving didn't make him less of a stranger, still it ruined her perfect excuse not to speak to him, because her parents also told her that if someone spoke to her, she was supposed to speak back, especially if that someone was a grownup. But something was seriously off about this grownup. Even his wave gave Kizmic the heebie jeebies.

I 'on't care, she thought. I'm just gonna haveta get in trouble 'cause I 'on't like him, so I ain't speakin' to him.

The man kept waving, like a little kid trying to make friends. When Kizmic didn't return his hello, he eased his hand back down by his side, shifted his weight from his right polished shoe to his left, then he gazed at her again. Kizmic squirmed as his dead wrong eyes began tugging on her t-shirt.

I gotta go in the house, she thought, but found she couldn't move.

He'd trapped her in the clutches of his gaze the way a vampire hypnotized and paralyzed his victims with his eyes. Kizmic's imagination ran wild, and in her mind's eye she saw the man float up above the banister, then start walking on air toward her. When his shiny shoes reached the alley, three short whistles startled the man, whose eyes fell off her, as if someone had shoved them away.

Now free of the creepy man's creepy gaze, Kizmic flung her head to the sky in anticipation. Old Man Graves whistled just like that.

There came a great noise that sounded like a million flags flapping in the wind. It wasn't flags, though. It was wings. The wings of about twenty-odd pigeons taking off. High above the trees, tipplers flew fast and tumblers rolled over backward in mid-flight. On the ground, Man 'n 'Em excitedly shouted their amazement.

At the sound of their voices, Kizmic tore down the stairs and tried to run out the back door. Magdalene stopped her with, "Did you finish unpacking those boxes?"

With the warm, soft sun lighting her face, she was enjoying the view of the trees and bushes on the side of the house in a way only her mother would—standing on a ladder cleaning the window above the kitchen sink. Kalaya was putting away pots and pans and sulking to beat the band, as their mother would say.

"Almost," Kizmic answered.

Magdalene sprayed Windex on the pane. "Kizmic, if you don't get back up there and finish unpacking those boxes, you're gonna wish you had."

"But Ma," Kizmic whined.

"What did I say?"

Kizmic was going to sigh her objection, but Kalaya beat her to it, sighing louder and heavier than she would have dared. The irritation Kalaya pulled into her lungs lifted her apple-sized breasts, which were getting bigger by the day to Kalaya's delight and Kizmic's horror. It seemed to Kizmic that Kalaya's breasts were where her attitude was coming from, because the larger they got, the meaner she became.

Magdalene turned to Kalaya. "You got a problem?" she asked, her chest rising with exasperation, as if to show Kalaya how small her breasts were compared to hers.

"No," Kalaya grumbled.

"Because if you do, I can solve it for you," Magdalene offered.

Kalaya stared hard at her mother. "I said I don't have a problem."

"Well, I suggest you stop sighing like you got one." She picked up the Windex, squirted some on top of the Windex already dripping down the window, then said, "And fix your face."

Instead of fixing her face, Kalaya fixed her lips to say something smart, but Turk rung the bell on Magdalene and Kalaya's latest round.

He had been up in the bathroom removing the old, crusty, yellow vinyl floor tile. With black kneepads over his blue jeans and sweat staining his red t-shirt, he stood in the doorway clapping his big hands and stomping one of his black boots on the floor to a song in his head. After warming up his audience, Turk belted out The O'Jays' "992 Arguments."

Magdalene pursed her lips and looked at him sideways. Kalaya gave him the evil eye and folded her arms across her breasts.

"What? Y'all don't like the song?" Turk grinned, feigning surprise. "Shucks. It can be y'all's theme song. Right before y'all start fussin' at each other, I can start singin' it. Man, we would be a hit." He sang the chorus, threw his hands up, then did a Temptations' spin.

Rejecting his idea and performance, Magdalene went back to her corner, so to speak, and started wiping the grime off the window and Kalaya went to her corner and continued putting away the pots and pans.

"I'm tellin' you we could go on the road with that right there." Getting no response, Turk shrugged his shoulders and asked, "Who wants Gino's?"

Kizmic and Kalaya immediately yelled, "I do!"

"Alright. Me and your mother are gonna run out—"

"Not until we finish in here," Magdalene said.

"Woman, I ain't liftin' another finger 'til I get somethin' to eat," he said.

"We just started."

"'Just started'!" Turk said. "Woman, do you know what time it is?"

Kizmic looked at her watch. It was going on two-thirty.

"We been workin' like Hebrew slaves since seven o'clock this mornin'."

Magdalene sat the Windex and rag on the pail shelf of the ladder. "I told you I want to get as much of this done as we can before we go back to work."

"And I told you we hungry, woman."

Magdalene sucked her teeth. Turk bopped over and grabbed the front side rails of the ladder as though he were spotting her. Then he shook it. The ladder rattled and the bottle of Windex clunked into the sink.

"Turk!" Magdalene screamed, hugging the ladder.

He stopped shaking it. "Now, me and your mother are gonna run to Gino's. What ya'll want?"

Kizmic and Kalaya yelled out their orders.

"I'm going to finish—"

Turk shook the ladder again.

"Man, if I fall off of here—"

Magdalene screamed as he shook it again.

"What?" Turk asked. "I don't understand what you sayin'. You just keep screamin'."

"Turk!"

"That's my name. Don't wear it out."

"Man, I'ma hurt you," she threatened, easing her way down.

The wonderful sound of their laughter bloomed throughout the house. When Magdalene was safely on the floor, she slapped him on the chest.

"You so violent," Turk smiled.

The second their parents drove off, Kalaya dropped the pot she had in her hand back in the box, stomped upstairs, and slammed her bedroom door. Kizmic hauled tail up the alley.

In Fatboy's yard was a pigeon coop about seven feet tall, made of wood, screens, and chicken wire. Thirty pigeons or more were cooing. To Kizmic, pigeons sounded like people talking under water. The gate to Fatboy's yard was off the hinges and leaning against the fence, so he stood in its place, blocking Kizmic's way into his yard. He was husky with a round waist, flat behind, and medium brown skin. Two gray and white pigeons sat on his right arm, a gray one was on his left shoulder, a white one stood in the palm of his left hand, and a pretty light brown and white pigeon was perched on top of his head.

"What you want?" he asked, looking her up and down with large, snarly eyes.

Even if Fatboy didn't have pigeons walking on him, she wouldn't have been fazed by his unfriendly tone. But it was especially hard for Kizmic to be intimidated by a boy with a pigeon on his head. Considering how often birds went to the bathroom, she surmised that Fatboy was pretty brave or pretty stupid.

"Can I hold one?" Kizmic asked.

Fatboy's jello cheeks jiggled as he broke into a yuk-yuk chuckle, like he couldn't believe she seriously thought she was worthy of putting her hands on any of his pigeons. He turned around to the rest of them and laughed a *Get-a-load-of-this* laugh.

He turned back to Kizmic. "My pigeons don't like girls," he laughed.

The pigeon on his head cooed, as if it were laughing with him. Then *BLOOP*. The boy dressed in pigeons had a blob of poop for a top hat.

His hair was cut low, but it was also thick, so it took a second or two for the poop to seep down to his scalp, then to his forehead. Without saying or showing on her face the *Ewwww!* screaming in her head, Kizmic watched the poop trickle down the middle of his forehead.

"What you lookin' at?" Fatboy asked.

That poop runnin' down your face, Kizmic wanted to say. But she didn't have to.

Just as the poop was sliding down his nose, Fatboy felt it.

"What the . . .?" He shook his left hand. The pigeon sitting on it flew over and landed on Man's arm. Fatboy put his hand to his nose. His eyes blinked. No way did he have pigeon poop on his head. No way did he have pigeon poop on his head in front of this girl. He turned to Man 'n 'Em and the looks on their faces said, *Yeah, man. That pigeon shit on your head.*

Kizmic was sure that had she not been there, Man 'n 'Em would have fallen all over the yard laughing. They would have clowned Fatboy for days, called him shit head and shit for brains. It would have been hilarious. And while they were all about having a good laugh, some things were more important. Maintaining solidarity in the face of their enemy was one of those things. It wasn't a matter of them suppressing their laughter, because they found nothing funny about this happening to Fatboy in front of Kizmic.

Fatboy's face wrinkled with embarrassment. He dashed up the porch steps and the pigeons that were on him flew into the coop as he flew into the house. Man 'n 'Em eyed Kizmic with mean mugs that accused her of pulling some girl trick that made the pigeon poop on Fatboy's head.

LATER IN THE DAY, when the sun was setting, Man 'n 'Em went into Steebo's yard and inside their clubhouse. Built from different sizes, types, and colors of wood, the rectangular structure ran the length of the medium-sized yard. It leaned slightly to the left and had one crooked, paneless window with a tacky, black curtain hanging in front of it. Kizmic, CJ, and Sleepy-eyed Ted always wanted to build a clubhouse, but their back yards were too small. The oak tree they played marbles under was the closest thing they had to a clubhouse.

Out of the small window bustled their voices, laughter, and The Spinner's "The Rubberband Man." When Kizmic walked up to Steebo's yard, his dog, PJ, a short, black-haired mutt, ran to the gate and greeted her with a loud, territorial bark. PJ's barking called Man 'n 'Em to the window. Seeing Kizmic, they closed the curtain, cut off the music and their voices, and acted like they weren't home.

Kizmic whistled and patted her thigh. "Here, girl!"

Cautiously, PJ came. Kizmic stuck out her hand. PJ growled deep in her throat then sniffed Kizmic's fingers. Smelling nothing threatening, she licked them.

A pair of harsh eyes peeked from behind the black curtain, then a voice full of frenzied infuriation tattled, "Steebo, man, she pettin' your dog!"

Steebo tore out of the clubhouse, bony arms flailing, eyes inflamed with frantic horror, as if Kizmic were a diabolical dognapper.

"Don't be pettin' my dog!" he squawked.

"I think she likes me," Kizmic said, continuing to rub PJ, who happily wagged her tail in Steebo's face.

Agitation made his pointy ears twitch. "Alright! When she bites your ass, don't say nothin'!" he said in a low voice so his mother, who was in the kitchen, wouldn't hear him curse.

"She won't bite me. Will you, girl?"

PJ answered by slobbering Kizmic's hand with friendly licks, which bruised her owner's ego.

"See. She likes me," Kizmic said, rubbing salt in Steebo's wounds.

Steebo gritted his teeth, balled up his fists, and raised his shoulders so high they touched his earlobes. He looked like one of those cartoon characters that got so angry the top of his head blew clean off. Kizmic should have let the poor boy's dog alone, but she couldn't believe he was about to flip his lid because she was touching PJ.

Unable to stand Kizmic putting her girlie hands all over his dog, Steebo started jumping up and down, stomping around the yard, hollering and screeching, "Stop pettin' my dog! Stop pettin' my dog! Stop pettin' my dog!"

Kizmic didn't mean to do it. Honest to God, she did not mean to do it. But seeing this boy have a sure 'nough conniption fit worse than—dare she say it—a girl, who could blame her? Still, she tried her best to hold it. She pressed her lips together as tightly as she could, but they started trembling, and before she knew it, the laugh slipped out of the corners of her mouth.

The second she heard it, Kizmic covered her lips and tried to act like she burped or coughed. Hey, she wouldn't have been at all embarrassed if he thought she farted instead of laughed.

Steebo straightened up and stared at her with hostile eyes that said, *I know the difference between a burp, a cough, a fart, and a laugh. And you laughed, you little heifer!* He stomped back to the clubhouse.

"Hey, wait! Can I come in?" Kizmic asked.

Steebo hurled himself around. His long, oval face changed from its natural chestnut brown color to rash red. "No!" he screamed worse than any girl she ever knew.

He slammed the clubhouse door.

And they won't let *me* play with them? Kizmic thought.

CHAPTER

8

TWO WEEKS WENT BY and Kizmic still had not found a way in with Man 'n 'Em. Then one afternoon, she overheard them talking about riding to Luckman Park. Kizmic didn't know how to get there, but she was going, and Man 'n 'Em were going to take her.

Kizmic barely slept she was so excited. By the seesaw, tick-tock of her wristwatch, she stopped trying to sleep around four-thirty and waited for the day to begin, which would be when her parents got up to get ready for work. Once they were gone, she could put her plan in motion.

Kizmic walked to the bathroom. She didn't really have to go, but it would help pass some time. She walked down the unlit hallway but stopped short of going into the bathroom when she heard noises coming from her parents' room. Kizmic tiptoed over and pressed her ear against the door, which muffled most of the sounds that rushed toward it looking for a crack or hole to cry out through. Most died in their search, but some more persistent notes found the small gap between the base of the door and the hardwood floor and slipped out. They weren't very strong notes to begin with and in their struggle for freedom, they grew weaker, so they were down several octaves by the time they reached the hallway. What Kizmic heard was really faint. But she heard it.

They're doin' *it* again? she thought with a sigh.

Her parents were always doin' *it*. They did *it* in the old house the night before they moved. They did *it* in the new house the first night they were there. They did *it* two nights ago. All they did was do *it*. Why her parents had to do *it* so much was beyond Kizmic. Why they had to do *it* at all was a question that had been bugging her since she understood that that's what they were doing. She had heard them doin' *it* a thousand times, still she had no idea what doin' *it* was. She knew it had a whole lot to do with kissing and touching and making a bunch of ooohs and ahhhhs sounds. But what was *it* exactly they were doing? Another thing Kizmic couldn't figure out was how long it took to do *it*. Some nights her parents did *it* like they only had two minutes to spare. Some mornings they did *it* as if they had two days. That morning her parents were doin' *it* like they had four days instead of two hours to get ready for work. If Kizmic didn't know any better, she'd swear they were taking a long time on purpose because they knew she had something planned.

At five-twenty, her mother and father finally rushed into the bathroom together, which meant it would take them a little longer to wash up because they would be in there playing. But at least they were moving toward the front door. An hour later, Magdalene walked into Kizmic's room looking nothing like the carefree woman Kizmic heard on the other side of the bedroom door. The woman that stood beside her bed was dressed in her pressed, spotless white nursing uniform and one of the colorful African print headwraps she bought from an African store. Those scarves smelled of Frankincense, and when her mother covered her entire head with them, Kizmic thought she looked like a queen wearing a jewel studded crown.

"Hey, Mama," Kizmic said then realized she should have pretended to be asleep. She didn't want her mother wondering what she was doing up so early.

"Hey yourself," she said, kissing Kizmic on the forehead. "What are you doing up so early?"

Dag! "Nothin'," Kizmic said, hoping she sounded convincing.

Magdalene squinted her eyes. "Why don't I believe you?"

Kizmic shrugged.

Magdalene walked onto the porch and into the soft blue glow of early morning. Kizmic followed her to see if the creepy man was standing out there waiting for her. He wasn't. In fact, there were no lights on in his house.

Guess he ain't up yet, Kizmic thought, but she had the strangest feeling that he was faking her out, hiding from her mother, and peeking at her from behind the shades.

"I don't know if I like you keeping this door open at night," Magdalene said, looking at the trees. "Anything can crawl or fly in here."

"Ain't nothin' comin' in here, Mama," Kizmic said.

Sleeping with the door open was one of the coolest things about having that room. She didn't want to give that up because her mother was afraid of a squirrel or a bat getting in.

"Put me down, Daddy!" Kalaya yelled.

Turk walked in with Kalaya slung over his shoulders. "Your wish is my command," he said, then dropped Kalaya on the foot of Kizmic's bed.

He was a playful man anyway, but Kizmic noticed he was even more so after he and Magdalene had done *it*.

"You play too much," Kalaya complained.

"Say what?" He reached out to grab her again.

"Nothing!"

"Cut it out, you two," Magdalene said.

Wearing a white tank top and red running shorts, Kalaya lay on Kizmic's bed facing the open door. Kizmic saw her sister's face reflected in the mirror on the dresser. Her eyes were consumed with frustrating curiosity. She was trying to figure something out. That something was the back porch. Kizmic had caught Kalaya in her room several times studying it. With the constructive mind of an architect and the cunning mind of a cat burglar, Kalaya inspected every beam and two-by-four. Her parents didn't notice Kalaya chipping away at it with her mind, because her mother was too busy laying down the rules.

"Turn around, Kalaya," Magdalene insisted.

Kalaya sighed and rolled over. The nipples of her plump breasts pressed against the cotton fabric of her tank top.

"Other than Plum, don't have nobody, and I mean *nobody*, in this house," Magdalene ordered.

"Who else am I going to have in here? I don't know anybody," Kalaya said.

"What?" Magdalene asked.

"Yes, ma'am," Kalaya yawned.

"And don't stay in bed all morning then sit on the phone all afternoon. I want you to do something to your room."

"Yes, ma'am," Kalaya said.

"And keep an eye on your sister," Magdalene continued. "I don't want her going out before ten, and I don't want her to leave the block." She turned to Kizmic. "In fact, why don't you play with the little girl across the street? She seems like a lot of fun."

Kizmic had to stop herself from bursting out laughing in her mother's face. Fun? The girl she met the other day? Umph! Other than her last name and the way Kizmic learned it, there wasn't anything fun about the girl that Kizmic could see.

With only two days left before her parents had to return to work, Magdalene put operation Get The House Straight into overdrive. So Kizmic was stuck in the house again, but this time she wasn't trapped in the middle of her mother and sister's bickering on top of not being able to go outside. Rather and gratefully, she got to work with Turk in the basement. Although, Kizmic never considered working with her father work.

While her mother taught Kizmic how to clean the house, her father taught her how to fix it. Instead of using a broom, mop, or cloth to wipe things down, dust things off, sweep or mop things up, Turk let her use a hammer, screwdriver, wrench, electric drill, and circular saw to help repair leaky faucets, running toilets, clogged sinks, broken light fixtures, plaster walls and ceilings. That wasn't work. That was Kizmic having a good ole time with her father.

The first day, she hung out with Turk sectioning off the large back part of the basement into a laundry room for Magdalene and a little workshop for him and Kizmic. On the second day, she and Turk turned the smaller front section of the basement into a family storage area. While shuffling things around, they came across a wood barrel top steamer trunk, like the one Captain Chesapeake had on the deck of his boat. It must have been buried in the cramped cellar on Proctor street, because Kizmic had never seen it before. She figured it had to be a hundred years old if it was a day, and from the faded travel stickers covering it like wallpaper, she believed that trunk had to have gone around the country at least three times.

Turk and Kizmic stood at either end of the trunk.

"Easy now. Old girl can't take too much pullin' and tuggin'," Turk said.

Gently they grabbed its tattered leather handles, which were hanging on by a thread or two, carefully picked it up, and sat it in a corner near the big, black oil tank and boxes of Christmas decorations. Kizmic ran a hand over the oak slats that wrapped around the trunk in almost a Tic Tac Toe grid. Pirates in movies had chests like these, she thought. Full of treasure. Peter Pan had a treasure chest bursting with gold. Kizmic wondered what treasure laid inside this trunk.

"Hey Daddy. Is this a treasure chest?" she asked.

Turk was neatly stacking boxes of old clothes against the wall near the front door. "Kinda."

"What's in it?"

"Memories," he said.

"Whose memories?"

Turk went back to his boxes. "Your mother's," he said, grabbing two broken portable heaters.

"Can I look in—" she started but was interrupted by a loud, gruff male voice from the alley.

"Iron man! They call 'im Christmas!" the man shouted.

A lighter, smaller girl's voice echoed him. "Iron Man! They call him Christmas!"

Kizmic and Turk frowned curiously at each other. Turk set the heaters on the workshop side of the basement next to an old lamp and box fan that also no longer worked. He and Kizmic then went out and stood at the back gate.

Coming down the alley was a man, thin, jet-black, dressed in a floppy, green bucket hat, black t-shirt, baggy, gray pants, and a pair of badly scuffed-up, brown work boots. He had big, ashy, rough hands, and long, hard fingernails caked with dirt. He was pushing an A&P shopping cart loaded with a metal folding chair, bicycle rims, vacuum cleaner, an ironing board, toaster, an old stereo, pieces of a screen door, and several large picture frames that didn't have any pictures in them. A little girl was walking happily beside him.

He gave the cart a giant shove. It rattled as it rolled ahead of him. He cupped one of his dirty hands around his mouth. "Iron Man! They call 'im Christmas!" He caught up to the cart, grabbed the bar and gave it another push.

The little girl cupped her small hand around her mouth and shouted, "Iron Man! They call him Christmas!"

"Mornin'. The name's Christmas. Willie Christmas," he said, stopping at their yard. His words were somewhat slurred, like he had been drinking all night and most of the morning.

"The iron man," Turk smiled.

"That's me. I live in the house right across the street from yours. Me, my wife, Shelly, and our little girl here, Charlotte."

Charlotte was ten years old, medium brown-skinned, with a chubby face. Dressed in a yellow sundress and sandals, the little girl gave Kizmic a bright, toothy smile and waved an excited hello. Despite her attire, Kizmic supposed Charlotte had to be pretty cool to hang out with her father roaming alleys picking up junk. Plus, her last name was Christmas. How could she not be cool?

Her mother probably makes her wear dresses, Kizmic thought.

Kizmic smiled and waved back. Charlotte then unraveled a jump rope she was holding and started showing off her dynamic jump rope skills. Instantly, Kizmic lost interest in her.

Pssshh! A girlie-girl, she thought, watching the two plaits on either side of Charlotte's head bounce up and down with her.

Christmas said to Turk, "Got anythin' you need hauled away, I'm your man. Got anythin' you need hauled away?"

"A couple of old heaters, a lamp, and a fan."

"Lemme put this stuff in my basement and I'll be right back," Christmas smiled a yellow-toothed smile.

He pushed his cart up the alley as Charlotte jumped rope home alongside him.

So, no, Kizmic was not going to be playing with Charlotte, but if saying she would was going to get her mother out of the house then . . .

"Yeah," Kizmic said to Magdalene. "She looks like she might be fun."

From her parents' bedroom window, Kizmic watched Turk and Magdalene kiss then get into their cars. Not long after Magdalene started her engine, Aunt Beana came up the alley then hopped in the passenger side seat. The two women looked like teenage girls on their way to school.

Kizmic went down the basement and wheeled her blue Huffy bicycle to the back door. Not the front, because that stupid cat was camped out on their porch again. Poking her head out, Kizmic checked for any sights or sounds of Man 'n 'Em. The coast was clear as the blue sky. With the cunningness of Wile E. Coyote setting a trap for the Road Runner, Kizmic quickly pushed her bike to the side of the house, where there was a narrow, concrete walkway. Butting up against it was a wider, grassy lawn that stretched to the backyard gate and was flanked by four feet tall hedges that walled it off from the alley. No one could see her bike there, and the second she heard Man 'n 'Em coming, she would be on it, riding after them.

They usually came outside around nine o'clock. At eight forty-five, while eating a bowl of Cheerios, Kizmic staged a stakeout at the back door. Nine o'clock on the nose Butch and PJ started barking.

"Here they come," she said and dropped the bowl in the sink.

Kizmic tore out the door, bolted down the steps, and—*BOOMP!*—ran smack into the creepy man with the creepy, crawly smile.

He was right in front of her, which scared the mess out of Kizmic, because she wasn't used to him being so close. Not that she could ever get used to someone as creepy as him. But on the upstairs back porch there was so much space between them. It was as though they were on two separate mountains on opposite sides of a long valley, so she felt comfortable, not in his presence, but in the fact that he couldn't touch her. He could gaze at her all day long, but he couldn't put his hands on her. He could make her feel naked, but that didn't make it so. But down on the ground there was nothing between them, no thousand-mile valley for him to cross. For him to get to her, he needed only to open his gate, stroll across the alley, open her gate, and step into her yard, where he could grab her and do whatever he wanted.

Why did she think that's what he wanted? To do whatever. What was it about him, about the way he gazed at her that made these thoughts worry her mind? What was the whatever he wanted to do?

For the moment, it seemed he only wanted her to stand still. Kizmic gathered this from the way *he* stood still. Not making any sudden movements for fear he would scare her off. But he was moving. His right arm was bent and moving slowly upward. The sun glinted off something shiny in the middle of his chest. Kizmic wanted to see what it was, but his gaze wouldn't let her. It wanted all of her attention. And it had it until Man 'n 'Em came riding down the alley and cut her off from the creepy man's hypnotizing, narcissistic gaze.

No longer trapped in it, Kizmic got to look at what he didn't want her to see. A 35mm Nikon camera.

Was he gonna take my picture? Kizmic wondered, frowning.

Reading her thoughts somehow, he put the camera behind his back as if to say, *No*.

Why would he wanna take a picture of me? He don't even know me.

Again, seemingly hearing the thoughts in her head, he smiled that creepy-crawly, jack-o-lantern smile.

Kizmic decided she didn't want to know. And to escape the question and him, she jumped on her bike and rode after Man 'n 'Em. But by the time she got to the corner, they were long gone.

Frustrated, Kizmic grabbed the handlebars of her bike, lifted the front wheel, then slammed it down on the pavement. "Dag!"

"You ain't gonna catch 'em like that, Shugga," a sweet-sounding voice said from behind.

CHAPTER

9

MANY OF THE STORES AND BUILDINGS around her way had nicknames. Belvedere Corner Store was called The Basement Store because it was in the basement of a house. People called The Ace of Spades The Jamaican Store because some Jamaicans owned it. They renamed Johnson's Grocery The Alley Store because it was in the alley off Cuthbert Avenue. Harvel's Paints was called The Paint Store because Mr Harvel sold paint. Ziggy's Cut Rate was nicknamed The Bar because it was a bar. Everyone called Super Pride Market The Market because it was, well, a market. Bel Park Tower was called the Old Folks' Home because old folks lived in the apartments of the eleven-story building. Blackstock's Corner Grocery was known as The Fish Store, because the owners, Mr Charlie and his wife, Miss Josephine, had a seafood hook up that helped them sell the freshest fish that side of Park Heights. The only joint that rivaled the Fish Store's lake trout was the Roost on Reisterstown Road, which, incidentally, was called Lake Trout. The Fish Store was the reason that cat, whose name Kizmic learned was Phyllis, stayed on her front porch.

There was a green metal dumpster in the back yard of the Fish Store and Phyllis staked it out hoping Mr Charlie would forget to close the lid so she could rummage through it and snag scraps of fish. The thing was, closing the lid to that dumpster was as second nature for Mr Charlie as closing and locking the doors to his Cadillac. So often times, Phyllis had to resort to using her feline, feminine wiles to try to get what she wanted. When Mr Charlie came out back carrying plastic trash bags full of fins, scales, and fish heads, Phyllis jumped off Kizmic's porch, hurdled the chain link fence that surrounded the back yard of the Fish Store, then rubbed up against Mr Charlie's leg, like a girlfriend trying to butter up her man so she could hit him up for money.

She would purr and meow, meow, meow (oh, how Kizmic hated that doggone sound!). All for nothing, because Mr Charlie said the same thing every time. "Sorry, Phyllis, ole girl, but I can't feed ya, 'cause if I do, there'll be no gettin' rid of ya."

Not that there was any getting rid of her that Kizmic could tell. No matter how many times Mr Charlie refused to feed her, Phyllis waited on Kizmic's front porch for him. And Miss Josephine was about to make it so that Man 'n 'Em had as much chance of getting rid of Kizmic as Mr Charlie had of getting rid of Phyllis.

In the hot summer of 1973, Miss Josephine came up from Mullins, South Carolina to live with her sister's family, and in just a few short months, she managed to do what the other single women in the neighborhood had been trying to do with fried chicken, collard greens, and potato salad, fried fish, string beans, and macaroni and cheese, fried pork chops, rice and okra, pig-tails and sauerkraut, ham hocks and black-eyed peas, homemade Pineapple Upside Down Rum Cake, and sweet potato pie. Miss Josephine snagged Mr Charlie. At least that's the way Kizmic overheard Charlotte's mother tell it to Magdalene and Aunt Beana.

As the single men went in the neighborhood, Mr Charlie was as good a catch as any. He was a tall, high-waisted man, very dark-skinned with a small Miller Beer gut. His eyes were big and brown with low hanging eyelids, which made him appear to be half a sleep or drunk. A sex symbol Mr Charlie wasn't; a kind, faithful, strong, and fun man, Mr Charlie was. And him being an entrepreneur didn't hurt. Rumor had it that the first time Miss Josephine walked into the Fish Store, Mr Charlie took one look at her with his half sleep eyes and fell madly in love.

The women tried to pin Mr Charlie's attraction to Miss Josephine and their disdain for her on something as superficial as her looks. She was a light-skinned woman with candid, smoky-gray eyes, short, wavy black hair, and a curvy South Carolina body that she kept draped in provocative but tasteful spring and summer dresses, fall and winter skirts, and occasionally a pair of pleated slacks. By anybody's standards, Miss Josephine was a gorgeous woman. But there were plenty of light-skinned, gray-eyed beauties around, so Kizmic didn't buy it. What she did buy was that Mr Charlie fell for Miss Josephine and the women disliked her because she had an unapologetic, outlaw, free spirit that allowed her to laugh, cry, scream, cuss, shout, sing, and dance without the least bit of fear, shame, or hesitation. That was why the kids in the neighborhood loved Miss Josephine. She didn't have many of the hangups their mothers had, so they could enjoy themselves when they were around her. And they could talk to her about things their parents were too busy or one-track-minded to understand.

After Kizmic calmed down from the little temper tantrum she'd thrown behind not being able to follow Man 'n 'Em to Luckman Park, Miss Josephine invited her into the Fish Store.

Inside was a glass counter full of the finest penny candy in the land: Mary Janes, NowLaters, Squirrel Nuts, Jaw Breakers, Tootsie Rolls, Bazooka Bubble Gum. Beside the cash register sat a jar of pickles and a jar of onion pickles. To the right of the candy counter was the seafood bin, where crabs, shrimp, oysters, catfish, and lake trout chilled on a bed of ice. Next to the seafood bin was a deli counter, on top of which sat two jars of pickled pigs feet. On the other side of the store was a cigarette machine and a tall soda freezer.

Miss Josephine reached into the freezer and grabbed an iced cold grape soda then handed it to Kizmic.

"All they say is, 'You can't do nothin' 'cause you ain't nothin' but a ole girl,'" Kizmic said as she drowned her sorrows in the syrupy drink. "And I can play ball better than all of 'em, Miss Josephine. All of 'em!"

Miss Josephine stood behind the counter listening with the sympathetic ear of a veteran bartender. When she felt Kizmic had wallowed in self-pity long enough, she smiled, then sauntered to the back of the store, where Mr Charlie stood at a table cleaning fish. Without worrying about the stinky smell of fish seeping into her pretty, yellow sundress or flying scales landing on it, she kissed her husband.

"I'll be back in an hour," Miss Josephine told Mr Charlie.

Still smelling and looking beautiful, she walked Kizmic to her house. "You need the top off a gallon of milk and a flathead screwdriver."

Kizmic would have taken the top off the empty milk container, but her father had already set out the trash. She opened the refrigerator and took the red top off the gallon of milk.

"I'll tell Mama it rolled under the stove." She covered the mouth of the jug with a piece of aluminum foil then went down to the workshop and got the screwdriver out of her father's toolbox.

"When I was a girl, we filled our tops with hula-hoops that had gotten bent," Miss Josephine said. "We'd hold a lit match against the hula-hoop and when it started meltin', we'd catch the drippings with our tops. But I don't suppose a girl like you ever owned a hula-hoop."

Ah, but Kizmic had owned a hula-hoop once. Not that it was her idea. After Kalaya started "smellin herself," her mother tried to turn Kizmic into a mini Kalaya, which made absolutely no sense to Kizmic since her mother was always mad at Kalaya. She got it in her head that Kizmic was a girl and, by God, she was going to play like a girlie-girl and play *with* girlie-girls. So she bought Kizmic all the trappings that girlie-girls were attracted to—jacks, bat-and-balls, jump ropes, a pink—PINK! When everybody in the world knew her favorite color was blue—hula hoop.

Her mother had to see that she was not the kind of girl who would be happy sitting on the floor tossing a stupid rubber ball in the air and picking up pointy pieces of metal; that she was not going to waste perfectly good daylight hitting a rubber ball with a wooden paddle; that she didn't want to repeatedly jump over a clothesline in the same doggone spot; and that she didn't want to stand around gyrating her hips trying to keep a hard piece of plastic from falling to the ground, especially not a pink one.

Holding it between two fingers, Kizmic asked, "What am I 'posed to do with it?"

"You can roll it up and down the street for all I care," Magdalene said. "But you better play with it."

Kizmic did exactly as her mother suggested. She raced alongside the hula hoop as she rolled it up and down the sidewalk like an old tire. She was having the most fun she ever thought she could have with a hula hoop until it somehow got away from her and rolled out into the street, where it was run over by a car.

Of course, there was no telling her mother that she didn't know she was being sarcastic when she told Kizmic to roll it up and down the street. Heck, Kizmic didn't even know what sarcastic meant. And there was no telling her mother that she didn't roll that stupid hula hoop out in front of the car on purpose. So after being yelled at about how money didn't grow on trees and being threatened with the promise of never getting another toy in her life, Kizmic was sent to her room for the rest of the day.

That's why I didn't wanna play with no ole, stupid hula hoop in the first doggone place.

"Okay," Miss Josephine said. "Start diggin'."

"Diggin'?" Kizmic asked. "What? Where?"

Miss Josephine pointed to the spot in the street where the tar had been softened by oil leaks. There were already some teaspoon-sized holes there.

"The boys fill their tops with tar," Miss Josephine said. "Some use candles. It's pretty, smells good, but it ain't heavy enough to me."

Kizmic dug up some tar and packed it into the milk top up to its rim. Afterward, with her yellow, high heels click-clacking, Miss Josephine walked Kizmic to the corner of Beaufort and Spaulding. Miss Josephine was famous for her high heels. The women hated her for them because they were just another reminder of the freedom she possessed that they envied. They couldn't admit that, though, so they laughed about those heels behind Miss Josephine's back. More than once, by more than just her own mother, Kizmic heard the joke cracked, "Who does she think she is? June Cleaver?"

But even as the old joke tickled them, they were thankful that Miss Josephine did not want to be and knew that no matter how much those catty women got on her nerves she could not afford to think of herself as June Cleaver, because June Cleaver's heels stayed in her house. Miss Josephine's heels click-clacked inside every child's house around their way as she strutted up alleys, around basketball courts, parks, and playgrounds. Basically, Miss Josephine's heels could be heard click-clacking whenever most mothers were preoccupied with work, cleaning, cooking, laundry, shopping, or negotiating with bill collectors. That click-clacking sound ended fights, cut short experiments with drugs, gave girls an excuse to say no when a boy's hand followed his mind up her dress, gave boys an out when they were punked into doing something that would get them sent to Charles Hickey Training School for Boys. To that end, the same women who hated and laughed at the freedom Miss Josephine strutted around in also didn't know what they would do without it, because she could be where they couldn't, when they couldn't.

Kizmic and Miss Josephine stopped in front of a board that was painted in the middle of Beaufort. Man 'n 'Em were standing around it one day when Kizmic ran up to them with her Crown Royal sack full of marbles and her beautiful clay Kizmic marble in her pocket for luck.

"Hey, y'all wanna play marbles?" she asked excitedly, believing no boy could resist such an offer.

"Marbles?" spat Redtop.

Kizmic noticed for the first time that his skinny, red-boned body was marked with scars and she wondered how he got them all.

Babyfrog tore up his face like he'd just eaten something that left a bad taste in his mouth. "Don't nobody 'round here play no marbles."

Kizmic dropped her bag to her side. "Well, what y'all gettin' ready to play right now?"

They walked away laughing, carrying the secrets to their favorite game to their graves. So they thought.

"It's a skully board," Miss Josephine told Kizmic. "Man 'n 'Em blocked off the street with some boards and buckets and painted this." She described how they used rulers and yard sticks to make sure the square measured seven feet on all four sides and had an area of forty-nine feet. Squares numbered one through twelve measured twelve inches, and the skull, which was the most important part, was painted perfectly in the center, with the number thirteen box smaller than all the rest and surrounded by four beautiful, menacing trapezoids. It was a handsome work of art.

"This game is as sacred to those boys as football," Miss Josephine said. "If you wanna play with them, you have to earn their respect by kickin' their butts in this game."

"But I don't know how to play."

"You ever play marbles?"

"All the time 'round my old way," Kizmic said.

"If you can play marbles, you can play skully." She held out her hand for the top.

Kizmic hesitated. Miss Josephine's long, manicured fingernails had a fresh coat of yellow polish that matched her shoes and sundress.

"I ain't gonna die if I get a little dirt on my hands, Shugga," Miss Josephine said and took the top. Her heels click-clacked onto the board. "Stand here in box one and hold the top between your thumb and middle finger." She stretched out her arm and aimed at the number two square. "Then you flick it."

The top flew across the air, fell right before the number two square, then slid into the box.

"Still got it," Miss Josephine smiled.

Boy, did she have a beautiful smile. It was like sunshine on the first day of spring.

"That's all there is to it," Miss Josephine said.

Kizmic stood in the first box, holding the top just the way Miss Josephine showed her. With a flick of her finger, it coasted then landed about ten inches off the board.

"Not bad," Miss Josephine said.

For an hour, she helped Kizmic practice and explained the rules of the game.

"You gotta make it from number one to number thirteen, then from thirteen to one. First player makes it back to number one wins. Now, you better make darn sure you don't wind up in that trapezoid 'cause the only way out is for another player to hit you out, and ain't none of them gonna do that." She looked at Kizmic's watch. "We'd better go. They'll be back soon."

"When's my next lesson?" Kizmic asked.

"Tomorrow, while they're up at Arlington playin' football," Miss Josephine said.

For close to two weeks, Miss Josephine and Kizmic snuck to the skully board. She had never known a woman so fascinating in all her life. A grown woman who not only knew how to play a boy's game, but was also willing to teach it to a girl. That went against every rule known to grownups. Girls got curls; boys got toys. *What was Miss Josephine doing? She ought to be ashamed of herself, all out in public, strutting around some skully board like she's five years old.* That's what Kizmic saw in the glaring looks Miss Josephine got from the women who walked by. *Ain't nobody got time for no kid games,* their twisted lips admonished. *I'm sure something in her house needs cooking or dusting or washing.*

The way they acted, you would have thought Miss Josephine was teaching Kizmic how to shoot dice.

No matter the stares, Miss Josephine kept right on. She taught Kizmic how to shoot without getting stuck in the trapezoid, how to knock a player's top out of a square or into the trapezoid, sweep another player's top off the board, how not to hunch, which was against the rules, and how to hunch and get away with it. Kizmic was an astute pupil. She studied every move Miss Josephine made, from the way she held her skully top between her soft, long fingers, to the way she balanced herself on her high heels when she stooped to line up her shots. Kizmic listened to every word Miss Josephine spoke with her adorable red lips, from the encouraging shout, "There you go!" to the marvelous suck of her teeth when a shot didn't go as planned.

While Kizmic started out only wanting to know how to play skully, she ended up knowing something far more valuable and wonderful—where Miss Josephine got the only flaw on her body. It could be seen at the hem of her dresses and skirts.

They had just finished a lesson and were walking back to the Fish Store when Kizmic asked, "How'd you get that, Miss Josephine?" and pointed at the long, raised scar slanted across her right knee.

"This beautiful thing?" Miss Josephine sang about it. "It's been a part of me since I was nine. I got it runnin' from these two little white boys. Jimmy and Henry. Every day, them knucklehead boys chased me and my sister home from school. One day we was runnin' so hard from them, I tripped over my own feet and fell on a piece of glass. Slit my knee wide open. Meat was hangin' out and everything. Blood was everywhere. Talk about somethin' that hurt and somebody who cried. Honey chile." She shook her head from the painful memory. "Me and pain ain't never got along too well. But that wasn't the only reason I was cryin'. My mama worked as a maid, cleanin' white folks' houses, makin' next to nothin'. So she didn't have no money to be buyin' stuff she just bought, and she didn't have no money to be takin' me to no doctor."

Miss Josephine caressed her scar as if it were the prettiest thing about her, and it occurred to Kizmic that Miss Josephine felt about her scar the way her Uncle Monty felt about his dead eye.

"I wasn't one to do a whole lot of fightin'," Miss Josephine said, "but I got to thinkin' 'bout how mad my mama was gonna be about spendin' money she ain't have. So, bloody knee and all, I got up and me and my sister whupped both them boys like nobody's business. And we took all their money."

"Took their money!" Kizmic's voice rose with astonishment.

"Every penny they had in their pockets. I don't think God'll keep me outta heaven for it. Might keep me out for some other stuff, but that I'm sure he'll forgive 'cause it wasn't like I took it to buy candy or some other foolish thing.

I bought myself some bandages and peroxide and a new pair of stockings. My knee was hurtin' something awful, but I never told my mama what happened."

"Never?"

Miss Josephine shook her head. "And you know what else I never did? Run from them boys again. They ran from me and my sister, though," she laughed. "The first time they did, I looked at their backs and thought, What a beautiful thing. And every time I get scared about somethin' and want to run, I just look at this knee and it reminds me never to run from anything or anybody."

CHAPTER

10

Under Miss Josephine's tutelage Kizmic developed a pop-shot so fierce
and a sweepsies so wicked that one day Miss Josephine ended her lesson ten
minutes after she started.

"I got a taste for a frozen cup," Miss Josephine said.

They walked across Belvedere and went up Beaufort to Miss Irene's.
From her big, shingled house that looked like it was covered in freshly
baked gingerbread, Miss Irene sold relief from the heat during the summer
months with her twenty-five cents frozen cups and ease from an angry
sweet tooth during the winter months with her thirty cents caramel and
candied apples, all three of which kept a steady flow of children at her door
year-round. She was a cute, brown-skinned, seventy-some-year-old woman
with short, permed, gray hair. She lived alone, for Stanley, her husband of
forty years, passed away twelve years ago, which was when she started selling frozen cups.

Miss Josephine got an egg custard frozen cup and Kizmic got cherry. They
were sitting on the steps of the Fish Store eating them when Man 'n 'Em came
back from playing football.

"Hey boys," Miss Josephine said sweetly to them.

"Hey Miss Josephine," they said.

Fifteen minutes later, Miss Josephine went inside the store. When she
came out again, she said, "Okay. Let's go make you some new friends."

She led the way, strolling at a pace that gave her heels that musical click-
clack and allowed Kizmic, in her tennis shoes, to shadow her stride.

"You gotta play this cool," Miss Josephine cautioned. "Act like you don't know nothin' about this game. And put that away," she said, looking at Kizmic's top. "Don't show them what you know 'til I give the signal."

"What's the signal?" Kizmic asked.

"Shhhhh," Miss Josephine said.

Kizmic was listening so intently to Miss Josephine's instructions that she hadn't realized they were already at the corner. Man 'n 'Em had clearly started a game, but when they saw Kizmic, they stuffed their tops in their pockets, then stood around the board, like they were just hanging out. Fatboy took a *Black Goliath* comic book from his back pocket and pretended to be reading it. Onion's dog, Butch, ran up to her. He was big, light and dark brown, a mix of Shepherd and something else. Kizmic petted Butch, who, loving her touch, rolled over on his back so she could rub his belly. Onion wanted to yell at her about touching his dog, but he didn't dare with Miss Josephine standing there. So he tried to vaporize her with his green eyes. Steebo was practically strangling PJ with her leash trying to keep her from running over to Kizmic.

"What you know good, boys?" Miss Josephine asked, her voice as enjoyable as a midday summer breeze.

"Nothin', Miss Josephine," they said in unison.

"Ah, come on. Everybody knows somethin' good," she laughed.

Man 'n 'Em stared at Kizmic with suspicion tinting their eyes. Maybe one of those jealous, busybody women told them about the lessons Miss Josephine had been giving her.

"I know Man knows somethin' good. Don't you?" Miss Josephine said.

Man's expression asked, *Why you gotta single me out?* But he said, "Yes, ma'am."

"I was just tellin' Kizmic that I used to play skully when I was a girl."

They smiled politely.

Kizmic looked at Miss Josephine. You're bombing, she thought.

Miss Josephine smiled, *Never, Darlin'.*

"Would you boys mind if I relive a little of my girlhood? Just to see if I still got it."

If Kizmic was reading the smirks on Man 'n 'Em's faces correctly, they were thinking:

First of all, no girl, or you, Miss Josephine, ever had what it takes to play a serious game like skully. Second of all, yeah we mind. We've been safeguardin' the secrets to this game from that girl ever since she ran up to us with that stupid bag of marbles, and you want us to hand everything over with one shot. Third of all, we don't play with no girls. Or you, Miss Josephine.

But how could they say no to Miss Josephine? She was a grownup, and kids did what grownups asked. Especially Miss Josephine.

Man dug in his pocket and handed Miss Josephine his top. She walked to square number one and pitched the top. It sailed past square number two and landed way off the board. Now, Kizmic had seen Miss Josephine make that same shot a dozen times. Twice with her eyes closed.

"Um! I guess I don't still have it," Miss Josephine said.

The boys' snickers said, *Yeah, like you ever did have it.*

"You wanna give it a try, Kizmic?" Miss Josephine asked.

Man 'n 'Em almost gasped. Steebo let out a loud snort. But it was all the rest of them could do to remain calm as they tried to figure out how to respectfully say, *Come on, Miss Josephine. Girls ain't allowed on our skully board. What kinda ole mess you tryin' to pull?*

Kizmic thought she would suffocate from the laughter she was holding inside.

Miss Josephine put her soft, lovely hands on Man's tense shoulders. "You boys weren't playin', right?"

Rather than lie to Miss Josephine, they cut their eyes to the ground, to the sky, to Man.

Miss Josephine gently massaged his shoulders, making him blush and relax. "Do you mind if Kizmic tries it?" she whispered in his ear.

The boys stared at Man, telling him with their eyes to stay strong, man. Ignore Miss Josephine's touch. But how was he supposed to do that? Miss Josephine had the softest hands anybody ever wanted to feel. Her sweet voice was humming in his ear. What else was a guy to do?

Kizmic slowly walked onto the board like she was totally lost. "Can I hold somebody's top?"

Peanut spit some sunflower seed shells into the gutter then half-heartedly tossed his top at her. Man 'n 'Em waited for Kizmic to shoot it to the moon or some place far off the board. Kizmic did not disappoint them. She chucked her top so hard and crooked that it rolled under a car.

"Pretty good," Miss Josephine said. "Don't you think so, boys?"

"Yes, Miss Josephine," they all said, straining to hold in laughter that would ask, *Are you blind, Miss Josephine?*

"Hey, I have an idea," Miss Josephine said.

Man 'n 'Em's suppressed laughter begged for this idea to be better than her last one.

"Why don't you play against one of the boys?" she suggested.

Their jaws dropped as their hope for a better idea was dashed with an utterly ghastly idea. Steebo was so appalled by the suggestion he dropped PJ's leash.

Brushing aside Man 'n 'Em's obvious, unspoken objections, Miss Josephine asked, "Which one of you is the championship player 'round here?"

They were reluctant to divulge that classified information, but finally Meatball named Man.

"Why don't that surprise me?" Miss Josephine smiled, buttering him up for the kill.

Man's dark skin turned a bright blushy red. Soon they were spilling their guts about him.

Redtop boasted, "Can't nobody beat him, not even them boys from Woodland."

"Yeah," Fatboy echoed, rolling up his comic book. "Man can whup anybody."

"Hmmmm. Is that right?" Miss Josephine asked.

"Yes, ma'am," Man said. Then he held his head down, averted his eyes, and mumbled, "But I don't play against girls."

"You don't what, baby?" Miss Josephine asked, sounding sincerely baffled, as if she'd never heard of such a thing as boys not playing with girls.

Man was trying to get up the courage to repeat himself when Diamond, Poochie, 'n 'Em flocked over to do what they did best—harass Man 'n 'Em.

Diamond Tilley was a twig of a girl with coffee brown skin, a pie-face, and long, pretty hair. She hung around a girl named Poochie and a bunch of other girls with girlie-girl names like Princess, Peaches, Candy, Cookie, Hope, Precious, Destiny, April, Tootsie, Lacey, Angel, Melody, and Ebony, better known as Diamond, Poochie, 'n 'Em. Diamond and Poochie were the leaders of the girlie-girls. Wherever they said was cool to go the other girls followed. Whatever they ruled was cool to do the other girls did. Whomever they declared was too uncool to be alive the other girls wished that person would keel over and die. The cool thing to do right now was hate and torment the boys as much as the boys hated and tormented them. The boys would run through the girls' four square or hopscotch games. The girls would stroll across the field in the middle of the boys' football or baseball games. The boys would ride their bikes past the girls while they were jumping rope and grab the rope. The girls would cut through the boys' basketball game and steal the ball.

Miss Josephine knew Diamond, Poochie, 'n 'Em would take advantage of any opportunity to stick it to Man 'n 'Em. With an innocent smile, she asked, "Man, why don't you like playing against girls?"

Diamond put her hands on her boney hips and asked, "Yeah, *Lesssleee Morgan,* why don't you play against girls?"

At the sound of his real name, Man stared sharply at Diamond. Leslie Morgan was the name his parents cruelly gave him at birth, and to Man they sounded like two girl names. Kizmic learned that day that the quickest and most amusing way to agitate Man was to call him by his real name.

"Yeah, *Lesssleee Morgan,*" Poochie teased between licks of a strawberry Tootsie Roll Pop. "Why don't you like playing with girls?"

Poochie was light-skinned with freckles, and kind of short. She had a slight dog tooth and a big mouth. She always had something to say about somebody and was always in the middle, behind, or around the corner of some he said/she said stuff.

"*Lesssleee Morgan!*" Poochie taunted.

"Don't call me that," Man warned her.

"What you gonna do?" Poochie laughed, knowing he wasn't going to do anything, not with Miss Josephine standing there.

"I'll tell you what Man's gonna do," Miss Josephine said. "He's gonna play against Kizmic."

Man's gumball-sized eyes narrowed like, *I'ma do what?*

"What's wrong?" Diamond heckled, "You scared, *Lesssleee Morgan?*"

All Man could manage in response was a huffy frown.

"Ain't nobody scared of no girl?" Onion said indignantly.

"Oh, be quiet, space invader," Poochie said with a suck of her dogtooth.

Kizmic would have thanked Diamond, Poochie, 'n' Em for their support if that's what it was, but it wasn't. They didn't like Kizmic because, number one, she was new to the neighborhood, and two, she acted like a boy and ran behind Man 'n 'Em.

With the girlie-girls putting on the pressure, hoping he would back down so they could call him a punk, Man grudgingly caved.

Kizmic stepped into the number one square. She raised her arm for her shot and looked over at Miss Josephine, her eyes asking, *Can I do it now? Huh? Can I can I can I?!* Miss Josephine inconspicuously reached down and sweetly caressed her scarred knee. That was the signal for Kizmic to cut loose, but before doing so, she needed to set the stakes of the game.

"Alright, this is the deal," she said. "If I beat you, I get to play with y'all whenever I want to."

The girlie-girls went, "Ooooh!" Miss Josephine smiled, impressed with Kizmic's risky move.

Man's eyebrows rose. "Beat me?" he asked.

"Yeah," Kizmic said.

Meatball pointed to Man. "You're gonna beat Man?"

"Yeah," Kizmic said confidently.

It was quiet for a second as Man 'n 'Em turned this thing over in their brains, trying to make sure they heard what they thought they heard. Then they burst out laughing, falling all over one another. They laughed so hard that Miss Josephine, Diamond, Poochie, 'n 'Em, and even Kizmic started laughing.

"Girl, what you been smokin'?" Peanut asked.

Man 'n 'Em settled down and huddled together again. At the end of their brief conference, Babyfrog turned to Kizmic with those big, froggy eyes that earned him his nickname and said, "Alright. But if Man beats *you*, you gotta leave us alone and play with them." He pointed his half-eaten Sugar Daddy Pop at the girlie-girls.

"Hey, don't be puttin' us in it," Diamond scoffed.

"You scared she gonna lose?" Man taunted.

Diamond, Poochie, 'n 'Em fiercely eyeballed the boys. They couldn't have cared less whether Kizmic won or lost. They were there strictly and simply to instigate and agitate the boys as much as humanly possible, not get stuck with some tomboy. And needless to say, Kizmic wasn't jumping at the bit to get stuck playing with a bunch of girlie-girls. So she had to ponder this unexpected challenge.

I ain't been playin' that long, she thought. I might not be able to beat him.

She looked at Miss Josephine, who winked her eye, telling her that she could.

Kizmic held up her thumb and pinky finger. As she and Man tangled their pinky fingers and pressed their thumbs together, they looked hard into each others eyes the way boxers mugged at each other just before the bell rung.

"Bet!" Man said.

"Bet!" Kizmic replied.

At that point, Kizmic flung Babyfrog's top to him then pulled out her red skully top. Man 'n 'Em were surprised to see that she had a top, but just because a girl could *make* a skully top didn't mean she could *play* skully.

Skully was an individual sport, but the boys huddled together as one and coached Man not only on how to beat Kizmic, but on how to whip her good. Kizmic's first shot landed in the number one square easily. Man 'n 'Em blew it off as a lucky shot. She went for the number two square and made it.

"Ahhhh, so what?" was their collective response.

She went for the number three square and made it.

Man 'n 'Em laughed that shot off too.

She went for the number four square. Made it. Went for the number five. Made it.

"Ain't nothin' but luck," Meatball laughed.

Number six. Made it.

Ain't that much luck in the world, was on Meatball's chubby face.

Man 'n 'Em stopped laughing and started paying attention to Kizmic's form and technique. What was she doing with a form and technique?

Number seven. Made it. Heck, Kizmic was starting to impress herself. Number eight. Made it. Nine. Made it! Miss Josephine was smiling proudly. Diamond, Poochie, 'n 'Em were cracking up at the boys.

Kizmic went for the number ten square and her top glided . . . dipped a little . . . then fell in front of the square, as if it had hit an invisible brick wall and slid down it.

"Dang!" she said.

It's alright, Miss Josephine mouthed to her.

Steebo whispered in Man's ear, patted him on the back, then set him loose. Man squatted down a few inches behind the start line. His long, dark brown legs sticking out the frayed ends of his cut-off denim shorts made him look like a grasshopper. He had a small, green top filled with tar. He vigorously scraped the bottom of it back and forth on the street. Afterward, he leaned over and blew away any debris with his thick lips.

Man had a funny way of shooting. Instead of holding the top between his fingers and flicking it, he sat it down behind the number one square, positioned his hand behind it, cocked back his middle finger with his thumb, then plucked it. Within two minutes, Man swiftly went from the number one square to thirteen by not only plucking his top in the squares with precision but also tapping Kizmic's top, which allowed him to skip squares.

Plucking his top inside the ninth square on his way back to one, Man 'n 'Em couldn't contain their gloating. They bragged about all the fun they were going to have now that Kizmic wouldn't be following behind them. Kizmic looked at Diamond, Poochie, 'n 'Em. They rolled their eyes at her.

I'll stay in the house before I play with them, Kizmic vowed.

But then something of a miracle happened. Going back to the number six square, Man's top hit a hair crack in the asphalt, flipped over on its side, rolled, then fell over in the trapezoid! In all the years Man had been playing this game, he had never ended up in the skull. Not once in all those years!

Steebo, Meatball, Redtop, Fatboy, Peanut, Onion, and Babyfrog could not believe what they had just seen, even though they were looking dead at his top laying tar-face down in the skull, like Man had walked over and carefully set it there. That was the only way they believed his top would ever end up in the skull. What made them accept it was the silence that came from Man as he stood outside the number eight box, his big eyes as wide as an owl's staring at something in the dark. That was when it all became real to them, and that was when the boys yelled, "Awww, man, Man!" Steebo actually jumped up and down in the middle of the street like a baby. Fatboy slapped his thigh with his comic book. Diamond, Poochie, 'n 'Em squealed and laughed in relief. Their laughter was the thing that shut Man's eyes. Kizmic only smiled a bit. She wasn't out to embarrass Man. She wanted to be his friend.

Technically, the game was over. The only way Man was getting out of that trapezoid was if Kizmic hit him out, and no matter how sorry she felt for him, she was not going to do that. But rather than concede, Man 'n 'Em insisted that Kizmic go all the way back to one. Man chewed his fingernails as she shot around his top. He waited for her to either make a mistake and tap his top out of the skull or take pity on him and purposely hit it out. He didn't care if she did a sweepsies and swept his top all the way up the block to Mack's Corner Store, so long as he was out of that doggone skull and back in the game. *Come on. Have a heart,* Man's facial expression pleaded.

I can't do it, Kizmic thought sympathetically, watching Man look up to the sky, as if he had resorted to praying for rain that was nowhere in sight in order not to lose to a girl.

Babyfrog wasn't going to waste time praying for rain. They needed something to put a stop to this madness right then and there, but the only weapon he had at his disposal was the knockers in his back pocket. As Kizmic prepared to take another shot that would get her closer to horning in on their fun for the rest of their natural born lives, Babyfrog got an idea. Grabbing the dingy white string of the knockers, he whipped the toy out of his back pocket the way a goldminer who just struck the mother lode yanked out that first gold nugget. Eureka!

Redtop looked him and the knockers up and down and asked, "What you gonna do with that?"

Babyfrog didn't answer. Holding the string between his thumb and forefinger so that the knockers were even, he began slowly moving his hand up and down, making the two red, acrylic balls clack together. At the sound of the first *CLACK!* everyone, including Kizmic, looked at him.

A conniving grin spread from Babyfrog's lips to Redtop, Fatboy, Steebo, Onion, Peanut, Meatball, and finally Man's lips. Babyfrog had given Man his rain.

"Babyfrog, man, you a genius!" Redtop said.

Babyfrog looked at Kizmic with a smirk that said, *I know.* Then he started clacking those knockers together above and below his hand to beat the band, as the grownups liked to say.

CLACKCLACKCLACKCLACKCLACKCLACKCLACKCLACKCLACK!

Kizmic wanted to take those knockers and clack Babyfrog over the head with them the way Bruce Lee cracked his enemies over the head with nunchucks. *Waahh!* She couldn't believe he was standing there doing that, but when she thought about it, she realized they were doing the same thing CJ and Sleepy-eyed Ted did when she was beating them at marbles and they meowed. No doubt Man 'n 'Em would have, too, had they known about her fear of cats.

CLACKCLACKCLACKCLACKCLACKCLACKCLACKCLACKCLACK!

Kizmic shook her head and looked at Miss Josephine, who was smiling in the face of Man 'n 'Em's attempt to distract Kizmic, whose concentration was completely blown, but not so much by the sound of the knockers as by Man 'n 'Em and every other boy's pitiful aversion to playing with girls. As if girls were not as good as them.

Well, daggit, I am as good as them! Kizmic thought. And y'all gonna play with me! Watch!

CLACKCLACKCLACKCLACKCLACKCLACKCLACKCLACKCLACK!

Kizmic tuned out that clacking the way she tuned out CJ and Sleepy-eyed Ted's meowing. And she did it with Miss Josephine's high heels, of all things. That clacking sounded just like Miss Josephine when she was walking, only way faster. But by associating that clacking to something she loved—the sound of Miss Josephine's walk—Kizmic, with grace and superhuman sportsmanship like restraint, completed the game as quietly as she had begun.

Man 'n 'Em moaned and whined and Diamond, Poochie, 'n 'Em cackled and howled.

"Thank you," Kizmic said, giving Miss Josephine the biggest hug she could give her.

"You welcome, Shugga. Now, promise me one thing."

"Anything."

"Give them a day or two to lick their wounds before you collect your winnings." She winked her eye at Kizmic then click-clacked on home.

CHAPTER
11

ONE DAY WAS ALL KIZMIC COULD STAND to give them. On the second day, she ran outside to get what Man 'n 'Em owed her. They were in the clubhouse. PJ and Butch greeted Kizmic at the gate.

"Hey," she said happily, and took a moment to pet them.

She knocked on the clubhouse door.

"Who is it?" a voice barked.

Who is it? They know doggone well it's me. She humored them anyway. "Kizmic."

After a long minute, she heard a lock unlatch, then the door squeaked open. Kizmic had been dreaming of being in that clubhouse and now she was just a step away. But Man blocked the door. His arms were folded across his chest, and he had a contemptuous spark in his eyes, like that of a man who knew he had gotten hustled at cards or pool.

Alright. I hustled you, Kizmic thought, as she waited for him to move. It wasn't like you left me a choice. And now you have to step aside and let me in. I won it fair and square.

Not so fast, Man seemed to say with a twist of his lips. "We goin' to Luckman Park," he announced.

"What? Now?" Kizmic asked.

Man 'n 'Em answered by filing out of the clubhouse. Man slammed the door then put on the combination lock.

They rode their skateboards. At Luckman Park was a hill, a steep hill with a sharp curve in the middle of it that they called Dead Man's Curve. Kizmic had been practicing how to curse. She hadn't perfected it the way Kalaya and Plum had. Her progress would have been better if she'd put a little more effort into it, but it took a lot of time trying to match up the right curse word with whatever was going on. It seemed like an awful lot of trouble just to say one word, especially if an adult heard you. So Kizmic rarely cursed and couldn't figure out why other people bothered. But when her stomach dipped as if she had dropped suddenly from a high place as she looked down the hill, Kizmic thought, Damn! And for the first time she totally understood why dag or darn wouldn't do.

"What a steep ass hill," she muttered to herself.

Dead Man's Curve said everything Man 'n 'Em wanted to say to Kizmic. *You wanna play with boys?"* it asked. *"Well, this is how we boys play!"*

That was fine with Kizmic because the concrete hill around her old way was steeper, and thanks to CJ and Sleepy-eyed Ted, she knew how to live through a ride down a hill like Dead Man's Curve.

Fatboy flashed a wicked smile at Kizmic. "Last one down is a rotten egg."

The nine of them took off and Man 'n 'Em quickly found out that Kizmic wasn't like the sissified girlie-girls in the neighborhood. She didn't ride down the hill on only her back wheels like Man, didn't zig-zag like she was maneuvering safety cones like Meatball and Babyfrog, didn't do a 360-degree spin like Steebo, didn't ride on only the front wheels of her board like Peanut, didn't flip her board over with her feet and land back on the deck like Onion, didn't do a hand stand on it like Redtop, but Kizmic rode her skateboard down and around Dead Man's Curve as fast and fearless as any of them, and she wasn't the rotten egg. Fatboy was.

Ha! In your face! she thought ecstatically.

"So what she can ride down a hill," Steebo said. "We playin' baseball tomorrow."

THUMP! THUMP! THUMP!

Kizmic stood in the middle of her bedroom throwing a rubber baseball against the wall and catching it with her glove.

THUMP! THUMP! THUMP!

She didn't know if they would let her pitch or play catcher, so she practiced throwing strikes and throwing someone out.

THUMP! THUMP! THUMP!

"Kizmic!" Magdalene yelled.

"Huh?" Kizmic asked.

"Stop throwing that ball against my wall. Go on outside with that mess."

She couldn't go outside. Man 'n 'Em would see her practicing and find out how good she was. From her nightstand, Kizmic picked up the baseball CJ and Sleepy-eyed Ted had given her. It had been a few weeks since she'd last called them. She was too busy trying to get Man 'n 'Em to play with her. She thought about calling them now, but she knew they wouldn't be in the house. Not on a nice day like this. She set the baseball back on the nightstand. She missed CJ and Sleepy-eyed Ted, although not as painfully as when she first moved. Man 'n 'Em helped relieve that pain, and she didn't want to feel it again. That's why she was going to kick their butts in baseball, too.

She grabbed her bat, threw an imaginary baseball in the air, then *CRACK!* And the crowd goes wild!

KIZMIC HAD A GUT FEELING Man 'n 'Em were not going to knock on her door that morning to tell her they were going up to Arlington. So, once again channeling her inner Wile E. Coyote, she went out front a little before nine (she didn't want to run into the creepy man in the back yard and that cat wasn't on her porch, thank God), sat on her bike with her Frank Robinson baseball glove hanging on the handle bar, and waited. Like clockwork, Man 'n 'Em sped down the alley, and as expected, rode by her house not even pretending they were going to stop and tell her to com'on.

Kizmic didn't call out for them to wait up like some old girlie-girl. She just started pedaling. Man 'n 'Em zipped across Belvedere. Kizmic made it to the center island of the four-lane, two-way street, but got stuck when the number 19 bus came down too fast for her to beat it across. By the time it and five other vehicles passed, Man 'n 'Em had disappeared around the first bend on Beaufort Avenue. Kizmic pushed her pedals hard. She hit the first bend but didn't see them. She surged around the second bend at Miss Irene's ginger-bread house and there they were.

"Whew!" she said and slowed her pace.

Man, Onion, and Babyfrog had baseball bats resting on their shoulders as they rode. Fatboy, huffing and puffing, sat down. While coasting to catch his breath, he casually glanced over his shoulder and spotted Kizmic. His face tightened with irritation. Fatboy stood and his knees moved up down up down up down as he raced to close the gap his brief break in pedaling had put between him and his friends.

"She right behind us, man!" he snarled when he caught up to them.

"What?!" They all snapped their heads around at the same time.

Seeing that Fatboy wasn't lying or joking, Man 'n 'Em sneered at her and stomped on their pedals, spinning their wheels double-time, as if they could lose her with the orange flag on Steebo's bike flapping and calling, *Yoo-hoo! We over here.* Besides that, she could see Arlington from there.

Kizmic didn't try to ride with them, rather she biked at a pace that kept her from falling too far behind. Something did make her lose sight of them for a minute, though. Standing out from the Colonial and Traditional single-family homes on the block was a majestic, three-story Victorian-style house, light lavender colored, trimmed in white. It had a wide porch that wrapped around its right side and a turret on its left. Stopping to admire it, Kizmic thought it looked like a castle. It even had a natural grey stone wall at the tower's base, the height of the white, wooden porch railing.

Her imagination took over and the story of a princess living inside that castle house began to write itself. The princess was beautiful, although Kizmic couldn't quite picture her face. She wasn't Cinderella. She was more like Rapunzel, trapped in the tower by an evil witch. Turning the page in her fairy tale, Kizmic lifted her head to the tower, but, except for the sheer, light blue curtains, the three tall open windows were as empty as the pictureless frames Christmas had in his cart. The street was empty now, too, for Man 'n 'Em were gone.

"Shoot!" Kizmic said, slamming the book closed in her mind.

She put her butt in gear by getting it off the seat and pedaling hard and fast. Crossing Hayward Avenue, she wheeled up the block and ran into a wall. Literally. Beaufort came to a dead end at a long, high retaining wall, like the one that surrounded the tower of the castle house. Only this wall was made of beautiful gray and burgundy stones of varying shapes and sizes that partitioned the school playground from the back yards of the houses that bordered it. The bright, yellow rays of the sun and the soft blue of the sky cast a bluish white light that intensely illuminated the stones' colors, the shadows falling on the wall from the trees, the red and green leaf vines creeping up it, and the green foliage laying at its feet. This bluish white light also brought out the rocky texture of the stones and the thick vein of mortar that crisscrossed the wall's landscape and took Kizmic's eyes on a trip from stone to stone the way the black lines on a roadmap took the eye from town to town, city to city, state to state. Mounted on top of the wall, running directly down its center, was a tall, green chain link fence. A stone staircase had been cut and hammered into the wall. Kizmic picked up her bike and climbed those stone steps. When she reached the top, her new neighborhood felt like home to her for the very first time.

There wasn't just a playground up there. It was a park, as big, if not bigger, than Johnston Square. Where she was standing, a foot pavement divided two fields. The first was a wide, grassy field to her right that extended some yards down to the blacktop in front of a red, portable building. On her left was a baseball field. To the left of that was another stone stairway and sweeping foot pavement that ran between a softball field and a play area that had swings, monkey bars, and a sliding board. Hopscotch and foursquare boards, and a three-lane, sixty meter straightaway track were painted in white on the asphalt, and classroom numbers were stenciled on it in yellow. Kids were playing on every square inch of grass, concrete, and asphalt with absolutely no thought of the school year looming inside the dark classrooms of the four-story, red brick building that sat in the background.

Man 'n 'Em were gathered around home plate picking teams. Kizmic parked her bike next to theirs near the stone wall, the top of which functioned as a ledge on the playground. She grabbed her glove, ran around the backstop fence, and joined them. Man and Peanut stood across from each other in the batter's boxes.

Man scanned the small crowd. "Meatball," he said.

While giving everybody the once over, Peanut blew a big bubble out of the gob of gum in his mouth. When it popped, he sucked it back in, and said, "Babyfrog."

They're gonna pick me last, Kizmic thought. But that don't matter. They still gotta pick me.

Man pointed to Onion. Peanut pointed to Redtop.

Man looked at Kizmic. His gumball-sized eyes inspected everything about her, from her green t-shirt to her blue jeans to her tennis shoes and back up again. Man then leaned to his right, looked around Kizmic, and pointed to... "Steebo. Ha! She's yours."

Peanut, Babyfrog, and Redtop moaned.

Digging a quarter out of his front jeans pocket, Fatboy, who was playing catcher for both teams, said to Peanut, "Call it."

"Heads."

Fatboy tossed the silver coin into the air. The sun flickered on and off the piece of change before it landed face down on the brown clay.

Losing the last pick and the toss, Peanut stomped to the pitcher's mound without telling Kizmic which position she was playing.

Guess I'll play first base, she thought, and started in that direction, but Babyfrog beat her to the piece of cardboard with a gloating smile.

I like playin' third base better anyway, she said to herself.

So that's where she headed. Redtop waited until she was practically on the base then cut in front of her and stood on the piece of cardboard. *Get outta here*, his smirk said.

Okay. Guess I'm playin' second base, she thought. But at least I'm playin'.

Fatboy picked up the piece of cardboard that served as home plate and shook off the dirt. He placed it back on the ground and straightened it with his foot. He then punched his fist in the pocket of his catcher's mitt and shouted, "Play ball!"

Kizmic wanted to play the game of her life. To do that, she needed to stay one hundred percent focused. The perfect strategy came to her when she pulled her Orioles baseball cap down to her eyebrows and thought, even with the sun glaring in her face, it was great baseball weather. The thing about the thought, though, was it didn't come in her voice but in the brisk, animated voice of a broadcaster like Chuck Thompson calling an O's games play-by-play on the radio.

It's a glorious day here in Charm City, the announcer in Kizmic's head said excitedly. *The sun is hot and beaming down on Arlington Stadium. Gonna make it hard for the players to see the ball but it's gonna be a good game, folks. They playin' for all the marbles.*

Looking at the empty green, wooden benches on either side of the sideline, the announcer said, *We got a packed house. Everybody's come to see the rookie, Kizmic Waters, coverin' second base and center field.*

Top of the first inning, Man, third baseman and manager of the team, is up at bat. Knees bent, high butt high, he looks like he's a power hitter. Peanut studies the strike zone. Here comes the windup . . . the pitch, fastball down the middle . . . Hooo! Swing and a miss!

"Strike One!" Fatboy yelled.

Man shakes that one off. He's calm. If you didn't see the play, you wouldn't know it's O and one. He's back at the plate. Pitch . . . low and outside.

"Ball!" Fatboy shouted.

One ball, One strike. Peanut's takin' a little time. Didn't like how that ball got away from him. Here comes the pitch . . . fastball . . . Swing . . . PING! And it's a hit! Ground ball to the left of second base. The rookie, Kizmic, dives. The ball is in her glove. Man is hustlin' to first base. Kizmic jumps to her feet, throws! And . . . He's out, ladies and gentleman! Hooo! What a play by the rookie. Mama gonna haveta go buy some Tide *today. Look at the fine dirt she got on her clothes after stoppin' that run.*

Alright, it's one out, no runs. Second baseman, Onion, comes to the plate. Got a lazy hittin' stance goin' on with the bat sittin' on his shoulder. Let's see what he's got. Here's the pitch . . . the swing. CRACK! It's a high fly ball to second base. What's the rookie gonna do with it. Easy out! Rookie's lookin' good so far.

We got a fantastic crowd here at Arlington Stadium. I bet the people on Park Heights can hear them. Two outs, bases empty.

"Com'on, Steebo," Man, Onion, and Meatball yelled and clapped from the sideline.

Steebo grabbed the wooden Roberto Clemente bat. Peanut's ready. Pitch . . . fastball to the inside . . . Swing . . . Hard hit, high ball to second base. Hooo! The rookie snatched it out the air. What a spectacular play! Listen to that crowd. I bet you can hear them cheerin' way over in Cherry Hill. They didn't know she could field like that. Look, even her teammates' faces are askin', How'd she get that high up? Did she climb a tree?

Okay, folks. The score is zip zip. Steebo's on the mound. Second baseman, the rookie, is up to lead us off here in the bottom of the first inning. We've seen her make three incredible plays. Now let's see if she can hit. She looks a little nervous over there choosin' her bat. Is she a wood girl or an aluminum girl? Okay, looks like she's a wood girl. She picked up the Hank Aaron Louisville Slugger. *Alright, let's see what she got.*

Kizmic taps the plate once and the bottom of her left tennis shoe twice with the bat. A little superstitious routine goin' on. She bends her knees slightly, holds the bat up and behind her right shoulder, and gets ready to swing. Steebo sizes her up. Here's the wind-up. There goes the pitch . . . fastball, low and outside.

"Ball!" Fatboy shouted.

Kizmic is okay with that gimme. It helped her shake off the jitters. She doesn't want to walk, though. She wants to show that she can hit as well as she can catch. Steebo stares at the strike zone. There goes the pitch . . . wild fastball, low and away.

"Ball Two!"

Steebo's gotta control his arm. Take his time and throw it straight down the middle. Here comes the pitch . . . fastball. The rookie starts to swing, pulls back just in time.

"Ball Three!"

Last chance to get it over the plate or she's walkin'. The crowd is so loud I bet people on Biddle Street can hear them. Steebo grabs the visor of his baseball cap, turns it back around to the front, and pulls it down low over his forehead. He throws the baseball hard in his glove, again and again and again as he eyes the plate. The rookie digs in, bending her knees a little more, lookin' to get that ball on the sweet spot of her bat. Steebo draws his glove with the ball inside it to his chest. He rears back on his right leg, lifts his left leg, high kick . . . the pitch . . .

WHACK!

The ball hit the side of Kizmic's upper thigh. Jagged lines of pain shot and burned out in all directions through her leg. The ball bounced off and rolled toward the mound like a well-trained pet Steebo sicked on her. Kizmic and her bat dropped on home plate simultaneously. On her hands and knees, Kizmic's face was all teeth as she bared, gritted, and sucked deep breaths through them. Ooh, she wanted to scream, *You did that on purpose! You little ...* But she stopped herself.

When a pitcher hit a batter intentionally, the trainer came out to check on the batter, the benches and dugouts cleared as players stormed the field and charged the mound in defense of their injured teammate. Boos roared throughout the stadium. The umpire gave the pitcher a warning or ejected him. None of that was happening.

Kizmic glared at Steebo and he grinned back at her and waited, not for her to get up and go to first base, but to cry. In fact, that's what all of them were doing, waiting for her to bawl. Kizmic wouldn't give them the satisfaction of watching her lie there like a wimp and whine like some old girl.

It was a struggle, but she leaned on her bat, and using her right leg, she slowly got to her feet. They weren't impressed. She had to get to first base. Kizmic walked lamely and with each step she grimaced and winced as the muscles in her thigh jiggled and pain wrapped around it with the tightness of an ace bandage. Man! She wanted to lie down on the base until her parents discovered she was missing and sent out a search party for her. But she couldn't. All she could do was hope her teammates wouldn't get a hit, because she wouldn't make it to second base. Even if they knocked the ball out the park, she couldn't hobble home. Thank God Redtop, Babyfrog, and Peanut struck out.

Because of the pain in her thigh, Kizmic didn't need the announcer in her head to keep her focused. She was on her game now. Anything that came her way ended up in her glove. And they made sure everything came her way. It was raining fly balls and pop-ups. She was sliding and diving for line drives and scooping up ground balls. She was leaping and flying around so much, Peanut started calling her Rocky the Flying Squirrel. Every time she got up to bat, she hit a single or a double. She hadn't hit a home run, yet, but her hits brought Babyfrog and Redtop home in the fourth inning, making it two to nothing. In the seventh inning, she hit another double and Redtop brought her home with a base hit, then Babyfrog hit Redtop home. By the top of the eighth inning, they were up four to two with Peanut striking Man, Meatball, and Onion out one, two, three.

Come ninth inning, the throbbing in her leg eased up somewhat. Kizmic limped to the mound. "Can I pitch?" she asked Peanut.

Chewing his wad of bubblegum, he said, "I don't know. Can you?"

"Why don't you gimme the ball and find out."

"You ain't gotta get smart," he said.

"Neither do you."

Peanut blew a bubble then sucked it into his mouth. "What's wrong? Leg hurtin'?"

"No," Kizmic lied. "I wanna pitch."

He looked at her sideways for a few seconds, spit his gum out at her feet, then turned the mound over to her.

Steebo was up. It took him forever to go stand at the plate. First, he was fooling around with picking a bat, like they had a hundred of them. They had three: two wooden and one aluminum Louisville Slugger.

"Man, what you doin'?" Man asked. "Get a bat and come on."

"Yeah, you ain't gonna hit nothin' no way," Redtop said.

"Shut up!" Steebo shouted.

He grabbed the aluminum bat. Whole game he only hit with the wooden Roberto Clemente bat. Now he was over there doing test swings like he was actually going to use it. To no one's surprise, Steebo dropped the aluminum bat in the grass, reached past the wooden Hank Aaron bat, then finally took the Clemente bat and stepped into the batter's box, or rather on the edge of it.

"How you gonna hit the ball standin' way over there?" Fatboy teased.

"Don't worry 'bout it," he said, and started tugging on his jeans and shirt.

Kizmic stood on the mound with her arms folded, waiting. Everybody knew why he was taking so long.

He scared I'ma hit him with the ball, she laughed to herself. Feeling the sting in her thigh, she thought, I oughta.

After playing with his clothes, Steebo went through this ritual that he didn't have all game. He tapped the bat on the plate not once, not twice, not three times, but ten.

"What you tappin' the plate for? That ain't gonna get you no home run," Meatball said. "You gotta hit the ball to get a home run."

"Man, forget you," Steebo said and tapped the bottom of his Pro Keds.

"Steebo, man, ain't no dirt on your tennis shoes," Onion said.

Finally, he bent over the plate and rested the bat on his right shoulder.

"Batter up!" Fatboy bellowed.

Okay. Here we go, Kizmic thought. She wound up to throw out the pitch, but Steebo took the bat off his shoulder.

"What?" Fatboy asked, looking up at him as he kneeled behind home plate.

Steebo pointed the bat at Kizmic. "You better watch where you throwin' that ball," he warned.

Kizmic said, "Oh, I'ma watch it, alright."

He got back in his batter's stance. Kizmic wound up and threw the ball, straight down the middle. Steebo didn't even swing. He just jumped away from the base.

"Strike One!" Fatboy hollered.

"Steebo, what you doin'?!" Man yelled. "What you jump away from the ball for?"

"She tried to hit me," he said.

"She ain't try to hit you," Babyfrog said.

"Yes, she did. You saw her throw that ball all close."

"She ain't throw the ball close," Man said.

Kizmic didn't say a word.

"All I know is she bet' not hit me with that ball."

"All I know is you better get a hit, man, or we gonna lose," Onion said. "And com'on. It's hot!"

Steebo went back through his sham of a ritual, straightening his clothes, tapping the plate, tapping his tennis shoes, then putting the bat on his shoulder. Kizmic threw the ball. Steebo ducked away.

"Strike Two!" Fatboy called.

"That ain't no strike," Steebo protested.

"That's a strike, man."

"How's that a strike?"

"You moved away from the ball. That's how it's a strike."

"That's 'cause she keep tryna hit me."

"No she ain't. You just scared," Redtop said.

"I ain't scared of nothin'."

"Well, then stand at the plate and stop jumpin' 'round like a rabbit." Redtop hopped around the field. Everybody laughed.

Steebo went back to the plate this time without any ritual. Kizmic pitched the ball straight down the middle again.

Fatboy caught it. "Strike Three! You're out!"

Steebo threw down the bat, mumbling about how he wasn't out and how he wasn't going to stand there and let that girl hit him with the ball. He never got a hit off Kizmic. Just like she planned. Sucka.

CHAPTER

12

Kizmic walked gingerly up the steps of the Fish Store but had to quickly move aside as Miss Josephine's niece, Tonya, and her best friend, Nikki, strolled out arm in arm, Tonya drinking a bottle of Coke and Nikki sipping an orange soda.

Kizmic often saw the two girls around the neighborhood and hanging out in the Fish Store. Always with each other. They had no interest in anyone else. Kizmic envied their close friendship, but she was especially envious of Tonya because Miss Josephine was not only her aunt but she was loved so by her that Miss Josephine called Tonya Luv.

Behind the candy counter, Miss Josephine leaned on her elbows with her pretty gray eyes softly marveling over a white, miniature bottle of Coca Cola and a pair of white high heel shoes no bigger than her palm. The bottle of Coke reminded Kizmic of the small, wax Nik-L-Nips on the second shelf of the candy counter, only it wasn't filled with flavored syrup. The heels were a replica of a blue pair Kizmic had seen Miss Josephine wear. Each had been meticulously carved out of bars of soap by Tonya with a red, folding pocket knife similar to the one Sleepy-eyed Ted used to carve their names and winning notches into the tree.

"Aren't these wonderful?" Miss Josephine asked.

Kizmic nodded, not really caring. She had more important things on her mind.

"I tell you, if Luv keeps this up, she's gonna be a famous sculptor one day. Mark my words. Now," she said, neatly setting the heels and Coca Cola bottle aside. "What's wrong with your leg?"

"Steebo hit me with a baseball," Kizmic said.

"Good Lord."

Miss Josephine helped Kizmic up the back stairs that led to their apartment above the store. It was a long, small place, but just right for her and Mr Charlie. Miss Josephine took Kizmic into the kitchen.

"Pull down your pants, sweetie," she said.

"Huh?" Kizmic said.

"I gotta see what's goin' on with your leg."

Kizmic hesitated. Her mother was the only person who had seen Kizmic in her underwear.

"You ain't got nothin' I don't have," Miss Josephine smiled.

Kizmic eased her pants down and looked up at the ceiling, feeling completely embarrassed.

"Now that's a doozy," she said.

Kizmic looked down and saw a dark purple, baseball shaped bruise on her thigh.

"Sit down," Miss Josephine said.

She reached inside the freezer and pulled out a metal ice cube tray. She got a towel from her linen closet, wrapped the ice in it, then gently pressed it against the bruise. It hurt like crazy.

With her elbow on the table and her chin resting in her palm, Miss Josephine looked at Kizmic. "You know they ain't gonna stop 'til you quit."

"I ain't gonna quit," Kizmic said.

"Well, what they got planned for you tomorrow?"

"Football, Redtop said."

"Football!" Miss Josephine snatched her hand from under her chin. "Kizmic, you can't play no football with them."

"Why not?"

"Shugga, they gonna beat the crap outta you, that's why not."

"I'll be alright."

Miss Josephine shook her head at Kizmic's stubbornness. "Well, let's get you home so your mama—"

"Nooooo!" Kizmic shouted. "If my mother sees this, she'll have a fit, and I won't be able to play with them no more."

"Kizmic, I can't keep this from your mama."

She didn't see why not. It wasn't like she was dying.

"I didn't even cry when it happened, Miss Josephine," Kizmic argued.

"You cryin' ain't what I'm worried about."

Miss Josephine lifted the ice-filled towel off the bruise. Kizmic turned away and her eyes fell on what she needed to tell Miss Josephine to keep her from telling her mother.

"Remember what you told me about your scar?" Kizmic said. "How you didn't tell your mother."

The sideways look Miss Josephine fixed on Kizmic said, *No this little girl ain't trying to use my scar against me.*

"Just give me 'til tomorrow," Kizmic pleaded. "If they don't let me in, I swear I'll let 'em alone."

Miss Josephine thought on it and thought on it some more. She looked at the bruise on Kizmic's thigh, then touched her scar. "All right," she said as reluctant as reluctant could be. "You got until tomorrow. But this is the deal. Tonight you put some ice on this leg and if it starts lookin' funny or gets to hurtin' really bad, you tell your mama, you hear?"

"Yes, ma'am."

Miss Josephine closed her eyes and threw her head to the ceiling. "Lord, your mama's gonna kill me."

FROM THE MOMENT THEY SET FOOT on the field, Man 'n 'Em gave Kizmic a message. They weren't playing to have fun, show off, or win. They were playing to make her quit trying to hangout with them. Playing with the once-and-for-all, conspiring, cheating, desperation that made her suspect that they had been standing beneath Miss Josephine's kitchen window and had overheard her swear to leave them alone if they didn't let her in today, and they were bound and determined to make Kizmic keep her promise. And from the moment Kizmic set foot on the field, she gave Man 'n 'Em a message. She wasn't playing to have fun, show off, or win either. She was playing for keepsies when it came to hanging out with them. Playing with the same once-and-for-all desperation that would make them think that she had been standing outside the crooked clubhouse window and had overheard them swear to let her in if she didn't leave them alone today. Except Kizmic doubted that Man 'n 'Em had made any such swear. If anything, Man 'n 'Em would have sworn to never let her in, and so she was bound and determined to make them break their promise.

Supposedly, it was Man, Steebo, Fatboy, and Redtop against Peanut, Onion, Meatball, and Kizmic. In reality, it was Kizmic against them all. Babyfrog was the quarterback for both teams because he played little league football at Grove Park Recreation Center, had a Terry Bradshaw jersey, and a pair of black and white Spot-bilt cleats.

Whether her team was on offense or defense, every play centered around Kizmic, and every ball Babyfrog threw to her was too short or too long, too high or too low, too hard or too soft, too far to the left or too far to the right. These on purpose bad throws had Kizmic diving, jumping, running up, running down, scrambling this way, scrambling that way, coming back over here, going back over there, falling forward, falling backward, falling to her knees to make a catch. Which, to Man 'n 'Em's frustration, she did, most of the time. Hurt leg and all. Adding to their irritation, Kizmic never once fumbled the ball. She held onto it even when they all piled on top of her, including her own teammates, under the pretense of trying to stop the other team from tackling her.

Kizmic was playing out her mind. Still, it wasn't enough, because it wasn't about the spin moves or head and shoulder shakes she used to evade tackles and make eleven first downs. It wasn't about the footraces she won that resulted in her scoring three touchdowns, despite being double, triple, and quadruple-teamed. It wasn't about the two touchdowns she prevented, one of which she foiled by herself, the other with the unintentional aid of Peanut, who, by tripping Kizmic, helped her stretch out and grab Fatboy's ankles before he crossed the goal line. It wasn't about the three interceptions she caught with Man and Steebo hitting her from behind. It wasn't about the four blocks she made with Redtop and Fatboy yanking on her chunky cornrows and pulling her down. It wasn't about the five fumbles she caused by stripping the ball out of Redtop and Steebo's hands. Nothing Kizmic did was enough, because it wasn't about any of that. It was about her being a girl. And they didn't know how many times they'd have to push her, trip her, blindside her, smush her face down in the dirt, and yes, even pull her hair to make her understand that they did NOT play with girls. Period!

"Alright, y'all. We gonna run the flea flicker," Babyfrog announced.

Down on one knee, he used a short twig for a pencil and the patch of dirt on the top of the field as paper. Kizmic, Peanut, Onion, and Meatball huddled around Babyfrog as he drew out the play.

"Onion, you go about halfway down the sidewalk," Babyfrog said, drawing a straight line in front of a small circle that represented Onion. He sketched more circles and lines in the dirt to illustrate what he wanted everyone to do. "Peanut, you run down to the second pole in the fence. Kizmic, you go straight down the middle to the third pole then do a little button hook."

"Right or left?" Kizmic asked.

Babyfrog hunched his shoulders. "I'on't care."

Of course he didn't care, because he wasn't going to throw the ball to her so much as throw it somewhere in her vicinity, which meant she was going to have to practically break her neck to catch it.

"Meatball, you cut back and I'ma hand you the ball," Babyfrog continued. "I'ma take four steps this way and then you throw the ball back to me and then I'ma throw it to Kizmic."

"On three," Babyfrog said and stuck out his hand.

Kizmic, Onion, Peanut, and Meatball stacked their hands on Babyfrog's. "Break!" they shouted then broke from the huddle.

"Thirty-One!" Babyfrog held the Voit rubber football out in front of him as he shouted. "Thirty-Twoooo!" He looked across the scrimmage line. Man, Steebo, Fatboy, and Redtop each had one foot back and the other forward.

"Thirty-Threeeee!" Babyfrog turned to his left. Onion and Meatball were set. He turned his head to the right. Kizmic and Peanut were ready to explode down field. "Hut One! Hut Two! Hut—"

"Get out the way!" Peanut suddenly yelled, his squinty eyes glaring down field.

In pink, yellow, bright green, and floral sleeveless summer dresses, Diamond, Poochie, 'n 'Em had traipsed onto the field, like kites that had floated onto the green grass after the wind had let go of their sails.

"Go on somewhere!" Steebo cried. "We tryna play."

Some of the girls rolled their eyes at them, some sucked their teeth, a few puckered their lips, others stuck their tongues out at them, two or three pooted their hands at them, and some acted like they didn't hear them and stood there giggling and running their mouths about nothing.

Wearing a flared, pink checkered dress decorated with pink and yellow daisies, Diamond stood straight, her small shoulders back, and her long, slim neck tirelessly balancing her head full of small, tight cornrows that swept away from her face and turned into individual plaits that cascaded down her back. Looking down her pug nose at Man 'n 'Em, Diamond stamped her freshly polished, white Buster Brown's-clad foot, put one hand on her imaginary hip and, tilting her head from side to side, told them, "You don't own the grass."

"Yeah," Poochie said, looking equally snooty and girlie in a two tier, yellow dress and two thick, long braids on either side of her head. "We can stand anywhere we want."

Oooh, I can't stand them, Kizmic whined. They get on my nerves. Always gotta be in the way. What's wrong with them?

"We gonna run you over if you don't move," Onion threatened.

Diamond, now with both hands on her nonexistent hips, said, "You ain't gonna do nothin'."

"Oh, yeah?" Man asked.

"Yeah," Diamond, Poochie, 'n 'Em yelled.

While they argued back and forth, Meatball ran over to the stone ledge and picked up a stick. He searched the grass and when he found what he was looking for, he poked it with the stick. He then ran toward the girls. "I'ma put this doo-doo on you."

Pandemonium broke out on the field. Diamond, Poochie, 'n 'Em scattered in all directions crying, "Stop!" with their hands raised above their curled, plaited, and ponytailed heads in surrender; screaming, "You better not put that on me, boy!" as they clutched the hems of their pretty dresses; and squalling "Ewww! Leave me alone!" with their white, knee-high socks falling down their skinny legs and bunching up around their ankles and sliding down inside their shoes.

They carried on as though there were ten Meatballs chasing after them with doo-doo sticks. But since there was only one of him, they took turns being terrified by watching Meatball chase other girls and waiting for him to spot them before they squealed, "Get away from me!" and took off running.

Finally, they retreated to the asphalt at the end of the field and behind the cool, summer orange dress of Miss Josephine, who was playing hopscotch with a group of younger girlie-girls. At least that's what she was doing on the surface. Kizmic, however, understood that beneath the clack of her summer orange high heels on the numbered blocks, Miss Josephine was watching and waiting to throw in the towel for Kizmic, because she knew Kizmic was stubborn enough to let Man 'n 'Em kill her before she threw in the towel for herself.

Back on the line of scrimmage, Babyfrog snapped the ball and pulled it into his chest against the number twelve on his jersey as he backpedaled. To Kizmic's total surprise, the play went as Babyfrog had drawn it in the dirt. Onion ran down along side the walkway and Man chased after him. Meatball cut back to Babyfrog and grabbed the hand-off with Steebo on his tail. Peanut sprinted down to the second pole, leaving Fatboy in the dust. Kizmic ran deep down the middle of the field, feeling exposed with just Redtop sticking her. When she passed the third pole in the fence, Kizmic stutter stepped, then jerked her body to the left. Redtop fell for it.

Gotcha, Kizmic thought, then cut to her right, juking the heck out of him. "Arrggghh!" Redtop growled.

Meatball flicked the ball back to Babyfrog, who, seeing Kizmic wide open, threw a hail Mary. The ball went up, up, up, then came spiraling down into Kizmic's hands then — *WHAM!*

Redtop drilled Kizmic so hard the impact was heard way on the other side of the field. The ball popped out of her hands.

"OOOOOO!" burst in the air from Miss Josephine, Diamond, Poochie, 'n 'Em, a bunch of other kids on the playground, some passersby, and the boys.

Knocked into the middle of next week, Kizmic was flat on her back, spread-eagled in the freshly, evenly mowed grass, the way she would be if she were lying in a few inches of snow making a snow angel.

I'm makin' a grass angel, she thought with a loopy wit and a lopsided smile on her face.

Except, she wasn't sweeping her arms out and above her head then back down to her sides and widening her legs then drawing them back together, bending the easygoing blades of grass into the shapes of the angel's heavenly wings and majestic robe. Kizmic was just stretched out there, staring at the sky. Not that there was much to look at. The blue sky was clear with nary a cloud, not even the pretty, white, fluffy ones in the shapes of bears, whales, or mountains, and the sun was so glaring that Kizmic had to keep her eyes squinted.

The ground was cushiony, though. That was a plus. Although, Kizmic didn't remember it being all that soft when she first landed on it. Landed? Why would she say she landed in the grass instead of laid? Come to think about it, why was she lying in the grass at all? Kizmic wasn't a lie in the grass for no reason type girl. She would lie in the grass around a dirt ring to play marbles, but she wasn't just lying in the grass; she was playing marbles. When she played baseball, she often wound up lying in the grass after diving to catch a fly ball, but she wasn't just lying in the grass; she was playing baseball. She also laid in the grass when she was playing foot — Oh, that's it! *I'm not out here just lyin' in the grass,* Kizmic thought with a slight chuckle. *I'm playin' football.*

She turned her head and saw the football a couple feet away and the last play came back to her, along with the realization that she wasn't simply lying in the grass, but rather Redtop had *laid* her out in the grass. And that she wasn't squinting from the bright sun. She was wincing from the raw, red, crashing pain in her head, stomach, and back that felt like someone had taken a running start then dropkicked her.

Kizmic was on the verge of letting every tear she had been wanting to cry since the day they moved spill out of her eyes. What a relief her mind told her it would be. *Just let it all out and everythang will be everythang. See that,* her mind whispered. *It feels good just thinkin' 'bout it. Com'on. Let it go.*

And by God, she would have. She would have bawled like crazy if it wasn't for Peanut. He was standing over top of her, eyes narrowed in anger, teeth gritted together like a mother's when her child performed out in public and she was quietly yelling at him to shut up that noise. Through his clenched face, Peanut was quietly yelling to Kizmic, *Don't you cry. Don't you dare cry!*

Are you crazy? she wanted to ask Peanut. *Didn't you see—didn't you hear how hard Redtop hit me? Of course I'm gonna cry. I got every damn right in the world to cry. After all, I am a girl.*

Oddly enough, Kizmic being a girl suddenly wasn't the point, which ticked her off. Here she was fighting to prove that her being a girl didn't matter, and they were fighting her tooth and nail to prove that her being a girl absolutely mattered. And now Peanut had his angry face in hers telling Kizmic that he didn't care that she was a girl, *You bet' not cry.*

Meatball, Babyfrog, and Onion rushed over to help Kizmic up. They pulled on her arms, which made the pain spread.

Every damn right in this world to cry, Kizmic thought.

So, Peanut's face scoffed. *That don't mean you gotta cry. You just wanna cry.*

Yeah, *I wanna cry,* Kizmic thought. *I wanna scream and holler and jump up and down worse than Steebo. I wanna cry sooooo bad!*

But just because she had the *right* to and *wanted* to, didn't mean she *had* to. If she let one tear fall, Man 'n 'Em would laugh, *See. Told you girls can't play.* And

Miss Josephine, who was carefully observing from the hopscotch board, so far believed that Kizmic was hurt but not seriously. If she cried, Miss Josephine would tell her mother everything and Kizmic would be sentenced to a life of bat 'n balls, hula hoops, and, at the most, Four Square. To tell the truth, the pain was so excruciating that Diamond, Poochie, 'n 'Em were starting to look kind of good. Still and all, Kizmic held back her tears.

"You alright?" Babyfrog asked, his big-bug eyes warm with worry.

Without a whimper, Kizmic said flatly, "Yeah."

"What you do that for?" Peanut yelled, jumping in Redtop's chest. He was too short to get up in his face.

"You ain't haveta hit her like that," Onion said.

"I ain't hit her no harder than I woulda hit one of y'all," Redtop said in his defense. "She shouldn't be out here if she can't hang."

"That's messed up, Redtop," Meatball said.

"Y'all ain't say nothin' when Steebo hit her with the ball yesterday," Redtop pointed out.

Nope, they didn't, but that was because one, Kizmic should have seen that coming, and two, he didn't hit her as hard as he could have. Redtop, on the other hand, unloaded on Kizmic, and *they* didn't know he was going to hit her that hard, let alone Kizmic.

Kizmic was confused. This was the first time any of them had defended her, and they weren't pretending to be upset because Miss Josephine was there. They were genuinely pissed off with Redtop for taking such a cheap shot.

"I should kick your ass," Peanut said, pointing his finger up in Redtop's face.

"You gonna get your ass kicked if you don't get out my face," Redtop said, slapping Peanut's finger away.

Man stepped in and shoved them apart. "Com'on. Let's finish the game." He looked down at Kizmic. "You still playin'?"

"Yeah she still playin'," Peanut snapped.

I am? Kizmic wondered to herself.

"Break!" Man, Steebo, Redtop, Fatboy, and Babyfrog broke from the huddle.

Kizmic stood on the line of scrimmage with Meatball on her left, Peanut on her right, and Steebo across from her.

Okay, so Steebo must be getting the ball, Kizmic surmised, since she was sticking him and every play revolved around her in some way, shape, or form.

"Hey, girlie-girl!" Steebo smirked. "I'ma shake you off like baby powder."

"Thirty-one!" Babyfrog yelled.

"That's what you think." Kizmic bent her knees and put her hands on her thighs, careful not to touch the bruise on the outer side of her thigh.

"Thirty-Twooo!"

"Watch me, now, watch me!" Steebo taunted.

"I'ma stick to you like Elmer's Glue," Kizmic said.

"Thirty-Threeee!"

Steebo put a hand above his eyebrows and looked in the distance, as if he were searching for somebody. "You 'bout to be like, *where he go?*"

"Set! Hut!" Babyfrog snapped the ball to himself.

Steebo did a little fake move to the right, then stepped to the left and zipped past Kizmic. "See ya," he laughed.

She took off up field after him. Oh, they goin' for it, she thought, as Steebo headed straight for the goal line.

About a third of the way, he suddenly stopped then shot left. Kizmic slipped as she tried to change direction. When she caught up to him, Steebo had his hand in the air, signaling to Babyfrog that he was open. Babyfrog prepared to launch the ball. His hand went up, but the football wasn't in it. He faked the throw as Redtop ran behind him and grabbed the ball in a classic Statue of Liberty trick play.

With the ball tucked in his cast-covered arm, Redtop rolled out wide to his right, dipped up the middle, and blew past everybody.

"Get 'im, Kizmic!" Peanut shouted.

'Get 'im, Kizmic'?! she frowned. Shoot! Now I know you crazy. I done took my hit for the day. *You* get 'im.

She was about to step right off that field when she realized the trick Man 'n 'Em hid inside the Statue of Liberty trick play. Steebo lured her up field so Redtop could get the ball. The thing was, he wasn't going to drive her into the ground the way he did before, but he was going to pop her.

If I stand here and take the hit. Which I bet they think I won't. And if I can't take a regular ole hit . . . Kizmic shook her head. I gotta. If I wanna hang with them, I gotta.

She sprinted to the right side of the field and blocked the goal line. Redtop was the only person moving. Man, Fatboy, Babyfrog, Meatball, Onion, Steebo, and Peanut had become spectators.

"Get 'im, Kizmic!" Peanut shouted again.

He startin' to get on my nerves.

Redtop grinned as he charged toward her.

Her stomach quivered as the memory of the last hit flashed in her mind. How 'bout I come back next week and let him hit me?

"Get 'im, Kizmic!" Peanut yelled.

Guess not, she laughed.

Redtop picked up speed, his knees moving up, down, up, down, up, down like pistons in an engine.

Gnawing pain stamped all over Kizmic's back. And he ain't even hit me yet.

"Get 'im, Kizmic!" Peanut and Meatball hollered.

Redtop's orange Pro-Keds skittered up field. Her heart was pounding in her chest.

"Get 'im, Kizmic!" Peanut, Meatball, and Babyfrog yelled.

She braced herself.

Redtop was three poles in the fence away.

"Get 'im, Kizmic!" Peanut, Meatball, Babyfrog, and Steebo shouted.

He was two poles in the fence away.

"Get 'im, Kizmic!" Peanut, Meatball, Babyfrog, Steebo, and Fatboy shouted.

One pole in the fence away.

She closed her eyes.

"Get! Him! Kizmic!" Peanut, Man, Meatball, Babyfrog, Fatboy, Steebo, and Onion yelled.

"OKAY!" she screamed, opening her eyes.

She and Redtop collided with a solid, giant thud. His momentum had her falling backward, but as she wrapped him up in her arms, she somehow flipped him over. He landed—*BOOM!* — on the ground and the ball popped out of his arm.

Kizmic could have picked it up and ran. But again, she wasn't playing to have fun, show off, or win necessarily. She was playing to show Man 'n 'Em that even after being laid out, she would take another hit like one of the boys rather than leave the field and hide behind Miss Josephine's dress, like one of the girlie-girls running from a doo-doo stick.

CHAPTER
13

SLEEP DIDN'T COME EASY for Kizmic. Her whole body hurt, but she was smiling as she lie in bed staring at the bright stars. All her hard work paid off. She was in.

After the football game, Man 'n 'Em unlocked the door to the clubhouse and moved aside. Walking on the sunlight, Kizmic entered, eyes opened as wide as her mouth. In the middle of the floor sat a small wooden table. Onion's Raleigh AM/FM portable radio, Steebo's electronic football game, and Man's latest issue of *Street and Smith's Basketball* magazine were on it. Nailed to the right wall were Peanut's amazing pencil drawings of Batman and Robin, Luke Cage, Spiderman, Green Lantern, Superman, Captain America, Black Panther, and The Falcon. The back wall had three crooked shelves on which Babyfrog displayed his jars of lightning bugs, Praying Mantises, spiders, and caterpillars, some of which were inside cocoons. In the corners were shoeboxes full of Fatboy's *Dracula, Blade,* and *Tales From The Crypt* comic books, Meatball's *Archie's Joke Book* and *Funny Li'l Joke Books,* and Redtop's Evel Knievel *Topps* cards. There were also cigar boxes filled with old skully tops, *Topps* football, basketball, and baseball cards. Everyone had that special thing that said they belonged in that clubhouse. Before they locked it up for the night, Kizmic placed a shoebox full of marbles inside. To top it all off, Redtop apologized to Kizmic by letting her sign his cast.

Being in with Man 'n 'Em had Kizmic wired with joy akin to Christmas night, when she laid in bed smiling because every last toy on her list was under the tree. One o'clock came before she finally dozed off. Her eyes were closed for less than thirty seconds when a scream ran through the streets and climbed into every open door and window. Kizmic sprung up as the scream scurried onto her upstairs back porch, across the floor, then jumped in bed with her. Right behind it came the slam of her bedroom door hitting the wall as her father opened it and ran in with a baseball bat. Wearing only a pair of blue jeans, Turk searched the room with the bat raised, ready to bash somebody's brains out.

"Kizmic!" Magdalene rushed in on Turk's heels.

She had on a red, fancy nightgown that exposed and covered her breasts at the same time. Her hair was tussled but still neat for that late hour and her face was damp with perspiration.

Falling on the bed, Magdalene wrapped Kizmic in her protective arms, and Kizmic liked to have died. Her mother touched every bump, bruise, and scrape on her body. "Are you okay?"

"Yeah," Kizmic whispered, trying not to let on how much pain her loving hug swaddled her in.

"Why did you scream like that?" Magdalene asked, kissing her forehead.

"That wasn't me," Kizmic said.

The dogs in the neighborhood were barking like a pack of wild, ferocious wolves.

Kalaya ambled in, rubbing her eyes and yawning. "What's going on?"

A voice, dark and wrathful with murder, blasted through the night. "Where you at mother—"

BOOM!

The explosion rattled the windows. No one moved.

"Was that a gunshot?" Magdalene's voice was crouched.

"Shotgun more like it," Turk whispered. "A pretty big one, too." Keeping low, he crept onto the back porch and leaned over the railing.

BOOM!

The blast shook the windows again. Kizmic, Kalaya, and Magdalene screamed.

Turk dropped to his knees. "On the floor!" he ordered.

Down they went. Magdalene pulled Kizmic off the bed, and she landed on the leg that had the bruise on her thigh. The pain that shot through her burned as if she had been hit by the ball again.

"Owe!" Kizmic shrieked, knowing her mother would think the hard fall to the floor caused her to holler.

BOOM!

The sound exploded in their ears.

"Turk," Magdalene called, "Who is that?"

"Sound like Tilley," he said.

"Tilley?" Magdalene asked.

Turk crawled over them. "Stay here." He ran to their bedroom and returned carrying his work boots.

"Turk," Magdalene called in a cautious tone.

"It'll be alright," he promised, shoving his feet in his shoes. "I'm gonna see what's got him so pissed and get that damn gun away from him 'fore he kill somebody."

"Don't you get shot fooling around with him," she said.

Turk kissed her quickly on the lips then was out the door.

Magdalene stayed on the floor for a few seconds then she rushed into her bedroom. Kizmic and Kalaya ran behind her. Their bedroom was dark except for two red candles burning on the dresser, which meant her mother and father had been doin' *it* yet again.

Magdalene blew out the candles. "Kalaya, turn on the light."

Kalaya did as their mother asked. Funny thing, though. Kizmic could still see the flames of the extinguished candles flickering in Kalaya's eyes as she looked at the album spinning soundlessly on the record player. Kalaya turned her attention to their mother, who had stripped off the negligee and flung it onto the bed. Kalaya picked it up and studied it with her eyes and her hands.

BOOM!

"Shit!" Magdalene said under her breath as she pulled on a t-shirt.

Kizmic trembled. "Mama . . ."

Slipping on a pair of jeans, she said, "It's going to be all right."

Kalaya placed the negligee neatly on the bed. "I'm coming, too." She ran to her room and got dressed.

Favoring not just her leg but every part of her body, Kizmic did the same.

From the relative safety of their front porch, they saw Diamond's father, Dale Tilley, standing in the middle of the street, flanked by his two sons, Derek and Dale Jr. Mr Dale looked to Kizmic like a soldier who had gone off the deep end. His boney legs were sticking out of a pair of red and white striped boxers. On his long feet were his brown work boots. His hair was matted all over his long head. The street lights beamed on him, illuminating the anger that reddened his yellow face and his long, skinny neck like a heat rash. Close to his scrawny, hairy chest, Mr Dale held his double-barrel shotgun.

"Where you at bastard!" Mr Dale hollered.

Keeping his hands raised and his eyes on Mr Dale's trigger finger, Turk cautiously approached him. "Tilley, man, what's goin' on?"

"Somebody was in Diamond's room." Under his bushy eyebrows, Mr Dale's squinty eyes were wide with fury and revenge.

"What?" Turk asked.

"Yeah! Some mutha climbed up that damn back porch, man, and came in her room."

Just saying what happened to his sweet, little girl sent Mr Dale insane. With his thick lips turned down into a grotesque, merciless frown, he lifted his thin arms, pointed the shotgun to the sky . . .

BOOM!

White smoke and fire exploded from the muzzle of the shotgun. "I'ma kill you!" he screamed.

BOOM!

Kizmic covered her ears and squeezed her eyes closed. Her hands only muffled the sound of the shotgun, which vibrated in her heart. Her nostrils were clogged with the eye-stinging smell of the smoke that hung low like clouds from a storm. When she opened her eyes, she half expected to see everyone laid out in the street, because it sounded as if Mr Dale had taken out the whole block in that last violent shot.

Mr Dale shucked the empty shells. They clattered as they hit the street. Dale Jr handed his father two more, which he quickly loaded with one hand.

"Go in the house!" Magdalene yelled to Kizmic and Kalaya.

"Mama, get Daddy away from him," Kizmic said.

"I will, baby. Now go in the house."

Kizmic and Kalaya stood in the doorway. The phone rung. Kizmic limped to answer it.

"What's goin' on around there?" Aunt Beana asked.

"Mr Dale's shootin'," Kizmic said, on the verge of tears.

"For what?"

"He said somebody came in Diamond's room."

"Where's your mother?"

"She's out there watchin' Daddy. He's tryna get the gun from Mr Dale."

Aunt Beana didn't ask anything else. She hung up the phone. By the time Kizmic got back to the door, Aunt Beana was running up the alley with Plum. Uncle Monty was away, hauling a truck full of televisions to Hurricane, West Virginia. Times like these were the only things that made him hate his job. "I need to be here watchin' out for my family in case somethin' go down," he said. Whenever Uncle Monty felt guilty about leaving Aunt Beana and Plum, she reminded him of the time she was walking home from the market and a guy pointed a knife at her and snatched her pocketbook. Uncle Monty was in the house watching a football game. She was a block from their marble steps, within screaming distance of her husband, yet, "I got robbed anyway. Somethin' can happen to me or Plum whether you here or in Timbuktu, and it won't be no fault of yours."

Aunt Beana ordered Plum in the house, then held Magdalene's hand as they watched Turk try to talk Mr Dale down.

"Come on, Tilley, man," Turk said. "Stop shootin' that gun 'fore you hit the wrong somebody."

Mr Dale pulled the trigger again. The *BOOM!* thundered over their heads.

Besides her father, Mr Charlie was the only other man brave or stupid enough to approach Mr Dale.

"Man, you better stop shootin' 'cause you ain't gonna have no bullets left to kill the son of a bitch when we catch him," Mr Charlie said.

Mr Dale turned to Dale Jr, who showed them the large box of shells he was holding for his father. In that moment, Turk grabbed Mr Dale and wrestled the shotgun from his hands.

"Gimme back my gun, Turk!" he demanded.

"Naw, man."

"You wouldn't be sayin' that if he was in Kizmic's room," Mr Dale said.

"You right," Turk admitted. "But I ain't givin' you back this gun. Least not 'til we find him."

"Who was it?" Mr Charlie asked.

Mr Dale shook his head. "I don't know."

"You out here shootin' up the gotdamn neighborhood and you don't even know who it was?" Mr Charlie asked.

"What'd Diamond say?" Turk asked.

Mr Dale's eyes were inflamed. "'The boogeyman was in my room'."

"What'd she say the boogeyman look like?" Mr Charlie pressed.

"She didn't see his face," Mr Dale answered, grabbing his head with his hands and pressing on it like his head was hurting so badly he wanted to rip it off.

Christmas stumbled from under his back porch, where he'd been sleeping for the past two nights.

While Kizmic didn't find Charlotte to be all that fun, she thought Christmas was one of the coolest dads around, because he wasn't just the Iron Man. He was the Bike Man, who fixed up bicycles and gifted them to kids whose parents couldn't afford to buy them bikes. If they needed a rim, seat, handlebars, breaks, inner tube, they didn't go to the store; they went into Christmas' basement, which had metal shelves stacked with all the junk he collected and sold —blenders, speakers, record players, telephones, sewing machines, waffle irons, typewriters, and everything he needed to restore the bikes he gave away. There was just one thing with Christmas. He had a terrible drinking problem, which had cost him his good job at the racetrack, and, every so often, his warm, cozy spot in bed next to Miss Shelly.

The other day, suffering from a miserable summer cold, Miss Shelly left work an hour into her shift in housekeeping at Provident Hospital. She came home and found Christmas passed out drunk with Black Betty, called so to distinguish her in conversation—gossip—from her white counterpart of the same name and vice, White Betty, who lived in the first unit of the green apartment building. Irked to no end, Miss Shelly dumped a bucket of water on them then put Christmas out.

"Hey Christmas," Turk called. "You see anybody?"

Still three sheets to the wind, Christmas shook his head.

"I coulda told you that drunk fool ain't see nobody," Mr Dale said.

"This drunk fool did," a voice crawled down from overhead.

Everyone looked up and there was White Betty perched in the window of her apartment.

When blacks migrated to the area in large numbers, "For Sale" and "For Rent" signs popped up like weeds in front yards. And blacks, who relished the idea of living in the very area that just yesterday they were only allowed to ride through on the bus on their way to work, started plucking those signs out of the ground like rare flowers. Turk kept his routine of listening to music when he came home, but instead of dancing in the house, he sat on the front porch sipping a beer and watching black and white people play musical houses. The black folks bopped their heads and tapped their feet to "Ball of Confusion" and "Why Can't We Be Friends" as they moved in. The Jews, looking as though the neighborhood had been invaded by some horrifying creatures, moved out without so much as a pluck of their fingers to "Touch A Hand, Make A Friend" or "Everyday People."

By July, all the Jews had scrambled to upper Park Heights or hightailed it out to the neighboring counties. All except for Harold and his wife, White Betty. A lanky, seven-foot-tall man with salmon pink skin, salt and pepper hair, enormous feet, and sunglasses hiding his eyes, Mr Harold stayed to himself. He went to work and came home, and that was all anybody ever saw of him. White Betty stayed in her window. She wasn't a mean woman; she was just a drunk. So occasionally, she talked loudly and made a spectacle of herself, but nobody cared because that was what drunks did.

Everyone's eyes were on White Betty.

Turk asked, "What'd you see, Betty?"

Her watery gray eyes sat like stones on her wrinkled, pale gray face. Her frizzy white hair glowed from the light of the television. "I saw the boogeyman," she slurred, as she wavered on her sill.

The grownups gathered under her window and waited for her thin, drunken lips to spit the name of the boogeyman down on them.

Seconds later, Turk gave Dale Jr the shotgun. "Take this home and hide it good!" He pointed to Derek. "Go get your father a t-shirt and some pants."

Several of the men picked up the shotgun shells and stuffed them in their pockets.

Afterward, Magdalene said to Kalaya, "Call the police. Send them to D. Tinkle's."

D. Tinkle. The man who lived in the pink house on Belvedere. The man who always gazed and waved to Kizmic when she was standing on her back porch. The man with the creepy, crawly, jack-o-lantern smile who tried to take a picture of her.

"All right, everybody, back it up," an officer commanded, cutting through the crowd standing in front of D. Tinkle's door.

He didn't look anything like the Officer Friendly who came to school and talked to the children about safety, Kizmic noted. He was white, stocky, clean shaven, but still very scruffy looking. He had small, blue, hardened eyes and a mouth trained to get the truth rather than to be hospitable.

Officer Not-So-Friendly's climb up D. Tinkle's steps was grave, solid, and authoritative. When he reached the door, he turned to the crowd. His long, piercing stare said he didn't want no crap from nobody. He took out his night-stick and *BAM! BAM! BAM!* on the door.

The block was eerily quiet.

"Who is it?" D. Tinkle's unnatural, unnerving, controlled voice seemed to sneak from behind his door and grope at the crowd outside. Kizmic felt it and she could tell by the way everyone flinched, squirmed, and twisted up their faces that they felt it too.

"He know who it is," Mr Dale said, angrily.

"It's the police, Mr . . ." Officer Not-So-Friendly hesitated, as though embarrassed by having to say the name. "Tinkle."

Without the "D" or Mister in front of it, his name made Kizmic think of little kids out shopping with their mothers and in the middle of it began dancing in the aisles, crossing their legs, grabbing their private parts, and announcing to everyone in the store, "Mommy, I gotta go tinkle!"

"Open up," Officer Not-So-Friendly commanded.

Obeying the order, D. Tinkle cracked open the door, but only as wide as the links in the short chain lock he still had on would allow. He peeped out and inspected the officer's badge, then stood on his tiptoes and peeked over Officer Not-So-Friendly's cap and casually glanced at the crowd. He then closed the door and the sound of the chain sliding slowly across its metal plate made the grownups suck their teeth and sigh impatiently. With sleep in his eyes and his bush mashed on both sides of his head, D. Tinkle appeared in the doorway, wearing yellow pajamas.

"Now you tell me, what grown man goes around wearin' yellow pajamas?" a woman in the mob questioned.

Men didn't wear pajamas was the sentiment of the grownups. Especially not men who didn't have any girl children running absentmindedly through the house, who at anytime could accidentally barge into the bedroom and get a shocked eye full of them in their birthday suits. Uh-uh! Grown men wore boxers. Look around that crowd and you'd be hard-pressed to find one grown man standing there in a pair of pajamas.

So the question, what grown man went around in yellow pajamas, stayed raised in the crowd like a red flag. And while Officer Not-So-Friendly may have agreed, yellow pajamas were not enough for an arrest.

"Yep," a man said. "Sure as he standin' there in those simple-ass yellow pajamas, he did it!"

"What can I do for you at this late hour, Officer Elliott?" D. Tinkle asked, his voice as even and sharp as a blade.

It sliced through Kizmic's gut.

"A house was broken into," Officer Not-So-Friendly explained. "The intruder, a male, tried to have his way with a young girl, a very young girl."

"Goodness," D. Tinkle said. Only he didn't say "Goodness" the way people said it when something horrendous happened. He said "Goodness" in the way people said it when they were talking about something wholesome, something innocent, something natural, something godly.

"You wouldn't happen to know anything about that, would you?" Officer Not-So-Friendly asked.

Cutting his eyes at the mob, D. Tinkle answered, "I'm afraid not."

Kizmic had a terrifying feeling that D. Tinkle wasn't afraid at all. His face was flat, void of any emotion. It was a Mr. Potato Head face before you stuck the happy eyes and smiling mouth in the holes.

Officer Not-So-Friendly quietly observed D. Tinkle for a few seconds, then turned to the mob and asked, "You got anything else?"

"Yeah," Magdalene said and presented White Betty.

White Betty was dressed in a flowery robe, reeking of vodka. In fact, she was so liquored up that Magdalene and Aunt Beana had to hold her up so she wouldn't slump to the ground.

"I seen 'im runnin', runnin' up da alley," White Betty slurred.

Her stinking breath lit up the air and plowed through Officer Not-So-Friendly's nostrils. He turned up his nose as he looked at White Betty, then turned to Mr Dale. "You got anything else?"

"I'm tellin' da truth, officer. I did see 'im. I was leanin' out my window and I seen 'im run up dat alley," White Betty insisted, not understanding why he didn't find her eye witness account credible.

"You got anything else?" he asked Mr Dale once more.

"Since when police stop takin' a white woman's word over a black man's?" someone in the crowd asked.

Like a victim studying faces in a lineup, Officer Not-So-Friendly scanned the black faces in the crowd with his steel blue eyes to ID the culprit who made the smart-ass comment.

Frustrated, Mr Dale answered, "Naw, I ain't got nothin' else."

"Well, then, I'm afraid we are going to have to get off this man's property. Sorry to have bothered you."

"That's quite all—" D. Tinkle began.

"Sorry!" Mr Dale snapped. "What you apologizin' to him for?"

D. Tinkle started smiling that bloody, jack-o-lantern smile, which infuriated Mr Dale.

"Keep on laughin' and I'ma—"

"Don't finish that statement," Officer Not-So-Friendly advised. "Or else—"

"Or else what?"

Mr Charlie stepped in front of Mr Dale. "Come on, man. Let's go."

"You gonna arrest me?" Mr Dale asked in an ain't-this-a-bitch? tone.

Turk, who was standing behind Mr Dale, grabbed him by the arm.

Mr Dale snatched away from him. "This bastard came into *my* house!"

Turk grabbed Mr Dale by both arms this time to hold him back.

"And tried to molest *my* daughter!"

Mr Dale was walking forward despite Turk pulling on his arms, so Mr Charlie put a hand to Mr Dale's chest and shoved him back.

"And you gonna stand here and threaten to arrest *me*!"

Seeing the two men struggling to restrain Mr Dale, Miss Josephine turned to the crowd. "Somebody go get Belinda."

A woman in a purple housecoat nodded her head full of pink rollers then ran up the street.

Miss Belinda was Mr Dale's wife, and she was still at home comforting Diamond, where she may as well have stayed, Kizmic thought. What good was she going to do? She was four-foot-nothing, ten pounds less than a featherweight, and as dainty and girlie as Diamond. If her father and Mr Charlie were having trouble holding back Mr Dale, how was this girlie-girl woman supposed to?

"I'm going to tell you one more time to leave this man's property," Officer Not-So-Friendly warned.

"Man, Fu—"

Mr Charlie put his face directly in front of Mr Dale's. "He ain't worth you goin' to jail."

"Man, get out my face!"

Kizmic saw that bloody smile creep across D. Tinkle's mouth, and it stretched wider and wider, provoking Mr Dale.

Mr Charlie now had both his hands in Mr Dale's chest, but the more her father and Mr Charlie pulled, pushed, and talked to Mr Dale, the more agitated he became. They were losing their grip on him at the same time Officer Not-So-Friendly was tightening his grip on his nightstick.

He's gonna beat Mr Dale, Kizmic thought. He's gonna beat 'im and take 'im to jail.

Kizmic hadn't told her parents about D. Tinkle, not about the way he waited for her on the upstairs back porch, the way he looked at her, the way he smiled at her, the way he waved at her, and especially not about him trying to take her picture. And watching Officer Not-So-Friendly's fingers wrap around that nightstick Kizmic now knew that she never, ever could, because there would be nothing to stop her father from trying to kill D. Tinkle and nothing to stop Officer Not-So-Friendly from beating and jailing her father.

"Hold him, Turk," Magdalene said.

Turk shot her an extremely annoyed look. "I'm tryin'."

"Oh, thank God!" Miss Josephine sighed.

Kizmic followed the relief in her voice and eyes. Miss Belinda was trucking down the sidewalk, four houses ahead of the robed woman who had gone and gotten her. That was the first time Kizmic had ever seen Miss Belinda move that fast. Usually, she switched along, admiring her stylish, sexy, tight-fitting clothes, fussing with her mid-length, black, permed hair, and constantly freshening her flawless makeup. But tonight, her hair was all over her head, her clothes were twisted, and, without her makeup, she couldn't hide the frantic look on her face. Kizmic could hardly believe that that was Miss Belinda.

"You don't want this, Tilley," Turk said, fighting to keep him from going on D. Tinkle's porch.

Miss Belinda disappeared as she cut through the crowd, and when she emerged, Kizmic saw *Miss Belinda*. Her hair was parted down the middle and gently framing her now calm, pretty face. She had adjusted the spaghetti straps of her red tank top, tightened the drawstring of her red sweatpants, and tied the laces of her red and white tennis shoes.

"You don't wanna go to jail," Mr Charlie said.

"You know what I wanna do?" Mr Dale yelled. "I wanna make sure this muthafucka don't *never* come near my house again, and if I gotta go to jail to do it then gotdamnit, I'm goin' to jail 'cause I'ma k—"

"Dale," Miss Belinda said.

Not "Dale!" as in *What the hell are you doing?!* Not "Dale!" as in *I'm scared, baby.* Not "Dale!" as in *Do somethin'!* Not "Dale!" as in *Get over here and stop actin' a fool!* Miss Belinda said, "Dale." Softly, coolly, sexy, like a wife who walked up on her husband trying to leave her for no good reason and she was reminding him of the good thing he was throwing away.

At the sound of Miss Belinda's voice, Mr Dale stopped fighting with Turk and Mr Charlie and turned his head to her.

Miss Belinda switched her itty-bitty self over to him. She patted Turk on the back. "You can let him go now."

Turk looked down at her like, *You sure?*

"I got him," Miss Belinda smiled. "You too, Charlie. He ain't leavin' me. Are you, baby?"

Mr Dale shook his head.

Turk turned him loose and Mr Charlie stepped back, but the two of them stayed within arm's-length of Mr Dale.

Looking up into her husband's angry eyes, Miss Belinda said, "What you out here carryin' on about? You know that man ain't worth us."

"I gotta let him know he can't get away with this," Mr Dale said.

Miss Belinda nodded in agreement.

"He came into our house and tried to touch our baby girl."

Miss Belinda continued nodding, letting him speak his peace, letting him get it all out.

He threw a finger in the cop's direction. "And he talkin' 'bout arrestin' me while he standin' up there grinnin'."

Officer Not-So-Friendly looked back at D. Tinkle, who had quickly dropped that awful grin and was looking straight face at the officer, like Mr Dale was crazy, seeing things.

"Bring your ass down here so I can wipe that grin off your face," Mr Dale yelled.

Turk and Mr Charlie moved to restrain him again, but Miss Belinda put up her hands and gestured for them to stay where they were. She then reached up, pulled her husband's face down to hers, and put her hands on the side of his eyes the way a trainer put blinders on a racehorse to make him see only what was in front of him.

"Shhhh, Dale," Miss Belinda said, not in a condescending tone, but in the highly respectful tone of a woman comforting her man, who had never dropped the ball when it came to protecting his family.

"But, Linda . . ." Mr Dale said.

"I know, baby," she said, sweetly. "But Shhhh anyway." She put her tiny arm around her husband's waist and led him away from D. Tinkle's house. But behind his back, she eyed D. Tinkle, putting him on notice that, *Oh, this ain't over, you mutha. This ain't over by a long shot!*

CHAPTER

14

JUST AS EVERY NEIGHBORHOOD had its share of cats, every neighborhood had its share of D. Tinkles. And just like a low-down, sneaky, dirty cat, D. Tinkle crept around and picked on little children, little girls, to be exact.

When her parents, uncle, and aunt moved to that Pimlico neighborhood, there were no signs warning them that there was a D. Tinkle in their midst. Nobody passed out fliers or mailed letters saying in all caps, BEWARE OF THE BUSHY-HAIRED MAN IN THE PINK HOUSE!!! Nobody knocked on their doors or called them on the phone and said, "Hey, watch out for that D. Tinkle dude!" Nobody nailed anything to the side of a building, plastered anything on a billboard, stapled anything to a utility pole, or even tacked anything up in their minds as a mental note to tell them about D. Tinkle, because they didn't know about him. The only thing they knew or cared to know about D. Tinkle was the color of his skin.

They watched D. Tinkle move in, but because he was yellow, high yellow at that, which meant he was black, the Jews continued to plant for sale signs in their front yards and blacks continued to pluck them up without giving anymore thought to D. Tinkle. Only the single, black women looking for a man thought to dig a little deeper into D. Tinkle, and they were the ones who found out that he lived alone, didn't have a girlfriend, made his living as a photographer, and had turned his basement into D. Tinkle Studios. They also learned that his name was D. Tinkle. What the "D" stood for nobody bothered to ask until after he painted his house pink, but by then it didn't matter. And anyway, how could knowing his first name have told them who he was and warned them about what he was? How could knowing that that "D" stood for Dennis, Darryl, Donald, Dwayne, or Dwight have told them that D. Tinkle

130

was a devil with an unspeakable, insatiable, vile appetite for a well known but fleeting delicacy—the forbidden, sticky, sweet taste of innocence that could only be found within the soft, ripe, vibrant, fleshy walls of little girls. And it was precisely because they did not know who or what D. Tinkle was that, for all the right, common sense reasons, without realizing they were doing so, the grownups had served D. Tinkle his forbidden fruit, his sweet meat on high, wooden platters.

Because of D. Tinkle Kizmic could no longer sleep with the moonlight shining on her bed or wake up with the sun warming her face, because she was no longer allowed to sleep with that back door open. For days after Diamond's scream tore through the night, fathers, brothers, uncles, and boyfriends slept on the upstairs back porches, waiting to catch D. Tinkle slithering up the railings like the snake they knew he was so that they could blow his Mf-in' head off! There was talk of nailing the window shut and having the older girls moved to that room. On her way to the bathroom late one night, Kizmic found Kalaya with the whole side of her face pressed against their parents' bedroom door, eavesdropping as they discussed the matter.

Joining her sister at the door, Kizmic heard her mother say, "He's not after Kalaya. She's too old."

Kalaya was grinning spitefully hard. She had been sulking about her parents taking that room away from her since the day they moved in, and now they were going to have to give it to her whether they wanted to or not, and they most *definitely* didn't want to. *Nan Nan-nah Nan Nan!* glittered in Kalaya's moonlit, gloating eyes.

"Yeah, but if we put Kalaya in there, we'll be up all night tryin' to keep her in 'stead of tryin' to keep him out."

"Caught between a rock and a hard place," Magdalene said.

In the end, Turk and Magdalene, like all the rest of the grownups, put an extra lock on the door and checked it before going to bed, because they left the children where they were. Feeling that her parents had taken that room away from her twice just to be mean, Kalaya refused to speak to them for three days.

Months passed and things gradually got back to normal, but the grownups remained on alert. Their parents being on guard made it easy for the children to push worries about D. Tinkle to the backs of their minds and focus on the joys of being kids. Kizmic, for one, had gotten on with the joys of being in with Man 'n 'Em, which to her surprise didn't solely revolve around baseball, football, basketball, riding their bikes and skateboards, or playing skully. Being in with Man 'n 'Em was finding out that Babyfrog had an easier time understanding the circles, squares, lines, and arrows his little league football coach drew on the board than the letters and numbers his math and English teachers wrote on the blackboard, so he was labeled "retarted" and put in the class for "slow" kids. It was learning that Man had the ultimate thing that said he belonged in the clubhouse, which were the blueprints of the clubhouse itself. He'd drafted them, like he did the plans for the pigeon coop, basketball hoop, and skully board. It was knowing that Onion's father was a deacon and his mother was a missionary in a church on Gold Street, and they made him and his brothers and sisters go to Sunday school and eleven o'clock service every Sunday, Bible Study every Wednesday night, and choir rehearsal every Saturday morning. It was figuring out that Steebo made such a big to-do about everything because he was the only boy in a house of five girls, six if you counted his mother, and they all gave him whatever he hollered for. It was finding out that Meatball only bought Popsicles for the riddles on the sticks and that he listened to his father's Redd Foxx and Richard Pryor albums when his parents weren't home. It was realizing that Redtop fancied himself the black Evel Knievel and that the scars on his body came from spills he'd taken jumping ramps on his bike, riding down steps on his skateboard, doing flips off banisters, falling out of trees, and off a garage roof that sat next to their house. The back bedroom of Redtop's house had a flight of stairs with a long, wooden railing that he often jumped over and free-fell onto the roof of the garage. It was a heck of a lot quicker and much more thrilling than running down all the steps. Being in with Man 'n 'Em was discovering that Fatboy's mother worked two jobs to support her family, that sometimes he and his older sister and brother had to cook their own dinner and go to the laundromat, and that his bike was orange and yellow because his mother couldn't afford to buy him a Sting-Ray, so Christmas fixed up one for him. It was seeing Peanut's four older brothers punch him as hard as they could, trying to make him cry, which he never did because that would make them hit him even harder. To suck up the pain, he would "Waahh!" "Ooooohhhh!" and "Aaaahhh!" like Bruce Lee.

So, for Kizmic being in with Man 'n 'Em was going to Babyfrog's football games and cheering for him and not allowing anybody to get away with calling him stupid. It was holding off on doing any serious playing every Saturday until Onion got done with choir rehearsal. It was ignoring Steebo when he whined because he didn't get his way. It was helping Man build stuff that he'd pictured in his mind and sketched out on paper. It was huddling around the television in Meatball's living room watching "Captain Chesapeake" for three weeks straight waiting to hear Captain C read the corny riddle Meatball mailed in to WBFF-TV. It was twice explaining to the social workers, who accused Redtop's mother of breaking his right arm a month after he got the cast off the left one, that he did a death-defying backward flip from the clubhouse roof and landed wrong. It was grubbing out on the pizza, cookies, and cornmeal pancakes Fatboy learned to cook and hanging out at the laundromat with him while his brother and sister washed their clothes. It was getting that

Peanut sucking up the pain from his brothers' punches was how he could tell Kizmic to suck it up the day Redtop tackled her so hard she wanted to boohoo all over the place. Most of all, being in with Man 'n 'Em for Kizmic was staying out of the feud her mother and sister insisted on waging against each other.

"I Wish" was playing on the radio inside the clubhouse. It was the Saturday before Easter. The April morning was warm and sunny. Hanging up bedsheets to dry on the clothesline in the back yard, Steebo's mother sang with Stevie Wonder as he lyrically reminisced about his outta sight childhood.

Kizmic and Redtop sat across from each other at the wooden table. In unison, they plucked three cards from the decks in their hands and slapped them facedown while both saying, "I! De! Clare!" Then they shouted "War!" as they plucked a fourth card from their decks and slapped them face-up.

"Ha!" Redtop laughed, collecting the whole lot after seeing Kizmic had thrown out a three of clubs and he had laid down a Jack of Diamonds.

Kizmic sucked her teeth. She didn't fare any better at the next hand, as Redtop flipped over a two of hearts and she a nine of clubs.

"Deuces wild, baby," Redtop smirked.

As Kizmic and Redtop continued their card game, Babyfrog fed leaves to the three grasshoppers he had in a mayonnaise jar. Man sat in a corner bopping his head to the music and looking over the plans he'd drafted for a tree house that every one of their parents said they couldn't build after Redtop broke his arm again. "You ain't gonna get me locked up 'cause you decide to flip your silly behind outta no tree house," his mother said. Lying on the floor beneath the window, Fatboy read a *Brother Voodoo* comic book his father had given him. Sitting with his back against the wall, Steebo had his squinty eyes focused on the small screen of his electronic football game as his thumbs pressed the arrow buttons, making the red blip run up and down the field. On the floor under his poster of Jim Kelly as *Black Belt Jones* Peanut worked on a drawing of Spiderman. In essence, they were lounging around waiting for Meatball and Onion to show up so they could go play skully.

Meatball was out with his mother shopping for a new pair of Easter shoes and Onion was at choir rehearsal practicing the solo he was going to sing at Sunrise Service. They all felt sorry for Onion having to spend so much time at church. None of their parents were slouches when it came to attending the House of the Lord, but they weren't fanatics like Onion's parents. Turk, Magdalene, Uncle Monty, and Aunt Beana were members of Brown's Memorial Baptist Church on Fulton Avenue, and they made Kizmic, Kalaya, and Plum go to Sunday school and worship service every Sunday unless Magdalene and Aunt Beana had to work, in which case Turk and Uncle Monty (if he were in town) always "overslept," thank God. They also didn't have to go if they were sick, but not with a little cold or something. They had to have pneumonia or broken bones in order to stay home. Weather didn't get them out of church either. Blizzards, thunderstorms, hailstorms, freezing cold, if the doors of the church were open, they're butts were in those pews.

Kizmic couldn't figure out if she actually didn't mind going to church or if the fact that her *not* going to church wasn't up for discussion made her not mind it. Kind of like school. She had to go whether she wanted to or not, so she didn't bother with minding it. That just made having to go worse. So rather than harp on the things that she disliked about church (having to go to school on Sunday, attend second service, sit next to Miss Mildred who shushed her if she made any noise and elbowed her if she fell asleep) Kizmic focused on the choir. It was the one thing she was certain she enjoyed not because there was no point in not enjoying it, but because she genuinely loved hearing the choir sing. Those men and women, boys and girls were as powerful as the preacher. From the moment they entered the sanctuary, thirty plus strong, wearing their grand, blue and white robes that had *BMBC* embroidered vertically on the sash, marching up the two aisles like soldiers, arms and legs moving in harmony to the organ and tambourines, altos, basses, tenors, baritones, and sopranos joyfully singing out in one voice, they set the spiritual tone for the entire two-hour service. Two and a half if it was Communion Sunday. Another hour and a half if they had second service. Kizmic had to confess, though, that of all the thirty-some voices, she loved her mother's the most, especially when she sang "Oh, Happy Day."

Her mother sang that song differently than she sang Aretha Franklin's "Respect," differently than she sang "He's An On Time God." And Kizmic didn't know why, but every time her mother sang "Oh, Happy Day," instead of seeing her on the choir loft, in her mind's eye, she saw her standing in the middle of the ocean. Not on a boat or raft. On the water itself, with the choir behind her. That's how they appeared to Kizmic last Sunday. After the organist played the intro to that great gospel song, her mother softly sang the first lyric and her alto voice became a ripple on the surface of the water that settled before reaching the shore. It was closely followed by a ripple made of the choir's voice when they sang in a hushed, chant-like way the same lyric, the last note of which they held so that it drifted closer to shore. As her mother led the song, the choir's ripples gradually swelled to waves that got bigger and bigger until the song reached a crest. That was when the choir took over the lead. Their voice rushed toward the coast, sweeping up her mother's voice. The two voices roared to shore and washed over the congregation. Ad-libbing words that sounded as if they were written lyrics for that song, her mother's voice rode rolling wave after rolling wave of the choir's voice, and filled the people inside Brown's with heavenly joy that compelled them to rock side to side in the pews, stand to their feet and shout, dance, clap, run, cry, stomp, wave their fans, their hands, their bulletins, and hold their arms up. Her mother sang out "Good God!" and a rejoicing, good-time smile covered her face, danced in her shoulders, shook her head, and made her jump up and down in her high heels. Kizmic was submerged in it all, not drowning, enjoying the soothing ebb and flow of her mother's voice as she made everything that had breath in that church praise His name. Then, as suddenly as the choir's voice rose, it calmed, and her mother's voice rippled over the ocean again, then settled as the choir's voice gently flowed to the coastline, bringing peace to the members of Brown's Memorial.

Sitting inside the clubhouse, Kizmic wondered if Onion's voice had the same effect on the members of his church when he sang.

By the teeter-totter of her wristwatch, it was eleven o'clock. Choir rehearsal was over. Onion should be on his way. Kizmic was anxious to go out and play because her mother would be calling her in around eight to straighten her hair.

She threw out a jack of diamonds as Redtop plopped down an ace of diamonds.

Man, this just ain't my day.

"Look what I got, y'all!" Meatball walked into the clubhouse with two white bags of Little Tavern burgers.

Meatball's father had "sugar" and wasn't supposed to eat fried foods, but every few weeks his mouth watered for sliders. So, he would send Meatball to buy three bags of the small, greasy, tasty hamburgers—one for him and the other two he gave as a bribe to Meatball and his buddies to keep them from blabbing to his wife.

Onion got there just as Meatball was handing everybody two burgers each. After woofing them down, they ran to the skully board.

The neighborhood was bustling with the usual Saturday clatters, clanks, and hums of mothers cleaning and preparing Easter dinner, the tinkerings, roars, and bangs of fathers fixing cars, doing yard work and home repairs, Christmas' cart rattling through the alleys as he yelled, "Iron Man! They call him Christmas!" and the hoots, shouts, and patters of kids playing. Diamond, Poochie, 'n 'Em were sneaking around looking for a safe place to play. They weren't hiding from D. Tinkle, though. They were hiding from a girl named Tori Pompey.

Like Diamond, Poochie, 'n 'Em, Kizmic avoided crossing Tori's path the way she avoided crossing Phyllis' path, because she had a serious thing about Tori, which was akin to her thing about cats. The thing was, even though Kizmic had never so much as been scratched by Tori, nobody could tell her that Tori wasn't lying in wait for the slim chance to leap on Kizmic and beat her to a bloody pulp. Where this thing came from, any kid in the neighborhood could say, because they had witnessed or been on the receiving end of the mean and nasty things Tori did to kids who made her mad, which wasn't hard to do since Tori stayed mad about something all the time.

Tori was a short, skinny girl with skin the color of peanut brittle and big, amber, almond-shaped eyes. Cat eyes, Kizmic thought the first time she saw her. Mean cat eyes. Her long face was always broken down in this hard, blustery mug that cast cold shadows over everything in her way. Her little hands were perpetually balled up into fists.

Kizmic didn't know nor did she care to know why Tori stayed on the warpath. She only knew that she didn't want to be within two feet of Tori when she went off. So, she stayed as far away from Tori as she could, which, unfortunately, wasn't very far considering she lived four doors down from Uncle Monty and Aunt Beana, whose house Kizmic ran in and out of as much as her own. Also, Tori went to Arlington and walked the same route going and coming. They ate lunch and had recess at the same time. Bottom line, staying out of Tori's way wasn't just difficult, it was darn near impossible. So Kizmic devised a diversionary tactic that eliminated any contact with Tori. If Tori was in the vicinity, Kizmic covertly kept tabs on her without making eye contact, and if she stepped in her direction, Kizmic went the other way. This seemed to allow her to fly under Tori's radar, but Kizmic quickly learned that that was only because Tori's sights weren't set on her.

For all her toughness, Tori wasn't nothing but an old prissy, girlie-girl. She wore frilly dresses, pleated skirts, stockings, knee socks, shiny white or black patent-leather shoes, flip-flops, and sandals. Her long, black hair was always done up in Shirley Temple curls, bangs, or ponytails that were tied with colorful ribbons or long, dangling plaits with rainbow barrettes clipped to them. She played girlie-girl games and played with girlie-girl toys. And of course, Tori liked to play those girlie-girl games with other girlie-girls, in other words, Diamond, Poochie, 'n 'Em. The only problem was Diamond, Poochie, 'n 'Em were petrified of Tori, so much so they hid from her. Every other day they moved their treasured games around the neighborhood like crooks trying to duck and dodge the police. It didn't do much good, because Tori hunted them down and made them play with her. That was how she got her one and only friend, Lynette Fleebish.

Lynette Fleebish lived on Cuthbert Avenue, a block where the houses didn't match. At the beginning of the street was a brick, ranch style home followed by a few wooden single-family homes. In the middle of the block were a group of red brick rowhouses and a few more wooden single-family homes. Then there was Lynette Fleebish's house, a detached adobe style home that stood out from every other house on the block, the same way Lynette Fleebish stood out from the girls her age. She had the staggering height of a varsity basketball player in high school and the pretty, smooth, black complexion of a Doberman pinscher, as well as its fearless bark. Thing was, she didn't have the bite of a mutt. So when Tori one day decided that they were best friends, Lynette Fleebish was too afraid to say otherwise. The friendship worked in Lynette Fleebish's favor, though, being that she liked to run her mouth but didn't have the fight in her to back up the mess she got started. With Tori as her buddy, Lynette Fleebish could get a bunch of stuff going then hide behind Tori's fists. Even still, Kizmic imagined that it couldn't have been too cool being friends with Tori. Lynette Fleebish had to temper every word that came out of her mouth, watch every cross-eyed look in her eyes, quickly apologize for every accidental step on Tori's toe to ensure Tori didn't take offense then beat the crap out of her.

Wearing brightly colored dresses, rainbow hair ribbons and barrettes, Diamond, Poochie, 'n 'Em hid from Tori in the alley, right up the street from the skully board, but because they disliked everything that made an alley an alley, they played on the edge of it.

"No hunchies!" Onion yelled at Kizmic for the thirteenth time in a single game.

Kizmic didn't hunch the twelve times Onion called it and she didn't hunch that time. The fact of the matter was this: while Man 'n 'Em respected Kizmic's unnatural ability to play skully, they still did not like losing to a girl, and they would do anything to avoid such an embarrassment, including accusing Kizmic of cheating.

Crouched down in the number twelve square with her shot all lined up going for the number eleven square, Kizmic said, "Boy, ain't nobody hunchin'."

"Yes you did. Didn't she, y'all?"

"Yeah," they all said, even though some of them weren't paying attention to the game.

Fatboy was reading a *Frankenstein Monster* comic. Peanut was practicing his karate chops. Babyfrog was playing with a worm in the dirt. Redtop was walking up the sidewalk on his hands.

Dismissing Onion's charge, Kizmic once again prepared to shoot, but something or rather *someone* got caught in her eyes. It was Tori stalking up the street with Lynette Fleebish in search of playmates.

Kizmic tried to get Tori out of her eyes, but she was trapped inside, like specks of dust that scratched and tormented her eyeballs, refusing to come out no matter how much Kizmic blinked or rubbed.

"You gonna shoot or just stand there lookin' stupid?" Man asked, putting on the pressure.

"Yeah, we ain't got all day," Steebo said, then popped a piece of Squirrel Nut candy in his mouth and smiled.

"Shut up," Kizmic said. "I got somethin' in my eye."

"She ain't got nothin' in her eye." Meatball turned his transparent, green, plastic visor to the side of his big head. "She just scared she gonna miss."

"I ain't scared I'ma miss nothin'," Kizmic said.

To ensure that she didn't miss, Kizmic waited for Tori to work herself out of her eyes on her own, which she did the minute Lynette Fleebish pointed to the girlie-girl fun fest going on in the alley.

"H-O-T spells hot!" Candy and Precious said, then began turning a jump rope hard and fast. It cracked like a whip as it struck the ground, narrowly missing the exposed toes of Destiny and Melody as they giggled and skipped the rope in their sandals. Singing the lyrics to the game "Donna Died," Peaches, Angel, Ebony, Tootsie, and Lacey surrounded Cookie, who was spinning around and around with one hand covering her eyes and pointing the index finger of her other hand so she could blindly choose the next player when the song ended. Sucking on an orange Lollipop, Hope rapidly moved her left leg back and forth, keeping a yellow hula hoop swishing and twirling above her knees. Princess' head was moving back and forth, making a blue hoop swish around her neck. April had her arms stuck out, moving them in small circles that whirled the pink hoops she had on them. Singing "Miss Mary Mack," Diamond and Poochie stood in front of each other crisscrossing their arms over their chests, patting their thighs, and clapping their hands to the beat.

"I'm next!" Tori said.

Tori didn't talk to you; she hissed at you. "What's your name!" "Where you goin'!" "What you doin'!" "What you got!" "Let me hold it!" "Where you live!" All the kids quickly and politely answered her hisses and prayed their responses didn't anger her. But if Tori was hellbent on beating you up, it didn't matter what you said or how you said it, you were going to get your ass whipped.

At the sound of Tori's hiss, Destiny and Melody tripped on the rope, Hope's hula hoop rattled as it hit the ground, and Diamond and Poochie lost their rhythm. They looked at Tori as if she were a cat burglar that had somehow managed to out slick their most sophisticated cat burglar detector. Lips twisted, Diamond and Poochie turned to the other girls with eyes that scolded and blamed them for letting Tori walk up on them. The girls pointed the finger at one another.

Well, obviously somebody had fallen down on the job, and now somebody was going to have to pay the price. Right off the bat, Diamond and Poochie let it be known it wasn't going to be either one of them. Tori was heavy-handed and to play a clap and rhyme game with her meant your palms and fingers were going to be stinging. None of the girls volunteered, so Diamond and Poochie had to choose which one would get stuck with Tori. While deciding, they began playing the clap and rhyme game that was sung to the tune of Bobby Day's "Rockin' Robin" song.

Diamond, Poochie, 'n 'Em sang that clap and rhyme almost every day. Most of the time with Tori and Lynette Fleebish. But for some reason only known to Tori, when they got to the part in the song that talked about somebody's sister being around the corner selling fruit cocktail, she took offense to the lyrics and yelled, "What'd you say about my sista!"

"Yeah! What'd you say about her sister?" Lynette Fleebish asked.

Now, people talked about Tori's sisters all the time. In fact, they talked about her whole family. It couldn't be helped. Her family did things that caused conversation. Her mother, Miss Vivian, was in her mid to late thirties with three daughters, Catherine, better known as Bootsy, Kelly, and, of course, Tori. Bootsy, the oldest, was tall, red-boned, and skinny. Kelly, the middle child, was shorter, high-yellow, and thick, and Tori was dark-skinned and thin. Gossip had it that other than the resemblance of their mother, those girls looked nothing a like because they had different fathers, all three of whom Miss Vivian was messing around with. There was talk about Bootsy that Kalaya got from the grapevine. "I heard she let *all* of Miss Hannah's boys do it to her," she told Plum, who, in turn, repeated the hearsay about Kelly. "They said she stole a box of Kotex out of Rite Aid. Just stuck it under her shirt and walked out the store."

See, there was lots to talk about when it came to Tori and her family, but nobody was fool or suicidal enough to talk about it to Tori's face. So, when Tori jumped in Diamond and Poochie's faces and yelled, "I said, what did you say about my sista?!" Kizmic knew they were itching to ask, "Which one?" And theoretically, they should have, because they had the size (Diamond was a good three inches taller than Tori and Poochie was at least four pounds heavier) and number (it was two against one) to handle Tori. Everybody knew that Lynette Fleebish was just going to stand on the side and boost up the fight. But between the two of them they possessed no more guts than two little, brown mice. They stared at Tori opened mouth, shaking under her cold, shadowy stare with their eyes pleading for her not to hit them.

"Hey! They gettin' ready to fight," Steebo said, prompting Man 'n 'Em to abandon the skully game.

"Come on, Kizmic," Peanut said.

Nope, Kizmic thought. If that was me, I wouldn't want nobody standin' around watchin' Tori beat me up.

Besides, who's to say Tori would stop at beating up Diamond and Poochie? She might look at Kizmic and decide to fight her, too.

"She ain't beatin' me up. I'm keepin' my behind right here." Kizmic flicked her top. It landed in the center of the number eleven square.

Poochie finally managed to mumble in an innocent, mousy voice, "We ain't say nothin' 'bout your sister."

"Yes, you did. I heard you," Tori insisted. "Now, take it back!"

"Yeah! Take it back!" Lynette Fleebish squawked like a parrot that hadn't learned any words of her own.

Not knowing how to take back something they never gave, Diamond and Poochie stood there. Tori took their silence and blank stares as fighting words and pounced on Diamond *and* Poochie the way an alley cat pounced on a poor, declawed house cat that had unwittingly allowed curiosity to lure it out of the back door. With claws that had been skillfully and meticulously sharpened on the thick bark of a three-hundred-year-old oak tree, Tori scratched the girls to shreds and caused them to not simply whine or whimper, but wail like children being abused in the most perverted, invasive way imaginable.

Their blood-curdling wails pierced the air like a police car siren and commanded the attention of mothers and fathers. Right when they started to wonder, *What in the hell?* the nightmare that loomed in the minds of all the grownups sent them scrambling out front doors, back doors, off porches, from under cars, off roof tops, and bus stops. Mothers came wielding cast iron skillets and butcher knives, fathers came clutching baseball bats, hedge clippers, crowbars, or tire irons. Anything that was handy, anything that was sharp, anything that was weighty, anything that would kill.

CHAPTER

15

The ground was literally vibrating as the grownups came running, running, running, like a bunch of raving lunatics, except they weren't making a sound. That wasn't like them. Usually, when grownups were angry, they screamed, yelled, hollered, cursed, and while their barks were nothing to laugh at, they still were nowhere near as worse than their bites. For them to be coming without so much as a grunt or growl, a hem or a hah was scary.

Mr Dale and Miss Belinda headed the stampeding mob. Kizmic saw her mother, father, uncle, and aunt coming right behind them. That they would come was not a surprise to Kizmic. They were her, Kalaya, and Plum's knights in shining armor. Since the day the three of them were born, their parents had always come to their rescue, amazingly turning nightmares into sugar plum dreams, wizardly plucking the knots out of long division, fractions, cursive writing, and spelling, magically making lost toys reappear right before their eyes, and astonishingly turning their cries into laughter when the why-can't-we-get-what-we-want, why-can't-we-do-what-we-want, somebody-touched-my-stuff blues caused them to act like the world would not be there in the morning. But to come like this, her father brandishing a tire iron, her mother wielding a huge butcher knife, her uncle swinging a long pipe, and her aunt gripping a baseball bat was insane!

The grownups came frantically searching, eyes darting up, around . . . no . . . down . . . down . . . down some more . . . right there! Within two minutes they had converged upon the alley, as though they had practiced their response to this alarming wail a million times in their heads. All the children had abandoned their games to watch and instigate the fight between Tori, Diamond, and Poochie, but now they were standing and staring in horror at the sight of their bloodthirsty parents.

The grownups' minds were so bent with the intent that their angry and revenged filled eyes only saw the source of the wail and never bothered with the obvious cause standing in front of them. Not that Tori made it easy for them to spot her as the cause, for in seeing fear in Diamond and Poochie's eyes that was taller and wider than any fear she could have provoked in them, Tori spun around. Her eyes ballooned in terror at the sight of the grownups coming, coming, coming. And in an instant, Tori, like a shape-shifter, changed from a bully to a frightened, helpless little girl.

That was the Tori the grownups saw when they reached them. They also saw Diamond crumpled on her knees. The two thin spaghetti straps that held up the halter top of her sweet, yellow dress were ripped off, so her undeveloped chest was exposed. Her barrettes were scattered all over the alley, and she only had on one sandal. Poochie lay flat on her back with the hem of her dress obscenely flung up above her waist, and everyone could see her pink panties. Her rainbow ribbons had been pulled out of her long hair and both of her sandals were on either side of the alley. Poochie's sweet eyes were filled with tears; Diamond's were stretched wide in a petrified stare. Both of their adorable pug noses were flaring and snotting. Their soft, full lips were quivering and their heads were shaking back and forth, as if they were begging not to be touched again.

Compelled by the overwhelming evidence cowering before them and reeling around in their heads, the grownups concluded that D. Tinkle had somehow managed to get a hold of these poor little girls, because no child on God's green earth screamed like that for the hell of it.

Mr Dale was beside himself with guilt, rage, and revenge, for he believed that he'd let D. Tinkle get his hands on his daughter not once but *twice* on his watch.

With their eyes, the enraged, guilt-ridden grownups began ransacking the neighborhood for D. Tinkle. Kizmic looked around as well, but not for D. Tinkle. She was looking for Kalaya and Plum. She spotted them up by the Fish Store lollygagging with Clive, Louis, and Donald Greenleaf, referred to by everybody, including their own father, as Hannah's Boys. Hannah being their doting, overprotective, and overbearing mother. Nobody bothered Hannah's boys because nobody wanted to be bothered by Hannah. Touch her boys in a harmful manner, say something out the way to her boys, look cross-eyed at her boys, Hannah was coming for you. She didn't care who the culprits were, how old they were, Hannah would show them that she didn't play when it came to her boys.

Kizmic ran up the street, hoping Kalaya and Plum could help talk some sense into their parents. The five of them were in their own little adolescent, hormonal world, oblivious to the chaos that had erupted. Louis was checking out Plum's body, which was filling out slowly but nicely. She wasn't as self-conscious about it as she used to be. A couple of years ago, she would have tried to hide herself from her head to her feet behind her journal. Now she was standing, not totally erect under Louis' gaze, but mellow with her journal in her left hand down by her slender thigh.

"How old are y'all anyway?" Louis asked, his thick lips moving as he chewed some gum. He was short, well-built, and had skin the color of a pecan.

Plum blushed and said softly, "I'm fourteen."

Donald, who was tall and skinny as a beanpole, stepped to Kalaya. "How old are you?"

Kalaya arched her back, a movement that made her chest rise and stick out. Donald ran a hand over the field of cornrows on his head and gaped at Kalaya's tender breasts.

Having his full attention and delighting in it, Kalaya said with a pretty, flirtatious smile, "Old enough to eat cornbread without gettin' choked."

What?! Kizmic thought. Old enough to . . . She couldn't even get it out, it sounded so stupid. Eat *cornbread*! What kind of dumb answer is that? You should be able to eat cornbread without chokin'. Somethin's wrong with ya if ya can't.

But apparently not in their teenaged world. Kalaya stood there grinning, convinced she had said the coolest, deepest thing there was to say on the matter. And Donald was grinning at her, completely impressed with Kalaya's slick intelligence.

Somebody needs to shoot both of them, Kizmic thought. *Old enough to eat cornbread without gettin' choked.*

"Don't you believe it."

The comment came from Clive. He had been standing there with his gangly arms crossed, not the least bit interested in Plum or Kalaya, or so it seemed.

Kalaya placed her hands on her hips and asked, "Don't believe what?"

He noted the striking curves in her hips then looked down his broad nose at her. "That you that old."

Twisting her lips, Kalaya scoped Clive out. He was a teenaged heartthrob, to say the least. Tall, cinnamon brown skin, thick, black, naturally curly hair, heavy, black eyebrows, long black eyelashes, large, dark brown eyes. Stylin' in his navy blue Adidas sweatsuit with white stripes, the jacket zipped down showing off his scrawny chest, and profilin' in his white Adidas tennis shoes, Clive reminded Kizmic of that Peter Wingfield song her father played called "Eighteen With A Bullet." Except Clive was only fifteen.

"What makes you think I'm not that old?" Kalaya asked.

Clive sniffed the air. "You still got Pet Milk on your breath."

Donald, Louis, and Clive busted a gut hooting.

Kizmic found their entire conversation utterly ridiculous. Here all their parents were about to commit murder and ...

They up here talkin' 'bout some daggone cornbread and Pet Milk.

Kizmic elbowed her way in between Kalaya and Donald.

"Whoa, Shorty," he said, stumbling back.

Glaring up at him, she said, "My name is Kizmic."

"Kizmic, what do you want?" Kalaya asked and had the nerve to be embarrassed by her.

You should be embarrassed about tellin' somebody you old enough to eat cornbread without gettin' choked, Kizmic thought as she pointed down the street.

"What's goin' on?" Kalaya asked, seeing the mob.

"They lookin' for D. Tinkle," Kizmic told her.

Plum's face dropped the goofy smile she was flashing for Miss Hannah's boys. "Who'd he touch?" she asked.

"Nobody," Kizmic said.

Like Kizmic, Kalaya and Plum had never seen their parents so enraged, so terrified, so condemning, so unforgiving, so filled with hatred. And the fear of what they would do to D. Tinkle when they laid eyes on him sent them running. Kalaya grabbed her mother, Kizmic grabbed her father, and Plum grabbed her mother and father. Frantically, they pulled on their parents to get their attention, but their fury had put them in a bottomless pit of wild hysteria where the girls could not reach them. All the other children followed their lead and tried to get their parents to look at them, to see that they were safe and that there was no need for them to commit the crime they would argue would be a public service.

Then it happened. They laid eyes on D. Tinkle. He was standing in the middle of the street in front of Kizmic's house. Nonchalantly standing there as innocent as a child, with Phyllis in his arms. Casually stroking her back, his long, thin, yellow fingers fanned out over Phyllis' body in a way that made them all uncomfortable. Phyllis squirmed under his fondling, but he refused to let her go.

The grownups took D. Tinkle's lewd display with Phyllis as a bona fide confession. Their eyes pronounced him guilty. Strangle holding the neck of a broken *Johnnie Walker Red* bottle, Poochie's mother, Miss Ruthie, gave the signal to charge. The other grownups lifted their weapons, ready to bolt down the street and bash him in the head, cut off his . . . and shove it down his throat.

The children continued to yell, scream, and yank on their parents, trying to get them to take a second look at the evidence so they could see that they had it all wrong. In the end, it was Lawyer Balil who overturned the guilty verdict handed down in the street. On the sidewalk in front of Christmas' house, he looked saner than any of the grownups out there, and that was just plain crazy.

Lawyer Balil was a Vietnam vet who had survived two tours in Nam, which everybody said left him a little off. To Kizmic, though, Lawyer Balil seemed as normal as everybody else. He worked at the Baltimore Gas and Electric Company reading meters. He was friendly and spoke to everybody. He helped her father fix his car a couple times. He walked his German Shepherd, Phoebe, before and after work. At midnight on New Year's Eve, he fired off a round from his shotgun.

What were they talking about? Kizmic wondered. Lawyer Balil was a nice, normal acting guy. But that's what the grownups said he was doing. *Acting* normal. But no matter how okay he appeared to be, they still said he was nuts, even more so for thinking they were crazy enough to believe he was sane. They had seen the news footage on television, showing soldiers shooting their way out of trenches, using the bodies of their fallen comrades as human shields. They read the news stories about soldiers coming home with no arms, legs, heads. They saw the photographs of the bodies on top of bodies on top of bodies, big bodies, little bodies . . . baby bodies. So, sure as the sun rose and set, whether he went to work every day or not, whether he walked his dog or not, whether he said hello or not, whether he fired his shotgun or not, the grownups knew Lawyer Balil was whacked out his mind. There was absolutely no way he could have seen the things he saw and did the things they knew he had to do in order to stay alive, and then make it back here sane.

"Ain't no way," Kizmic heard her father say. "He's just a bomb without a lit fuse. Give him some time, though. Somethin's gonna light it."

But for the moment, Lawyer Balil stood with a cool sanity in his eyes that stared at the crazed, condemning mob of grownups and made them ask the obvious. *Do you really think the man is that stupid?*

Then and only then did the grownups turn their eyes back on Poochie and Diamond, and this time they actually saw Tori, not the nightmare in their minds. As quickly as they had picked up their weapons, they put them down. Then they unleashed their fear, anger, and embarrassment on the girls.

"What y'all out here screamin' like that for?" Miss Ruthie picked Poochie up and pulled down the hem of her dress.

"That wasn't me," Tori denied and pointed. "That was them."

Poochie and Diamond looked at each other in utter amazement.

Miss Belinda straightened up Diamond's dress. "What ya'll screamin' like that for?" she demanded.

"She hit us!" Poochie explained, pointing a shaky finger at Tori.

"Oh, for heaven's sake!" Magdalene yelled.

"Jesus Christ Almighty!" Aunt Beana groaned.

"Tori!" Miss Vivian called, making her daughter jump. She had an old bed slat in her hand. "What you out here fightin' 'bout now?"

"They were talkin' 'bout Bootsy," she claimed.

"Yeah," Lynette Fleebish said.

"No we wasn't!" Poochie said, appealing to her mother. "We were just singin' a song and then she hit us!"

"I don't care what she did," Miss Belinda said. "You don't go 'round screamin' like that. Y'all liable to get somebody killed." She looked at her husband, who was glaring at D. Tinkle, who was still standing there stroking a squirming Phyllis. Mr Dale kept his eyes glued on D. Tinkle with relief but also disappointment.

D. Tinkle loosened his grip on Phyllis. She jumped out of his arms, ran over to Lawyer Balil, and started rubbing against his leg, as if she were trying to scrub D. Tinkle's touch off her. Lawyer Balil took one last look at the mob that was now no more than a group of people, then walked slowly down the alley to his house. Feeling vindicated, D. Tinkle smiled then headed up the alley to his house. As Kizmic watched him walk away, she recalled the jump rope rhyme the girlie-girls had made up.

They can run, run, run as fast as they can.
They can't catch me. I'm the boogeyman.
I can get you in the tub, where we can rub and scrub, scrub.
I can get you in your bed, cut off your sweet, pretty head.
I can get you under the porch, set you on fire like a torch.
I can get you in my house, make you squeal like a mouse.
And when I'm done having my fun,
your mama and daddy gonna run, run, run.
But they can run, run, run as fast as they can.
They can't catch me.
I'm the boogeyman.

CHAPTER

16

Yeah, Kizmic's life seemed pretty hazardous at times, what with her having to sidestep a rabid cat, a child molester, and a temperamental bully. But Man 'n 'Em made ducking and dodging Phyllis, D. Tinkle, and Tori Pompey all worthwhile.

For two marvelous, funfilled years, Kizmic basked in her child's paradise. She likened herself to Peter Pan. Man 'n 'Em were her Lost Boys and her Pimlico neighborhood was her Never Land, where she played skully, hung out in a cool clubhouse, raced pigeons, ate penny candy, drank soda, ripped and ran the whole day and never, ever grew up.

The morning after Labor Day still had the mouth-watering smell of grilled chicken, hamburgers, and hotdogs from the last of the summer cookouts. Kizmic woke up excited. She would be in the sixth grade today, and other than hoping that Miss Habeebulah wouldn't be her teacher, Kizmic lay in bed without a worry in the world.

Her bedroom door opened, and Magdalene, who had taken her customary first day of school off, rushed in and laid Kizmic's freshly ironed school clothes on the foot of her bed.

"I tell you, summer flew by as fast as Christmas break," she said. She then paused and looked down at Kizmic, her eyes sparkling. "My little girl. Next year you'll be in junior high." She shook her head as if she couldn't believe it.

That's right, Kizmic said to herself. She hadn't given much thought to this being her last year in elementary school, because nothing was going to change.

Kizmic smiled up at her mother.

"Now, get out of that bed." Magdalene kissed her on the forehead then closed her door.

Kizmic lazed in bed a few moments more.

"Kalaya!" she heard her mother yell. "Don't make me come back in there."

That was her cue to get up. Kizmic yawned, stretched out her arms, and felt two dull aches on her chest. She had been experiencing that tenderness there on and off for a couple of weeks, and while she attributed it to playing football, she didn't remember Man 'n 'Em tackling her or her tackling them any harder than usual.

She placed her hands over the two aches ...

What are those?

Sitting up, she looked down at her chest. The cartoon faces of the Jackson Five on her pajama top smiled at her. There was something under those smiles, though. Kizmic put her hands over the aches again, squeezed, then yanked them away.

No!

She jumped out of bed, ran over to the mirror, and ripped off her pajama top. Her eyes widened with disbelief. There were two marshmellow sized lumps on her once flat chest. No. Not lumps. Brea — brea —

As if someone had let the air out of her, she slumped on the bed. "This can't be," she said, shaking her head. Tears stung her eyes. "This can't be. Mama said...Mama said..."

Suddenly, her door swung open again.

"Up!" Magdalene shouted then froze when she saw tears rolling down Kizmic's face. "What's wrong, baby?" She kneeled in front of Kizmic and wrapped her arms around her.

Kizmic laid her head on her mother's shoulder and cried. After a while, Magdalene gently pushed her back. "Come on. Tell me what's wrong, Kizmic." It was then that she noticed her baby girl's budding breasts. "Awww, Kizmic."

Magdalene took her in her arms again as Kizmic burst out crying.

"It's nothing to cry about," Magdalene said.

"Yes, it is. You said this wouldn't happen," Kizmic sobbed.

"Huh? When did I say that?"

"After Kalaya bled on the steps."

Magdalene frowned. "'Bled on the steps'? You mean back on Proctor Street?"

Kizmic nodded.

"Baby, I don't know what you're talking about. When did I tell you that you wouldn't grow breasts?"

"Not me. Daddy."

Knowing her mother would probably yell at her for eavesdropping, Kizmic reluctantly told her about listening at the top of the stairs. "You told Daddy not to say it, 'cause 'if we don't claim it, it won't happen'."

Magdalene pulled Kizmic to her again and rocked her soothingly back and forth.

"And I didn't," Kizmic said, holding her mother. "I didn't claim it. So, why'd it happen?"

"Because, baby, you're growing up."

"I don't want to," Kizmic whined. "I don't want these *things* on my chest. And I don't wanna bleed on the steps."

"You're not going to bleed on the steps."

"Maybe not on the steps, but I'm gonna bleed one day, right?"

"One day. Yes."

Kizmic dropped her head and started crying in her mother's arms again.

"Summer's not the only thing that flew by," Magdalene sighed, softly rubbing Kizmic's back.

ON TOP OF WAKING UP in the morning and discovering she had grown breasts, Kizmic got to school and found out that she was in Miss Habeebulah's class. Miss Habeebulah seemed tall, but only because she wore high-heels. She had nutmeg brown skin, a stack perm with a wreath of soft curls around her oblong face, and vigilant, brown eyes. Standing in front of the class in a fashionable black and white pleated blouse and black pants waiting for everyone to be seated, Miss Habeebulah didn't appear as bad as the talk on the playground sketched her out to be. Once the last kid was sitting down, Miss Habeebulah licked her red lipstick-covered, wide lips and began to live up to every bit of her horrible reputation.

First, she made the boys sit on the left side of the room and the girls on the right.

"I've come to learn that you boys and girls learn better when you're not next to one another," Miss Habeebulah said.

Kizmic, Man, Onion, Steebo, and Redtop looked at each other totally dumbfounded.

"How she just gonna move us like that?" Steebo asked.

"We always sit together," Onion said.

"Not this year," Poochie said with a smirk.

Kizmic pouted as she joined the girls on the other side of the room, feeling awkward. Not herself, especially with bre ...

"Kizmic Waters," Miss Habeebulah called. "You will sit there."

She pointed her ruler at a desk near the back of the room. Kizmic shuffled toward it and saw Diamond was to the right of her, Aunt Josephine's niece,

Tonya, was to the left of her, Poochie was behind her, and Lynette Fleebish was sitting in front of her.

Oh, come on! I don't wanna sit with none of them. Kizmic dropped her books on her desk and flopped down in her seat. Lips poked out, she looked around the room. Well, at least I ain't sittin' next to Tori, she thought, trying to see the bright side of things.

But there was no bright side being in Miss Habeebulah's class. All day long she called on kids even if they didn't have their hand up. She called on Kizmic three times and made her come to the black board all three times. She gave math and English homework on the *first day*! And said they were going to have a quiz on Friday!

Man! This school year ain't startin' off on the right foot, Kizmic thought, sinking down in her seat.

OF COURSE, KIZMIC DIDN'T TELL Man 'n 'Em about the rotten, low down, dirty trick Mother Nature had pulled on her. She went around like normal, trying to do everything she always did. But those little bumps got in the way of all the things Kizmic loved. When she rode her skateboard, they pulled her forward and made her lose her balance. When she played basketball, they bounced up and down and made her throw up bricks or air balls, and when she played skully, they distracted her by brushing against her shirt every time she lifted her arm to take aim at a square. The feel of the soft cotton fabric of her undershirt against her young, sensitive nipples tingled within her. The sensation was like nothing Kizmic had ever sensed before, and every time it happened, she dropped her top or overshot the square.

At night Kizmic got down on her knees and prayed for them to go away. When she woke up the next morning and they were still there, she got down on her knees and prayed, "Well, if you ain't gonna make them go away, can you please at least stop them from growin'?" Three days later, Aunt Beana asked Magdalene, "When you gonna take Kizmic to get a training bra? Her little nipples are justa stickin' out." Needless to say, Kizmic was more than a little hot with God.

Magdalene had been trying to take Kizmic bra shopping for over a week, but Kizmic managed to avoid that very public, very embarrassing mother-daughter outing by arguing that "those things" weren't big enough for her to have to wear a bra. Truth was, the real issue had nothing to do with size. To go shopping for a bra was to officially tell herself that she did indeed have them, and Kizmic wasn't trying to tell herself no such thing. But what she didn't want to tell herself didn't matter in the least. The fact of the matter was not only did she have "those things," but, apparently, that tingling sensation she felt inside when her undershirt rubbed against her nipples, let everyone know she had "those things," because they could see them poking through her shirt.

After that horrific realization, Kizmic willingly went with Magdalene to Kmart, which was having a "Blue Light Special" in the women's lingerie section. It was packed with women holding bras up to their breasts or their daughter's, talking about A cups and B cups and double D cups and *triple D* cups! Kizmic swore she would die if her breasts ever got anywhere near that big. The other girls there were pushing out their busts trying to turn their triple A-cups into C-cups.

"Is this her first bra?" some woman asked Magdalene.

"Yeah, it is," Magdalene said tickled pink, sharing Kizmic's personal business with some stranger.

"Hmmm," the woman said, sizing up Kizmic's breasts. "She looks like a double A to me."

Like somebody asked her, Kizmic thought, wanting to hide her chest from the woman's intrusive eyes. What's wrong with you, lady? Stop lookin' at me.

"I was thinking the same thing," Magdalene said and held up a white bra with lace trim.

Oh no, Kizmic protested. I might have to wear a bra, but it ain't gonna have no lace all over it.

Turned out she was a size twenty-eight double A, which confused Kizmic. The double anything bras the women had in their hands were way bigger. So how could she be a double A? Kizmic decided that it didn't matter as long as her breasts were tiny.

Mistaking Kizmic's confusion for disappointment, the woman said, "Don't worry, dear, they'll get bigger."

Again, like somebody asked her.

One cold December morning, Kizmic stood naked in front of the mirror and stared at her body, which she was beginning not to recognize. Her beautiful flat chest had swelled even more. She was now a twenty-eight A, which meant she had breasts. Boobs. Tits. Tiddies. Her hips were no longer straight, but had a slight roundness to them, almost as dangerous as the bend on Dead Man's curve. The smooth, innocent brown skin between her legs had sprouted fuzzy, inky black pubic hairs in the shape of an upside-down triangle. She called it her Bermuda Triangle, because she found herself lost in its warmth brought on by an invisible sensual sensation that stiffened Kizmic with fear, craziness, and uncertainty. But what Kizmic felt mostly about her body's transformation was betrayal because it was doing something to her that she didn't want to do—grow up.

The following week, Magdalene took Kizmic to see Dr. Helen Zollicoffer, who had delivered Kalaya, Plum, and Kizmic. Kizmic laid on the examination table while Magdalene stood beside it, keeping Kizmic from jumping up and running out of the room by holding and caressing her hand. After Dr. Z finished examining Kizmic, she peeled off her latex gloves and picked up Kizmic's chart. Twelve years of her life was scribbled down on the pages inside that file, all of her cuts, falls, colds, infections, stomach viruses, and immunization shots recorded in chronological order. Now it held the presumed date she would begin menstruating.

"Around late September. Maybe November," Dr. Z told Magdalene. "I can't say for certain, of course. But for sure by the end of next year."

AROUND THE SAME TIME those two despicable lumps formed on her chest, Man 'n 'Em realized that even though Kizmic could shoot a basketball like a boy, catch a football like a boy, pop wheelies on her bike and skateboard like a boy, crack home runs like a boy, take a punch like a boy, play skully like a boy, Kizmic Alexandria Waters was no boy. She was a girl. And Man 'n 'Em started acting as if they had been standing on a patch of land and discovered that it was an uncharted island, and since they were the original inhabitants, they laid claim to it and was determined to explore and uncover all its earthly secrets and riches.

At first Kizmic thought Man 'n 'Em had accidentally squeezed her tiny breasts, grabbed her behind, or touched her crotch as they tried to strip the football, but then she realized that they (she couldn't tell who exactly because they would all be piled on top of her) were trying to strip *her* because they tackled her whether she had the football or not. When they played basketball, whichever one was sticking Kizmic would check her all over her body, except for Onion. He would stare really hard at her, like he was thinking about touching Kizmic somewhere he had no business, but would end up brushing his hand across her shoulder or arm when he reached in to steal the ball or foul her. Even with baseball they found some way to touch her. It got so Kizmic began hating all the games she loved, which was making her hate Man 'n 'Em. And she did not want to hate them.

Between morning drills, classwork, home assignments, and quizzes, Kizmic wrote letters in her notebook to Man 'n 'Em. However, her *Dear Man 'n 'Em Letters*, as she called them, resembled word-find puzzles, with a bunch of words jumbled up all over the pages as she sought to find the right one to express the feelings in her head and in her heart. So, she never gave them to Man 'n 'Em.

She was writing one such letter to Babyfrog when Diamond had Kizmic pass Lynette Fleebish a note in class that read, "My mother said if you let a boy play with your titties, they'll get as big as your head." That's what ran through Kizmic's mind when they were in the clubhouse and Peanut, the one who had

had her back from the start, came up behind her and not only groped her breasts but copped three quick nasty pumps on her behind before she realized what the heck he was doing.

Ewwwww! It was so disgusting feeling his "thing" against her and hearing him grunt "Uhn, Uhn, Uhn," as he humped on her. Instinctively, Kizmic balled up her fist, but found that it didn't hold the anger she needed to serve up the Battle Royal she knew would break out when she hit Peanut. What her fist did do was hold Kizmic inside the ten seconds that followed the nasty, unspeakable thing Peanut had done to her. Inside those ten seconds, she was able to pretend that the boy who felt her up was not the same Peanut who was going to punch Redtop on her behalf. Inside those ten seconds, Kizmic was able to pretend that the boy who put his "thing" up against her behind was not the same Peanut who made skully tops for her. Inside those wonderful ten seconds, Kizmic was able to pretend that she actually saw shock in Peanut's eyes, like his hands cupping her breasts and his pelvis pressing against her butt, of all the breasts and butts around their way, was just as much of a surprise to Peanut as it was to Kizmic.

What's that song the Doobie Brothers sang? "What A Fool Believes." Well, call her what you may. Kizmic believed it and tried her damnedest to stay inside those ten seconds. The only thing she tried harder to do was to become friends with Man 'n 'Em in the first place. If a Brooklyn Bridge salesman had come along riding on an Arabber's horse-drawn fruits and vegetables cart hawking the once in a lifetime opportunity for Kizmic to live the rest of her life inside those ten seconds, she would have gladly handed over every penny she had. And you could bet your last dollar that the money wouldn't have gone to waste because once Kizmic was inside those ten seconds, she would never, ever click together the heels of her high-top Converse tennis shoes and wish to go home, because that space in time was no place like home. That space in time was like a fairytale, because Man 'n 'Em saw her as one of the boys there.

Despite the unlikelihood of a Brooklyn Bridge salesman coming her way, Kizmic was still unwilling to say "uncle," but then Peanut laughed and betrayed her again. In front of everybody. It was as if he'd pulled down her pants while she was standing in the hallway at school. Nothing Man 'n 'Em had ever done to Kizmic hurt her more. Not the time Steebo beaned her with the baseball or even the time Redtop tackled her like he was trying to kill her. And it was those gropes, those filthy, have-ya-lost-your-freakin'-mind humps! and Peanut's rotten laughter that made it impossible for Kizmic to pretend for one more second. The hands of time spun forward. Eleven seconds later, Kizmic let loose the lies, her wish for a Brooklyn Bridge salesman, and the belief that Man 'n 'Em would ever see her as just one of the boys again.

Sad, humiliated, and just plain old pissed off, Kizmic clocked Peanut in the face so hard he fell straight to the floor. Embarrassed at having been popped by a girl, Peanut scrambled to his feet and leaped on Kizmic. The weight of his anger forced Kizmic backward then sent them falling to the floor. The whole clubhouse rocked. Peanut, who had landed on top of Kizmic, sat up, glared down at her, balled up his tiny fist and, as if she were one of his older brothers, he punched her in the nose with all his might. Blood gushed out of Kizmic's nostrils and splattered all over her face and all over Peanut's knuckles. Man and Babyfrog yanked Peanut off her. Meatball helped Kizmic to her feet. That's when blood dripped out of her nose and onto her shirt. Everyone, including Peanut, stood and stared in horror.

Tackling a girl too hard while playing football could get you in trouble, not too much, though, because people would say if she couldn't take the hit, she shouldn't be on the field. Purposely hitting a girl with a baseball would get you yelled at for sure. But hitting a girl with your fist, oh that was grounds for some serious punishment time. Maybe even a whuppin'. Yeah, she hit him first and hit him hard, but when her parents and his found out *why* she hit him . . .

"Oooo! Peanut, man, you in trouble!" Steebo said, as Kizmic ran out the clubhouse door.

The only thing that could save Peanut was if Kizmic didn't tell on him, but they knew she would. That's what girls did. Shoot, they told on boys if they looked at them too hard. And Kizmic was a girl. Everything they felt up on her said so.

Kizmic may have been a girl, but she was a smart girl. She knew doggone well that she couldn't run up in her house with a bloody nose.

"I ain't no nurse, you know," Miss Josephine fussed as Kizmic once again sat at her kitchen table. "And I can't keep keepin' stuff like this from your mother. Now what the hell happened this time?"

Pressing a cold towel to her nose with her head held back, Kizmic told Miss Josephine all about her troubles with Man 'n 'Em. Miss Josephine sat and listened. When Kizmic was done, she turned Kizmic's thoughts around in her head.

"Well, Kizmic," Miss Josephine said finally after a long silence, "sounds like you've been goin' through something. But I've got to be honest. This ain't a conversation I should be havin' with you. You need to go home and talk with your mama and daddy."

"I can't, Miss Josephine. They won't understand. Mama don't want me playing with Man 'n 'Em anyway. And Daddy'll kill Peanut."

Miss Josephine looked across the room, eyes not really on anything, just contemplating what she should do. "I don't feel right talkin' about this with you, but I'll tell you this and then I want you to go home and talk with your mama and daddy, ok?"

Kizmic nodded.

She took a deep breath. "You are a pretty little girl, Kizmic. I know you don't wanna hear that, but you are. And you're growin' up and so are those boys. And they see you differently, and pretty soon, you're gonna start seein' them differently."

"No, I'm not," Kizmic denied.

Miss Josephine shook her head. "Kizmic, it's not the end of the world. It's the beginnin' of a whole new part of your life."

"So you sayin' I should let Man 'n 'Em feel all over me?"

"Oh, no, Darlin'. You need to put them in their place about that. What I am sayin' is those boys ain't never gonna be friends with you, not the way you were before. And one day, you're gonna want a boy to . . . touch you that way."

Kizmic held her head back and closed her eyes, thinking, Ain't no way in this world am I *ever* gonna want some ole, nasty boy touchin' me like that! I don't care what Miss Josephine says.

After the bleeding stopped, Kizmic walked home, thinking for the first time that Miss Josephine didn't have a clue about anything. For all Miss Josephine said, I may as well of gone and talked to Kalaya and Plum.

CHAPTER
17

FEBRUARY BROUGHT THREE SNOWSTORMS. The first came on a Wednesday night, nice and easy, covering the city in the four inches of snow the meteorologists predicted. The second came the following Monday, quiet, gently dumping the six inches of snow the weather reporter predicted. The third came that Sunday night and continued the following day, President's Day, only it wasn't a storm; it was a blizzard that not one weatherman picked up on their radar. It came with winds, thunder, and twenty-two inches of snow that buried the city, shutting everything down, schools, businesses. Nobody could move except on foot, and even that was iffy depending on where you were walking. Cars and busses got stuck, forcing people to abandon them in the middle of the street, making it difficult for ambulances, police cars, and fire trucks to get through to their emergencies and for snowplows to clear the way. Turk's job shut down for two days. Uncle Monty was on his way home from Philadelphia but got stranded in Delaware. Magdalene and Aunt Beana got snowed in at Holy Cross Monday night and volunteered to stay Tuesday night because they were short-staffed.

Five o'clock Wednesday morning, Turk received a call from his boss ordering all employees back to work.

"I ain't gonna do no whole lot of talkin'," he said to Kizmic, Kalaya, and Plum. "Y'all know the rules."

Kalaya yawned, as if she were too tired to think about rules, so she certainly didn't have the energy to break them.

"When are Mama and Aunt Beana coming home?" Kizmic asked.

"Tonight, around seven or so. The roads should be a lot clearer by then," Turk said, looking out the window. He kissed them. "Be good."

"We will," the three of them promised.

"Old Man Winter has shut the city down." The disc jockey's smooth, warm voice came from Onion's radio, which was sitting on the back porch banister. "But we're still rockin' here at V-103."

A bright yellow sun rose through a large snow cloud floating above a rainbow. Not in the sky. On the back of Kizmic's blue ski jacket as she kneeled behind the three-foot tall wall of densely packed snow near the porch.

Around eight-thirty, Man 'n 'Em knocked on her front door. Ever since she and Peanut traded blows, none of them had touched her, but she hadn't really given them the chance. Kizmic stood on her porch with her lips puckered and arms folded.

Onion elbowed Peanut.

Stepping forward, he said, "I'm sorry for hittin' you."

"You sorry for pumpin' on me?" Kizmic asked, surprising them and herself.

Lowering his head to his snow-covered boots, Peanut said, "Yeah. I was just playin'."

"Well, I don't play like that."

"He ain't gonna do it again," Man said. "Are you?"

"No," Peanut answered.

"What about you, Man?" Kizmic asked.

Man's gumball-sized eyes widened. "What?! I ain't do nothin'."

"Yes, you did. You been touchin' me. All y'all been touchin' me."

"Not me," Onion said.

"I know, but you don't say nothin' when they do," she argued.

Onion hung his head in shame.

Finally saying it, getting it off her chest almost felt better than punching Peanut. Almost. Wanting to hit them all, Kizmic glared at Man 'n 'Em the way the murderer said the old man's eye stared and tortured him in Edgar Allan Poe's "The Tell-Tale Heart."

They fidgeted and squirmed under her gaze until Man said, "Alright. We ain't gonna touch you no more."

Kizmic unfolded her arms and tromped down the steps. Peanut shrunk back in line with his cohorts.

"Swear," she demanded, glowering at them.

"Swear," they all grumbled.

After that, she, Man 'n 'Em spent the better part of the morning shoveling her back yard and constructing four three-foot tall walls for their snowball fight.

Widow's peak peeking from under his evergreen trapper hat, Peanut sat with his back against the wall next to their mound of snowballs. "See where they at," Peanut said.

"*You* see where they at," Kizmic told him.

"Chicken." Peanut looked across the yard to the other snow wall, behind which Redtop and Onion laid low. "Pssst!" he called. "Where they at?"

Also sitting with his back to the wall, wearing a black ski jacket and ski pants, Onion hunched his shoulders. That was as far as he was willing to go to risk getting hit in the face with a snowball.

In his brown Bomber ski jacket, Redtop was on one knee beside their pile of snowballs, staying low enough to keep the royal blue pom-pom of his beanie from going above the wall.

"Don't forget that curfew tonight, Ladies and Gentlemen. Mayor says y'all better be in your house by seven or you're going to be in the big house by seven-O-one," DJ Ross laughed. "Y'all stop all that lootin' out there now. Ya makin' it bad for the rest of us who just wanna hang out in the street or go get a pack of cigarettes."

"One of y'all look," Peanut ordered.

"Why don't you look?" Redtop grinned.

Frowning, Peanut said, "Somebody gotta look. We can't sit here all day."

Kizmic volunteered. She tugged the braided tassels dangling from the ear flaps of her white, blue, and yellow striped knitted hat, pulling it way down on her head. She put her mitten-covered hands on the ledge of the wall. Slowly, she pulled herself up and cautiously scoped out the battlefield. Steebo and Meatball were hunkered down behind the first snow wall in the back of the yard. Fatboy was behind the second wall. All Kizmic could see of them were the top of Steebo's black trapper hat, the orange pom-pom of Meatball's hat, and the top of Fatboy's green camouflage aviator cap.

Ducking back down, she gave her report, adding, "Man and Babyfrog must be lyin' on the ground or hidin' behind the trees 'cause I don't see—"

"Hold up!" Peanut said.

They listened to the air.

"It's two-fifteen in Charm City," announced the DJ. "And we 'bout to get down to the nitty gritty." Over top of his voice were the shouts and laughter of other kids in the neighborhood playing, car tires spinning in the snow, people shoveling out vehicles and walkways. Below all of that was the *CRUNCH . . . CRUNCH . . . CRUNCH . . . CRUNCH . . . CRUNCH CRUNCH CRUNCH* of one of their enemies on the move.

Snow soaked through the knees of Kizmic's jeans as she crawled to the end of the wall to sneak a peek at whoever was trying to sneak up on them. Butch and PJ came into the yard, leaping through the snow to keep from being swallowed up by it. Butch jumped on Onion, licking his face. PJ ran to Kizmic, wagging her tail and panting, her tongue hanging out the side of her mouth.

She petted and hugged PJ, then whispered, "Go get Steebo. Go 'head, girl. Get Steebo."

PJ trotted to the first snow wall and Kizmic waited for her to draw Steebo out in the open.

"What's up, Baltimore?" an excited caller shouted. "I'm Lawrence from Edmondson Village and V-103 plays all the jams."

"That's right. Y'all heard it," said the DJ. "Now I'ma give y'all a li'l Heatwave to groove to on this cold winter day. Let's get it."

"Boogie Nights" started playing and an epic snowball fight commenced. Kizmic stuck her head out from behind the side of the wall and — *WHACK!*— was hit smack in the face with a snowball by Babyfrog, who was hiding in the center of their battlefield behind the huge snowman they made that had a nose and eyes made of tar they had popped out of old skully tops, skinny twigs for arms, and a green Elmer Fudd cap on its head.

"Awwww!" Kizmic screeched, falling back behind the wall. Her nose, mouth, and cheeks were stinging from the cold ball of snow.

"Bombs away!" Man yelled.

He, Fatboy, Steebo, and Meatball jumped up from behind their snow walls and laid down cover so Babyfrog could run from the snowman and take shelter. Snowballs were flying every which way as Kizmic, Peanut, Onion, and Redtop returned fire. In a sheer kamikaze move, Redtop charged the open field toward Steebo and Meatball's wall with a snowball in each hand. He jumped on top of the wall.

"Boom! Boom!" he laughed, bombing them up.

Out of ammunition, Redtop did a backward flip off the wall, landed on his feet, and ran back behind his wall and didn't get hit by one snowball *and,* amazingly, didn't break any part of his body. The battle lasted for an hour. Butch brought it to an abrupt end when he sniffed the snowman, circled it, then lifted his hind leg and peed down its back.

The snow turned yellow and melted as Onion yelled, "Butch! Get away from there!"

They practically rolled around in the snow laughing.

"When you gotta go, you gotta go," Meatball chuckled.

Peanut threw his last snowball and hit the tree. "Let's go in the clubhouse," he said.

Everybody seconded the motion except Kizmic. They had had a great day together. Still, she was skeptical about being in such close quarters with them.

"I'll be there in a few minutes," she lied.

Onion grabbed his radio, and they all headed up the alley to "Le Freak" by Chic.

"They ain't freakin' me," she said.

Kizmic trudged through the nearly waist-high snow on the side of the house. When she got around front, Kizmic saw her mother walking down the street.

"Hey, Ma," Kizmic said. "What you doin' home?"

"I came to check on you," she said, giving Kizmic a hug.

"You walked all the way?"

"It wasn't that far. Besides, the roads are so bad it would have taken me longer to drive. What you been doin' since I've been gone?"

"Nothin'. Helped Daddy shovel the front and the parkin' spaces," Kizmic said, pointing to the two green, metal porch chairs sitting on the street in front of their house.

"Good. Now, how long have you been out here in this cold?"

"Not long," Kizmic lied.

"Yeah, I bet," Magdalene smiled as they walked up the porch steps.

"Reasons" by Earth, Wind and Fire was playing on Turk's stereo. Ahead of her mother, Kizmic stopped in her snowy tracks when she saw that sly-faced Angelo from Proctor Street (whose family now lived down on Woodland) in the living room lying on top of Kalaya. That icky ole Angelo that was the boyfriend Turk and Magdalene told Kalaya she was too young to have was lying on top of Kalaya with his shirt off. That punk Angelo Kalaya talked to on the phone at night when their parents were asleep was lying on top of Kalaya with his pants down so Kizmic could see his white Fruit of the Loom drawers. That nasty Angelo Kalaya sneaked in the house when their parents were at work was lying on top of Kalaya with one of her breasts in his mouth.

What's he got that in his mouth for? Kizmic asked, mortified.

Even more horrifying and puzzling was Kalaya lying there with her eyes closed, moaning like having her breast in Angelo's mouth was the warmest, most sublime feeling she had ever experienced on this earth.

Kizmic stared at them so hard her vision blurred. Rubbing her eyes and squinting brought them back into focus. She tilted her head to the right, then tilted it to the left, as if a better angle would explain why he was sucking on Kalaya's breast.

Maybe it was the intensity of Kizmic's stare, or perhaps the feeling he was being watched, or the cold air blowing on his behind that made Angelo open his eyes and turn his head toward the hall. He looked at Kizmic gaping at him and he didn't even blink. He kept right on sucking Kalaya's breast, like it tasted so good nothing could make him spit it out. Then that despicable little creep winked at Kizmic.

Ewwww! You nasty, no-good dog! Kizmic thought, utterly disgusted.

Done toying with Kizmic, Angelo's eyes rolled up in his head as he closed them. But no sooner had his eyelids lowered than they sprung up again. His jaw dropped and Kalaya's breast fell out of his mouth as Angelo's eyes filled with someone Kizmic, in all her shock and revulsion, had forgotten about.

Mama! Oh, god! "Kalaya! Mama!"

Kizmic didn't realize she was screaming this until Magdalene said, "Shut up that noise!"

Kalaya's head turned, and she started pushing Angelo, who struggled to get off her. His hands, knees, and feet kept slipping, like he was trying to scramble off a slippery mountain. Kalaya got her knees against his chest and shoved. Angelo fell on the floor with a thump. He hopped to his feet and stood erect with his chest heaving, eyes bulging, and his Levi jeans down around his skinny, hairy ankles.

Magdalene was as red as her coat and hat. As red as blood. Anger trembled her clamped lips as her eyes flicked from Angelo to Kalaya, from Kalaya to Angelo. She walked slowly into the living room. Angelo pulled up his pants and tried to face her mother like a man, but it was hard to act like a man when you were shaking like a little boy.

Angelo bolted. Left Kalaya in there to fend for herself without so much as a *Well, it's been nice knowin' ya.*

What a punk! Kizmic thought.

"We weren't doing anything," Kalaya said, putting on her shirt.

The anger that had wired Magdalene's lips shut began to bubble out the corners of her mouth. Soft as snow falling, she said, "You weren't doing anything." A little louder, as if Kalaya disagreed, she repeated, "You weren't doing anything." Finally erupting, "You weren't doing anything!"

Kalaya and Kizmic jumped. A clatter came from the stairs. Kizmic looked and saw an ink pen rolling down the steps. Plum was standing on the landing.

"Mama," Kalaya whimpered with tears in her eyes. "I mean . . . he . . . he wanted to, but I-I-I said no. I said no, Mama."

The slap came when Kalaya closed her eyes to squeeze out her tears. It could have been called a sucker punch, but a blind man could have seen that coming. It was so hard that Kalaya's head snapped to the left and stayed there.

"Mama!" Kalaya screeched.

Startled, Kizmic stepped back. Her mother had beaten them before, yeah. Sure. With a belt, and even then, they had to really and truly deserve it. But she had never, ever slapped either of them.

As quietly as a thought, Plum slipped upstairs.

"Kalaya," Magdalene said in a voice so calm it made the tears Kizmic had for Kalaya pour down her face. "Get out of my sight before I kill you, girl!"

Kalaya ran up the steps two at a time.

SEVEN O'CLOCK, Kizmic stood at the kitchen table and poured King Syrup on two slices of bread. She usually enjoyed this gourmet sandwich after school with a glass of grape Kool-Aid, but she was hungry and her mother hadn't come out of her room to fix dinner.

The front door opened. A blast of cold wind brought in Turk and Aunt Beana's voices, which echoed through the silent house. Kizmic couldn't remember ever dreading the sound of her father's voice, but her stomach sank when she heard him say, "Hey, baby girl."

Kizmic looked up with a tear-stained face.

Turk's brow furrowed. "What's wrong?"

Kizmic said nothing.

Turk sat down in the chair and turned her toward him. "Where's your mother?"

Kizmic's head dropped to the floor. "Upstairs."

"Where are Kalaya and Plum?" Aunt Beana asked.

"Upstairs."

Turk kissed Kizmic on the forehead. Aunt Beana hugged Kizmic then followed Turk upstairs. Kizmic came up after her father opened their bedroom door. The room was dark.

"Magdalene," he called out hesitantly.

A sniffle came back. Turk switched on the light. Magdalene was lying in bed, still dressed in her uniform.

"Magdalene?" His voice was low and large with concern.

He rushed in to comfort his wife. Aunt Beana stood in the doorway. Kizmic tip-toed into the bathroom where she could be out of sight but still hear.

"What's wrong, baby?" Turk asked.

"I hit her," Magdalene sobbed into his chest. "I hit her."

"You hit who, baby?"

"Kalaya," she said.

"Okay," Turk said, trying to calm her down. "Is she dead?"

"No," she said sorrowfully, lifting her head and looking him in the eyes. "I slapped her, Turk. I slapped her in the face. I've never hit her like that before. I feel awful." Magdalene collapsed in his arms again.

He stroked her back and kissed the top of her head to soothe her. "What'd she do?"

Magdalene's back stiffened as she suddenly grew silent.

"I know you didn't slap her for no reason."

Magdalene took a deep breath then exhaled, "She . . . had a . . . uh . . . a boy in here."

"Oh crap!" Aunt Beana groaned.

"She had a what?" he asked.

Kizmic cringed and shrink away from the door.

"She had a boy in the house," Magdalene repeated.

"A boy?" Turk repeated with his voice clenched between his teeth. He rose to his feet. "What boy?"

"Angelo."

"Angelo who?"

"From Proctor Street."

"Proctor Street?! What the hell is he doin' over here?"

"They moved down on Woodland," Magdalene said.

Turk said nothing for a minute. Then he asked, "Where in the house?"

"The living room. On the couch," she told him.

Turk's face hardened. "Just sittin'?"

"Turk, I wouldn't have slapped her if they were just sitting."

"S-s-so w-w-wh-wh-what? Theeey w-w-was . . . was ha-havin'..."

Her father was stuttering like Porky Pig.

"No," Magdalene assured him. "But they weren't far from it."

He scratched his head. "She sat right in my face this mornin', actin' like she wasn't up to nothin'. And all she was doin' was waitin' for me to leave so she could bring some pissy ass boy up in my house! On my couch!" He stamped toward the door.

"Turk, wait!" Magdalene grabbed his arm.

"Wait! Wait for what? Her to let some punk get her pregnant?" He yanked his arm from Magdalene's grip and marched out to the hall.

Aunt Beana jumped in front of him. "Let me get her, Turk," she pleaded.

He bit his bottom lip and averted his damp, angry eyes to the ceiling. "Go get her. Go get her ass now!"

Aunt Beana burst in Kalaya's door. Kalaya and Plum were huddled together on the bed, dread dripping from their eyes.

"You," Aunt Beana said, pointing to Plum, "Go downstairs. Kalaya, your parents want to talk to you. Baby girl, for your own sake, don't say nothin' stupid out your mouth. Just listen. You hear me? Listen!"

Kalaya nodded, seeming to practice what Aunt Beana instructed her to do. After Aunt Beana and Plum left, Kalaya plodded to her parents' room, face still red with her mother's anger.

"So you wanna have boys in the house when we ain't here, huh?" Turk asked her.

Kalaya stared at the floor. "No." Her voice was just loud enough so they couldn't accuse her of not answering.

"No? Your mother said you had one up in here. She lyin'?"

"No," Kalaya said softly.

"Then you wanna have boys in the house while we ain't home."

Following Aunt Beana's advice, Kalaya kept her mouth closed.

"So what? You think you grown?" Turk asked. He started walking slowly around her. "Think you a woman now?" His voice reeked of sarcasm.

Kalaya watched him with her eyes, flinching with every step he took. "No."

"But you had a boy up in here like you grown, right?"

Kalaya was holding her breath, trying not to cry, but doing so also held her voice.

"Answer me!" Turk yelled. His voice trampled through the house and through everyone in it.

Kalaya jumped, Magdalene jumped, Kizmic jumped.

"No," Kalaya whimpered as the tears fell.

"Oh, you cryin'?" He stopped circling and watched the tears run out of Kalaya's eyes. "Was you cryin' when Angelo was on top of you?"

Why's he being so mean? Kizmic wondered.

"I bet you wasn't," he said. "Did it feel good? Did you like it? Was it fun?" Kalaya didn't answer because Turk kept talking. "What'd he say? No, let me tell you what he said. 'You know I love you, girl.' Ain't that what he said? 'I ain't gonna tell nobody.' You believe him, don't you? Well, I got news for you, little girl. The only thing that boy love about you is what you got in your pants. And once you give it up, he ain't gonna be sittin' up in your face talkin' 'bout how much he love you. He's gonna be braggin' to his buddies about how easy you are. And if you get pregnant . . ."

The word echoed in Kalaya's eyes. *What you mean pregnant?*

Turk laughed, reading her expression. "And you know what that boy you so in love with gonna do? He gonna look his mama in the eye and say it ain't his; he gonna look his daddy in the eye and say it ain't his. And he gonna look *you* in the eye and say, 'It ain't mine.'"

Kalaya started crying so hard her whole body shook.

"Go 'head. Get it all out," Turk said. "And while you cryin', just remember this: The *only* people allowed to have sex in this house are me and your mama. You got that?"

Sobbing, Kalaya answered, "Yes."

That night Turk sat in the recliner, staring at the couch, drinking beer, and listening to the Stylistics singing their heart-broken song "You're A Big Girl Now."

CHAPTER

18

THE REST OF FEBRUARY REMAINED cold and snowy. Things eased up for a second in the first week of March, when Mother Nature gave them two spring-like days. One day temperatures reached fifty-five degrees. The second day of that warm spell hit sixty-two, if you could believe that. Most people couldn't but took advantage of it anyhow, especially with it being a Saturday.

On their bikes, Kizmic, Man 'n 'Em cut through the side streets and came out on Reisterstown Road across from Lucille Park, pedaling to Towanda Park.

"Last one there is a rotten egg!" Redtop yelled.

"That ain't fair," Steebo whined. "You just called it."

Hearing Steebo whine made the first real smile of Kizmic's in months spread over her face like the purple petals of a Venus Looking-Glass. She was riding free with her friends, feeling warm and easy.

At Towanda, they threw down their bikes, then took off running on the open field.

"Last one to the woods kisses a duck's butt!" Meatball shouted.

Like a ball of laughter rolling up a throat, Kizmic ran zigzag with her arms stretched out. She didn't care about being the last one. She was flying.

Huffing and puffing, they ran across the baseball diamond, then into the woods. The trees were not as trusting of Mother Nature as they were. The elms, dogwoods, and hawthorns seemed to know that this was pneumonia weather, so they stayed huddled together, resembling shirtless castaways trying to keep the littlest member of their crew from catching frostbite.

Kizmic bounced along with Man 'n 'Em, using that slight tomboyish bop her mother always complained about, even though she had one of her own. On the path, they turned the railroad tracks into balancing beams. The nine of them were walking on either side when they heard the moans of a woman just below the chirping of the birds.

"You think somebody got hit by a train?" Steebo asked.

They hushed and waited for their ears to tell them which way the moans were coming from. Man's ears caught the direction of the sound first. He pointed right.

There was a rhythm to the moaning, an "Um-um-um-um!" Underneath it was an "Ah-ah-ah-ah!" And below that there was the chirping of bugs, the screeching of small creatures hiding from view, and the whistling of the birds nesting in the trees. It sounded a lot like one of Miss Josephine's crazy jazz albums, where all the musicians seemed to be playing a different song, but somehow it all blended harmonically together.

Stretching and squinting their eyes, they searched the woods for the person making the sound. Through a cluster of tall, thin trees, they saw a girl. She was bent over with one hand on her skinny knee and the other pressed against the trunk of a tree, in the middle of the heart that had "Liz and Jim '65" carved above it. The blue skirt she had on was hiked up way over her hips, exposing her long, red-boned legs, and her small behind. Despite her efforts to brace herself, her body rocked back and forth.

"She must be sick on the stomach or somethin'," Kizmic said.

"Nuh-uh. She ain't sick," Babyfrog said.

In the middle of a moan, the girl briefly raised her head and they got a glimpse of her face.

"It's Bootsy!" Fatboy said.

Bootsy. Tori's older sister.

"And ... that's ... that's Twin!" said Redtop.

Yep. Standing behind Bootsy was Twin. Everybody called him Twin because he had a twin brother. Both boys were tall, skinny, and dark-skinned. They looked so much alike that it was difficult to tell them apart, so everybody called them Twin. Maybe if people hung out with them more, got to know them then they would be able to tell one from the other by something different in the color or shape of their eyes, or some flex in their voices, or some birthmark, but they didn't have any friends because they weren't very nice. They stayed in trouble and had even spent time at Charles Hickey for shoplifting and stealing a car. Either Twin was bad news.

What she doin' hangin' around with him? Kizmic wondered.

The answer came when Kizmic saw that Twin's pants were down around his ankles, and Peanut said in an excited whisper, "Hey! They're doin' *it*!"

Kizmic, Man 'n 'Em ducked behind a large, fallen oak tree, stiff with the stillness of opossums, gawking with the sparkling sight of owls, and listening with the keen hearing of bats. They watched Bootsy and Twin with the dazzled, shameless curiosity of twelve-year-olds that had for a long time been hearing about people doing *it* but had never actually seen *it* being done. Now, there *it* was being performed right before their eyes, and oh, what a sight *it* was.

So many things fell into place for Kizmic. The moaning and groaning that came from her parents' room when they were doing *it*. Kalaya and Plum talking about how they had heard that Bootsy had done *it* with all of Hannah's boys. Her mother telling her she was growing up. Man 'n 'Em feeling her up. Peanut humping on her behind. Miss Josephine saying she was going to like boys in that way some day. Kalaya and Angelo on the couch that snowy January day. It was all right there up against that tree with Bootsy and Twin.

A coldness in the air suddenly swooped down. It stung Kizmic's cheeks and turned Man 'n 'Em's excited breaths to frost. From heavy snow clouds, large fat flakes showered down upon them, blanketing the woodlands with that wonderful wintry quiet. The snowflakes decorated Bootsy's long black hair the way Kizmic's mother used to decorate her hair with barrettes. Bootsy and Twin's frosty breaths became heavier as the snow crystals fell on her red-boned behind and melted, turning into droplets of water. Bootsy lifted her head. Her girlish face was twisted in a frown, not one of pain, but of concentrated pleasure. She opened her mouth, stuck out her tongue, and tasted the cold flakes.

Kizmic didn't understand how a girl who still loved to catch snowflakes on her tongue could be out there doing something as grownup as *it*. Looking at Man 'n 'Em's still, intense stares, Kizmic saw that Miss Josephine was right. They would never again see her as just one of the boys.

But I ain't *NEVER* gonna want no boy to do that to me. 'Specially not out here.

Man 'n 'Em were so lost in what Bootsy and Twin were doing that they didn't see Kizmic back away nor did they hear the soft crunch of her snow-soaked tennis shoes as she left tracks that led away from her vacant spot at the trunk.

Twin let out a loud, long moan. The unexpected noise startled the flock of black crows roosting in the trees. A roar of wind came from overhead. Hundreds of flapping black wings turned the patch of gray sky above them almost pitch black as the birds flew out of the trees. Kizmic stood amazed. The birds did not fly away. Some flew around in a circle. Others flew back and forth, as though they were doing the Hustle.

KALAYA WAS PUNISHED FOR LIFE after Magdalene caught her and Angelo. She was allowed to go to the school, because it was the law, but she had to come straight home. She couldn't talk on the phone or have any company, not even Plum, whom Aunt Beana punished for not telling somebody that Kalaya had a boy in the house.

Who was she gonna tell? Kizmic wondered in Plum's defense. Wasn't nobody home.

Not that Kizmic thought for one second that Plum would tell on her best friend, but still....

One good thing did come out of the whole Kalaya and Angelo incident. Magdalene and Kalaya weren't arguing anymore. How could they? They weren't speaking to each other. Except it wasn't like their normal not speaking to each other where Kalaya gave Magdalene the silent treatment because she believed Magdalene punished her unjustly or didn't let her have something she thought was rightfully hers or wouldn't let her do something Kalaya felt she should be allowed to do or ran off at the mouth until Magdalene got pissed and told Kalaya to shut up before she slapped the taste out of her mouth. It wasn't their normal not speaking to each other where Magdalene waited for Kalaya to get over whatever wrong she felt her mother had done her. Even Kalaya, with all her craziness, knew she was lucky to still have a head after the stunt she pulled with Angelo. Naw, Kalaya wasn't speaking to her mother because she didn't know what to say that would make Magdalene stop being mad at her. And Magdalene wasn't speaking to Kalaya because she didn't know how to talk to her daughter without yelling at her about that day.

Things changed, though, one Wednesday night. They were sitting at the dining room table eating pork and beans and hot dogs for dinner. It wasn't the most elegant or nutritious meal her mother made, but it was quick and tasty. Turk, Magdalene, and Kalaya ate their hot dogs on buns with the works—onions, relish, ketchup, and mustard—and their beans in a bowl. Kizmic cut her hot dogs up in a bowl and mixed them with the beans and some sugar. She ate it all with two pieces of bread (taken from the middle of the loaf, where the slices were softest) and a tall glass of ice-cold milk.

Turk sat at the head of the table eating and drinking and looking to his right at Kalaya, then to the other end of the table at Magdalene. Kalaya was slouched in her seat across from Kizmic, eating and drinking mechanically with her head down. Magdalene stared into her bowl of beans, barely eating at all. Turk was angrier than anybody about what happened, but he had somehow come to terms with it and had put it behind him, and thought it was time Magdalene and Kalaya did the same.

Turk cleared his throat. "Kizmic."

"Huh?"

"What happened in school today?"

"Nothin'," she said and put a spoonful of beans in her mouth.

"Really? Nothin' at all?" he pushed.

"Nope," she said, shaking her head.

He widened his eyes and jerked his head at Magdalene and Kalaya in a help-me-out-here way.

Kizmic didn't want to help him out. She liked the quiet. Granted, the silence wasn't exactly peaceful. It was disturbing to tell the truth. Family members not talking to one another wasn't normal. But Kizmic feared that if her mother and sister broke the silence, which was getting louder and louder with each passing minute, they would start arguing again. And Kizmic would take the cantankerous silence over their fighting any day.

"Nothin'," Kizmic repeated.

Baby girl, Turk's eyes pleaded as he poked out his bottom lip.

Kizmic thought about it for a second then, Uh-uh. Nope. Not doin' it.

Turk put his hands together like he was praying.

Kizmic sucked her teeth. Alright, alright, Kizmic sighed. But when they start fightin', don't blame me.

"So, what'd you say happened?" Turk asked.

"Um . . ." Kizmic said, trying to think of something, because nothing happened other than, "Miss Habeebullah is makin' us do a project."

"Oh, yeah?" he asked, exaggerating his enthusiasm to hear about an ordinary school assignment.

Magdalene and Kalaya didn't raise an eyebrow let alone their heads in interest.

"What do you haveta do?" Turk asked, twirling his index finger, signaling for her to elaborate.

Kizmic played along. "She told the class anything but told me that I can't do it on skully."

"Really?" he asked.

"I told her it was my favorite thing."

"Uh-huh," Turk said with his eyes on Kalaya.

"And you know what she said?" Kizmic asked, no longer talking to coax Kalaya into opening her mouth, but venting to let her parents know how unreasonable Miss Habeebulah was being.

"What?" Turk asked.

"'Find another favorite thing. You're too old to be still playing skully.'"

"Did she really?" Turk asked.

"Yeah. Plus, she said I'm too old to be wearin' my watch." Kizmic held up her arm and showed her father her Teeter Totter watch. "Said it was for little kids *and* it's too loud. Am I too old to be wearin' this watch?"

Turk laughed and picked up his hotdog. He took a bite then said, "Kalaya . . ."

Wait a minute. I wasn't finished, Kizmic thought, eyeing Turk, who mouthed a thank you.

Kalaya lifted her head. Kizmic hadn't looked Kalaya directly in the face since the day her mother slapped her. The redness from her mother's hand was gone and so was the hostility that used to cover Kalaya's face like mascara.

"Anything interestin' happen in school today?"

Kizmic expected Kalaya to say no and drop her face back in her bowl. But to everyone's surprise, she actually talked.

"Coach Little asked me to come out for track," she said.

Turk eyed Magdalene. "Track?"

Kizmic dunked a piece of bread in her bowl, soaking it with the sweet tomato sauce, and ate it as she watched her mother look up from her meal with only her eyes and met Turk's stare. The idea of Kalaya running track triggered something inside them.

Suspicion was Kizmic's first guess. Kalaya didn't want to do any kind of physical activity that would cause her to sweat out her hair or get sweat stains on her clothes, and she was talking about track.

She just tryin' to get out the house, Kizmic said to herself, chewing a spoonful of beans and hotdogs.

"Yeah." Kalaya scooped up the rest of her beans.

"Who is Coach Little?" Turk asked.

"One of the gym teachers. She coaches the girls track team. She said she's been watching me in Mr. Milburn's class and she thinks I'd make a good hurdler."

"Hurdler?" Turk asked, elbowing Magdalene with his eyes.

Oh, now she really lyin', Kizmic thought. Kalaya jump over hurdles? Yeah, right.

Magdalene didn't say a word, which was not like her at all. Whenever they did something good, especially in school, she praised and encouraged them. This conversation she left in Turk's hands.

"You gonna do it?" he asked.

Kalaya shrugged. "I don't know. I might. It'll give me something to do other than sit in the house all day."

She ain't runnin' no track, Kizmic thought.

Well, Kalaya did join the track team, and according to Coach Little, whom Turk and Magdalene called to make sure Kalaya wasn't trying to pull a fast one on them, "If Kalaya puts in the time and the work, she can easily be one of the best hurdlers in the city."

Kalaya put in the time and the work and discovered that she had a hidden talent. She could run. Not just run fast. Kalaya could sure 'nough *book*! And the biggest discovery of them all was that she enjoyed it, even more so after she found out that Angelo was going with some other girl.

Dang! Kizmic thought. She risked her life foolin' 'round with him and he dropped her like a hot potato.

The thing was, track didn't just get Kalaya out of the house; it made her forget all about Angelo as she became the object of a bunch of new boys' desires. She went to track practice from three in the afternoon until five-thirty, Monday through Friday, and sometimes Saturdays. On the Saturday mornings Coach Little didn't call for practice and after church on Sundays, Kalaya jogged around the neighborhood. Kizmic went from thinking she had the most uncool, girlie-girl sister there was to bragging to Man 'n 'Em about how she had the coolest big sister in the world.

The whole family got in on supporting Kalaya. Kizmic rode her bike alongside Kalaya during her runs around their way, helping to pace her. Turk made a hurdle out of PVC pipe so Kalaya could do her drills. Uncle Monty and Aunt Beana gave Kalaya money to buy the things she needed. Plum, who was a reporter for Northwestern's newspaper *The Compass*, wrote an article about her. And Magdalene, who seemed to know everything Kalaya needed and where to get it, took her shopping for spikes, shorts, sports bras, sweatsuits, and running shoes.

After they'd come home from one of their shopping sprees, Magdalene came into Kizmic's room with a small, clear case. Inside was a sky-blue Timex Snoopy watch. His big paw was on the two and his little paw was on the six.

"So I *am* too old to be wearin' my Teeter Totter watch?" Kizmic asked.

Magdalene held up her thumb and forefinger, leaving a tiny space between them. "Maybe just a little."

CHAPTER

19

IN THREE WEEKS, Miss Habeebulah was going to call Kizmic to the front of the class to present her project. A project Kizmic didn't have. She had been poking around in her room for ideas for weeks but came up with nothing. Zilch. And zilch was what Miss Habeebulah was going to give her for a grade if she didn't come up with something by Wednesday, April 11.

Sitting on her bed, staring at her Teeter Totter watch on her nightstand next to the baseball with CJ and Sleepy-eyed Ted's phone numbers written on it, Kizmic went down to the cellar of her mind and rummaged through things that had interested her at one time or other for some reason or other and she dug out the dusty, hundred-year-old steamer trunk with the Tic Tac Toe grid made of oak slats that she'd helped her father move when they were straightening up the basement a while back.

Not knowing how the trunk could help with her project, Kizmic kneeled on the concrete floor in front of it. Dust, deep cracks, long scratches, and slanted scrapes coated and scarred the brown wood. Age had eaten away the shine of the brass lock, hinges, latches, handle caps, and corner clamps, making rust their new fancy color. Still in all, the trunk hadn't lost its beauty or its sturdy will to be. More importantly, it had made the move with them, which meant this old, raggedy trunk had been through more than time and rough travels.

The initials W.E.B. were engraved on the metal lock plate. Kizmic traced the "W" with her finger. If the trunk was full of her mother's memories like she remembered her father saying, then who was W.E.B.?

172

She released the two drawbolt latches but couldn't open the trunk because while there was no padlock on the metal staple under the hasp, a key was needed to unlock the fastener. From Turk's workbench, Kizmic grabbed a key in the form of a flathead screwdriver. She inserted its tip into the keyhole and for several frustrating minutes poked and fiddled ("C'mon, old girl") until something clicked inside the locking mechanism and the rusty, metal plate popped loose.

The hinges moved stiffly and creaked like arthritic joints as Kizmic lifted the lid. A heavy odor of old and mildew rushed out, hitting Kizmic in the face like a January gust of wind, stinging her eyes and the inside of her nostrils. She turned away, squeezing her eyes closed, pinching her nose with one hand, fanning the air with the other, and shouting *Pee-yoo!* in her mind instead of out loud because she didn't want the smell to get in her mouth.

When the air cleared, Kizmic rubbed then opened her watery eyes to words printed in capital letters with bold, black ink screaming at her: **NEGRO ... BURNED ... SHOT ... WHITE ... LYNCHED ... DRAGGED ...TORN ... MOB ... HANGED ... KILLED ... SLAUGHTERED ... MUTILATED ... RAGE ... HUNTED ... AMBUSHED ... SLAIN ... CLUBBED ...**

The words came from a collage of yellowed newspaper headlines that were glued and taped to the underside of the lid. *The Bryan Daily Eagle*, *The Tacoma Times*, *The Cleveland Call and Post*, *The Jackson Miss Daily News*, *The Rock Island Argus*, *The New York Amsterdam News*, *The New Orleans States—Item*, *The Omaha Daily Bee*, *The Chicago Tribune*, *The Baltimore Sun* were just a few of the newspaper titles that lined the trunk.

Some headlines and subheadings Kizmic could read clearly. Others were torn or so badly faded that they looked as if they had been composed on a typewriter that was missing several letters and she could only make out pieces. **MOB BREAKS IN JAIL, HANGS THREE NEGROES FROM LIGHT POLE, MOB TAK NEGRO FROM COURT , HANGS HIM FROM —, BERT MOORE AND DOOLEY MORTON LYNCHED TREE, CHANDLER LYNCHED, JESSE WASHING LYNCHED AND BURNED, FOUR NEGROES LYNCHED, NEGRO BEAT, HA , BURNED.**

Whether she could read the whole headline or not, Kizmic felt that every story of this paper tapestry was the same. **NEGRO MAN FOUND HANGING FROM TREE ON SYCAMORE LANE, NEGRO WOMAN HUNG FROM BRIDGE** —Just different people. **TWO NEGROES LYNCHED —, THOMAS MILES LYN—, NEGRO MAN AND NEGRO WOMAN LYNCHED IN WOODS.** Different places. **NEGRO UND IN DITCH, NEGRO FOUND IN RIVER, NEGRO IN FIELD.** Different ages. **NEGRO MAN SLAUGHTERED IN ATLANTA, GEORGIA, FOUR NEGRO BOYS LYNCHED IN RUSSELLVILLE, KENTUCKY, 100 NEGRO SHOT, NED, CLUB TO DEA E. ST. LOUIS RACE**

WAR, —YEAR-OLD EMMETT TILL FO ND **TALLA** ATCHIE RI**—** Different times. **Wednesday, June 16, 1920**, **Thursday, January 15, 1942**, **Friday, July 20, 1935**, **Saturday, August 21, 1926**, **Monday, May 15, 1916**, **Tuesday, April 4, 1950**, **Sunday, July 1, 1917**.

These stories weren't in the history books she read at school during Black History Month. Those stories briefly talked about slavery and how Harriet Tubman freed some slaves before Honest Abe freed them all. They talked about how Rosa Parks refused to give up her seat to a white man and started the Civil Rights Movement with Dr. Martin Luther King. Those stories said blacks were yelled at, called nigger, pushed, knocked down, jailed, had dogs sicked on them, had water hoses turned on them, soda poured over their heads, ketchup squirted on their clothes. But none said anything about the gruesome things printed in these headlines.

Kizmic had never been scared reading those stories, not even when she read of Dr. King's assassination. She didn't feel scared when every night for a week they all sat in the living room and watched the mini-series *Roots*. She felt mad and sad seeing Kunta Kinte whipped until he said his name was Toby. She got irritated with Diamond, Poochie, 'n 'Em for calling her Kizzy, but she wasn't scared. *These* stories, however, unnerved her the way the white people on the news fighting against blacks attending their schools unnerved her, the way the white people staring at them as though they were outlaws who had ridden into town on black horses the day they moved in unnerved her.

"You know we grew up in Lynchburg, South Carolina, so we used to white folks doin' a heck of a lot more than just lookin' at us hard," her father had chuckled that day to put her at ease and to let the white people know that they had no intentions of hightailing it out of town before sundown.

But if these stories were what they were used to white folks in Lynchburg doing instead of just looking at them hard, then it was no chuckling matter. Her mother, father, Aunt Beana, Uncle Monty—Shoot, her whole *family!*—were lucky to be alive.

"Why?" she asked. "Why would they kill people like that? What was wrong with them? They had to be crazy," she insisted.

3,000 WATCHED NEGRO BURNED, FIVE HUNDRED GATHERED AT LYNCH PARTY, FIFTEEN THOUSAND WATCHED NEGRO LYNCHED

"*Fifteen Thousand?!*" Kizmic said aloud to make sure she read it right. Sometimes she had to do that, read things out loud so she could understand them. Endless passages from boring, classic novels, long chapters in social studies textbooks that went on and on about the government, confusing descriptions of cells and planetary rotations in science textbooks, Kizmic had to read that stuff out loud with her finger following each word to make the information stick in her brain.

She moved her face closer to the lid and put her finger under the words. **"'FIFTEEN THOUSAND WATCHED NEGRO LYNCHED'**," she read. "And none of them stopped it? All fifteen thousand of them watched someone be killed and no one stopped it?"

Kizmic turned her attention to the contents of the removable tray. It held a bunch of roadmaps, an old Bible with gold lettering stamped on a black, tattered, leather cover, several copies of *The Negro Motorist Green-Book*, one copy of *Scott's Blue Book*, a pamphlet by Ida B. Wells-Barnett entitled *Lynch Law in Georgia*, a *Jet* magazine, and a 78 record with a red label that read "Commodore Classics In Swing." On side A was the song "Strange Fruit" by Billie Holiday and her Orchestra. Side B she and her orchestra recorded the song "Fine and Mellow."

Kizmic picked up the *Jet*. It was small enough to fit in the back pocket of her jeans. Dated September 15, 1955, the front cover featured Beverly Weathersby, an attractive, young, black woman, light-skinned, vibrant smile, permed, curly hair, wearing a long string of pearls and a one-piece bathing suit that flattered her gorgeous, centerfold body. When Kizmic went to leaf through the magazine, it opened to page six as though it were dog-eared. A headline printed in capital letters with bold, red ink talked about the murder of a Chicago kid. Below the heading was a photograph of a smiling, handsome, black boy dressed in a white shirt and black and white tie sitting next to a pretty woman with a bright, proud smile. His name was Emmett Louis Till and her name was Mamie Bradley. Kizmic had seen the kid's name and face before.

She searched the collage and there was a photo of the boy wearing a hat under the torn and faded *St. Louis Argus* headline, **—YEAR-OLD EMMETT TILL FOUND TALLAHATCHIE RI—**

Pages six and seven in *Jet* told her the rest of the horrendous, true story. Sunday, August 28, 1955, Fourteen-year-old Emmett Louis Till whistled at a white woman. Her husband and brother-in-law later kidnapped Emmett Till, beat him, shot him in the head, crushed his skull, used barbed wire to tie his lifeless body to a 200-pound iron cotton-gin fan, then threw him into the Tallahatchie River.

Kizmic's eyes watered again. Not from the strong, musty odor. They were tearing up from the horrific words she read. "He was only fourteen," Kizmic said to herself. "Two years older than me. Two years younger than Kalaya and Plum. How could they do that to a fourteen-year-old boy? All he did was whistle." Her voice cracked as she spoke. "Just—" Kizmic poked out her lips and blew. A thin, short, tuneless whistle sounded.

She turned the page and came face to face with the photographic image of the words from page six: "beat," "shot," "crushed," "barbed wire," "cotton-gin fan," "Tallahatchie River."

The magazine fell from her hands and Kizmic started running. Running faster than the times her imagination had gotten the better of her and made her see red, sinister eyes glowing in a dark corner of the basement. Tearing through the basement faster than the times she was positive she heard the low growl of some monster lurking behind the furnace. Bounding the steps two and three at a time when she thought a decaying hand would reach from under the basement stairs and grab her ankle. Kizmic ran. But she wasn't running from imaginary monsters. She was running from the *real* heinous monsters who savagely gouged out Emmett Till's eye because he whistled at a white woman. Running as he must have tried to run. Running for her life.

Her heart was banging against her chest like the fists of someone trying to break down a locked door. Finally, after feeling like she had been running in place for miles, she made it to the top step. The door was shut. Fear told her it wasn't going to open. That she would be trapped down there with those monsters. And they were coming for her. Kizmic drove her hands into the basement door with such force it swung open and hit the wall.

"Kizmic!" Magdalene screamed, startled out of her mind.

She was at the kitchen table chopping up potatoes and a head of cabbage to put in the pot of pig knuckles boiling on the stove.

"What in the world is wrong with you?!" she snapped. "You scared the life out of me!"

Kizmic stood there unable to talk, eyes full of fright. Her chest and shoulders rose and fell rapidly as she struggled to breathe as though something were wrapped around her neck, cutting off her airway. Tears ran like a river down her face.

Seeing the distressful, delicate state her daughter was in, Magdalene put down the knife. "Kizmic," she called quietly to keep from upsetting her any further.

Kizmic stared at her mother, wanting to run to her, but she couldn't move. Something had her by her arms, her legs, her feet.

"Baby, what's wrong?" Magdalene asked, taking slow steps toward her.

Kizmic watched her mother coming for her and it gave her the courage and strength to break free from what was holding her in that spot. She ran and threw herself into her mother's waiting arms. And she cried.

Kizmic's whole body was shaking. Magdalene held her tightly, almost swaddling her with her arms, trying to calm her, trying to assure Kizmic, with all her might, that she was safe.

"Baby, I can't help you if you don't tell me what's wrong. Now tell me."

"They ... killed ... him," she sobbed.

"Who killed who?!"

Between heaves, she said, "...Emmett...Till."

"Emmett Till?" Magdalene grabbed Kizmic by the arms and stepped back. Bending to look directly in her eyes, she asked, "Baby, what are you talking about?"

"In your trunk," Kizmic wept. "He's dead in your trunk."

"Dead in my tru—" Suddenly, it all made sense. "Awwww Kizmic..." Magdalene sighed, wrapping her up in her arms again and letting her cry it out.

CHAPTER

20

Magdalene sat Kizmic down at the kitchen table then went to the sink and wet a paper towel.

"Now, how did you get in that trunk?" she asked, wiping her daughter's sad, tear-streaked face. "It was locked. I lost the key ages ago."

"Promise you won't get mad?" Kizmic asked.

Magdalene stopped wiping. "I'm not promising anything."

"I ... I used a screwdriver to get it open," she confessed.

"What?! Why? What were you looking for?"

"Somethin' to do my school project on," she said innocently. "I thought I might find something cool in there."

"Yeah, well, next time ask before you go poking around in grown folks' stuff."

"I'm sorry," Kizmic said.

Magdalene continued to clean her face as if it would wipe away all that Kizmic had seen in that trunk.

"Mama?"

"What?"

"The men who did that to all those other black people, were they crazy?"

"No," Magdalene said flatly.

"Well, what were they then?"

"Killers. Of course, they don't want anybody to know that's what they are, so they hide behind racism. 'Oh, I hate black people,' they say. 'Black people this. Black people that.' And the world lets them slide, because you know, it's just hate. And if they didn't hate, then they wouldn't kill. They're good people. Got children, go to church. When the truth of the matter is, they kill not because they hate, but because they love killing. It has nothing to do with the color of our skin. Believe me, if black people weren't here, they would kill each other. Even with us here they kill each other and blame it on us. None of those people were guilty of any of the so-called crimes they accused them of. Those white people just like killing. You can't do what they did to Emmett Till and all those other black people unless you are a stone-cold killer. That's what they are. That's all they are."

Magdalene stopped talking and turned away. Kizmic got the sense that her mother was struggling with whether or not she had gone too far in telling her all of that. But Kizmic had opened that trunk. Her mother could close the lid, yes, but that wouldn't close Kizmic's mind off to the things she'd read, the things she'd seen, and the fear she was now feeling. And so, her mother had to explain things to Kizmic in a way that would allow her to live with those senseless deaths and still find joy in life.

"Why'd you put all those things in that trunk?" Kizmic asked.

Magdalene cleared her throat. "I didn't," she sighed. "It's not my trunk."

"But Daddy said it was yours."

"No. That one belonged to my great-grandfather, Walter Edward Boss. Your great-great-grandfather," Magdalene smiled.

"So he put all those newspaper clippings in there?"

"Uh-uh. My grandfather did. Horace Boss. His father gave it to him when he started traveling. He went around the country photographing black people who had been lynched. He believed that if the world saw what was happening to us, then it would stop. He took thousands and made two copies of each picture. He kept one for his records. The other he mailed to the government. But the lynchings kept right on and the government said nothing, did nothing. Hell, white people were taking pictures of themselves standing with the corpses and putting them in photo albums, like they were pictures of them in the park having a picnic. Some lynchings they actually *did* have picnics. Got dressed up, brought their children, blankets, picnic baskets, and they sat on the grass talking, laughing, eating, drinking, having a good old time. They called them 'lynch parties' and they made postcards out of the pictures they took and mailed them to their friends and family."

"Postcards?" Kizmic asked, mortified.

Magdalene nodded grimly.

"And nothin' happened to the people that did it? They didn't go to jail?"

"No."

"Not even the men that killed Emmett Till?"

"No, baby," she said sadly. "That's why my grandfather quit taking the pictures. He said if white people could look at a picture of Emmett Till's body, where the only way his mother could identify her son was by the ring he was wearing that belonged to his father, and still let the men who murdered him go free, then no picture in the world could make the lynchings stop. So, he stopped. My grandmother was happy. She nearly worried herself to death when he was traveling, worried he would come back lynched. It was by the grace of God he didn't."

"Where are the pictures?" Not that Kizmic wanted to see them. She was just curious about where he'd put them.

Her mother shrugged. "Nobody knows. One rumor is he took them out to the woods and burned them."

Magdalene paused and stared off again.

Needing to know the rest of the story, Kizmic asked, "What's the other rumor?"

She looked at Kizmic and said, "Come on."

Magdalene kneeled in front of the trunk as though she were kneeling at the altar. She looked at the headlines, closed her eyes, raised her head to the ceiling, and said, "Lord Lord Lord."

After exhaling a deep breath, Magdalene pulled out the removable tray, sat it on the floor, and situated herself in such away that Kizmic couldn't see around and therefore couldn't see inside the trunk. She paused and smiled reminiscently at a wide brim, black hat with a yellow feather tucked in the bow of the hat band. Magdalene dusted it off and placed it on top of her head. She then began rifling through the trunk, pulling out pictures of various sizes and laying them facedown on the tray as she went.

Those pictures must be really bad if Mama don't want me to see them.

Magdalene sat aside at least fifteen to twenty photographs in that manner until she came upon one in particular. Holding it up, she said with pride, deep affection, and a hint of heartache, "This is my grandfather."

A distinguished-looking black man in his sixties stood in front of a big tree on a bright day. On his head was a wide brim, black hat with a feather tucked in the bow of the hat band. The same hat that was on her mother's head. He had medium dark brown skin and a dimple in the center of his chin. His entire top lip was buried under a bushy, gray moustache that was allowed to grow just past the corners of his smiling mouth, the left side of which held a smoking pipe. He was tall, very tall, dressed in a black, three-piece suit and a light-colored bowtie. Hanging around his neck was a strap attached to a small, rectangular black box that he looked down adoringly at as he held it in his wrinkled hands.

"What's that?" Kizmic asked.

Magdalene smiled. "A camera."

"A camera?" Kizmic repeated, taking the photograph out of Magdalene's hand and studying it.

Ciro-flex was printed on a plate above a lens. Directly below that lens was another that had a numbered silver ring around it. The word *Rapax* was writ-ten between the outer ring and the top of the lens. Two silver knobs were on the right side of the box. It was the most fascinating camera Kizmic had ever seen. It looked more like a secret black box with a combination lock, inside of which you hid your most prized possessions.

Continuing the story about her grandfather, Magdalene said, "The other rumor, which I believe is more likely, is my grandfather donated the pictures of the lynchings to an organization that collects stuff like that to keep a record of our history."

"What happened to the camera?" Kizmic asked, tracing the black box with her finger, wondering how it worked.

"He threw it into the Tallahatchie River the day the white men who killed Emmett Till walked out the courthouse with their wives and children to go off and enjoy the rest of their lives."

Dag! Kizmic hoped that the tale was a false rumor and that the camera was still around there somewhere so she could tinker with it.

"He said every time he looked through the viewfinder, all he saw were dead black people. I'm the only one he told that to, because he wanted me to pick up where he left off."

Kizmic's eyes ballooned. "He wanted you to take pictures of dead peo-ple?!"

"No," Magdalene laughed. "After Emmett Till, he started taking pictures of 'Negroes full of breath, full of life,' he said."

She moved aside and motioned for Kizmic to join her at the trunk. Ex-pecting to see more frightening headlines, Kizmic braced herself then hesi-tantly peeped inside. To her surprise and relief there were no gruesome stories lining the walls of the trunk, only plain brown paper that she could barely see because the trunk itself was filled from the bottom to the top with thou-sands of 3x5, 4x4, 5x5, and 8x10 black-and-white photographs that captured black people in the most spectacular fashion doing everyday, ordinary things: walking, sitting on porches, swimming, farming, driving, standing on corners, walking in the rain, picnicking, buying ice cream, riding horses, bowling, go-ing to the movies, shoveling snow, looking out windows, talking on the phone, snapping string beans, playing baseball, scrubbing marble front steps, shoot-ing pool, rioting, dancing, listening to music, playing instruments, voting, teaching, playing cards, preaching, learning, protesting, praying.

"My grandfather wanted me to keep taking pictures like these for him," Magdalene told her. "But I only wanted to do one thing back then."

"What?" Kizmic asked.

"Ummm," was all her mother said.

Magdalene plunged her hands into the sea of photographs, pulling out handful after handful until she reached the bottom, where she came across a Weston Master II light exposure meter, two steel film developing tanks, a box of General Electric flash bulbs, plastic sleeves of negatives, white boxes of slides, a shoebox full of undeveloped Kodax black-and-white 120 film, and a worn, brown leather case, inside of which was the Ciro-flex Model E twin lens reflex camera her grandfather was holding in the photograph.

"I thought you said he threw it in the river!" Kizmic said, astonished that the camera was right in front of her.

"That was his Rolleiflex," she said. "His first camera. He loved that thing. Cost him a lot of money. It broke his heart to get rid of her. At the time he couldn't afford another Rolleiflex, so he bought this one. It didn't cost as much, but he loved it just the same and used it to take all of these."

The camera looked even more fascinating to Kizmic than it did in the photograph. Eager to hold it, she stuck out her hands, but her mother went and drifted down memory lane somewhere. Kizmic thought she'd only be gone a second or two, but she was actually strolling, taking her own sweet time.

"Mama," Kizmic called, but she was gone. Awwww, com'on, she sighed, irritably.

With nothing else to do except wait impatiently for Magdalene to come back (Any day now, Mama) Kizmic looked through the photographs and found one of twelve black boys ranging in age from around ten to twelve playing marbles in the dirt. Some had on shirts, ties, and slacks like they had just come home from church; others were dressed in t-shirts, jeans, and tennis shoes like they had been playing since they'd gotten up that morning. All the boys' eyes were focused on the marbles. The knuckle of the shooter's forefinger was pressed on the ground and his thumb was sticking out. So, he'd already taken the shot, but Kizmic couldn't tell from the marbles or the boys' smiling, serious, and pins-and-needles faces if he made it or not. But that wasn't the point of the picture. Capturing the moment was her great-grandfather's goal. Telling the story of *that* day that *that* group of boys kneeled and squatted in the dirt to play marbles was what he set out to do when he aimed his camera at them. That was a story worth holding and looking at over and over again. And it occurred to Kizmic that she had no stories of CJ and Sleepy-eyed Ted to hold, because in all the years she'd played with them they had never once taken a picture together.

It would've been nice to have a picture like this of us playin' marbles, she thought, which made her realize that, like CJ and Sleepy-eyed Ted, I ain't got no pictures of me and Man 'n 'Em.

No one would know their story. No one would know how they played skully and baseball and football and basketball. No one would know about their clubhouse and how they rode their bikes and skateboards down Dead Man's Curve. No one would know they even knew one another, let alone know that they were best friends unless …

I take a bunch of pictures of us with that camera! she thought, excitedly.

"Mama," Kizmic called.

And I can use the pictures for my project!

"Mama!" she called again when Magdalene didn't respond.

Visualizing the pictures she would take of her and Man 'n 'Em, Kizmic came to believe that the trunk was *indeed* a treasure chest, full of priceless memories captured by a little black box.

"Mama!" she yelled.

"You say something, baby?" Magdalene asked, finally moseying on back to the present.

Kizmic paused. She couldn't blurt out any old stupid thing. That camera meant a lot to her mother. She wasn't going to hand it over if she thought Kizmic was going to treat it like a toy. Whatever came out of Kizmic's mouth had to assure her mother that she would cherish that camera as much as—no—*more* than her mother did, *more* than even her grandfather did.

Thinking, thinking, thinking, Kizmic cast her eyes down at the photographs of the black housewives, firefighters, secretaries, doctors, husbands, police officers, children, dentists, milkmen, nurses, bus drivers, beauticians, boxers, singers, politicians, lawyers, soldiers, cabdrivers, crossing guards, construction workers. They were a sharp contrast to the grisly pictures captured in the headlines taped above, and that contrast took away the fear that had consumed Kizmic when she first opened the trunk and filled her with a breathtaking desire to capture not just her life with Man 'n 'Em but life period the way her great-grandfather had done.

But she had a hard time trying to express that to her mother, so she ended up saying, "Mama, I promise not to break it. I promise I'll take care of it. I promise I won't play with it. I promise not to let anybody touch it. Just let me have it."

Magdalene listened to Kizmic's plea with intense, scrutinizing ears.

"Please."

Saying nothing, Magdalene sat the Ciro-flex down in the tray beside the photographs she didn't want Kizmic to see.

She ain't gonna let me have it, Kizmic thought, disappointedly.

Magdalene reached into the trunk and fished out a Ricohflex Model VI twin lens reflex.

"He had *two* cameras?!" Kizmic asked.

"Yeah," she smiled. "This one is mine. I took that picture of him with it."

Kizmic frowned at the photograph of her great-grandfather holding his Ciro-flex. "But you said you didn't wanna take pictures."

"I didn't. That's the only picture I took with this camera." Magdalene pointed to the photograph of her grandfather. Beside it she placed a picture that was of her at sixteen, tall, lean, and fit, dressed in a dark colored sweatsuit and white Adidas tennis shoes. Like her grandfather, she too was standing next to a big, leafy tree on a bright sunny day, only she had the reservoir in Druid Hill Park behind her. In her hands Magdalene held the Ricohflex against her chest, looking down at it the way her grandfather looked down at his Ciro-flex in the picture she had taken of him.

"We stood across from each other and snapped these pictures." Touching the hat on her head, she took another nostalgic stroll down memory lane. She didn't stay as long, though. When she returned, Magdalene cradled Kizmic's face in her hands. "You have that hooked look in your eyes that my grandfather hoped to see in mine when he gave me this camera." She picked up the Ciro-flex and held it out to her. "I'm sure he would love for you to have it."

Before leaving the basement, Magdalene gathered up the pictures she'd placed facedown in the tray. As they walked up the steps, Kizmic opened her mouth to ask about them, but thought it best that she stayed out of grown folks' stuff.

The Ciro-flex and Ricohflex sat on the coffee table in the living room next to her great-grandfather's hat. The Ricohflex was smaller, lighter, didn't have as many knobs to fiddle with, its leatherette was peeling, and its geared lenses were stuck. Still, it was an amazing camera. But the Ciro-flex had stolen Kizmic's heart. Its buttons, knobs, dials, latches, levers, and lenses mesmerized her. She pressed a lever on the top, backside of the camera and a hood popped up like the lid of a Jack-in-the-box. Only no colorful clown sprung out. Inside the hood was a viewfinder. Kizmic realized then that her mother and great-grandfather weren't simply looking at the camera in those pictures. They were looking down at the ground glass that displayed the image coming through the upper lens, which her mother said was the "viewing lens." Holding it waist-level, Kizmic turned the focusing knob and watched the lens bed move forward and backward. She peered down into the viewfinder and had to do a double take when she saw things in reverse on the cloudy screen.

"Whoah! Everything's backwards!"

Magdalene smiled at Kizmic's delight and amazement. "Let's get these things cleaned up."

Her mother's mechanical prowess further delighted and amazed Kizmic as she watched her take the cameras apart, tiny screw by tiny screw, clean every compartment, every component, then reassembled them.

"It took me a while to get up the nerve to tell my grandfather that I didn't want to be a photographer," Magdalene explained. "So, I ended up learning a few things."

Over the next couple of days, she taught Kizmic how to use the light meter to set the aperture and shutter speed, open the film compartment, and, using a damaged roll of film, Magdalene showed her how to load and advance the film with the winding knob. Framing was the hardest and coolest part. She had to get used to seeing things that were on her right be on the left in the viewfinder and whether to hold it waist-level or chest high to get the subject in the center of the screen, because, as she learned, while the upper lens showed her the subject, the lower lens, or "taking lens," took the actual picture.

Suffice it to say, taking pictures with her grandfather's camera was an adventure that was ten times more fun than her mother's Kodax Ektra 1 or even her Polaroid Instant camera where the pictures developed right before her eyes.

One evening, as Kizmic was working at mastering the camera, Turk played side A of the 78 that was in the trunk. Her great-grandfather had taken several pictures of that glamorous, jazz singer walking on Pennsylvania Avenue and singing in clubs around Baltimore. Between the eery sound of the piano plinking underground and Billie Holiday's tormented voice turning her gloomy lyrics into photographic images, Kizmic could see the "Strange Fruit" she sang about in the newspaper headlines wallpapering the trunk. All of it made her more determined than ever to continue her great-grandfather's work, not so much for him but for the people who were killed.

Kizmic fell asleep with the camera on her nightstand next to CJ and Sleepy-eyed Ted's baseball and her Teeter Totter watch. In her sleep, she was chased by fifteen thousand raging white people dressed in their Sunday best, carrying ropes, guns, knives, picnic baskets, and cameras. Wearing a long, white dress, Billie Holiday walked down Pennsylvania Avenue holding a magnolia blossom to her nose to block out the stench of black death swinging from the trees and light poles, twisting her red lips as she whistled "Strange Fruit" while Kizmic's great-grandfather Horace photographed the whole deadly scene with his beloved Rolleiflex camera dripping wet from the Tallahatchie River.

MAGDALENE TOOK KIZMIC to a photography shop and bought three rolls of 120 Kodacolor film. Capturing the world inside the viewfinder of her Ciroflex made Kizmic feel as though she were creating pictures instead of merely taking them, because it required her to do more than simply point and shoot. She had to think about lighting, shadows, framing, whether her subject was still or moving. Those were the most difficult shots to get. She often had to use the sports viewfinder, which was a square hole cut into the back of the hood that allowed her to quickly line up the shot. Kizmic used it to take a picture of Christmas and Charlotte as they pushed his cart loaded with metal through the alley and to photograph Kalaya sprinting around the block. She used the viewfinder and magnifier when she took snapshots of the men playing dominos on the supermarket parking lot and when Mr Charlie and Miss Josephine posed in front of the Fish Store for her. She used it as well to get closeups of Plum typing on her Underwood typewriter, candids of Magdalene and Aunt Beana talking in the kitchen, shots of Turk sitting on the back porch eating raw oysters, and of course pictures of Uncle Monty behind the wheel of his big, blue rig.

Mostly, though, Kizmic kept her camera trained on Man 'n 'Em. She photographed Man making a killer shot with his skully top, Fatboy feeding his pigeons, Steebo playing fetch with PJ, Onion teaching Butch tricks, Redtop popping wheelies on his bike, Babyfrog holding a Praying Mantis, Peanut doing a flying drop-kick, and Meatball reading his joke books.

She only had one problem. The camera drew Diamond, Poochie 'n 'Em. Kizmic had to be selective with her shots and creative with her angles or else they would have been in every picture, either hanging around or hanging on Man 'n 'Em, because Man 'n 'Em were now trying to satisfy their budding sexual curiosity by preying on the girlie-girls. But it could hardly be called preying since Diamond, Poochie 'n 'Em were willing participants, because Man 'n 'Em were helping them satisfy *their* budding sexual curiosity. Poochie, however, was only curious about one boy. Onion. And he seemed curious about her. In class last week, Poochie made Kizmic pass him a "Do you like me? Yes or No" note. And although Kizmic tried her best not to, she found herself wondering which box Onion checked.

Kizmic was able to snap one very precious photo. She asked Man 'n 'Em to meet her at the skully board earlier than usual one morning. Diamond, Poochie 'n 'Em weren't outside yet. When they got there, Kizmic positioned Man 'n 'Em around the skully board. She walked to a dark brown Oldsmobile Cutlass Supreme parked on the right side of the street, a little ways up from them. Looking through the viewfinder, she turned the focusing knob until their image was sharp. Carefully, she placed the Ciro-flex on the hood of the Oldsmobile. Kizmic then pulled out a ten-inch shutter release cable and a silver mechanism (about the size and shape of an aspirin tin) called a Haka Autoknips timer that would trip the shutter. She screwed the shutter release cable into the fitting below the taking lens then connected the Autoknips timer to the cable button and set it for five seconds. She cocked the shutter then released the timer. It whirred like a wind-up toy as Kizmic ran to join them.

"Everybody say skully," she said.

Click!

The shutter fired with them shouting it and Redtop standing on his hands, Peanut posed in a karate stance, Meatball's tongue stuck out and eyes crossed, Man's arms raised in a double bicep pose, Babyfrog striking a Heisman trophy pose with his right leg up, right arm out, and left arm back, tucking away an imaginary football, Steebo standing with his arms folded and his squinty eyes squinty, smiling, Fatboy leaning to the side with his arms stretched out as if he were flying like Superman, Onion frozen in the middle of doing the robot, and Kizmic standing next to him, smiling bright as anything and happy as she could be because years and years from now somebody was going to look at that picture and see that they didn't just know one another, see that they didn't just play skully, but *see* that that picture told a story of a time in their lives when they were best friends. And that was a story worth holding and looking at over and over again.

Standing on the corner of Elmer and Belvedere with the bright yellow sun beaming over her shoulders, Kizmic held her head down and eyed the Jamaican Store. The tan brick, box-shaped building was perfectly framed inside the viewfinder of her Ciro-flex. She turned the focusing knob forward then a tad back, sharpening the green, red, and black Ace of Spades sign above the entrance. The glass door was propped open and the people perusing the two small aisles and coming in and out of the store walked on and off the focusing screen like thespians coming on and off stage. To the right of the door, after the Ice Bread Eggs Milk Cigarettes and Coca-Cola signs, Kizmic saw the head and shoulders of the owner, Mr Peter, in the lone square window that was covered by a black metal grate. He was behind the counter ringing up sales. His long, thick dreadlocks were tucked under his red, black, yellow, and green, knitted tam hat.

Liking the look of the shot, Kizmic cocked the shutter, but before she could snap the picture, Bootsy suddenly appeared on her screen. Wearing a red halter top and tight, jean shorts, Bootsy posed in the doorway, holding a cherry blow pop in her hand, shoving out her big breasts.

With a foxiness in her eyes, Bootsy asked, "You gonna take my picture or just stare at me?"

Kizmic swallowed. Everything about Bootsy made her nervous. Every time she saw her, Kizmic thought of that spring February day when Bootsy caught snowflakes with her tongue.

"You mind not blocking the door, hot stuff," said a woman who was trying to go inside.

Bootsy looked down and smiled at the woman with just the left side of her mouth. She was indeed hot stuff. She stepped out of the woman's way, popped her blow pop in her mouth, then sashayed down the street. Kizmic watched Bootsy until she disappeared around the corner. Swinging back around to her original subject, Kizmic bumped into D. Tinkle.

His hands clamped on her arms. "Watch out, now," he said, grinning that crooked Jack-o'-lantern grin of his.

"Oh, I'm sorry, Mr Tinkle," Kizmic said, inspecting her camera to see if the collision caused any damage.

"That's quite all right," he said, pressing down on her with that slimy grin.

Kizmic made sure she didn't make eye contact with him. "If you look into his eyes, you'll get paralyzed, and he'll drag you in his house and do *it* to you," Diamond, Poochie 'n 'Em said. Kizmic focused on the 35mm Nikon EM swinging on a black strap draped around his neck.

"That's a pretty sophisticated camera you have there, Miss Kizmic," D. Tinkle said.

"Uh-huh."

"Mine isn't nearly as intricate as yours." He released her from his clutches, only to hold her again with the hard, black body of his camera. He wrapped his long, skinny, yellow fingers around the zoom lens and moved the long, black cylinder back and forth, back and forth, back and forth, back and forth. "This is how you focus with mine. Do you want to touch it?" D. Tinkle asked in that weird, soft, slow voice he had that sounded like a funeral director's.

Click-clack Click-clack. Kizmic heard Miss Josephine's heels then Miss Josephine herself. "What no good are you up to, Tinkle?" She grabbed Kizmic tightly by her shoulders. So tightly that it hurt.

"Hello, Mrs. Blackstock. How are you?" D. Tinkle said as polite as a boy scout.

"You know me, Tinkle," Miss Josephine said. "I'm lovely, of course."

"But of course," D. Tinkle said.

Miss Josephine fixed her eyes on D. Tinkle's camera, sized it up.

"You're embarrassing me, Mrs. Blackstock," he said.

"You shouldn't be embarrassed," Miss Josephine said with a smile. "You should be ashamed."

"Ashamed of what?" D. Tinkle asked. "Showing Kizmic my lens?"

"Exactly," she said.

"Kizmic and I share the same love for photography. It's perfectly normal for me to show her my lens."

"It's more normal to show a grown woman. So why don't you show it to me?" She reached down and started roughly pumping the shaft of the lens.

"Now, Mrs. Blackstock, you are a married woman." His voice implied that Miss Josephine was the one who should be ashamed of herself. "Your husband might get a little jealous if I show you my lens. And he's a big man. I fear he will break me in two."

Miss Josephine laughed. "Yes, he would, I imagine. And if Kizmic's father catches you showing his little girl your little lens, he *will* break you in two."

"Yes. He's told me as much," D. Tinkle said with a sigh that expressed his boredom with these constant, annoying threats.

"Well, then why don't you take your . . . lens on in the house before somebody gets hurt."

D. Tinkle put his hand over Miss Josephine's. He gently pulled it off his lens then slowly brought it to his mouth. Miss Josephine lifted her head. With a smile that boarded on a sneer, D. Tinkle put her wrist up to his nose and breathed her in.

"Yeah, I know," Miss Josephine said, staring at him with hard eyes. "If I was thirty years younger, right?"

D. Tinkle glared at Miss Josephine as if she were the type of woman that needed to be slapped or maybe even punched to put her in her place. Stomped on to keep her there.

Miss Josephine snatched her hand away then grabbed Kizmic by the arm and escorted her down the street. "You tryin' to get your daddy locked up for murder?"

"No."

"Next time just walk away. You don't need to be lookin' at nothin' he got. You hear me, Kizmic? Nothin'."

"Yes, ma'am. You gonna tell my parents?"

"No. We'll have to bail your father out of jail tonight." She stopped and pointed her finger in Kizmic's face. "But if I catch you near him again, you won't have to worry about your parents. I'll beat you silly myself!"

CHAPTER

21

KIZMIC STOOD IN FRONT OF THE CLASSROOM at a table, on which were her great-grandfather's maps, his father's Bible, and *The Negro-Motorist Green-Book*. To the left of Kizmic, leaning against the blackboard, were two poster boards. The first had the photograph of her great-grandfather taped at the top and several of the pictures he'd taken taped below it. The second was covered in twenty-six pictures Kizmic had taken. There would have been more, but in getting used to the camera, she over exposed and double exposed and under exposed a bunch of shots.

Kizmic had her classmates on the edge of their seats as she described with pride and enthusiasm and some dramatics how her great-grandfather risked his life traveling around the country trying to put an end the lynchings of black people with his camera. She held up *The Negro-Motorist Green-Book* and talked about how it saved his life by directing him to hotels and homes that accepted blacks, restaurants that would serve him, and barbershops where he could get a haircut. She even pointed out the Clark, Majestic, and Reeds hotels, Y.M.C.A. on Druid Hill Avenue, Gorden's restaurant on Druid Hill Avenue, and other places in Baltimore City the book listed that catered to black people. Sadly, the list wasn't all that long. And of course, Kizmic got to show off her prized Ciro-flex camera. "My mother's grandfather passed it down to her and she passed it down to me," she happily told her class.

At the end of her presentation, kids gathered around the poster boards and oohed, aahed, and squealed as they pointed at themselves, asking how she put it together, when she took that shot, offering nickels and candy in exchange for the photos.

"Do you know this Bible is almost ninety years old?" Miss Habeebulah asked, gently skimming through it.

Indeed, Kizmic did know. Magdalene had her and Kalaya all up in their family tree by way of the family register in the middle of the Bible. Their great-great-great-grandparents, Joseph and Florah, were at the top of the tree written in her great-great-grandfather's meticulous print. Joseph was born in 1838 and Florah was born in 1841. Both of them were slaves. Both of them "belonged" to Howard and Meredith Boss. They had five children—Irma, Florence, Walter, Thomas, and Mary. One day in the summer of 1859, while Howard was away on business, Meredith sold Irma and Florence behind her husband's back because he was looking at them.

Kizmic asked, "Lookin' at them how?"

With a raise of his thick eyebrows and a scratch of his head, Turk passed the buck to Magdalene to explain. Magdalene widened her eyes and passed the buck back to Turk.

"He wanted to have sex with them," Kalaya said plainly, not understanding why her parents were having such a hard time spitting it out.

"Kalaya," Magdalene said, not understanding why she had to be so blunt.

Kalaya shrugged. "It's true."

"But you said they were only ten and twelve years old." Kizmic was disgusted.

"They were," Magdalene said.

Before her mother opened their family's Bible, Kizmic had only read about slaves in textbooks. Now she was hearing about four slaves listed on the discolored pages of their family Bible and two were little girls who had some nasty old man trying to do *it* to them.

"There were D. Tinkles back then too," Turk said. "More than anybody will ever tell."

"So his wife was one of the good slave owners, then," Kizmic surmised.

"There were no 'good' slave owners," Turk said matter-of-factly.

"But she sold them to protect them, right?" Kizmic asked.

"No," Magdalene said in the same brutally honest tone she'd answered no when Kizmic asked if the men who lynched all those black people went to jail. "She couldn't have cared less about any slave. She sold Irma and Florence because she was trying to protect her marriage, trying to protect their reputation by making sure her husband didn't have any mulatto slaves running around their plantation."

"Which I bet they already had," Turk said. "She probably just ain't want no more."

Going from branch to branch, limb to limb, twig to twig, Magdalene went on down the line decade after decade, explaining that Joseph and Florah were so heartbroken by the loss of Irma and Florence that they vowed never to have another child for Howard to lust after and Meredith to sell off.

"Then Lincoln gave them freedom," Magdalene said, "but Joseph and Florah didn't believe white people wouldn't take it back. Florah had this saying: 'You can't trust white people. They'll give you water in a broken glass.' They waited seven years before having Walter. Trusting that God wasn't going to let white people round them up again, they had Thomas then Mary." Her finger slid along a tree branch. "She married Richard Purvey and they had a son named Kermit."

"Kermit? Like 'Kermit' the frog?" Kizmic laughed.

"No," Magdalene smiled. "'Kermit' as in 'Kermit.'"

Kizmic and Kalaya snickered.

Turk croaked, "Ribbit."

"See, you're the reason they act like that," Magdalene said, trying not to laugh herself. "Anyway. Walter married Helen Grace and they had three children—Fountain, Elizabeth, and Horace."

"Fountain?" Kalaya laughed. "What's up with these names?"

"We think his name was actually Fontaine, which is French for fountain," Magdalene said. "Somehow it got mispronounced and misspelled and Fountain stuck."

Turk said, "A lot of black people's names got changed back then. Some only had first names and just tacked their owners' last names onto them."

Heading on down the tree, Magdalene said, "My grandfather Horace married a woman named Harriett Matthews and they had my mother, my Aunt Sally, my Uncle George, and Uncle James."

"There's Grandma and Granddad," Kizmic said. "And you, Aunt Ella, Aunt Katherine, Uncle Raymond, Daddy, and . . . and us!"

Kizmic took the Bible from her mother and touched her name, which was written in her great-grandfather Horace's newsprint script. People only wrote important things in the Bible, things they never wanted to forget. For Kizmic, seeing her name listed in something as important as the Bible meant that her being born was important and was never to be forgotten.

"Look, Kalaya." Kizmic handed her the Bible.

Kalaya smiled at her name at first. Then something about it caught her attention and she pulled the Bible closer to her face. She held up her right hand and began touching the tips of each finger with her thumb, counting. She lifted her head and stared off into the hallway. Whatever Kalaya was trying to make sense of about her name wasn't adding up. Her lips moved slightly as she mouthed something to herself. Scrunching up her face, Kalaya redid the math in her head and on her fingers again and again, and then her eyes widened and brightened as something pulled the string and turned on a lightbulb in her mind. She turned to Magdalene, squinted her eyes, and asked, "You were in high school when you got pregnant with me?"

Kizmic was stunned. She never gave any thought about how old their mother was when she had them. She always assumed she was old enough. Grown. Not a teenager. But that was grown folks' business. Her mother's private business. Kalaya had no right asking questions like that. It made Kizmic uncomfortable, as uncomfortable as the time she stood outside their parents' bedroom door after Kalaya dared her to knock on it because she *knew* they were in there doing *it*. That's how that question felt. Like Kalaya had stood in the doorway of their bedroom and asked their mother when she did *it* with their father.

Magdalene didn't respond right away. Not because she was stunned by the question like Kizmic. From her calm expression, she fully expected Kalaya to ask it sooner or later. She just seemed to have had a different sooner or later in mind. That appeared to be the thing that threw her *and* Turk off and delayed her answer, which Magdalene didn't give until Kalaya said, "Mama . . ."

Magdalene looked Kalaya straight in the eye. "No. I'd already graduated when I got pregnant with you."

She took the Bible out of Kalaya's hands and closed it.

"This is some serious history," Miss Habeebulah said, handing the Bible back.

You tellin' me, Kizmic thought.

"Your great-grandfather was an incredible man. My grandfather would say he is a 'credit to our race.'"

Kizmic bopped all the way back to her seat. She didn't know what being a "credit to our race" meant, but if Miss Habeebulah said that about her great-grandfather, it had to be a good thing.

Miss Habeebulah called Man to present next, but another teacher knocked on the door and asked for her assistance. No sooner had she stepped out of the room, Tori Pompey barked, "Hey Kizmic!"

Kizmic's first instinct was to run into the hallway and find Miss Habeebulah or some teacher to protect her.

"I know you hear me callin' you."

Yeah, I hear you, Kizmic thought with a grim, heavy sigh. She turned around to see Tori descending upon her with those vicious cat eyes. Her nerves and imagination assaulted her. She saw Tori laying her out right there in the middle of the classroom.

For what, though? Kizmic wondered. I ain't do nothin' to her. I was so busy with my presentation that I ain't even know she was in school today 'til she called my name.

Everything Kizmic said was stupid. Nobody had to *do* anything to Tori for her to want to kick your butt.

"Where's my picture?!" Tori asked. A rock-hard frown sat on her face.

"Huh?" They were pretty much the same height, but Kizmic had the weird sensation that she was looking up at Tori.

"Why you ain't take no picture of me?" Tori asked.

"Yeah!" Lynette Fleebish said from her seat. "Why you ain't take no picture of her?"

Awww shut up! Kizmic cut her eyes at Lynette Fleebish. You always got somethin' to say. To Tori, she thought, 'Cause I ain't wanna take no picture of you, but said, "'Cause I didn't see you."

"You see me now," Tori said.

"Yeah!" Lynette Fleebish cosigned. "You see her now."

"Take my picture!" she ordered.

"Yeah!" Lynette Fleebish shouted. "Take her picture!"

No! Kizmic cried to herself. I only got two frames left and I'm savin' them to shoot the sunset and the moon tonight.

The last few days the sun had been so pretty and golden as it sat down on the rooftops for the evening, and the moon was shiny and bright white, with a glow that Kizmic just had to have on film.

I ain't missin' that takin' no picture of you, Kizmic said to Tori in her mind.

Tori took a stomp back, planted her fists on her small hips, and shoved what she called a smile on her face. It was more of a grimace, which Kizmic was certain would crack her lens.

"She ain't standin' there for her health," Lynette Fleebish said.

"Yeah," Tori barked. "Take the picture!"

I don't wanna, Kizmic whined inside. But then she thought about her own health and what would happen to it if she didn't take Tori's picture. She pressed the release lever and snapped opened the hood. Okay. I can take a picture of the sunset and get the moon the next time Mama buys me some more film. Hopefully it will still be bright.

Kizmic sighed irritably, wishing she had the guts to tell Tori to take a flying leap. Not having the guts, she reached for the light meter. Without it, she wouldn't know what to set the aperture and shutter speed on to expose the frame to the correct amount of light so the picture . . .

. . . would come out right, Kizmic smiled to herself, leaving the light meter on her desk.

"Hurry up!" Tori barked.

"Okay." Kizmic flipped up the magnifier and looked down at the ground glass. Tori sat backward and blurred in the box. She turned the focusing knob until Tori's smileless smile slowly sharpened. "Say cheese."

"Cheese!"

Kizmic cocked the shutter, fired, and cracked up. I hope it comes out dark as I don't know what, she thought, turning the winding knob to the twelfth and last frame.

"Come on, Lynette, take a picture with me," Tori said.

What! Kizmic screamed in her head. No! Uh-uh! It's bad enough I wasted a frame takin' a picture of you. I ain't wastin' another one takin' no picture of Lynette Fleebish. I don't even like her. I don't like neither one of you!

Lynette Fleebish jumped up from her chair and stood next to Tori. She threw this goofy, uneven smile on her face that appeared as if someone had pasted it on. But at least it was a smile.

I'on't care. I ain't takin' no picture of them. I'ma just pretend to push the button. Shoot, they won't know. And when they ask me about it, I'ma say the picture didn't come out right like the other one. Wastin' my film. They ain't pay for it.

"What's that?" Poochie asked, pointing at the back of Lynette Fleebish's dress.

"What's what?" Lynette Fleebish spun around, trying to see what it was.

She looked to Kizmic like a dog chasing its tail.

Tori grabbed Lynette Fleebish by her shoulders and stopped her from spinning. Her back was now facing the camera. Kizmic adjusted the focus and brought sharply into view a heavy, dark cherry-red colored stain on the back of Lynette Fleebish's orange dress. Immediately, she recognized the stain. It was the same color and shape as the one Kalaya left on their marble step back on Proctor Street. Kizmic jerked her head up.

Bug-eyed, Kizmic said in a whisper, "She got her *friend!*" Then she accidentally pressed the shutter button. "Gotdaggit!"

The other girls recognized the stain as well, although their source was not Kalaya. It was a book by Judy Blume called *Are You There, God? It's Me, Margaret.* Diamond, Poochie 'n 'Em had been reading it and passing it around. When the book came to Kizmic, she wrinkled her nose, held it between two fingers, and passed it on as if it contained some incurable disease. She didn't need to read a fictional account of some crazy girl who couldn't wait until her breasts grew and her "friend" came. She had Kalaya. If Kizmic could have written herself in as a character, she would have told Margaret, "Havin' breasts and gettin' your 'friend' ain't nothin' it's cracked up to be." Lynette Fleebish standing in the middle of the class with her "friend" all over the back of her dress for the whole world to see was proof of that.

"She got her *friend!*" the girls said one after the other, turning the recognition into an echo that rippled around the classroom. "She got her *friend!* She got her *friend!* She got her *friend!*"

Redtop looked at her chair, and in the same innocent tone Kizmic's father asked, "Who cut themselves?" when he saw the blood on the stoop, Redtop yelled, "That's blood! Ewww! She bleedin'!"

Diamond stared open-mouthed at Lynette Fleebish, like at first she hadn't quite bought this period thing, but now . . . Wow!

"Stop lookin' at her all stupid!" Tori yelled at Diamond. Then she threatened to punch in the face the next boy that let ewww out of his mouth.

At the sound of the commotion, Miss Habeebulah rushed back in the room. "What's going on?" she asked.

"She bleedin'!" Redtop shouted, pointing at Lynette Fleebish, who stood in the middle of the floor. Embarrassment had erupted all over her face.

"Oh, for heaven's sake," Miss Habeebulah said. She took her sweater off the back of her chair, wrapped it around Lynette Fleebish's waist, then escorted her to the nurse's office.

For the first time in their lives the girlie-girls ran over to Tori instead of away from her. They wanted answers to the million and one questions they had about Lynette Fleebish and her period. Kizmic sat like a statue at her desk with a horrified look on her face that revealed just how close to death she had come.

"Is this her first time?" Diamond asked.

Relishing in the attention, Tori doled out the information in bits and pieces to ensure their interest in her didn't fade too quickly. "No."

"How long she been gettin' it?" Poochie asked.

"Since she was ten."

"Ten!" the girls shouted.

That's how old my mother was, Kizmic thought.

"How do you know?" Diamond asked.

Kizmic was surprised at how boldly Diamond, Poochie 'n 'Em questioned Tori. Apparently, fear had taken a back seat to their curiosity.

"'Cause she helped me when I got mine," Tori admitted.

Kizmic, Diamond, Poochie 'n 'Em sucked in a collective shocked gulp of air. Diamond, Poochie 'n 'Em moved in closer around Tori and she told them that she came on her period during a family cookout. Miss Vivian sent her to the store to get her "personals" by herself. Tori was scared to death. She didn't know what kind to get, what size, and she was embarrassed, especially since the cashier was a cute guy. She walked up and down the aisle five times. On the fifth time, Lynette Fleebish was grabbing a box of Kotex off the shelf. Tori asked her for help. Lynette Fleebish walked to the register and boldly purchased both packages. She went home with Tori and showed her what to do. They'd been friends ever since.

During their bathroom break, girls rushed into the stalls and groaned with disappointment when they didn't see their "friend" in their underwear.

Before Kizmic pulled her underwear down, she silently prayed, God, please don't let my "friend" be here.

God answered her prayer.

"IT'S NICE TO SEE you have interest in something besides skully," Miss Habeebulah said.

She and Kizmic were in the hall putting her project on display in the glass case next to the front office. When the bell rang at the end of the day, Miss Habeebulah asked Kizmic to stay after. "I want the entire school to see what a talented photographer you are," she said.

Kizmic loved the praise she received from Miss Habeebulah and the other teachers who commented on the beauty of her work, but to tell the truth, those pictures were the last thing on her mind. Lynette Fleebish had come on her period in class, in front of everybody!

And Miss Habeebulah's puttin' up pictures like it ain't no big deal, Kizmic thought.

"This one is my favorite," she said, pointing at the picture of Diamond, Poochie 'n 'Em double dutching. "I could do that when I was a girl." She smiled and Kizmic could see in her eyes that she was looking back at her twelve-year-old-self jumping rope. "You know what the best thing is about pictures like these?"

"No, ma'am," Kizmic said.

"You can freeze-frame your childhood. It goes by so quickly." She sighed. "Nice watch, by the way."

KIZMIC WALKED ACROSS the school playground carrying the bag that had all the things she used for her presentation and her Ciro-flex hanging around her neck. Not that she could take a picture of anything that caught her eye since she didn't have anymore film. As she went down the stone stairway, she saw Onion running up Beaufort.

"Hey, Kizmic," he said.

"Hey," she said, confused as to why he'd come back to school. "I thought you went home with Poochie."

"I walked home with Man 'n 'Em," Onion corrected.

"Who walked home with Poochie."

Onion laughed. "*Diamond, Poochie 'n 'Em.*"

Kizmic sucked her teeth. "Anyway. What you doin' back up here?"

"I came to see why Miss Habeebulah made you stay after school. Was it 'cause of Lynette Fleebish?"

"No," she frowned.

What happened to Lynette Fleebish was humiliating enough without having to talk about it with a boy. And just think, she had a picture of it.

Ewwww! I'm rippin' that thing up as soon as I get it back.

"Well, what'd Miss Habeebulah want?"

"To put my pictures in the display case in the front hall."

"I guess so. They're really nice," Onion smiled. "That one you took of Peanut doin' that flyin' drop-kick got him thinkin' he really Bruce Lee now."

They laughed together.

"You know what, though?" Onion asked. "I like the picture you took of us at the skully board the most."

"Me too," she said.

Kizmic loved that photo so much that she spent the extra money to have two copies printed—one she glued to the poster board, the other was in a pretty picture frame her mother had given her, sitting on her nightstand with the baseball from CJ and Sleepy-eyed Ted and her Teeter Totter watch.

"I've never seen you smile that hard." Staring softly and directly in her face with his green eyes, Onion said, "You look pretty."

Kizmic stutter stepped but managed, thank God, to cover it up by pretending to lose her grip on the bag. Tripping, even if she didn't fall, would have added embarrassment on top of the nervousness that was hopping around in her stomach like jumping beans because Onion said she looked pretty.

That was the first time Onion, or any boy for that matter, had used the word "pretty" in association with her. It was an odd thing for him to say. Almost as odd as him coming back to the school to walk her home. Kizmic didn't know what to do with any of it. So, she concentrated on securing the bag in her hand and acted like she didn't hear him say a word.

Seeing Kizmic struggle with the bag prompted Onion to reach for it and say something else odd. "You want me to carry that for you?"

"No," Kizmic replied.

"You got it?"

"Yeah...Yeah, I got it."

Kizmic clutched the bag tightly and kept her eyes straight ahead. Needing something to do with his hands, Onion put them in the front pocket of his jeans. They crossed Hayward. When they reached the alley before the castle house, Onion asked, "So when's our next photo shoot?"

"I don't know. I don't have anymore film."

"Can't you ask your mama and daddy to buy you some more?"

"Yeah," Kizmic said. "But not 'til next week."

Her parents never discussed their financial situation in front of their children, but sometimes Kizmic could hear them late at night talking about how the mortgage wasn't late until this date so they could hold off on paying it and pay the gas and electric bill which was already a day late. But then again, "We'd better pay the mortgage, because the lights will be on inside and we'll be standing on the sidewalk," her father would joke. Either way, they definitely had to pay the car insurance by this date, and the phone bill was due the next week, and her mother's car payment was due by the first but wasn't late until the tenth so they could put the check in the mail on the ninth, and don't for-get that Kalaya and Kizmic both needed new clothes.

"I know how you can get some money," Onion said, breaking into her thoughts. "I got a cousin who delivers the newspaper around his way and they pay him."

Kizmic's interest stood up. "Really? How much?"

He shrugged his shoulders. "Enough to buy his own clothes and stuff and sometimes he helps his mother buy food. He has to get up early, though. Around five, and he's done before he has to go to school."

"For real?" Kizmic's eyes widened.

Onion nodded. "It's easy money. You should do it."

CHAPTER

<h1 style="text-align:center">22</h1>

KALAYA SAT AT THE DINING ROOM TABLE picking at her fried potatoes and onions, cutting her eyes at Magdalene and returning them to her plate when Magdalene glanced back at her. Kizmic could tell she was thinking. No, plotting was more like it. That girl was always up to something. Although Kizmic didn't have much room to talk in that area today, because she was doing some plotting of her own.

Ever since Onion told her about his cousin making money delivering newspapers, Kizmic had been waiting for the right time to ask her parents about her getting a paper route. She couldn't think of a single reason they could come up with to object to her little venture. Film was expensive; to have it developed was expensive. If she had a paper route, she could make some cash to buy film, have it developed, and they wouldn't have to come out of their pockets. It was a win-win for everyone. But in the three days since learning about this incredible money-saving opportunity she had for her parents, Kizmic hadn't had a chance to bring it up because of Kalaya.

Things had been going smoothly between her mother and sister ever since Kalaya started running track. They were talking and laughing and joking and loving each other like they used to back on Proctor Street. Magdalene didn't miss a meet. She was Kalaya's unofficial second coach, as a matter of fact, and they got tighter after Kalaya lost to her rival.

Kalaya ran the 100- and 300-Meter Hurdles and was the anchor leg in the Mile Relay. A girl named Gladys Stackhouse who went to Walbrook competed in the same events. Gladys was dark-skinned and compact with protruding, focused brown eyes, quick, muscular arms, and fast, powerful legs. She ran every race as if she would cease to be if she didn't cross the finish line before everyone else. The first two times they raced, Kalaya proved to Gladys that her life would go on if she came in second. But the third time they met on the track, Gladys blew by Kalaya like she was standing still. The fourth time they raced, Gladys did blow by Kalaya, but only because Kalaya, who had the lead, crashed into the next-to-last hurdle and ended up limping across the finish line in last place.

"You're running not to lose to her," Magdalene told Kalaya during their workout session in the back yard. "Run your race."

The entire family was in the stands at Mervo High School for Kalaya's fifth meet. In the 100 Meter Hurdles, Gladys made it look easy. She sprinted out the gate, cleared the first hurdle at top speed, then one-two-three-four-jump-one-two-three-four-jump-one-two-three-four-jump. Her form, stride, and rhythm were flawless. Kalaya was running stiff, no rhythm, hardly any form, hitting several of the hurdles with her knee and trail leg. When Gladys crossed the finish line, she strutted like a peacock in Kalaya's face. In the 300 Meter Hurdles, Kalaya got out the blocks ahead, but Gladys came back strong. Everyone got nervous because it looked like she was going to walk Kalaya down. Luckily, Kalaya kicked it in at the end and leaned for the win.

"She still not running her race," Magdalene observed.

"She will," Turk said.

At five o'clock, teams started warming up for the Mile Relay. Northwestern was in lane six and Walbrook was in lane five. The official signaled for the runners to take their mark. The gun sounded and off the girls went, flying around the curve. Northwestern's first and second leg had a smooth hand-off, and they were running just a stride behind Walbrook. The crowd was screaming.

Some dude said, "Gladys is gonna smoke that girl."

"You wanna put some money on that?" Turk asked.

The guy held up ten bucks.

"You may as well put that in his pocket right now," Uncle Monty said.

Northwestern was looking strong, but something went wrong on the hand-off. The third leg left too soon and had to go back for the baton. With Walbrook in the lead, Gladys was out of the gate a full three seconds before Kalaya. No matter, because Kalaya didn't get caught up in the mistake her teammates made. She got the baton and started rolling. Gladys was stroking and she could feel Kalaya coming to get her. The crowd roared.

"Run your race, baby girl," Magdalene said quietly then yelled, "Run your race!"

"Look at her move," Aunt Beana said.

The two girls were approaching the finish line. It was going to be tight. Kalaya dug in. So did Gladys. All you saw were elbows and knees. Then came their heads as they both leaned.

The officials had a difficult time determining who crossed the finish line first. People in the stadium were biting their nails and arguing about who was the winner, as if they had the last word. Kalaya and Gladys paced around, catching their breath and trying not to appear worried, each girl putting up a front that said, *The race is in the bag*.

Three minutes later, the official announced the winner to be, "Lane . . . Six! Northwestern!"

A thunderous roar resounded throughout the stadium. Some people were cheering, some were cussing.

"See, that's what I'm talkin' 'bout!" Turk said proudly, pocketing his ten dollars.

Kalaya ran up in the stands and hugged her mother. It looked like nothing would be able to tear them apart again. Then Kalaya asked Magdalene that disrespectful question after seeing her name on the family register inside their great-great-grandfather's Bible, and she'd been showing her tail ever since. Not overtly or outrageously. She was doing subtle things, like standing in a doorway of the kitchen, eyeing Magdalene as she cooked or washed dishes, sitting on Turk and Magdalene's bed watching Magdalene wrap her hair in one of her beautiful headscarves, listening intensely and intently to every word that came out of Magdalene's mouth as she talked about her day, the soaps, a phone call she'd had with her mother, a letter she'd received from one of her sisters, a picture her brother had mailed to her, a random conversation she'd struck up with a cashier at the store.

All of this made Magdalene irritable. Sharply she would ask Kalaya, "What are you looking at?" And Kalaya would say, "Nothing," like it was really nothing and walk away. "Why are you looking down my throat?" she'd ask. And Kalaya would shrug and walk away.

"She's getting on my nerves, Turk," Magdalene complained one night. "She keeps looking at me like I'm a liar or some kind of hypocrite."

"Don't worry," Turk said. "It'll pass."

"You know what she's thinking, don't you? That this gives her license to do as she pleases."

"Well, I ain't got no problem lettin' her know that that ain't what that means."

Kalaya moved her broccoli around on her plate as though they were chess pieces, plotting, plotting, plotting.

Kizmic looked at the Ciro-flex she'd set next to her plate. She had missed some once-in-a-lifetime shots because she didn't have any film. All she needed was for her parents to say yes to the paper route and she wouldn't miss another shot.

I'd better ask now, she thought, before Kalaya says or does something to tick Mama off.

"I'm going to the movies with Clive tonight," Kalaya announced.

Too late. Awww man!

Kalaya said it the way she had been saying a lot of things lately, like Magdalene and Turk had no say-so in what she wanted to do. And what she wanted to do other than run track was hangout with her new boyfriend, Clive Greenleaf. Yep, the same Clive who a couple of years ago questioned whether Kalaya was old enough to eat cornbread without gettin' choked. Whatever the heck that meant. One of Hannah's boys, Clive.

He started sniffing around Kalaya the first time he saw her out on one of her runs. It was about ten o'clock on a Saturday morning. Kizmic was riding her bike alongside Kalaya as she ran on the sidewalk down Belvedere. In the middle of the block, Kalaya saw Clive dribbling a basketball up the street. Immediately, she slowed her stride and straightened her back so that her chest would stick out. But she no longer had to do that to make her breasts appear bigger, because they were bigger, so her chest stuck out like that naturally. What wasn't natural was the way Kalaya began swinging her arms across her chest and turning her upper body left and right instead of keeping it forward and her arms driving straight. She looked as though she was about to stumble and fall, like those women running from a serial killer in a horror movie.

When Clive noticed Kalaya, he accidentally bounced the ball off his big foot. It rolled and hit the wall of the Paint Store. Quickly, Clive ran and picked it up, then, sucking on a Sour Apple lollipop, he watched with his eyes popping out of his head as Kalaya came his way.

Kalaya had a body on her to begin with. Track made it worse, for it chiseled muscles in her arms and legs, toned her already flat stomach, sculpted the curves in her hips, and defined the roundness of her behind. And the outfits she got to wear. The hottest tank tops, the coolest shorts, the most fashionable sweatsuits, and the latest tennis shoes and track spikes that accentuated and displayed her feminine, athletic build. For Kalaya, the best part was Turk and Magdalene couldn't say anything about how clingy, short, and revealing her clothes were because she was in "uniform."

Kalaya was looking pretty cute in her uniform that morning. She'd spent a half hour combing her hair into a ponytail and wrapping a yellow headband around it. Then spent twenty minutes putting on a yellow and white Lightning Bolt sweatsuit, white sweat socks, and white Nike tennis shoes.

Kalaya ran past Clive. Although, by the time she reached him, she wasn't running; she was jogging.

He let her get to the corner then, taking the lollipop out of his mouth, yelled out, "Hey girl."

Kizmic didn't waste time wishing Kalaya would keep jogging. She stopped pedaling before Kalaya turned around.

"What you want, Clive?" Kalaya asked, jogging—*bouncing*—in place.

He lowered his big, brown eyes to her bouncing breasts then said, "You goin' the wrong way."

"Why you say that?"

"'Cause . . . I'm back here," he grinned.

That was his irresistible pickup line.

Ooooohhh. He's such a playboy. Kizmic rolled her eyes to the sky.

Kalaya sucked her teeth and smiled.

"Com'ere, girl. Let me talk to you for a minute," he said, tossing the basketball from one hand to the other.

Kalaya stopped bouncing. "You called me. So you com'ere."

Clive caught the basketball in his left hand then held it against his side with his long, now very muscular arm. He was wearing a red, white, and blue Bullets basketball jersey with the number 41 and Unseld on it and a pair of blue Bike Coach shorts. He had to be five inches taller than he was two years ago. His shoulders and chest were broader. His legs were still skinny but strong. He had fuzz above his upper lip and thin, patchy hair under his chin. Kalaya thought he was finer than fine, and he knew it.

With a slick, deliberate bop, Clive stepped to Kalaya. She liked that she stood only as tall as his chest and that she had to tilt her head way back to look up at him.

Still holding the basketball against his side, Clive took the Sour Apple lollipop out of his mouth. "Where you runnin' to?"

"I'm not running; I'm training."

"For what?"

"Track team."

"Oh, yeah? What school you go to?"

"Northwestern."

He nodded. "I go to Mervo."

"I know."

"How you know?"

"I went to the basketball games last year and saw you playing."

"Then you know I got skills." Clive put the lollipop in the corner of his mouth and started dribbling the ball.

Showoff, Kizmic thought, riding her bike around in a circle in front of the Paint Store, wanting Kalaya to come on.

"You alright."

"'Alright'?" Clive scoffed. "Girl, what you talkin' 'bout?"

"We won," Kalaya smirked.

"That don't mean I'm a scrub."

"I didn't say you were a scrub. I said you were alright."

"'Alright' is the same as bein' a scrub in my book."

"Means you're nice in my book."

Kizmic groaned loudly. That means you're both stupid in my book.

Kizmic couldn't take it. She rode down Litchfield, leaving the two of them there talking nonsense. A few days later, Clive and Kalaya were boyfriend and girlfriend. Why Kalaya would even want another boyfriend after what happened with Angelo made absolutely no doggone sense to Kizmic.

Mama and Daddy almost killed her. Angelo's runnin' around with some other girl.

Kizmic looked down at the piece of cornbread on her plate. Maybe when she was old enough to understand exactly what it meant to be old enough to eat cornbread without gettin' choked, all the crazy stuff Kalaya was doing would make sense. Until then . . . Kizmic picked up her cornbread and took a bite.

"What movie, Kalaya?" Magdalene asked.

"The Crest. Because it's Friday the 13th they're having an all-night horror show. They're showing *Halloween*, *Invasion of the Body Snatchers*, *The Hills Have Eyes*, *I Spit On You're Grave*, and *Last House on the Left*."

Turk shook his head as he chewed a piece of fried fish.

"No," Magdalene said. "You are not staying out all night."

"I won't be out; I'll be inside the theater," Kalaya argued.

"No."

"Why?" Kalaya asked.

"Because I said so, that's why," Magdalene said.

"I'll be back before—"

"You won't be back before anything because you're not going."

And just like that the bond mother and daughter had reestablished when Kalaya joined the track team disintegrated.

Kalaya went back to shoving her food around her plate. Plotting, plotting, plotting.

Now that Kalaya had pissed their mother off, Kizmic was hesitant to ask about the paper route, but she was tired of waiting for her parents to give her money for film, and besides, asking for a paper route wasn't the same as asking to stay out all night with a boy. "Hey Mama—"

"Well, I'm spending the night with Plum," Kalaya interrupted.

Awww, come on, Kalaya!

"No, you're not spending the night with Plum," Magdalene said.

Kalaya sucked her teeth.

"Suck your teeth at me one more time, hear, and you'll lose them."

"This ain't right," Kalaya whined.

Magdalene set her fork down on her plate and propped her elbows on the table. "You wanna know what ain't right, Kalaya?" Before Kalaya could respond, she answered, "That you walk around here thinking you're the only one with a damn brain in this house. That you think you can ask to go to the movies with Clive, and when we say no, come right behind it and ask—no—*tell* us that you're spending the night at Plum's. And your father and I aren't supposed to be smart enough to put two and two together. We're not supposed to be smart enough to know that Beana is working a double tonight and won't be home to keep you from sitting up all night in a theater with Clive. If that's where you're going at all." Magdalene picked up her fork. "That's what ain't right."

Kalaya rolled her eyes and speared a piece of fish with her fork.

"Roll those eyes at me one more time and you'll lose those, too."

"I can't do anything around here," Kalaya complained.

"Yes, you can. You can do the dinner dishes," Magdalene said. "And if you got anything else smart to say, the bathroom could use some cleaning, too."

That raging quiet engulfed their house again, leaving nothing except the sounds of forks scraping on their plates as they ate and their glasses of iced tea being sat down on the table after they drank. Relief from the silence came when someone knocked on the front door. Kalaya jumped up to get it and to get away from Magdalene, who told Kalaya to sit down and finish her dinner.

"I'm not hungry," Kalaya pouted.

"Sure you are," Magdalene said, getting the door to get away from Kalaya.

Kalaya flounced back down in her chair. "You make me sick," she said under her breath. Only it wasn't quite under enough.

"Kalaya!" Turk shouted.

Magdalene spun around. "What did you say?"

"Nothing," Kalaya lied.

"Oh, now I'm deaf?"

Kalaya put two forkfuls of potatoes and onions in her mouth.

You should have done that before, Kizmic thought.

"I make you sick, huh? Well, being that you're sick, how about you keep your ass in this house the whole weekend. See how sick I make you then."

Magdalene stomped to the door.

Turk glared at Kalaya. "When you gonna learn to keep your mouth shut?"

After Mama kills her, Kizmic concluded.

Kizmic lay in bed staring at the ceiling. Thanks to Kalaya she couldn't ask her parents about the paper route.

I'll ask them tomorrow, when Kalaya's not around. Hopefully they'll say yes.

She rolled over and fell asleep. Not long after the creak of her bedroom door awakened her. Through groggy eyes Kizmic watched someone tiptoe over to the back porch door. She assumed it was her mother, because she often checked to make sure the door was locked. She closed her eyes and was headed back to sleep when she heard the door being unlocked.

"Mama?" Kizmic called.

"Shhhh!" Kalaya said.

"Kalaya?" Kizmic sat up in bed and rubbed the sleep out of her eyes. "What are you doin' in my room?"

"Nothing. Go back to sleep."

Kizmic switched on the lamp and looked at her watch. Snoopy's paws said it was eleven-twenty. Kalaya opened the door and sneaked out onto the porch. Kizmic hopped out of bed and followed.

A "Psssst!" came from below.

Kalaya leaned over the railing and looked down. If the tight jeans and even tighter pink blouse Kalaya was wearing didn't tell Kizmic that her sister wasn't dressed for bed but a night on the town, or rather a night at the movies, Clive Greenleaf standing in the alley under the street lamp was a dead giveaway. The question was, how was Kalaya going to get to the movies from the upstairs back porch?

The long, whistling, moonlit drop between the porch and the ground was a deterrent, but only for those who were not as slick as Kalaya, who had spent hours on the sly studying that back porch with a mischievous mind and had been rewarded with the brilliant discovery of the ladder cleverly hidden in the beams and railings. A tricky ladder indeed, but a ladder nonetheless. And you didn't have to be particularly athletic or coordinated to make it down without breaking your neck. All it really took was thought, patience, guts, and determination. Kalaya had all the thought, patience, guts, and determination in the world when it came to doing things she had no business doing. And with a handful or two of defiance dumped in that mix, Kalaya swung her long legs over the railing as if she were doing nothing more than stepping over a hurdle on the track.

Kizmic grabbed her sister by the arm. "What you doin'!"

"Let me go, Kizmic. You're gonna make me fall."

"Come on, Kalaya," Clive yelled.

"I'm coming," Kalaya half whispered and half yelled back.

Kizmic had that I-oughta-tell-Mama look on her face, but Kalaya knew she wouldn't dime her out. They had grown beyond telling on each other. They now kept an eye on each other to make sure neither went too far. Tonight Kalaya was going too far as far as Kizmic was concerned. Worry broke out over Kizmic's face like a rash. What if their parents woke up and discovered she was gone? What if she got hurt?

"Look, Kizmic. Mama doesn't have to work tomorrow, so I'll be back way before she and Daddy get up. The Crest ain't that far. It'll be okay. *I'll* be okay. Okay?"

Against everything inside her that was screaming don't let her go, Kizmic sighed heavily and let go of Kalaya's arm.

"That's my little sister," Kalaya smiled. "Oh, yeah. You'll probably be sleep when I get back, so leave the door open."

"Leave the door open? Are you crazy? What about D. Tinkle?"

"He ain't stupid enough to come in here."

"But Mama might and I'll get in trouble."

"All right then close it but don't lock it."

Facing Kizmic, Kalaya squatted then gripped the beam with her left hand and held fast to one of the thick, wooden spokes of the railing with her right hand. Slowly, she lowered herself down until her feet landed on top of the porch railing below, the last rung on that hidden ladder. Once on the ground, Kalaya ran up to Clive. They kissed then sprinted off into the night and straight into trouble, Kizmic thought. She turned to go back inside and saw D. Tinkle standing on his porch.

Kizmic stayed awake all night long. She worried about Kalaya, worried about D. Tinkle, worried about her mother or father waking up to find Kalaya had snuck out of the house and that she knew and didn't say anything.

Finally, around five o'clock, the latch on the back gate clinked. Kizmic ran down the hall and listened at her parents' door. The familiar squeak of the bed sent Kizmic rushing back to her room.

Kalaya climbed up the hidden ladder like it was nothing. "Where's Mama?" she asked.

"In bed. They're . . . you know."

Kalaya headed inside, filling Kizmic's room with the heavy odor of cigarettes.

"You been smokin'?" Kizmic asked, a little louder than she meant.

"Shhh!" Kalaya said, frowning.

"What you doin' smokin'?"

"I only had one," Kalaya admitted.

Kizmic pinched her nose. "You smell like you had a whole pack."

"That's because Clive and 'Em were smoking through the whole thing. Gave me a headache."

Kalaya opened the door. Coast being clear, she made a beeline to her room. When she reached it, Kalaya looked back at her parents' still closed door with a triumphant smile.

CHAPTER

23

OKAY. THIS WAS THE DEAL. No matter what anybody said, no matter how old she got, no matter how much cornbread, Wonder Bread, Schmidt Blue Ribbon Bread, or any other kind of bread she ate without choking, Kizmic was never, ever, *EVER* going to understand the crap Kalaya pulled last night.

Sneakin' out the house and goin' to the all-night movie after Mama and Daddy said she couldn't go. Something bad coulda happened to her out there. D. Tinkle could've climbed up the railin' and come in here and tried to do *it* to me. Mama and Daddy could've come in here and I coulda got in trouble. All 'cause she out smokin' cigarettes, runnin' behind some daggone *Clive Greenleaf.*

These were Kizmic's thoughts as she rode her bike up Reisterstown Road. And the more she thought about how much trouble *both* of them could have gotten in, the madder she got, the harder she pedaled.

She had spent the last hour at Lucille Park, watching a baseball game. She went there so she wouldn't run into Man 'n 'Em, who had snuck off with Diamond, Poochie 'n' 'Em. Not that she cared. They could stay gone with them the rest of their natural born lives.

Doggonit. They get on my nerves. One minute we're goin' to play skully, the next minute Diamond, Poochie 'n 'Em come grinnin' up in their face, and they start talkin' 'bout "We be right back."

Not that she cared that Man 'n 'Em were with Diamond, Poochie 'n 'Em, but the more she thought about the twenty minutes she spent shooting around the board waiting for them to come "right back," the madder she got, the harder she pedaled.

Kizmic turned right on Nelson Avenue. Man 'n 'Em hardly ever hung out around there so she wasn't in danger of them seeing her and having Diamond, Poochie 'n 'Em swear out that she was following them.

She followin' us. Why she followin' us? Kizmic imagined Poochie saying.

I don't need to follow them. Shoot! Onion was the one who came back up to the school lookin' for me. And he came lookin' for me this mornin' too.

At nine-thirty, Kizmic was on the upstairs back porch looking at the wisps of white clouds in the azure sky on the ground lens of the Ciro-flex, wishing she had film to capture its beauty. She panned her camera to the left and D. Tinkle slithered onto the lens, smudging it. He stood on his upstairs back porch watching her through his zoom lens. Kizmic looked up from the viewfinder and D. Tinkle moved his camera away from his face. With his ghoulish jack-o-lantern smile, he said, *I know a secret.*

D. Tinkle knowing what they did the night before made Kizmic uneasy for a bit. Then she decided, So what he knows. He can't tell nobody. And even if he did, we can say he's lyin'. It's not like he took a picture. Or did he? she feared, looking at his camera.

She didn't see anything in his hands last night, but it was dark. Before she noticed him spying on them, he could have taken twenty shots with that zoom lens.

"Hey, Kizmic!" Kalaya yelled. "Onion's at the door."

Kizmic closed the lid on the viewfinder and went inside. Out front, Onion was sitting on her porch petting Phyllis. Kizmic lifted her foot to shoo Phyllis away by stomping as she did all the time, but she caught herself. For the last three years, she had managed to keep her fear of cats a secret from Man 'n 'Em. When she first met them, Kizmic hid it because they would have exploited her fear in the same way CJ and Sleepy-eyed Ted had. Now it seemed stupid to be afraid of a cat and she didn't want Onion to think she was stupid.

Kizmic eased her foot down. Hearing a noise behind him, Onion got up and stared at her. No, he didn't stare; he gazed, his green eyes tender and reflective.

What's he lookin' at me like that for? I wish he'd quit it. He's making me feel weird.

Purring loudly, Phyllis walked in and out between Onion's legs, rubbing her bluish-white body against his jeans and eyeballing Kizmic, like she was going to tell her secret any second.

"Hi," Onion finally said.

Hi. Not hey, like normal, Kizmic noted. But Hi, as in *Hi.* She answered back, "Uh . . . hey . . . um . . . Onion. What's up?"

"I came to see if you asked your parents about the route," he said, reaching down to rub Phyllis.

"Uh-uh. I didn't get a chance. I'ma ask them tonight."

"Oh, okay. Well, we're getting ready to play skully. You comin'?"

After last night, a nice fun game of skully would do her good. "Yeah."

"Alright. Com'on," Onion said, going down the steps.

Phyllis stretched out in the middle of the porch, staring at Kizmic with her sapphire blue eyes, seemingly saying, *Yeah, com'on.*

Kizmic stayed behind the screen door. Go away, you stupid cat.

"Kizmic, you comin'?" Onion asked when he looked back and saw her still inside the house.

"Yeah. Hold up."

Kizmic ran out the back door and up the alley. When she reached the corner, Onion looked at Kizmic, back at the porch, then again at Kizmic. He smiled as if she had performed a magic trick that had teleported her.

There's more than one way to get around a cat, Kizmic smiled to herself.

They went to the Fish Store to get Man 'n 'Em and some candy.

"So, you scared of cats?" Onion asked as they strolled up the sidewalk.

"No," she said, dropping her eyes. "I just don't like 'em."

"Ain't nothin' to be ashamed of. Lots of people are scared of cats." Stopping at the bottom step of the Fish Store, Onion smiled, "I won't tell nobody."

Miss Josephine was behind the counter handing Steebo a small brown bag of candy. "What you know good, Kizmic?" she asked.

"Nothin', Miss Josephine." She looked in the display case. "Can I have six Squirrel Nuts, six Mary Janes, and a pack of grape Now Laters?"

"You sure can, darlin'." While filling Kizmic's order, she asked, "What's goin' on, Onion?"

Onion didn't answer. He was standing back and off to the side of Kizmic. His mouth was open and he was gazing at her again.

"Check it out," Redtop said and plucked his fingers in front of Onion's face.

He didn't even blink.

Redtop plucked his fingers again. "Earth to Onion."

His green eyes stayed dreamily on Kizmic. Man 'n 'Em snickered.

"Onion!" Redtop plucked his fingers three times.

He snapped out of his trance. "Huh!"

Man 'n 'Em roared.

"What?" Onion asked, furrowing his forehead, looking confusingly around the store for the joke he missed.

"*You* that's what," Man chuckled.

They all laughed Onion into the corner by the cigarette machine.

Miss Josephine dropped the Squirrel Nuts into a bag. "I think Onion might be a little sweet on you."

"No he ain't," Kizmic said emphatically.

"Hmmmm," Miss Josephine smiled, reaching for the Mary Janes.

Kizmic looked over her shoulder at Onion. Why'd she say that? He don't like me like that.

"Yeah, you do," Babyfrog said to Onion.

He likes Poochie, Kizmic thought.

"What was you doin' at her house this mornin' then?" Steebo asked.

I know for a fact that she likes him.

"Tell the truth," Man said.

She passed him that note in class last week. *Do you like me? Yes or No.*

"Alright then. What was you lookin' at her like that for?" asked Peanut.

He musta checked "yes" 'cause she was in almost every picture I took of him, messin' up my shot with her funny-looking self. I swear, he can't go nowhere without her looking for him. I'm surprised he made it to my house without her.

Kizmic stared hard at Onion, who looked past the boys' taunts and smiled at her. She gave him a half smile back.

"Ahhh-Ha!" Meatball bellowed.

"Hey Miss Josephine." Diamond, Poochie, 'n 'Em pranced into the store with their sweet smells, nicely combed ponytails, braids, puffballs, and straightened hair, their long eyelashes batting, their full, rosebud and narrow lips puckered, and their small breasts and little curves filling their pretty dresses, skirts, and shorts.

"How you doin', girls?" Miss Josephine asked.

"We good," they said.

Why they all gotta speak at the same time? Kizmic shook her head.

"Hey Onion," Poochie squealed and skipped over to him.

Actin' like she didn't know he was in here.

Poochie put her cheek to Onion's and whispered something in his ear. Something sweet?

I'on't care, Kizmic thought, digging in her pocket for a quarter.

Onion whispered something back in Poochie's ear.

Kizmic narrowed her eyes. He better not be tellin' her that I'm scared of cats.

Whatever he said made Poochie cackle and take him by the hand. The two of them then walked out the door together.

Kizmic handed Miss Josephine the quarter, took her bag of candy, and said, "Told you."

And she hadn't seen Onion since.

Again, not that she cared, but she knew he was with Poochie, and the more she thought about it, the madder she got, the harder she pedaled.

Poochie, Poochie with the big fat—Ha Ha Ha! Yeah, I heard 'em laughin' in the clubhouse, teasin' Onion about Poochie bein' his girlfriend.

And for the last time, not that she cared, *but* the more Kizmic thought about it, the madder she got, the harder she pedaled and pedaled up Garrison Avenue, pedaled and pedaled down Litchfield, pedaled and pedaled up the alley, pedaled and pedaled until she hit the breaks on the sidewalk in front of her house.

Sweating and breathing heavily, Kizmic leaned on the handlebars, heart almost pounding out of her chest.

"I was about to call you. Come on in here and get your hair done for church," Magdalene said.

She and Turk were sitting on the porch, each with a can of Pabst Blue Ribbon Beer in their hands. It was seven-forty-five. The sun had gone down, but there was still a good hour of daylight lingering, and it was a pleasant sixty-three degrees. Any other time, Kizmic would have pitched her weekly fit about having to go in the house so early on a Saturday night, but, looking up the street at the deserted skully board, she decided that there was nothing and nobody to pitch a fit for.

Kizmic wheeled her bike toward the basement front door.

Noting her uncharacteristic response, Turk asked, "What's wrong with you?"

"Nothin'," Kizmic sighed.

Lowering the kickstand, Kizmic parked her bike by her great-grandfather's trunk.

I should ask them now, she thought.

Her mother and father were feeling pretty mellow. On a high from her secret rendezvous, Kalaya was in her room quietly and obediently serving out her weekend punishment. If ever there was a time to broach the subject of the paper route it was now.

"All the boys in this neighborhood and she has to like one of Hannah's boys," Kizmic heard her mother say as she stood at the screen door.

"I don't care whose boy he is, I bet' not catch him up in this house," Turk said then took a long swallow of beer.

"Hannah can come at me with some old mess if she wants to. She don't know, I'm just as crazy about our girls as she is about her boys." Magdalene sipped from her can. "She's gonna fool around and get more than her feelings hurt."

All right, so her parents weren't all that chilled. But there was only so much chilling they were going to do with Kalaya as their daughter.

Turk and Magdalene sat back in their chairs, taking swigs of beer, and listening to Kizmic's vacuum cleaner salesman type pitch. Her anxious enthusiasm had her talking faster than normal and she couldn't answer many of the questions Magdalene threw out, but she had the basics down. "I can deliver the paper right around here and they'll pay me."

Rubbing his clean-shaven chin and looking off into the distance, Turk rolled her spiel around in his mind. After a minute, he said, "Sounds like an okay deal."

Alright. One down, one to—

"Not with D. Tinkle on the prowl, it doesn't," Magdalene said.

Magdalene's words were a sobering slap across Turk's face. He turned his can of beer up to his mouth and gulped until he had swallowed every drop. He burped, said, "Sorry, baby girl," then went into the house, visibly upset with himself for forgetting that that slimy weasel lived not just in their neighborhood, not just across the alley from his family, but in the world, period.

Kizmic went to work on her mother. If she cracked her, the paper route was in the bag.

"Come on, Mama," Kizmic begged. "I'll be careful. I know how to watch out for D. Tinkle. And anyway, he's scared of Daddy. He ain't gonna bother me."

Magdalene shook her head. For the first time Kizmic could sympathize with Kalaya. Here she was with something she really and truly wanted to do and her mother was standing in the way. Now Kizmic wasn't about to go around her mother by climbing down the back porch, but someway, somehow, she was going to have her paper route.

"But I need the money to buy film," Kizmic argued.

"We'll buy you film. Just not every week," Magdalene said.

"But I need it every week," Kizmic insisted.

"You *want* it every week. You don't *need* it."

"But—"

"I said no, Kizmic!" she shouted, the way she often did when Kalaya refused to let a thing go.

Kizmic groaned in frustrated despair.

"That man is dangerous," Magdalene said, speaking in a much calmer tone. "All he's doing is waiting for somebody not to be paying attention. And yeah, make no mistake about it, your father and I will kill him if he touches you, but that's not going to take away the hurt. This paper route is just the thing D. Tinkle is looking for. You'll be out early in the morning by yourself and—"

"No she won't."

Kizmic jerked around and saw Onion standing on the top step.

Having a partner to help her with the route wasn't something Kizmic considered. And while Onion brought the whole paper route thing to her attention, she never imagined he did so with the intent of tagging along. But the way he ran everything down to Turk and Magdalene, that was his plan from jump.

Why didn't he tell me? Kizmic wondered. I could have told Mama and Daddy that he'd be with me from the get-go and we wouldn't have gone through all this aggravation. Unless, she paused, looking up the street at the skully board. He didn't tell me 'cause he wasn't really thinkin' 'bout helpin' me. He's only doin' this 'cause he feels guilty for ditchin' me to be with Poochie.

In which case, Kizmic's first impulse was to say bitterly, Bump him! I don't want him to help me. Go on back with Poochie somewhere.

But the truth was, she may not have wanted his help, but she sure needed it. Onion was the sole reason Magdalene caved in. But even though she agreed to let Kizmic do it, she called his mother and tried to plant worries in her head about the route interfering with choir rehearsal, cutting into his sleep time, and exposing him to all sorts of danger so she wouldn't let Onion do it. Luckily, Magdalene's fear tactics didn't work. They did, however, force Kizmic to understand that the bottom line of this whole thing was, no Onion, no route. And Kizmic was determined to have her route. Which meant she had to let that Poochie thing go.

MAGDALENE CALLED *The Baltimore Afro-American*, *The Baltimore Sun*, and *The News American* papers. The routes for *The Afro* and *The Sun* in their area were covered. The one for the *News American* was not. Early Wednesday evening, a tall, slender black man named Mr. Bollinger was sitting at their dining room table discussing route P-15.

Clothes, fingers, and breath smelling of the Pall Mall cigarettes he smoked, Mr. Bollinger explained, "Forty-five customers need the morning paper and fifty-seven need the morning and evening. It's a decent size route for somebody just starting out. Not too big, not too small. Only about eleven, maybe twelve blocks total." Spreading out a map of the area on the table, he said, "Belvedere starting at Cuthbert, going down to Elmer, Garrison starting at Linden Heights then down to Litchfield, and Beaufort going up to Arlington. It should take about a half hour, forty-five minutes to complete in the morning. Fifteen minutes more in the afternoon. You'll make about three dollars and some change a day, not including tips."

"Tips?" Kizmic asked.

"Yeah. Customers generally tip. If the service is good, that is," he said. "You know, if you throw their paper on the porch instead of in the bushes, if you don't dent up their storm door throwing the paper against it, if it's dry when it's raining or snowing, if they get it whether it's raining or snowing." He laughed.

Oh, they gonna get good service. Kizmic started doing the math in her head. A roll of film cost almost four dollars. To get it developed costs about three dollars. He said I'ma be makin' three dollars a day. Three dollars times seven is . . . *Twenty-one dollars*! *Plus tips*! Man, I'ma be buyin' film and gettin' it developed left and right!

"All I need now is for your parents to sign this consent form," Mr. Bollinger said, sliding a piece of paper in front of Turk.

"Soon as I sign this, you gonna haveta start payin' rent," Turk joked.

"Wait a minute, Turk," Magdalene said.

Awww no!

All along her mother had been squawking what-ifs and what-abouts and suppose-thises, and suppose-thats, trying to find any small thing that would go with her reservations, but she found nothing until Mr. Bollinger handed her the customer list to review. On page two, fourth address down. 3515 W. Belvedere Avenue. Yep. D. Tinkle's house.

Gee whiz!

He couldn't have a lifetime subscription to *The Baltimore Sun*, could he? No. He had one for the morning *and* evening editions of *The News American*, which meant Kizmic would be stopping at his house twice a day, seven days a week!

With that D. Tinkle was going to single-handedly put an end to Kizmic's career as a papergirl before it got started. But Kizmic, having already dreamed of the rolls of film she would buy and the pictures she would take, was not about to let him keep her from doing the only thing that had made her happy since her body turned on her.

Kizmic looked at her mother, who had this I-got-ya-now smirk in her eyes. What Magdalene didn't see was that Kizmic had a little something in her eyes as well. Tears. Yep. Big, fat, crocodile, sweet, brokenhearted tears that only a sure 'nough girlie-girl and Daddy's girl could cry. Kizmic didn't know she had it in her to stoop so low, but, hey, desperate times called for underhanded measures.

Turk grabbed a napkin from the holder in the center of the table. "Calm down, baby girl," he said, handing it to her. He then took Magdalene into the kitchen.

Mr. Bollinger gave Kizmic a look that said, *You just puttin' on.*

Kizmic blew her nose in response.

When her parents returned, Turk said, "You walk mighty wide of that dude, you hear me?"

Voice hitching, Kizmic whimpered, "O-O-O-kay."

Magdalene was too through with Turk for his gullibility and with Kizmic for her theatrics. She was done trying to talk everyone out of letting Kizmic have this route. She just had one last thing to say on the matter. "I don't care how much money he owes," Magdalene said, "don't you set FOOT in his house!"

"In fact, don't even go on his porch," Turk said. "Stand on the sidewalk and throw his paper up there. If it lands in the bushes—"

"Leave it," Magdalene said.

"And if I ever catch you with so much as a foot—"

"Or half a toe," Magdalene cut in.

"On the bottom step of that man's stoop, you're gonna wish I hadn't!" Turk threatened. "Do you understand me!" the two of them asked in unison, even though it was nowhere near a question.

"Here you go, young lady." Mr. Bollinger handed Kizmic a large, white, canvas bag with *The News American* written on it in big blue letters and a small notebook which listed the names and addresses of her customers, as well as columns that showed who paid and when.

"Welcome aboard," Mr. Bollinger said. He stood and shook Turk and Magdalene's hands. "One piece of advice. Walk that route so you'll know it a week from now."

Six o'clock Tuesday morning, Kizmic was awakened by the booming roll of thunder. She jumped out of bed and yanked open the door to the back porch. The whole sky was one gigantic dark gray cloud. Rain, cascading down in sheets, splattered all over her feet. It was raining so heavily and fast that it sounded like a river was flowing down the alley.

"Dang!" Kizmic said.

Today was the first day of her route and it was pouring.

"Oh, well." She shrugged her shoulders, closed the door, and climbed back in bed.

Not a second later, Magdalene stormed into her room, like she was standing outside Kizmic's door waiting for her head to hit the pillow again.

"Oh, no," she said, snatching the covers off Kizmic. "Your customers are waiting for their paper." *See, I tried to talk you out of this, but noooo. You turned on the waterworks*, she was actually saying.

She can't be serious. Don't nobody expect me to come out in all this mess. Yeah, Mr. Bollinger said somethin' about customers gettin' their paper even when it's rainin', but come on. I can wait until it slacks up, right?

Kizmic clomped downstairs in her rain boots at six-forty. Turk brought in a bundle of newspapers that had been tossed on their front porch sometime that morning. The headline read "**MARGARET THATCHER DREAMS OF BEING FIRST WOMAN PRIME MINISTER**."

They had to be rolled, rubber-banded, then delivered to . . . how many people? Kizmic looked out the door. The rain was coming down harder than it was before.

Turk cut the thin, white plastic strip that was wrapped around the papers with a pair of scissors. "I would help you, baby girl, but I gotta go to work." He handed her his green rain slicker.

"It's too big." Kizmic wanted to cry so bad the back of her throat hurt.

"I know," Turk said. "You put your sack over your shoulder, right? Then put on my slicker. It'll keep you and the papers dry."

Turk had Kizmic do a dress rehearsal. Hanging well past her knees, the slicker looked like a big, green, plastic dress.

He sat his wide brim, yellow rain hat on her head. "There ya go."

Kizmic couldn't see herself, but she knew she looked like an idiot.

Turk kissed her cheek to cover up his amusement. "You gonna be alright," he said. He kissed Magdalene, looked back at Kizmic, and smiled before walking out the door.

Kizmic stared at the stack of newspapers, convinced that she was not going to be all right.

"I gotta go to school after I get done," she realized out loud.

"That's right," Magdalene said in that annoying maybe-next-time-you'll-listen-to-me tone.

"I ain't even eat breakfast yet."

"You better go eat a bowl of cereal real quick," Magdalene said. "I don't want to hear that you were late for school because you were hungry."

Onion opened the screen door. "Wow! That's a lot of papers!"

He had on a long, bright yellow rain poncho with a hood and black rubber boots that came all the way up to his knees.

"Don't laugh," he frowned. "My mother said I couldn't come out 'less I put it on."

"You look cute," Magdalene said. She gave Kizmic a big hug. "You two be careful and have fun. And remember what your father and I said about D. Tinkle. Not half a toe."

Aunt Beana came into the house. She whistled "Wow!" at the sight of the papers, looked back outside at the rain and whistled again, then gave Kizmic a sympathetic hug.

"I give it a week," Magdalene laughed to Aunt Beana as they rushed down the steps to the car.

Kizmic took offense to her mother's comment, but she was giving it less than a week before she called it quits herself.

Shoot! I'm givin' it right here and now. This is crazy. And it's quarter to seven. "How we gonna rubber band all these newspapers in fifteen minutes?"

"Easy," Onion said. He got down on his knees, grabbed a paper, rolled it up, wrapped a rubber band around it, and tossed it in the sack. "Ain't nothin' to it but to do it."

"But I don't wanna do it," Kizmic said, staring out at the rain.

"Are you for real? We play football in rain harder than this. Com'on. I'll race you."

Onion divided the newspapers into two even piles and dropped the rubber bands in a heap between them. He then placed the bag to their right within their reach. Kizmic kneeled in front of her stack.

With playfulness in his eyes, Onion said, "One . . . Two . . . Three . . . GO!"

They each snatched a newspaper and started rolling. There was definitely an art to rolling newspapers up neatly. Kizmic rolled, unrolled, and rerolled six papers before she got it right. By then, Onion had twelve perfectly rolled and rubber-banded papers in the bag.

Kizmic looked at him through squinted, suspicious eyes. "You've done this before."

Unable to deny it, Onion grinned. "Only a few times with my cousin."

"That's cheatin'."

Fessing up to that as well, he said, "Yeah, you right. Let me make it up to you, though. Check it out. There's a rhythm to it. Paper, roll, rubber band, toss. Paper, roll, rubber band, toss. See?"

Hands covered in black ink, Kizmic grabbed a newspaper. "Paper . . . roll . . . rubber band . . . toss."

Onion's green eyes were big and bright. "You got it."

Kizmic smiled back, feeling proud of herself.

By Snoopy's paws they'd finished at five minutes after seven. School started at eight-fifteen. In order to get there on time, they had to be done with the route no later than seven-fifty. Kizmic still hadn't eaten breakfast. Onion had eaten before he came. Another trick he learned helping his cousin.

They didn't ride their bikes.

"I'm tellin' you, with all this rain, it'll be faster if we walk," Onion said.

The bag stuffed with newspapers was heavy. Onion offered to carry it, but Kizmic wanted to bear the load herself. They decided to start up on Garrison, worked their way down to Belvedere, and deliver the papers to the four customers on Beaufort on their way to school. Kizmic didn't have to pull out her customer book because, having taken Mr. Bollinger's advice, she and Onion had walked the route five times, setting to memory the houses on her list. This allowed Onion, who very much wanted to take some of the weight off Kizmic, to carry several papers under his poncho and work one side of the block while she worked the other.

Somewhere along the second block, she and Onion turned the route into a competition, in which they competed to see who could deliver papers the fastest. Kizmic found that there was an art to that too, and mastering it was based on four things: house, distance, aim, and arm.

Garrison was made up of long, tree-lined blocks of two-story rowhouses, some of which had fairly large porches. Kizmic had no trouble throwing the paper from the sidewalk onto the porches without hitting the door or windows. The problem came with the houses that were like the ones on Proctor Street, in that they didn't have porches, just steps, made of red brick instead of marble leading up to their doors. These entryways were tucked between theirs and the neighbors' sunrooms, which jutted out from the red brick facades. To keep the paper from hitting the door, clipping the side of the sunroom and landing in the grass or on the sidewalk, or bouncing off the top step and landing on the sidewalk or in the grass meant standing in the right spot in front of the house, keeping her eye sharply on the target, and pitching, tossing, flinging, slinging, throwing, or chucking the paper with the right amount of force, steadiness, and fluidity. Onion of course had it down. Kizmic was almost a pro at it by the time they got to the corner of Garrison and Cordelia.

Rain and all, Kizmic had an absolute blast. She couldn't believe she had thought of quitting or that she was actually going to get paid for essentially hanging out with Onion, boning up on her pitching and frisbee throwing techniques. That part of it became real when several of her customers came out to retrieve their papers and pay their fifteen cents. Some even gave her a nickel tip for keeping the paper dry. Unfortunately, this slowed Kizmic down, because she had to stop to record their payments in her book, but before leaving Litchfield, she had nearly half the money to buy a roll of film.

This is the greatest job in the world! she grinned.

It was seven-forty when she and Onion reached Belvedere. The rain had slacked up, but it was still coming down pretty good. They were drenched. The rowhouses on that block got them out of the rain, though, for they were able to go house-to-house by going over the banisters that separated the porches. Until they reached D. Tinkle's house. From Mr. and Mrs. Douglas' porch, Kizmic tossed D. Tinkle's paper onto his black welcome mat.

Not half a toe, Kizmic smiled.

CHAPTER

24

THE DAYS AFTER THAT FIRST RAINY MORNING were full of sunny, blue skies. Kizmic was up, dressed, and eating breakfast before her mother could come in her room and question if she had had enough of the route. Onion was there every morning with a canvas bag to carry his half of the load, arguing that having to come back and forth to get papers from Kizmic was keeping him from really kicking her butt.

They rode their bikes, which was another art to delivering newspapers that Kizmic quickly mastered. It was all in how fast she pedaled, what side of the street she was on, and the flick of her wrist. Being right-handed made throwing the papers on the stoops and porches awkward when she was on the right side of the street. It required her to throw overhand or in a backhand motion as if she were throwing a frisbee or making a backhand shot with a tennis racket. Either way, Kizmic hardly ever missed.

Being on their bikes sped up the completion of the route considerably. Her customers were the only thing that slowed her down. Some told her to hold up so they could pay, which Kizmic didn't mind in the least. Some met her on the sidewalk to give her candy, cookies, or Pop-tarts. She certainly didn't complain about that. Some called Kizmic over to tell her how much more reliable and pleasant she was than their old paperboy and how much they appreciated not having to fish their papers out of the bushes or puddles on their walkways, or being startled by the newspaper striking their doors and windows. Of course, Kizmic didn't complain about that. Some held her up by chit-chatting, although that was mainly the widows and widowers. They didn't keep her long, just long enough for Kizmic to suspect that those lonely men and women didn't really read the paper. They just enjoyed having "company" stop by twice a day. Kizmic didn't mind that either.

In just two weeks, Kizmic met every customer on her route except for D. Tinkle and whoever lived in the castle house on Beaufort. Kizmic completely understood what her father meant when he told her to walk mighty wide of D. Tinkle, but did that stop Turk from going to D. Tinkle's house and again threatening to kill him dead if he ever put his hands on his daughter? Of course not. So even with having to go to D. Tinkle's house, Kizmic didn't have to walk mighty wide of him because he walked mighty wide of her. So much so that he placed his weekly payment in a yellow envelope and taped it to the banister between his porch and Mr. and Mrs. Douglas'. He included a generous tip only once, because Turk returned it, telling Kizmic, "I don't want you thinkin' you owe him somethin'." After that, D. Tinkle's payment wasn't a penny over what was due.

The people in the castle house seemed to be walking mighty wide of Kizmic as well. She had never once laid eyes on anybody that lived there, but her payment, which always included a ten-cent tip, was in a white envelope with "Papergirl" written on it and taped to the lavender front door every Sunday morning. Which let Kizmic know that someone in that house had seen her.

Sitting on her bike in front of the castle house, Kizmic wondered who lived there and why they never came out, not even to sit on the red and white metal glider bench. The windows in the tower were open, but from them Kizmic couldn't hear any sounds of life going on inside. Kizmic got the sense that the house was holding its breath, waiting for her to leave.

Onion rode up to her after delivering his last paper. "You see anybody?"

Kizmic shook her head and tossed the evening paper on the porch. She purposely threw it hard so that it would hit the lavender door. Eagerly, she and Onion waited for someone to come investigate the noise. No one did.

"You know why, don't you?" Onion asked.

"No. Why?"

"'Cause, girl, an evil witch has a black Repunzel locked up in there."

Kizmic chuckled, "Boy, you so stupid."

"You don't believe me?" he asked.

"Uh-uh," Kizmic said, shaking her head.

"I'll prove it to you," Onion said. He slung his empty bag over the handlebars of his bike, walked into the front yard and over to the grey stone wall at the foot of the tower. He cleared his throat, cupped his hands around his mouth, and shouted, "Hey Repunzel! It's me, Prince Onion."

His voice bounced up and down the quiet street like the red rubber ball they played with in gym.

"Long time no see, girl," Onion yelled. "Why don't you let down your long cornrows so I can climb up there and save ya, sweet thang?"

Cringing in embarrassment for him and laughing at him, Kizmic glanced around to see if anybody was watching the show. Fortunately for him, she was his only audience.

"Repunzel! I know you hear me callin' you." He held up his arms to surrender his heart to the brown-skinned maiden. "I luv you, girl!" When she didn't show, Onion said, "Alright then. Be that way."

"You lucky I ain't got no more film," she said.

Onion got back on his bike. "I wish you did. It would have been a nice shot."

"You don't get embarrassed about nothin', do you?" Kizmic asked and started pedaling.

"Naw, I get embarrassed about a lot of things," Onion said, riding beside her. "I just don't let it stop me from doin' what I wanna do most of the time."

"What'd you wanna do at the castle house?"

"Make you smile like you did in that picture we took at the skully board."

Again, Onion's comment embarrassed Kizmic, making her wobble some on her bike as she shied away from it and his warm, closed-mouth smile. She put both hands on the handlebars to regain her balance (because she most definitely was not going to fall off her bike in front of him) and looked at her front tire as they rode down the street.

"You wanna see what embarrasses me more than anything?" Onion asked.

Facing him again, Kizmic said, "Yeah."

"Alright, but you gotta pinky swear not to tell Man 'n 'Em."

Pinky swear? Kizmic thought. This must be serious.

Coasting down Beaufort, Kizmic and Onion hooked their little fingers together.

THEY THREW THEIR BIKES DOWN on the walkway in front of Onion's house. His parents had gone to the market. The only one home was his older sister, Tracy. She was in the living room, laid out on the couch, eating potato chips, drinking soda, talking on the phone, and watching *Gilligan's Island*.

"Com'on," Onion said, grabbing Kizmic's hand and heading up the stairs.

"Hold on, Cedric." Tracy took the phone away from her ear. "Where you think you going?"

"To show Kizmic somethin' real quick," Onion told her and kept walking.

"Yeah, well, it'd better be real quick," she yelled behind him. "Mama and Daddy'll be back here soon."

"Alright," he yelled back.

Kizmic often went into Sleepy-eyed Ted's room with CJ to admire his marble collection. Since they moved, being in the clubhouse was the closest she had gotten to being in a boy's room, until she walked into Onion's bedroom, which he shared with his fifteen-year-old brother, Francis. So technically she was in *two* boys room. Her mother and father would whup her behind if they knew where she was. But it wasn't like he was Angelo or Clive. He was Onion. That's what she would tell her parents if they ever found out, which she was going to make doggone sure they didn't.

Onion's side of the room was filled with movie memorabilia. He had autograph books with signatures from Pam Grier, Diahann Carroll, Ruby Dee, Ja'net DuBois, Jim Kelly, Lawrence Hilton-Jacobs, Larry Fishburne, Richard Roundtree.

"You really met all of them?" Kizmic asked enviously.

"Yep," Onion beamed.

His walls were wallpapered with autographed photos of movies stars and movie posters—*Cooley High, Corn Bread, Earl and Me, Cleopatra Jones, Sparkle, Black Belt Jones, Blacula, Super Fly, Shaft, Claudine, Coffy*. There were stacks of *Ebony, Right On*, and *Jet* magazines, *Muriel Magnum* cigar boxes full of movie ticket stubs, and four wooden cassette tape holders. One held tapes with music on them. The others held tapes of shows and movies he recorded off the television—*Charlie's Angels, Diff'rent Strokes, Good Times, Happy Days, Laverne and Shirley, The Jeffersons, Welcome Back, Kotter, Quincy, Wonder Woman, Eight Is Enough, Fantasy Island, What's Happening, Little House on the Prairie, Threes Company, The After School Special, The ABC Sunday Night Movie, The CBS Tuesday Night Movie, the CBS Saturday Night Movie*. Most important in the collection, as far as Kizmic was concerned, were *kolchak: the night stalker* and *Ghost Host Theatre*.

She put the tape of *kolchak* in Onion's General Electric tape recorder, pressed play, and smiled when she heard Kolchak whistling the theme song. She had not seen all the episodes because she couldn't always sneak downstairs at eleven-thirty to watch it and because some genius took it off the air.

"Why'd you record these?" Kizmic asked.

"So I can listen to 'em and practice the lines," Onion said.

"For what?"

He gave Kizmic a scrutinizing look, wondering if he could really trust her to keep his secret. "I'ma be a movie star," he said, pushing aside his embarrassment.

"A movie star?" Kizmic asked. "Since when did you want to be a movie star?"

"Since I was in kindergarten," Onion said. "I was a red traffic light in the school play. I had one line. 'Red says stop!' I rehearsed that line every day for two weeks. And when I stood on stage and said it, everybody clapped. That's when I caught the actin' bug."

"How come you don't act in any of the plays at school?"

"'Cause our church has a lot of plays and I'm usually in those."

"Why don't you want Man 'n 'Em to know?"

"It's just something I want to keep to myself until I get better at it."

Green eyes sparkling with fame, Onion stared at a poster of Diana Ross and Billie D. Williams from *Mahogany*. "One day you gonna go to the movies or turn on the TV and you gonna see me."

The audacious way Onion spoke this, as if it were already in the works, made Kizmic believe that one day she would. And why not? He was certainly as cute as Todd Bridges. Might even be cuter, she thought to her surprise.

ON COLLECTION DAY, Kizmic usually cleared twenty-two dollars and some change. She should have had close to twenty-seven, but some of her cheapskate customers acted like they didn't hear her ringing their bells, knocking on their doors, or tapping on their windows. With the money she earned, Kizmic did exactly what she said she would do. She bought rolls and rolls of film and took loads and loads of pictures and got them developed left and right. Her room was turning into a regular photo gallery with all the boxes of negatives, photos, and picture albums. Some pictures she liked so much she taped them to the wall above her bed.

Every collection day, Kizmic also tried to give Onion a cut.

"You earned it," she told him. "You come out here every day with me, rain or shine."

Onion refused to take the money. "I come out here every day 'cause I like . . ."

He paused. In his eyes, Kizmic could see him mulling something over in his mind.

"You like what?" she asked, nudging him.

"I like hangin' with you," he said. "And I wanna help you become a famous photographer."

"What you talkin' 'bout, Onion?" Kizmic asked in her best Gary Coleman voice.

"Not bad," he said, impressed. "But for real. You keep takin' those pictures like you do and you gonna end up goin' all around the world and your photos are gonna be on the front page of newspapers and magazines," he said in that same determined, fortune teller voice he used to announce to her that he would become an actor. "And when I become a famous movie star," he said, brushing lent off his imaginary tuxedo, "I'ma get you to take my picture."

One evening after dinner, Onion rode up to Kizmic's house on his bike, told her to grab her camera and stuff, and hop on.

"Where we goin'?" she asked.

"You'll see," he said.

Kizmic held onto the sissybar with one hand and held onto her camera with the other, even though she had the neck strap attached to it. She could never be too careful with her Ciro-flex. She kept her feet raised as Onion pedaled up the street. Sitting behind him, Kizmic realized that she hadn't ridden on the back of his bike before. Didn't have a reason to. She didn't have a reason to then, really. She could have gotten her bike and followed him. But Onion was so excited and insistent that she didn't think about it until he was forced to stop at the corner to wait for a break in traffic and spotted Man 'n 'Em coming down the street, pointing in their direction and elbowing one another.

Peanut blew a bubble with his gum. After it popped, he sucked it back into his mouth and smirked, "What's up, y'all?"

"Nothin'," Onion and Kizmic said in unison.

"You got a flat tire, Kizmic?" Man asked.

Kizmic said, "Yes," and Onion said, "No," at the same time.

Well, at least we got our stories straight, Kizmic thought.

Chewing a Slim Jim, Meatball took note of Onion's tape recorder, which he'd slid onto the left handlebar, and Kizmic's camera and light meter, which was also hanging around her neck with a black nylon rope. "Where y'all goin'?"

"Nowhere," Onion and Kizmic said together.

"Where y'all goin'?" Onion asked.

"Nowhere," Redtop said.

They started walking away with Fatboy singing, "Kizmic and Onion sittin' on his bike. K-I-S-S-I-N—"

"Sike!" Meatball yelled.

That don't even make sense, Kizmic thought, annoyed as could be.

Onion laughed it off. Kizmic wanted to get off his bike, but Man 'n 'Em would have really teased her then. If she stayed on the bike and Miss Josephine came to the door of the Fish Store, she would be like, I knew it.

Onion's round head swiveled left and right as he watched the cars. Kizmic watched out for Miss Josephine. A gap finally opened in traffic and Onion rode them out from between the rock and the hard place. When he got to the median, Poochie started squalling his name. Looking behind them to her left, Kizmic saw Man 'n 'Em standing in front of Diamond's house with Diamond, Poochie, 'n 'Em.

"What she doin' on his bike?" Poochie loudly asked Man.

"I'on't know," he said.

"Where they goin'?" she demanded Peanut tell her.

"I'on't know," he said.

Poochie ran to the curb and started screaming, "Onion!" in that pestering voice of hers.

Onion stood up and started pedaling faster. Poochie's "Onion!" chased after them. Onion pressed play on the tape recorder and Heatwaves "Groove Line" drowned her out.

He took Kizmic to Arlington. It was crowded, as usual, with kids playing and shouting. A group of ten- and eleven-year-old boys were playing football.

Kizmic hadn't played football with Man 'n 'Em in months and, boy, did she miss it.

They walked to the end of the field and onto the asphalt. Onion sat his tape recorder on the ledge of the stone wall.

"What you want me to take pictures of?"

"Me."

"For what?"

"My portfolio, girl."

"What's a portfolio?"

"It's like a picture album with headshots and full body shots. All the big stars have 'em."

"Onion, I don't know how to take those kinds of pictures."

"Sure you do. Just pick up your camera and start shootin' like you been doin' and I'ma be like—" He threw his head to the sky. "Bam!" He crossed his arms and broke his mug all the way down. "Bam!" He put his hands on his hips and blinked his eyes in a feminine manner. "Boom!"

Kizmic couldn't help laughing.

Onion patted his short, curly hair in place, straightened his blue and white striped, long sleeved t-shirt, smoothed out the wrinkles on his straight-leg Levi jeans, and wiped smudges off his blue and white Nike tennis shoes. While he was sprucing himself up, Kizmic used her light meter to set the aperture and shutter speed. Big trees in the neighboring back yards that ended at the stone wall hung over the fence and shaded the area. It was almost seven-thirty and the sun was starting to go down. Kizmic had to take all of that into account to get the right exposure.

"I'm ready," he said.

That makes one of us, Kizmic said to herself, but focused her camera on him anyway.

Onion pressed play on the tape recorder and started dancing to KC and the Sunshine Band's "I'm Your Boogie Man," which, like all the songs on his tape, he'd recorded off the radio. He froze in the middle of a move and posed.

Kizmic looked down at his reversed image and timidly took the shot.

"Easy Peasy," he said.

The first three shots weren't easy peasy. The shutter stayed open way too long. They were going to be overexposed for sure.

"Don't worry about it. Let your hair down," he said, shaking his head as if he had long locks. "Have fun like me and everything'll be copacetic, girl."

To loosen Kizmic up, Onion persuaded her to do the funky chicken with him to "Ain't Gonna Hurt Nobody" by Brick. As Regi Hargis killed it on the guitar, Onion backed away, put his right hand in the front pocket of his jeans, looked down his left shoulder at the ground, and smiled.

In her head, Kizmic visualized what she wanted that shot to look like on film, then did everything she needed to do to produce the image. She motioned for him to come from under the trees so she could take full advantage of the early evening light. After setting the shutter and aperture in accordance to the light meter, she cocked the shutter, framed Onion's body from just below his knees to the top of his head, focused, then *Click!*

Beautiful! she thought.

From that shot on, Kizmic did start shooting like she'd been doing, only with a little more thought, confidence, and creativity. To the tune of Kool & The Gang's "Hollywood Swinging," Onion folded his arms across his chest and gazed far off, walked to his right while looking to his left, tilted his head with his forefinger against his temple as if he were deep in thought, sat cross-legged on the ledge laughing, stood wide-legged, looked directly into the camera pointing his finger. He loved the Ciro-flex and the Ciro-flex loved him. Kizmic loved them both. She got down on her knees for a wide shot, stretched out on her belly to get a medium body shot, got on top of the ledge to take a full body shot, and stood in front of Onion for a closeup.

"You're a natural," Kizmic told him.

"So are you."

Between shots they got down to Rick James' "Bustin' Out," Gene Chandler's "Get Down," Cheryl Lynn's "Got To Be Real," and Earth, Wind & Fire's "September." Kizmic had used two rolls of film before she knew it. With just two shots left on the third roll and The Jackson Five singing "Enjoy Yourself," Onion sat on his bike and told Kizmic to get in the picture with him. She placed the camera on the ledge and set the timer. Onion scooted up on the seat and Kizmic sat behind him. He then reached back and grabbed her hands and pulled her arms around his waist. Kizmic had wrapped Onion up in her arms a gazillion times when she tackled him in football right there on that field. But this was way different. Without a ball to try to strip from his hands or a first down or touchdown to prevent him from making, she focused on things that she never paid attention to before. Like how warm his body felt. How a week later, his hair still had that fresh barbershop cut smell. How his creamy, high yellow skin smelled of lotion and his t-shirt smelled of laundry detergent.

Tide, Cheer, or Bold? Kizmic wondered and laughed big and loud at herself for trying to figure out what kind of laundry detergent Onion's mother used to wash his clothes. Ridiculous.

Click!

"Let's do it again," Onion said.

Kizmic reset the timer, but in her haste to beat it, her foot crashed into the sissybar. The shutter fired as she, Onion, and the bike toppled over. Lying on the ground in a heap, she and Onion died laughing.

QUARTER AFTER EIGHT, they headed home, walking leisurely down Beaufort with their footsteps in sync.

"Those pictures are gonna look so good, I'm tellin' ya," Onion said, pushing his bike.

Kizmic nodded in agreement. "I'ma put them in to get developed tomorrow."

They neared the castle house and her eyes automatically went to the tower. The veil-like curtains stirred a bit as though blown on by a light breeze. Soft, bird-like music fluttered out the windows. Something by Minnie Rippleton, it sounded like.

"You know what I got to see the whole time you were takin' my picture?" Onion asked.

Eyes still fixed on the tower, Kizmic asked, "What?"

"That smile you had at the skully board."

She met his gaze. "You really runnin' that in the hole, you know?"

"Yeah, but you don't smile like that all the time," Onion observed.

"That's 'cause I don't feel like that all the time," she replied.

"Well, what do you feel when you smile like that?"

Kizmic looked straight ahead and in her mind's eye she saw herself playing marbles with CJ and Sleepy-eyed Ted, riding CJ's skateboard down the concrete hill, walking into her own bedroom, seeing Man 'n 'Em for the first time, beating Man at skully, stepping into the clubhouse after Redtop had run her over on the football field, taking pictures with her great-grandfather's Ciro-flex. "Joy," she told him, smiling.

No sooner had their feet touched the pavement in front of the Fish Store than Poochie squalled, "Onion!"

"Guess I'll see you in the mornin'," he said.

"Yep." Kizmic started down the street.

"Hey Kizmic," Onion called.

"Yeah?" she asked, turning around.

Looking tenderly at her, he said, "I had a good time today."

"Me too."

Poochie got in Onion's face and started giving him the blues. "How you just gonna keep ridin'? I know you heard me callin' you."

Kizmic didn't hear his response because she'd gotten distracted by Clive, who was being given the blues as well, by his mother.

Wearing a denim, cap sleeved Maxi dress, moving like a black glacier, Hannah Greenleaf clomped up the steps to Kizmic's house in her brown clogs.

"Uh-oh," Kizmic said.

Clive loitered on the sidewalk. "Awww com'on, Ma!"

"Boy, get up here."

With loathing, Clive did as he was told. "Why you doin' this, Ma?"

"'Cause you hard-headed, that's why," Miss Hannah said.

Kizmic stepped lightly onto the porch. "Hey Clive."

"Hey Kizmic," he mumbled.

She looked at Miss Hannah. She was a heavy woman. Not in the over-weight sense, although she was probably carrying a good ten pounds more than was recommended for her five-foot-six height. Miss Hannah was solid, imposing, ordered, stern. Big, loose curls made by pink rollers and a big tooth comb were all over her head. Her thin, harsh eyebrows crashed into the bridge of her hard, broad nose.

"Hi, Miss Hannah," Kizmic said.

She eyeballed Kizmic with marble-like brown eyes that reflected her un-shakable opinion of the person she was looking at. In a husky voice, she grunt-ed, "Hi." Then, "Where's your mother?"

"In the house, I think," Kizmic said.

"Go get her."

"For real, Ma?" Clive asked.

"As a heart attack," Miss Hannah barked.

Turk and Magdalene were snuggled up together on the couch watching the CBS Tuesday Night Movies premiere of *The Little Girl Who Lives Down The Lane* when Kizmic went inside and said, "Miss Hannah's outside, Mama."

Magdalene got up from the couch. "Good Lord, what in the world does she want?"

"You know she ain't here to borrow no sugar," Turk said, following Mag-dalene to the door.

"Hello, Hannah," Magdalene said.

"Your girl was in my house," Miss Hannah spat, as if Kalaya setting foot through her door left a bad taste in her mouth.

Magdalene stepped out onto the porch. "What girl?" she asked, knowing full well Miss Hannah meant Kalaya.

"Kaliea or whatever the hell her name is," she said with a snarl on her thick lips.

Magdalene crossed her arms and said, "Her name is Kalaya, and I don't believe you."

Miss Hannah placed her hands on her wide, square hips. "I don't care if you believe me or not, but you better keep that little . . . girl of yours out my house."

The two women locked evil eye to evil eye. "Kizmic, go get your sister." Only her mother's mouth moved.

"Black Betty said she saw Clive," Miss Hannah yanked him by the arm, never looking away from Magdalene, "sneakin' his little girlfriend in the back basement door around three-thirty yesterday."

"Black Betty, Hannah?" Magdalene questioned. "She was probably drunk as a skunk and don't know who she saw, if anybody."

"Oh, she saw somebody. Didn't she?" Miss Hannah said, gritting her teeth and squinting her eyes at Clive, whose eyes became twice their size when Kalaya came outside.

"She's lying!" Kalaya shouted.

Plum stood beside Kalaya, nodding in her friend's defense.

"Watch your mouth, Kalaya," Turk warned.

Kalaya turned and addressed Turk and Magdalene. No, she hadn't been an angel since the Angelo incident, but her parents seemed to have gotten over that and now trusted her. And she was not about to let Black Betty mess that up and make them start surveilling her again, not now that she learned how to sneak out the house.

"I had practice," Kalaya said. "We've been getting ready for the City Championship. Coach Little got mad and made us do three extra laps. I didn't get home until almost six-thirty."

Kizmic breathed the breath she had been holding since Miss Hannah first laid out her accusation. Kalaya had been doing a lot of crazy things lately, so Kizmic wasn't sure if Black Betty was lying or not. Turk and Magdalene didn't openly show their concern that Kalaya had defied them by messing around with Clive, but they put their happiness that Kalaya had a solid alibi on full display.

"It wasn't her, Hannah," Magdalene said.

Convinced that Black Betty saw what she said she saw, Miss Hannah snatched her evil eyes away from Magdalene's and fixed them angrily on her son. "So what slut did you have in my house this time? Was it this one?" Miss Hannah asked, jabbing a finger at Kalaya.

"Hannah, don't be calling my daughter no slut," Magdalene said.

Ignoring her, Miss Hannah asked, "Was it?"

Turk put a restraining arm around Magdalene's waist.

Clive stood there looking really scared and really stupid. Not only did he get caught sneaking a girl in the house, but now Kalaya, who had been so busy making sure her parents knew that she wasn't guilty, just then realized that Clive was cheating on her.

At the same time, Magdalene figured out Miss Hannah's game plan. A crowd had gathered to watch the show. Miss Hannah was going to make sure Kalaya left her son alone by humiliating her in front of them with Clive's confession.

"Take that home, Hannah," Magdalene said.

"Who was it?" Miss Hannah asked.

"I said take that home." Magdalene tried to wriggle free of Turk's grasp.

"Clive!" Miss Hannah yelled.

He recoiled. "A girl named Gladys."

"Ooooooo!" gasped the crowd.

Gladys Stackhouse. The girl Kalaya had been battling on the track had taken their fight to the street and had run up behind Kalaya and ran off with her boyfriend. Before anybody could stop her, Kalaya slapped the mess out of Clive.

"Ooooooo!" the crowd gasped again.

Turk let go of Magdalene and grabbed Kalaya. Miss Hannah looked like she was about to go crazy. She snatched Clive behind her and shielded him with her body. Her eyes narrowed so sharply that they could hardly be seen as she balled up her fists.

Magdalene jumped in front of Kalaya. "Don't you put your hands on my child!"

Turk had to let go of Kalaya so he could hold Magdalene.

"Well, tell your . . ." She looked Kalaya up and down. "*Child* to keep her hands off my boy."

"Kalaya, apologize," Magdalene said, keeping her eyes on Miss Hannah.

"He cheated on me, Mama!" Kalaya said.

"I don't care. Say you're sorry."

Miss Hannah said, "She ain't got to apologize. All she got to do is stay away from my son."

"Oh, you don't have to worry about that," Magdalene assured Miss Hannah as she marched down the steps.

"See! What'd I tell you about messin' with trash?" Miss Hannah said.

"Your mama!" Magdalene yelled.

CHAPTER

25

After the Clive incident, Kizmic thought Kalaya would be boo-hooing all over the place. But the next morning she went about her business like nothing ever happened.

"Clive's a clown," Kalaya yawned when Kizmic went into her room to check on her. "I was gonna break up with him anyway." She pulled the covers over her head to catch a few more z's before she had to get up.

Onion did the same thing. Came and helped with the paper route like Poochie hadn't screamed on him about riding Kizmic on his bike. She wondered if they broke up, too. But she didn't ask him about it and Onion didn't tell her about it. She learned that they were still "boyfriend and girlfriend" when they got to school and saw Diamond, Poochie 'n 'Em waiting for him by his locker.

Clowns, Kizmic thought.

"Live Life Like There Is No Tomorrow," Miss Habeebulah said, reading the quote she had written on the blackboard, underscoring it twice.

It was a week before graduation. All the other sixth-grade classes were having end-of-the-year parties. They were talking and laughing, playing music and dancing, drinking soda and punch, eating hotdogs, hamburgers, chips, potato salad, cake and ice cream. And what were they doing? Classwork!

Sucking their teeth, moaning and groaning, rolling their eyes, and swearing to themselves that Miss Habeebulah was the meanest teacher in the world, they slammed open their notebooks and grudgingly copied the stupid quote off the board.

"Now, I'm not saying for you all to live your lives recklessly," Miss Habeebulah said, walking up and down the aisles, stopping at the desks of students who hadn't jotted it down and moving only when they had picked up their pencils and started scribbling. "I'm telling you that we don't know if there is a tomorrow. So live each and every day to the fullest. And that means being the *best* person you can be, doing whatever it is you want to do in the *best* way you can do it. And I promise you that your today will be everything you dreamed life could be and more."

Oh my God! What is wrong with this woman? Kizmic brooded.

A roar came from the classroom across the hall as A Taste Of Honey's *Boogie, Oogie, Oogie* began to play. Kizmic put her elbow on her desk, rested her chin in her palm, and waited for the pop quiz. That's what usually followed one of Miss Habeebulah's inspirational speeches, which she used to pump them up and make them believe they could do anything, including pass her quizzes.

Why we gotta sit here and listen to this? Why can't we have a party like everybody else?

"Kizmic," Miss Habeebulah called.

"Huh? I mean . . . yes, ma'am?"

"I have a poem I want you to read."

Kizmic hated reading out loud, especially in Miss Habeebulah's class, because she wouldn't let them sit at their desks. She forced them to go to the front of the room, and the entire time they were reading, their classmates sat on the edge of their seats waiting for them to mispronounce words so they could laugh at them later. Whoever got called on to read, stood up there sweating and shaking, trying hard not to mispronounce words, which only made them mess up words that they knew, so they got teased anyway.

"Come on now. Hurry up," Miss Habeebulah said, waving her hand.

Kizmic got up from her desk and tried to ignore the snickers as she shuffled up the aisle.

Miss Habeebulah handed her a book entitled "The Poems of Dylan Thomas."

"Kizmic is going to read a poem called 'Do Not Go Gentle Into That Good Night.' Now pay close attention to the words."

Miss Habeebulah nodded to Kizmic for her to begin. She cleared her throat and buried her face in the book. In a monotone voice, Kizmic read the words without trying to understand a single thing that came out of her mouth. She didn't have to. Miss Habeebulah always ended up having to explain the poems, because they couldn't figure out on their own what the heck the poets were talking about. All Kizmic wanted to do at the moment was get through that Dylan Thomas poem without messing up any words so nobody could laugh at her. She stammered, lost her place a couple times, and Miss Habeebulah had to tell her to speak up, but nobody could tease her when she was done.

"Thank you, Kizmic. Now I know you all are thinking that this poem is just about dying," Miss Habeebulah said.

"That's 'cause it is," Steebo said.

"No it's not, Keith. This poem is as much about living as it is about dying. Dylan Thomas wrote it about his dying father. And what he wanted was for his father to fight death. To not go peacefully. Rage against it. Holler. Kick. Scream. Go out fighting. Swinging."

Redtop threw up his hands. "Like my man said—dying."

"No, Tony—living," Miss Habeebulah said. "There are several ways to rage against death. And that is to live. Live life to the fullest. Holler. Kick. Scream. Go out fighting. Swinging. All the people Thomas talks about in the poem rage because they didn't do everything they wanted and needed to do in life. If you 'rage'—that is *live*—while you're living, when you are in the mighty grips of death, you'll have no reason to carry on."

What the heck is she talkin' about? Kizmic wondered.

Someone knocked on the door. Miss Habeebulah glanced at it then addressed the class again. "I forgot to tell you all one other important thing. While you're striving to be the best you can be, have a little fun."

Fun? Kizmic scoffed with the rest of her classmates. What does she know about havin' fun? All she does is teach, teach, teach. If we look like we're about to have fun, she gives us a test. Talkin' 'bout some fun.

Miss Habeebulah opened the door and a man walked in with six boxes of pizza. The class looked at one another with their eyes wide and their mouths gaping open. After paying the pizza delivery man, she had some students go with her to the teacher's lounge. They returned carrying sodas, potato chips, pretzels, ice cream, and a big, yellow sheet cake with *Congratulations* written on it in red frosting.

Miss Habeebulah was the best teacher in the whole world! they declared unanimously.

The sounds of them partying back joined the festive sounds of the other sixth-grade classes. At the front of the class, girls danced together doing the bump and the rock while the boys were in a group pop locking, doing the footwork, the robot, and the electric boogaloo until Onion took center stage. To the claps and cheers of his classmates, he spun around, tossed his head back, and kicked his leg up like Michael Jackson to *Blame It On the Boogie*.

A natural, Kizmic thought, watching him from her desk.

She wasn't simply referring to his dance moves. She was also talking about the poses he did in the pictures she'd taken for his portfolio. They were in an envelope inside her notebook.

She was positive that Onion was going to trip out when he saw the photographs, because she tripped out herself when she picked them up from the store.

Kizmic ate a forkful of cake and strawberry ice cream, then reached inside the cubbyhole of her desk and slipped the pictures out of her notebook.

With her hands resting on the rim of the cubbyhole, she looked through them. There were thirty-six in all and other than those first three shots, which were overexposed like she figured, the pictures were amazing and they revealed things about Onion that Kizmic hadn't known. For instance, Kizmic didn't know that Onion's high yellow skin was so smooth or that his hair was that thick and brown and curly until she saw the closeup photographs of him with the daylight illuminating his round head and wrapping around his ears, jaw, and chin. The shots of him looking directly into the camera drew Kizmic's eyes to Onion's, and she realized that his eyes weren't just green but were an arresting jade. The profile shots of him looking away from the camera called Kizmic's attention to his strong nose. The pictures of him smiling attracted her to his thick, charming lips. The full body shots of him looking serious, sad, playful, menacing, shy, and confident made Kizmic see how cute Onion was. He looked like a movie star. She could see girls everywhere decorating the inside of their lockers with these pictures, staring dreamily at them on the pages inside *Right On, Ebony,* and *Jet* magazines, taping poster-sized reprints of them on their bedroom walls. They would gaze on and off at these pictures as they wrote letters to Onion, telling him that they were a Gemini, Leo, Sagittarius, that they'd seen and loved all his movies, thought he was super-fine, and wished they could meet him one day. They would look at the pictures of him on his bike and fantasize about what it would be like to sit behind him with their backs against the sissybar and their arms around his waist.

Kizmic pulled out the photo of them sitting on his bike with *her* arms around his waist. It was fun, she would tell those girls. She slipped off into a daydream where she could feel the warmth of Onion's body, smell his hair and clothes, and hear her laughter as she teased herself for trying to figure out what kind of soap powder his mother used to do his laundry.

Lynette Fleebish came to her desk, sat down and fiddled inside the cubbyhole. When she got up again, she asked a question that didn't penetrate Kizmic's daydream until she was walking away. Snapping awake, Kizmic looked up from the photograph and right at the back of Lynette Fleebish's yellow dress, which had a red stain that resembled the top of one of Miss Irene's apples after she had dipped it in the pot of sweet, hot, liquid candy and placed it on the plastic wrap to harden. As Kizmic stared at the candied apple stain, she heard the question Lynette Fleebish had asked: "Hey Kizmic. Is there anything on the back of my dress?"

"No," Kizmic had answered, gazing fondly at the picture of her and Onion laughing as they fell off the bike.

That stain on the back of Lynette Fleebish's dress and the question she'd asked told Kizmic two things. One: Lynette Fleebish's *friend* had come. Two: Kizmic was in big trouble.

As Lynette Fleebish walked up the aisle to rejoin the party, boys started giggling. Girls punched them and yelled, "It ain't funny!"

Tori stopped dancing and her eyes immediately fell on the red stain on Lynette Fleebish's dress. She ran to the aid of her one and only friend. Miss Habeebulah once again wrapped her sweater around Lynette Fleebish's waist and told Tori to go with her to the nurse's office. As they were leaving, Lynette Fleebish whispered in Tori's ear. Tori turned around. Her horrible cat eyes glared at Kizmic, who sat as though cemented in her seat, thinking, Awww shit!

WHEN THE BELL RANG, signaling the end of the school day, Kizmic ducked out the back door and was immediately surrounded by Tori, Lynette Fleebish, Diamond, Poochie, 'n 'Em, Man 'n 'Em, and almost everybody in her class. As she made her way off the playground and down Beaufort, the crowd of instigators jumped around like a bunch of buffoons. They had been waiting for this fight all afternoon. They were hungry for it, had bet Monday's lunch money on the winner, had decided to risk being punished or getting a whuppin' for coming home late just to see one shove, one punch, one kick.

With two blocks to go before she reached home, Kizmic hugged her faded, denim, loose-leaf notebook against her budding breasts and walked in the middle of the street, looking straight ahead. Being mindful, she placed one foot in front of the other (step, step, step, step, step) as if she might forget how to walk if she didn't consciously think about doing it. Kids she passed in the halls or saw around her way got swept up in the horde as well. The crowd was like a storm cloud around Kizmic. Dark. She couldn't see anything beyond it. Booming. She couldn't hear anything other than its rolling thunder. Natural. She couldn't do anything to break it up. All Kizmic could do was seek shelter by ignoring the crowd's instigating shouts ("Yeah! Go on and kick her!"), egging-on laughter (Ahhh ha! Hah hah!), and goading reenactments of her stumbling forward but not falling when briefly she stopped concentrating on walking and tripped over her feet. (Look, y'all! She went Oof!).

"You saw it," Lynette Fleebish swore, tromping behind Kizmic. She was now dressed in a green blouse and blue jeans that her mother brought up to the school so she wouldn't miss the rest of the party. "I saw you see it."

"You ain't see me see nothin'," Kizmic said, steady walking, knowing that she never even looked up from her desk. So how could she see it if she didn't look?

Crossing Hayward Avenue, Kizmic thought to herself, One more block and I'm home.

The crowd knew this, too. They grew anxious about the possibility of there not being a fight, so they stepped up their instigating efforts and started screaming for Lynette Fleebish to do something. So far all she did was talk a whole bunch of junk about how she was going to whup Kizmic's ass. But the crowd didn't have their lunch money riding on the woof tickets Lynette Flee-bish was selling, and they certainly were not putting their freedom or butts on the line to watch her follow Kizmic home.

Don't say nothin' else to her, Kizmic told herself. She managed to climb up out of the storm cloud by fixing her eyes on the tower of the castle house. She ain't gonna do nothin' except run her mouth. Just keep walkin'. Step, step, step, step, st —

Kizmic bumped into something that forced her two steps back. She looked down. Tori Pompey was standing like a boulder in her path.

Her first instinct was to haul ass. She wasn't as fast as Kalaya, but she could out run Tori. Heck, she could be on her front porch before Tori realized she had taken flight. But what if cars were flying up and down Belvedere? She wouldn't be able to cross it before Tori caught up with her. What if Phyllis was lounging on her porch? She wouldn't be able to run up on it.

Fear started having a field day inside her stomach, making it dip and flip and turn all around. Then Kizmic remembered the conversation she had had with Miss Josephine about the scar on her knee and how it reminded her nev-er to run from anything or anybody. Kizmic had been running from Tori for three doggone years and daggit she was tired. If Miss Josephine could stand up to two white boys, she could stand up to one Tori, right?

Peeking up into Tori's vicious cat eyes, Kizmic answered, Naw. Uh-uh. Can't do it.

She was too scared to stand there and stand up to Tori Pompey. The only problem was she was also too scared to run. She was like a petrified deer caught in the bright, deadly beam of headlights.

Growing a spine that sprouted out of Kizmic's obvious fear of Tori, Ly-nette Fleebish came and stood beside Tori with a we-gonna-beat-your-ass grin on her face.

I gotta fight both of them? Kizmic felt as if she were in a bad dream that kept getting worse and worse.

"Nuh-uh. Hol' up." Peanut pushed his way through the crowd and stood in front of Kizmic. He had grown a few inches, but he was still shorter than all of them. His temper was as big as ever, though. Puffing out his small chest and glaring up at Tori and Lynette Fleebish, he said, "Y'all ain't gonna bank her."

"Yeah," Meatball said as Man 'n 'Em joined Peanut.

"What y'all think this is?" Onion asked.

Kizmic breathed a sigh of relief. She was feeling so alone, but she wasn't. Man 'n 'Em had been patrolling the outer edge of the ring the whole time. They couldn't fight for her, but they could make sure it was a fair fight. And with Man 'n 'Em backing her up, Kizmic wasn't going to back down from Ly-nette Fleebish or Tori.

"One of y'all gonna fight her head up or there ain't gonna be no fight," Peanut said, head bobbing up and down as he spoke. "Now which one of y'all it's gonna be?"

Tori frowned down at Peanut like she wanted to squash him. She took the gold chain with her house key on it from around her neck and handed it to Lynette Fleebish. "I'ma fight her."

"Awww, shucks!" and "Awww, sookie, sookie now!" rose from the crowd as they shoved and elbowed one another in order to get a good view of the beat-down Kizmic was about to receive. But some instigators were crying foul. If Tori had been a contender in this fight from the get-go, they wouldn't have bet their lunch money, because everybody and their grandmother knew Kizmic Waters could not beat Tori Pompey.

With Tori in the ring, they wanted to call off the bet, and soon the crowd was fighting amongst themselves. Kizmic looked at the spectacle. She felt a hint of ironic vindication watching a group of kids who had bet money on her ass whupping kick one another in the behind. It wasn't only funny to Kizmic; Tori found it amusing as well. The two of them stood in the center of that ring and laughed as they watched the crowd go at it. For a split second, Kizmic forgot all about why Tori was standing in front of her.

Wwwhhoooooohh!

That's what it sounded like to Kizmic.

Wwwhhoooooohh!

Like the roar of a *747* zooming across the clear, blue sky. No. Like a heat-seeking missile. *That's* what it reminded Kizmic of as it soared up and across the little bit of space between them. It even had the nerve to be whistling as it cut the "ting" off the hooting and the "lering" off the hollering from the crowd. And while she spent a whole second narrowing down what it sounded like, Kizmic couldn't have cared less if it blasted through the air like a sonic boom, because Tori Pompey's skinny, brass knuckles fist was splitting the air open right in front of her face. And by the time Kizmic yell to herself, Man, she 'bout to sucka punch you! it was too late for her to even blink to protect herself.

Something went *Wick-up!*

Like Fourth of July fireworks, Kizmic's left eye exploded into bright, booming red, orange, and yellow lights. The blow knocked her mind against the back of her skull, where it rattled off, then went staggering around the way Christmas staggered home from The Bar every night. The crowd of hooting and hollering kids shouted, "WHHOOOOOA!!!" at the same time. But to Kizmic it sounded as if the "WHH" began in one kid's mouth then the "OOO" came out of another kid's mouth then another kid's mouth then another kid's mouth until it looped all the way back around to the first kid's mouth then the "OOA!" punched the air.

After the violent blow and multi-colored lights came this pain, this white hot, pulsating stream of pain that filled Kizmic's eye to the brim then trekked across her face to her ear with speed greater than she had ever felt or believed hurt could travel. Ooooou! Talk about somebody wanting to holler. Kizmic wanted to scream like nobody's business, but her voice didn't just leave; it ditched her. Scared as a rabbit, it hopped down the deep hole of her throat and hid in the dark with its eyes closed.

Tori yanked her fist out of Kizmic's eye and, My God! that hurt more than the punch itself. The pain found Kizmic's frightened voice and dragged it kicking and screaming out of its hiding place. When it reached the back of her dry tongue, she let loose a dreadful howl that sounded like hot air being stomped out of a balloon. Kizmic also let loose her notebook and covered her eye with both hands.

Between her blue Trax tennis shoes, Kizmic's notebook hit the asphalt with a clang! Its three metal rings sprung open and eight months worth of math, English, science, and history assignments littered the streets, along with the envelope containing Onion's photo shoot and her *Dear Man 'n 'Em Letters*, which she'd totally forgotten about.

"Gotdaggit!" Like all she needed now was for Diamond, Poochie, 'n 'Em to put their jealous, gossiping eyes on them.

Dazed and trapped in a circle of tormenting laughter, Kizmic felt as if she had been forced to play a game of A Tisket A Tasket and it had gone terribly wrong. But wrong was the only way a game like that was gonna go, according to Kizmic. It wasn't an innocent game of Duck, Duck Goose. It was a game about losing a letter written to a love. Except Kizmic hadn't written any letter to any love. She'd written some letters to her best friends, and while her words and thoughts were scrambled and scattered all over the pages, anyone reading them would get the gist of what she was trying to tell them.

 Getting her hands on those letters and stuffing them in the pockets of her jeans, ripping them up, or eating them if it came down to it, took precedence over everything. But, as if her battered eye felt some kind of way about taking a back seat to a bunch of corny letters, it got to throbbing tightly, like a heart on the verge of an attack, and turned a hot blue-black. Strangely, it didn't immediately swell shut as she feared. Instead, her eyelid stayed rolled up like a stubborn window shade as Tori danced around her the way Leon Spinks danced around the ring after he had beaten the heavyweight championship out of Muhammad Ali, making her father cry. Before that night, Kizmic didn't know her father owned any tears.

Thrilled by the punch, the kids started imitating Rocky Balboa after he'd run up the seventy-two stone steps of the Philadelphia Museum. They jumped up and down, pumping their black fists toward the sky to the tune of "Gonna

Fly Now" instead of thrusting them in the air to "Ungawa! Black Power!"

Kizmic lifted her head and something, or rather *someone*, a boy, caught her blue-black eye. He was inside the castle house, perched in the center window of its tower. A sun bigger and brighter than any afternoon sun that shone all year was poised in the sky behind the tower, showing off its brilliance, beaming tremendous shafts of light directly into Kizmic's blue-black eye, making the boy a painful sight for her to behold. But she held him nonetheless because she had been waiting for three years to find out who lived in that house.

Squinting and wincing, Kizmic strained to keep the boy in focus. He looked to be around her age—twelve. Maybe even a little younger. He was medium brown-skinned with a bald head.

Bald as Kojak, Kizmic thought, as mystified by the boy's hairless head as she would have been if she had come across the Headless Horseman, because boys that age didn't shave their heads.

While marveling at the boy's clean-shavened head, she saw that he was yelling about something. The window was open, but Kizmic couldn't hear him. He was too high up and the crowd was too loud. But she could tell by the way his mouth opened wide then closed, then opened wide then closed again that he was yelling. Kizmic could also tell that he was yelling for somebody, because he kept turning his head, looking back inside the house. After the third or fourth yell, he frowned, then disappeared from the window, almost as suddenly as he had appeared. Then, as if to say there's nothin' else to see here, folks, Kizmic's throbbing, blue-black eye twitched, burned, itched, and slammed shut like a door.

Her left eye. Her picture-taking eye. The eye she looked through the small magnifying glass and sports finder in the viewing hood of her Ciro-flex to focus her shot, yeah *that* eye was swollen shut! Because of Tori.

Kizmic focused her good eye on Tori, and for the first time she was looking down not up at her, because she could now see that Tori was not taller than her. She wasn't bigger than her. She wasn't stronger than her.

Kizmic couldn't help but to laugh at herself. For years she had been absolutely convinced that if Tori so much as plucked her on the back of the head with her finger, she would die. Today Tori had hit her as hard as she could with her *fist*, and Kizmic was still breathing. Why? Because Tori was a short, skinny, girlie-girl with a big mouth.

With that, Kizmic glared into Tori's cat eyes with her one good eye, balled her hands into fists, and proceeded to beat the hell out of her.

Stunned by Kizmic's seething, fearless resolve to kick her ass, Tori could barely shield herself from the heymakers Kizmic was swinging that connected to Tori's cheek, her arms, chest, stomach. It got so bad that Tori ducked her head and started swinging her arms like windmills to get in some licks.

The crowd was going wild until a couple of them asked, "Who dat?" Some others said in alarm, "Uh-oh!" That was followed by a bunch of them saying, "Com'on, yo!"

The patter of the crowd scattering and a rhythmic click-clacking filled the street until the only person standing in front of Kizmic was Miss Josephine in a pair of red, two and a half inch heels.

Cuddling Kizmic's face in her soft hands, Miss Josephine smiled and said in her light, southern voice, "Now, I know you don't think I can keep *this* one from your mama."

CHAPTER

26

Mr Charlie was laying catfish on a bed of ice in the display bin when Miss Josephine walked in with Kizmic. At the sound of her heels, he wiped his hands on his long, white apron and looked up with a big smile on his face that dropped to a frown when he laid his brown eyes on Kizmic's blue-black eye.

"What in the hell happened to her?" Mr Charlie asked, looking at Kizmic as if she had something the health department would shut his place down for if they knew she was anywhere near his store.

"She got into a little fight, that's all," Miss Josephine said. She strutted behind the counter and gave him a quick kiss on the lips.

"A little fight?" Mr Charlie questioned, grimacing.

"She'll be alright," Miss Josephine said. "Magdalene's not home yet so I'ma take her upstairs and put some ice on her eye, try to keep some of the swellin' down."

"You better hurry up," Mr Charlie said, in a tone that sounded like he thought it was a little late for ice.

Magdalene was hot!

"Who does she think she is putting her hands on you over some crap like that?" she yelled after Kizmic told her what happened.

Kizmic sat at the kitchen table while Magdalene got the aluminum ice tray out of the refrigerator. Even though Miss Josephine said that she had iced Kizmic's eye pretty good, Magdalene still insisted on icing it herself, like Miss Josephine's ice wasn't cold enough or something.

She pulled on the handle. Ice cubes cracked and popped out of the sections. She wrapped the ice in the towel.

"Hold your head back," Magdalene told her.

Kizmic sucked in her breath as the cold stung the thin, sensitive skin. Soon, though, her eye felt better because she couldn't feel it.

"I don't know what her problem is, but she's not going to solve it by beating on you," Magdalene fumed. "She might go around here whupping up on everybody else's child whenever she feels like it, but she's not going to be whupping up on mine. Soon as I change my clothes, we're going down to her house. She's not getting away with this."

Kizmic let out a heavy, exasperated sigh. The last thing she wanted was for her mother to drag her to Tori's house and perform in front of the entire neighborhood.

The telephone rang. Magdalene snatched the receiver off the hook. "Beana. Girl, I'm about to go off around here."

"What happened?" Aunt Beana squawked.

"That damn Tori. She punched Kizmic in the eye," Magdalene said, like she still couldn't believe Tori had the audacity to put her hands on her child.

"For what?!" Aunt Beana's voice blared out of the phone, echoing off the kitchen walls.

"Because some girl came—"

Kizmic didn't want to hear her mother relay the details of the fight. Holding the freezing towel to her eye, she got up.

Magdalene took the receiver from her ear. "Where are you going?"

"To the bathroom," Kizmic said.

"All right, but come right back down." Magdalene put the phone to her ear again. "Beana, you should see my baby girl's eye."

Kizmic closed the bathroom door and stood at the mirror with her head down. She'd only seen what her eye looked like from the reactions of people who had seen it, and if Mr. Charlie's "What in the hell happened to her?" and her mother's, "Beana, you should see my baby girl's eye" were any indication as to how bad it was, Kizmic wasn't sure she wanted to look.

She raised her head and slowly pulled the towel away from her face.

"What the f—!" Kizmic said in a mortified whisper, ready to fight Tori all over again.

She put the icy towel back over her eye and pressed hard, trying to speed up the healing process. After ten minutes, she strained to part her eyelids. They didn't budge. Kizmic put the towel back on her eye for a few more minutes, then tried to pry her lids apart again. She did this repeatedly until her eyelids separated slightly. Her blue-black eye now looked like Uncle Monty's dead eye.

Kizmic went into her bedroom and snatched her Ciro-flex off the nightstand. CJ and Sleepy-eyed Ted's baseball fell onto the floor. She opened the viewing hood and flipped up the magnifying glass. Kizmic then closed her right eye, took a deep, hopeful breath, and peered down at the ground glass. The bruised skin around her eye began to defrost, making it sting a bit, but through the slit between her eyelids she could see the reverse image of the collage of photographs she'd taped to the wall.

Kizmic sighed with relief. She could still take pictures. Happy, she looked down at the ground glass again, but this time her blue-black eye functioned like a cheap crystal ball from Woolworths, and showed her the past instead of the future. Sparing her the agony of reliving the punch, it jumped back in time to the moment her notebook hit the ground, exposing her *Dear Man 'n 'Em Letters.*

"Gotdaggit!" she said, realizing she had left her notebook in the middle of the street.

"Kizmic!" Magdalene called, hearing her try to sneak out the door. "Get your tail back in here."

The News American truck pulled up. The driver got out, tossed a bundle of papers on the porch, then drove off.

"But Mama, I gotta go—"

"Go where with your eye looking like that?" Magdalene asked, coming out into the hallway.

"Do my route," she replied.

Magdalene unwrapped the blue, gold, and black headscarf from around her hair. "Kizmic, I'm not thinking about that route."

"But the people are gonna be waitin' for their papers."

"Well, they can wait until your father gets home."

"That'll be too late."

There was a small commotion out front as Man 'n 'Em hopped off their bikes at her house.

"Told you I saw the truck," Redtop said.

"You act like you the only one that saw it," Steebo argued.

Babyfrog said, "I saw it before both of y'all."

"Yo, Kizmic," Onion shouted, walking up the steps. "Bring out the bag of rubber bands."

Magdalene shook her head. "You're not doing that route by yourself."

By myself? Did her mother just get struck blind? Did she not see Man 'n 'Em out on their front porch? "Mama—"

"No, Kizmic."

"But if I stay in the house, everybody's gonna think I'm scared," she said.

"I don't care what they think. And besides, I told you we were going to Tori's house so I can talk to her mother."

"Mama, you don't need to talk to her mother. It ain't like I stood there and let her hit me. I got some licks in too. I ain't scared of her no more."

Magdalene draped the headscarf over the banister. "Come here."

Kizmic walked wearily over to her mother.

"Lift your head up." Magdalene gingerly examined Kizmic's eye with her warm fingers, which defrosted and roused the pain that had been frozen. It sat straight up in her eye, like a guard that had been caught sleeping on the job, and began aching at a furious rate, trying to make up for lost time.

Kizmic had to resist the urge to grit her teeth. Any sign of pain and her mother was not going to let her out the door. Holding her breath, she rocked back and forth in her mind, waiting for the pain or her to lose oxygen and pass out.

"Don't you go looking for a fight," Magdalene said. "And if you find yourself in one, don't come back here with your other eye looking like this one."

Finally able to breathe, Kizmic ran out onto the porch.

"DANG!" Man 'n 'Em hollered, gawking at her eye.

"I ain't know she hit you like that!" Peanut said.

"Can you see?" Steebo asked, squinting his squinty eyes at her.

"Yeah, I can see," Kizmic said.

Meatball laughed. "I don't see how."

"Yo, man, it's purple," Redtop observed.

They got all up in her face to get a closer look.

Amazed, Fatboy said, "It sure is."

Kizmic stood there and let her friends tease her, feeling like one of the boys again.

Throwing punches at the air, Steebo said, "You should take a picture of that so you'll always remember the day you beat Tori's—" He looked in the house to see if her mother was in earshot. "Ass."

"Bet she won't be botherin' you no more," Meatball said.

"Here." Man handed Kizmic her notebook. "I tried to pick up all the papers but everybody was steppin' on 'em and kickin' 'em all over the place. And then Miss Josephine came, so I just picked it up and ran."

"She don't need none of that stuff no more anyway," Babyfrog said. "School's over."

"All jokes aside," Onion said. "You okay?"

"Yeah," Kizmic smiled.

Onion smiled back.

"Ooouuu," Meatball said and started making kissing sounds.

Fatboy started singing, "Kizmic and Onion sittin' on the porch. K-I-S-S-I-N—"

"Torch," Meatball laughed.

"Shut up," Onion and Kizmic said.

Kizmic took her notebook in the house and found that not only were her *Dear Man 'n 'Em Letters* missing, the pictures of Onion's photo shoot were gone too.

"We're gonna do Beaufort first," Kizmic said after they were all packed up.

"Why?" Onion asked. "We always start up on Garrison."

"Just 'cause," Kizmic said and rode her bike toward Belvedere.

Man 'n 'Em followed. When they got to the castle house, there were no signs that a fight had ever taken place, which meant there were no signs of Onion's photos or her *Dear Man 'n 'Em Letters*. There wasn't even a sign that the bald-headed boy had been in the window.

CHAPTER

27

SATURDAY MORNING, wearing a sleeveless, pink fuchsia floral dress, pink stockings, pink shoes, hair done up in soft, bouncy curls, Kizmic looked at herself in the mirror, ready to bawl her eyeballs out. Not because that dress was worse than any other dress Magdalene, abusing her mother authority, forced Kizmic to wear, including the gaudy ones she bought her for Easter. Not because no matter how many times Kizmic reminded Magdalene while they were shopping that her favorite color was blue, daggit, BLUE! her mother still went overboard with the pink *and* flowers to boot. No. Kizmic wanted to cry because that dress was her graduation dress.

In an hour, she was going to walk out of the blue, metal doors of Arlington Elementary as she had done every June since third grade. Only this time, she was not going to walk back through them at the end of the summer. She passed to the seventh grade and come September, she would be walking through the doors of Pimlico Junior High.

"Whoop-de-do," Kizmic said, turning away from the mirror.

Her whole life as she loved it was coming to an end, and there wasn't anything she could do about it. Nothing. Just had to let it go. Like she had to let her life on Proctor Street go when they moved, and with it, CJ and Sleepy-eyed Ted.

Kizmic picked up the baseball they'd given her, then slipped on her glove. The worn, tan leather balanced out the pink in her dress and the glove on her hand made her feel like she could hold onto some of what growing up was taking away from her.

Tossing the baseball in the glove again and again, Kizmic stared teary-eyed at Man 'n 'Em on her picture wall. She was taking fewer and fewer photographs of them playing baseball, basketball, football, and, believe it or not, skully. They were outgrowing those games, at least outgrowing playing those games with one another. And Kizmic had a sad feeling that by the time they graduated junior high, they wouldn't be playing together at all.

"Girl, if you don't put that filthy thing down," Magdalene said, swinging open her door.

Kizmic quickly wiped away tears that had started to fall and sat the glove on the bed. Holding onto the baseball, she sighed as her mother patted her curls and swept invisible dirt off her dress.

When Kizmic was presentable again, Magdalene gushed, "My beautiful baby girl. Your Daddy and I are so proud of you."

Turk and Kalaya came in.

"You ready, slugger?" he smiled with a wink.

"My eye is still purple," Kizmic sulked.

"That's all right," Kalaya said, putting her arm around her little sister. "It matches your dress."

THE AUDITORIUM INSIDE ARLINGTON was packed. Families and friends sat shoulder to shoulder in the rows of black metal chairs, cheesing, bragging, and snapping pictures of their children, who were on the wooden stage also sitting in black, metal chairs, in alphabetical order.

On the end of the third row from the back, Kizmic gazed out at the audience, remembering all the times she sat in those very same seats enjoying the school's Christmas, Thanksgiving, and Black History Month plays, math and spelling bees, talent shows, or some other assembly. Arlington had been like a second home to her. Now it was kicking her out, the way a parent kicked a grown child out into the world.

The graduation ceremony went along as they had rehearsed. They recited the Pledge of Allegiance, the school pledge, sang the school song, George Benson's "The Greatest Love of All," and the National Black Anthem, "Lift Every Voice and Sing." Of course, they received standing ovations at the end of every performance. After all of that pomp and circumstance, Principal Redd walked up to the podium. Tall, light-skinned with a white-hot desire to eradicate ignorance in the black community, Principal Redd spoke in the same drill sergeant tone she used when she told them to stop playing in the hall, get out the bathroom, stop running down the steps, stop actin' a fool, go to her office, have a good day. "Young ladies and gentlemen! Today is the day that you move from childhood to young adulthood."

A sharp pang cut through Kizmic's stomach. She was on the verge of tears again while all the other kids on stage cheered and clapped. Kizmic told herself to cut it out. She couldn't sit there sniveling, not unless she wanted her mother to come running up on stage to see what she was carrying on about. And when she did, what was Kizmic supposed to tell her? *Oh, I'm up here blubberin' like a baby 'cause I don't wanna grow up. I'm sorry for gettin' you all upset, Mama. Go on and sit back down. I'll be alright in a few . . . years.*

Principal Redd said, "You have the opportunity to go on and accomplish things your parents only dreamed of. The road has been paved for you. All you have to do is walk it and never give up, no matter how bleak your journey gets. Fight for what you want in life."

But I did fight, Kizmic replied in her head to Principal Redd.

She'd been fighting growing up since the day Kalaya's *friend* appeared on their stoop. What good did it do? She still grew up. Her breasts, which hadn't gotten any bigger but certainly hadn't shriveled up and disappeared like she prayed to God for them to do, were proof of that.

"Stand tall, young people," Principal Redd continued. "Be yourselves and be *somebody*. And don't listen to the people who tell you that you can't. My mother had this saying: 'Can't died when God said I believe I'll make a world.'"

Several in the audience showed their agreement with her grandmother by shouting, "Amen!"

"The future is yours, young people. Grab a hold of it." Principal Redd clutched the air in her right hand. "And don't let go for nothin'!" she said forcefully, shaking her fistful of future.

Applause erupted in the room. Hands folded in her lap, Kizmic looked around at Man 'n 'Em, and in their smiling faces she saw the tight, excited grip on the future they held in the fists that they pumped in the air.

Miss Habeebulah came to the podium, pumping her fist in solidarity. "Class of 1979, please stand," she said.

Kizmic took a deep breath and rose. This is it. The end of the line.

When she walked across that stage, she would take the beginning steps to the end of her childhood life, for in a few short months she would spend all her time and energy making sure her *friend* didn't embarrass her in class the way Lynette Fleebish's *friend* embarrassed her almost every month, wishing some boy that she thought was the cutest thing ever would talk to her, like Plum, and getting her heart broken by some boy that she'd risk breaking her neck to be with, like Kalaya.

"Eric Adams," Miss Habeebulah called, smiling at the fact that the first graduate to receive a diploma was one of her students.

Wearing a handsome tan suit, Onion waltzed coolly over to Principal Redd and accepted his diploma as though he were walking the red carpet to receive his Oscar. Not only did he look like a movie star to Kizmic, he looked honest-to-goodness cute.

Thinking that about Onion, saying that about Onion, and feeling that about Onion had let the cat out of the bag. She had grown up, and the proof of that wasn't just in her tiny breasts, but also in the way her sitting on the back of Onion's bike with her arms around his waist left her wondering about more than whether it was Tide, Cheer, or Bold she smelled on his clothes. Since that day, Kizmic had been wondering if Onion liked her the way Miss Josephine said he liked her. Wondering if he liked her hair and her clothes, if he thought she was as pretty as Poochie, even though she wasn't light-skinned. If he wanted to kiss her.

With pride, Miss Habeebulah said, "Kevin Carter," into the microphone, and Fatboy, who had a little stage fright, walked quickly to Principal Redd with his head down.

Kizmic's heart pumped dread throughout her body. There seemed to be nothing she could do about her fate other than to go on and give up the ghost. Except something in the back of her mind questioned if she really had to just lie down and take this.

What else am I supposed to do? Kizmic asked.

"Tori Pompey," Miss Habeebulah's voice boomed from the speakers.

Kizmic's left eye twitched as she watched Tori promenaded over to Principal Redd, and then the something inside her said, *Fight.*

I *did,* Kizmic insisted.

But in truth, she hadn't. She whined. Avoided. Closed her eyes like a two-year-old playing hide-and-seek, believing that because she couldn't see anyone or anything, no one and nothing could see her.

Okay, so she had been going through life with her eyes closed. But they were open now and Kizmic needed to know what she could do to save her childhood.

Miss Habeebulah pulled the microphone closer to her mouth, then with admiration and excitement called, "Antwon Smart."

Babyfrog ran across the stage with both fists in the air. Man 'n 'Em hollered, clapped, and whistled as loudly as they could, because they knew that by passing the sixth grade, Babyfrog had won the fight of his life. Kizmic couldn't sit that one out. She joined Man 'n 'Em in the celebration of their friend's extraordinary accomplishment, and while she was clapping, hollering, and stomping, she heard Dylan Thomas' poem "Do Not Go Gentle Into That Good Night" in her head.

"There are several ways to rage against death," Miss Habeebulah had explained. "Live life to the fullest. Holler. Kick. Scream. Go out fighting. Swinging," she'd told the class. At the time it made no sense to Kizmic. Now everything was clear. The something inside Kizmic wasn't telling her to fight to save her childhood; it was telling her to fight while letting it go.

I get it, Kizmic thought, relieved. "If you 'rage'—that is *live*—while you're living, when you are in the mighty grips of death, you'll have no reason to carry on," she remembered Miss Habeebulah saying.

Maybe that's why Dylan Thomas' father didn't rage, Kizmic thought. He lived his life to the fullest. Dang! I wish I had said that in class. Miss Habeebulah would have thought I was the smartest kid in there.

"Andre Wallace," Miss Habeebulah called happily.

Peanut bopped over to Principal Redd, brushing imaginary dirt off the jacket of his black suit. He was just too clean. Couldn't nobody touch him.

That's gonna be me this summer, Kizmic decided. Nobody's gonna be able to touch me 'cause I'ma live the end of my childhood like I've never lived before.

"Kizmic Waters," Miss Habeebulah smiled.

Walking over to Principal Redd, Kizmic knew she was doomed to sit around hoping Onion liked her, not the way Miss Josephine said he liked her, but the way *she* liked him. Hoping that he thought her hair and clothes looked nice, that he thought she was as pretty as Poochie, even though she wasn't light-skinned. Hoping that he wanted to kiss her like she had been wanting to kiss him ever since they fell off his bike.

Smiling and gazing at Onion, who was smiling and gazing at her as she walked across the stage to receive her diploma, Kizmic thought, Yeah, all of that's gonna happen. But I'ma go out swingin'.

CHAPTER

28

ALL RIGHT. FIRST AND FOREMOST, if Kizmic truly wanted to have one last fling with childhood, she was going to have to chuck all those feelings that had her betting that she smelled Cheer on Onion's clothes that day she sat on the back of his bike with her arms around him.

Those feelings were behind her getting a black eye. If she hadn't been thinking about Onion in that way, she would have heard Lynette Fleebish ask about her dress and wouldn't have gotten into a fight with Tori and lost her *Dear Man 'n 'Em Letters* and her pictures of Onion's photo shoot. Which, by the way, were still missing. Lord only knew where they were and He wasn't talking. Those feelings were only going to have Kizmic trying not to mess up her hair instead of trying to hit a home run, trying not to get her clothes dirty instead of trying to score a touchdown, trying not to get all sweaty and funky instead of trying to nail a jump shot, so that Onion *would* think that she was prettier than Poochie, even though she wasn't light-skinned, and would want to kiss her too. Yep, those feelings had to go.

Second, in order to seriously go out swinging, Kizmic needed to come up with a foolproof plan. She went to Rite Aid and paid a dollar for a small, blue diary with a lock, like the ones Plum had. In it, she plotted how she was going to live out the end of her childhood, from the first skully game, to the fourth baseball game, the eighth race on their bikes, the twelfth basketball game, the sixteenth football game, the twentieth skateboard ride down Dead Man's Curve, the twenty-seventh game of Pitty Pat, to the last shot on the thirtieth roll of film inside her Ciro-flex. This was going to be a summer to remember.

Monday, June 4, 1979, Kizmic awoke before five, retrieved her diary from under her mattress where she'd hidden it from her nosey mother, and reviewed her schedule for the day.

7:00 do route with Onion. 9:00 ride skateboards and take pictures of us at the top of Dead Man's Curve. 10:30 play football. 12:45 play with Fatboy's pigeons. 1:30 go swimming. 4:00 do route with Onion. 5:30 play Go Fish in the clubhouse. After dinner ride bikes. 8:00 play skully until it gets dark.

What was that saying about the best-laid plans?

Kizmic sat on the steps of her back porch with her Ciro-flex around her neck and her right foot on the deck of her skateboard, pushing it back and forth. By the paws of her Snoopy watch, it was eleven twenty-seven, and Man 'n 'Em had yet to come outside. On a gorgeous summer day like today, they usually hit the streets by nine. Onion wasn't even out. He had come at seven to help with the route, but because they didn't have school, he didn't eat break-fast. He said he was going home to eat then come right back.

At eleven fifty-five, Man 'n 'Em came straggling out. Onion claimed to have fallen back asleep. Man, Steebo, and Meatball said they didn't get up until ten-thirty. Peanut said he was drawing. Redtop and Fatboy said they were watching television, and Babyfrog said he was trying to catch some weird-look-ing bug that had gotten in his house.

They ended up skipping riding their skateboards and football. They fed Fatboy's pigeons, but instead of going swimming afterward, they played skully. For all of fifteen minutes. In the middle of an unprecedented historic game, in which Redtop was beating the pants off everybody, Diamond, Poochie, 'n 'Em strolled up wearing their shorts, sundresses, and sandals.

Last year, Man 'n 'Em would have sent them screaming away with an in-sult, a loud burp, a fart, or a boogie on the tip of one of their fingers. Those were the good old days. This new day, Man 'n 'Em stopped playing skully and started chasing Diamond, Poochie, 'n 'Em around instead of away. And they giggled and squealed and ran as slowly as they could so that Man 'n 'Em could catch them. It was ridiculous. Especially the way Poochie called Onion's name in that whiny, irritating, girlie-girl voice of hers. "Onion, stop."

The next day, Kizmic got up early, opened her diary, drew a line through the stuff they didn't do the day before, and read the agenda she'd written for Tuesday, June 5, 1979.

7:00 do route with Onion. 9:00 ride skateboards. 10:30 play football. 12:45 take pictures of us playing with Fatboy's pigeons. 1:30 go swimming. 4:00 do route with Onion. 5:30 play Tonk in the clubhouse. After dinner ride bikes. 8:00 play skully until it gets dark.

Man 'n 'Em showed up at twelve-forty with the same excuses. They had just enough time to go back home, change into their swimsuits, and run the four blocks to C.C. Jackson Recreation Center. Sitting on the corner of Garrison and Park Heights Avenue, across from the Enoch Pratt Free Library and connected to Park Heights Elementary School, C.C. Jackson was a red brick, two-story building and a magnet for children. With their rec cards in their pockets, they flocked to C.C. Jackson from all over the community to hang out with their friends playing pool, air hockey, ping pong, chess, checkers, taking art, dance, music, poetry, and martial arts classes, shooting hoops on the indoor and outdoor basketball courts, lifting weights in the small weight room, attending and participating in fashion shows, talent shows, Valentine's Day dances and Halloween parties, which featured one of the scariest haunted houses in the neighborhood. Outside the building, kids played baseball on the little league field, football on the open field, and soared through the air on the swings and glided down the sliding board on the playground. But the main attraction at C.C. Jackson was its swimming pool.

Enclosed behind burnt red, wrought iron fencing that sat on top of a retaining wall made of wood beams and flanked by green trees on its Garrison and Park Heights sides, the five-lane pool went from two feet to five feet deep. In the summer, kids walked, rode their bikes, caught the bus, or a ride from their parents and lined up as early as eleven o'clock in the morning to be the first wave of kids to dive in the pool when the gate opened at twelve. Every ninety minutes until six o'clock, the lifeguards cleared the pool and let in another stream of kids.

Kizmic, Man 'n 'Em got to C.C. Jackson at 1:15. Twenty to twenty-five kids were already in line, eagerly awaiting their turn to take a dip in the cool, blue water. Between the rec's main door and the pool's gate, mothers hovered over their squealing toddlers as they waded in a wide, square kiddie pool, some lying on their bellies in the ankle high water, eyes closed, holding their breath, kicking their legs, and stroking their arms, imitating the kids in the big pool.

Baking under the scorching sun and breathing in the wonderful smell of chlorine, Kizmic, Man 'n 'Em peered through the gaps in the iron rods and watched the first group of swimmers enjoy their last fifteen minutes of inner city heaven. At one thirty-five, the lifeguards opened the gate. Kids rushed in, flinging their towels, clothes, and shoes at the foot of the wood and iron wall. Wearing a pair of green and white striped swim trunks, Meatball ran across the concrete deck, yelled, "Geronimo!" then belly flopped into the deep end of the pool. Man followed by coolly diving in then turning over and floating on his back in his Hawaiian trunks with *Ahhh!* written all over his face. Redtop did a handstand on the edge of the pool, then fell in backward. Steebo, whining about the water being too cold, eased himself in using the ladder, shivering and teeth chattering. Fatboy, complaining of the same thing, sat on the side of the pool, sticking his toes in and out of the water and wincing. Babyfrog,

Onion, and Peanut got a running start, yelled, "Cannonball!" jumped in the air, pulled their legs to their chests, and hit the water with three big splashes.

In a corner, under the overhanging tree branches, Kizmic watched her friends, wishing there were some way she could have brought her camera. But that wasn't the only reason she hadn't jumped into the pool. Her bathing suit, or rather what was under her bathing suit, made Kizmic reluctant to take off her t-shirt and shorts. The admiral blue one-piece was like the bathing suits she'd worn her whole life. Except now she had breasts and a cute, little behind, and that bathing suit put them on full display. She wanted to keep her t-shirt and shorts on, but that was against the rules written on the sign at the entrance that explicitly stated that all swimmers must wear swim attire.

Onion climbed out of the pool. His yellow skin sparkled with droplets of water. His trunks were the same color as Kizmic's bathing suit.

Twins, she thought dreamily, watching him walk over to her.

"Why you ain't get in yet?" Onion asked, looking at her clothes.

His eyelashes were longer and darker wet. Their dampness brightened the green in his eyes.

"Kizmic?" Onion called.

"Huh?"

"I said, why ain't you in the water?"

"Oh . . . um . . ." Snap out of it, girl. You messin' up your summer. "'Cause . . . I—"

"Hey Onion," Poochie called in that drive-Kizmic-out-of-her-mind voice.

Diamond, Poochie, 'n 'Em crowded around Onion with their hair protected underneath white, red, blue, and yellow rubber swim caps and lured Man 'n 'Em out of the pool with their colorful, two-piece bathing suits, showing off their breasts, behinds, and legs. The only thing missing was a horn honking as Man 'n 'Em's eyes turned to hearts and bulged out of their heads.

"You like my swimsuit, Onion?" Poochie asked.

With her hands in her pockets, rolling her eyes to the sky, Kizmic thought, If you gotta ask him, then the answer is no.

Poochie turned this way and that, modeling her red and white polka dot bikini for him. Now, she was flat-chested as flat-chested could be, but everything else about her was so lean and dainty and poised and lovely that her breasts were a tiny, desirable eyeful.

A spellbound Onion gaped at her and said, "Yeah."

Knowing her darling body had him wrapped around her little finger, Poochie smiled victoriously and tugged on his arm. "Let's get in."

"You comin'?" Onion asked Kizmic.

Shaking her head, Kizmic said, "Uh-uh."

"Why not?" he asked, looking disappointed.

"Come on, Onion. It's hot," Poochie whined with pouty lips.

"I forgot my swim cap," Kizmic lied, rolling it up in her towel. "My mother said I can't get in without it."

"Yeah, 'cause chlorine will make your hair fall out." Poochie patted her white swim cap. "That's what my mama said."

Ain't nobody ask you what your mama said, Kizmic thought.

Poochie started pulling on Onion hard enough to drag him away.

"So what you gonna do?" he asked, no longer resisting.

"I'ma go home and get it. I'll be back," Kizmic lied.

WEDNESDAY, JUNE 6, 1979, Kizmic woke up early, crossed out the things they didn't do on Tuesday, and looked over what she had planned for the day.

7:00 do route with Onion. 9:00 ride skateboards. 10:30 play football. 12:45 feed and play with Fatboy's pigeons. 1:30 go swimming. 4:00 do route with Onion. 5:30 take pictures of us playing Pitty Pat in the clubhouse. After dinner ride bikes. 8:00 play skully until it gets dark.

Man 'n 'Em came out again at noon and, to Kizmic's delight, they rode their bikes up to Arlington and played football. The day was cloudless, easy, and hot. A small breeze blew, and the sky was blue with big white clouds. It was so nice.

The game was good, too. Kizmic hadn't played with Man 'n 'Em since her breasts had grown and they started feeling all over her. Today, they tackled her, but they didn't touch her breasts or her behind. The only thing that threatened to derail her fun happened when Kizmic and Onion tackled each other. Depending on who did the tackling and how they fell, Onion would lie on or under Kizmic long after they had hit the ground, gazing into her eyes. Kizmic would avert her eyes but bury her nose in the scent of his shirt and the great Cheer, Tide, or Bold debate would commence in her head.

At one o'clock, the score was fourteen to seven, in her team's favor. In the huddle, Kizmic told Babyfrog to run wide to the right, shake Peanut, then cut left, and she would drop the ball right in his hands. Standing behind Meatball, Kizmic hollered, "Hut! Hut! Hut!" But before she could holler "Hike," Diamond, Poochie 'n 'Em strutted across the field. In their yellow, red, orange, pink, white, and green summer dresses and short sets, they looked like tall sunflowers enjoying the day.

"Ahh F—Phooey!" Kizmic said out loud. She felt like jumping up and down and screaming the way Steebo did when he was having a temper tantrum. Then it occurred to her. She hadn't seen Steebo do that in a good while.

"Onion," Poochie whined. "Come here."

Of course, Onion went running like some old puppy dog, tongue hanging out, tail wagging. The rest of 'Em ran over to Diamond 'n 'Em.

A few giggles later, Man said, "Hey, Kizmic, we goin' to Miss Irene's to get frozen cups. You comin'?"

Diamond, Poochie, 'n 'Em flung unwelcoming, venomous, catty glares at Kizmic.

Onion came over to her. "Come on. We'll finish playin' later."

No we won't, Kizmic sighed to herself.

"Onion!" Poochie screeched.

"I think I'ma hang up here a little while."

"By yourself?" Onion asked.

Like you care, Kizmic thought.

He stared at her like he did care.

"Onion!" Poochie stomped her pink Jelly sandals in the grass.

"I'll catch up with y'all later," Kizmic said.

"You sure?"

"Onion!" Poochie screamed. She twisted her lips so hard that they looked like they were now on the side of her face.

"Yeah, I'm sure," Kizmic said. "You better go on 'fore Coo—"

Onion's green eyes widened and his mouth dropped open.

Kizmic could only laugh at her slip. "I mean *Poochie's* tonsils fall out."

Onion smiled and pointed a cautionary finger at her.

They left, riding Diamond, Poochie, 'n 'Em on the backs of their bikes. The day seemed to cloud over once Man 'n 'Em were gone. Brooding, Kizmic tossed the football up in the air and caught it about a dozen times before she hopped on her bike and headed home. As she was coming up on the castle house, she saw Man 'n 'Em and Diamond, Poochie, 'n 'Em leaving Miss Irene's house. Kizmic looked up at the sky so they wouldn't see her staring resentfully at them. Her glance skimmed the tower and there was the baldheaded boy.

Kizmic almost ran into the curb when she saw him perched in the window like a bird.

She had to take her eyes off him and drop the football to regain her balance. She got off her bike and looked up at the window, but again the boy was gone. The only thing there was that soft, bird-sounding music. Minnie Riperton's "Memory Lane."

He was there, Kizmic thought. I know good and well I saw him. I'm not crazy; I'm not imaginin' things.

Almost as if the house said, "Sike up!" the front door squeaked open and a girl emerged. Kizmic frowned and tilted her head in confusion. She expected to see the baldheaded boy, not his sister, assuming that that was who she had to be because they were the spitting image of each other, except for the Angela Davis sized Afro she had on the top of her head.

Wearing green shorts and a light blue t-shirt that had Astrea from the *Space Sentinels* cartoon flying across it in her pink jumpsuit and yellow cape, the girl bounced down the steps with her hands behind her back. She looked to be about twelve and was the same height as Kizmic. Her body was skinny, straight up and down skinny, with no visible signs of encroaching adolescence. She had pretty, zestful brown eyes. But there was something odd about them. Something not there.

With a sunny smile brightening her thin, acorn brown face, she said, "Hi. I'm Journey."

Her introduction gushed with the excitement of a person meeting someone she had heard fantastic stories about, and now that she was standing in front of her, well, there was nothing like seeing people for yourself.

Kizmic should have introduced herself, but her mind was stuck on the girl's name. "How'd you get a name like Journey?"

"My mother said she went through hell and high water to bring me into this world. So, she named me Journey."

They laughed at the joke.

"I'm Kizmic."

"I know. You're our papergirl." Fascination shimmered in Journey's strange eyes. "I have something that belongs to you."

She took her right hand from behind her back and held out a few sheets of wrinkled notebook paper stamped with footprints. Kizmic recognized them immediately. Her *Dear Man 'n 'Em Letters*!

"I didn't read them," she said. "Well, actually, I read the first one. That's why I picked them up. I figured you didn't want them laying in the gutter."

You figured right. Kizmic was grateful but embarrassed that Journey knew what those letters were about. But it could have been worse. Diamond, Poochie, 'n 'Em could have read them.

"I also found these." Journey took her left hand from behind her back and gave Kizmic the envelope with the pictures of Onion's photo shoot.

Kizmic almost cried, she was so relieved. "Thank you."

"You're welcome." Journey's eyes dropped to the football. "Can I hold that?"

"Sure." Kizmic picked the ball up off the ground and gave it to her.

Journey smiled at the faded, scuffed up ball like it was a shiny, brand-new toy. She rubbed it and squeezed it and tossed it up in the air. Her strange eyes sparkled as she waited for the ball to fall back into her open hands.

"Go long," Journey said.

Kizmic looked at her skinny arms and laughed. "You mean short?"

Journey smirked, then walked out into the street. With the fingers of her right hand spread across the laces, Journey solidly gripped the football as she cupped it with her left hand. "You're still standing there?"

Kizmic folded up her letters, stuck them inside the envelope with the pictures, then put the envelope in her back pocket. Thinking this thin girl couldn't possibly have much of an arm, Kizmic only jogged a little ways up the block. But she had to pick up her pace because Journey didn't just toss the ball up in the air like a girl. She cocked it behind her ear, then hummed that sucker.

"Whoah!" Kizmic said. She hustled back, back, back—whew!—back . . . and caught the ball on the tips of her fingers.

Journey cracked up. "Was that short enough?"

Man! Kizmic thought, but refused to give a cocky Journey the satisfaction. Instead, Kizmic gripped and cupped the ball. Okay. She can throw, but can she catch?

Kizmic hummed the ball just as sweet. Journey ran back, back, back, and back some more, then her blue The Winner II tennis shoes left the ground as she jumped up and snatched the ball out of the air.

Kizmic stood in the middle of the street, stunned and thoroughly impressed. Journey landed and threw the ball back to her. She was winded, though, and sweating.

"Where's your brother?" Kizmic asked.

Journey closed her eyes and concentrated on taking deep breaths. "I don't have a brother," she panted after she'd collected some oxygen in her lungs.

"So who was that in the window?"

"Me," she said.

Eyeing her Afro, Kizmic said, "But the person I saw didn't have no—"

"I know." Having regained her strength, Journey held up her hands.

Kizmic threw the football. Journey caught it, walked up her front steps and into her house. Kizmic followed.

CHAPTER

29

With each step Kizmic recalled every last lecture her parents gave about going into a stranger's house.

It ain't like I'm goin' in D. Tinkle's house or something, she reasoned, walking through the lavender door.

Standing in the foyer, Kizmic was immediately struck by the calm inside. It was the middle of the afternoon and all the lights were off, even in the kitchen, which was straight ahead. Rays from the sun, however, streamed through the windows and cast soft shadows and daylight in every room. Minnie Riperton singing "Return To Forever" floated down from upstairs. To the right, double glass doors opened into the circular room on the first floor of the tower. Kizmic walked in and was astonished to find that it wasn't much bigger than their clubhouse. Its barrel-shaped walls were peach-colored and its round floor had the same beige wall-to-wall carpeting that ran throughout the house. A comfy, cream loveseat sat in the middle of the room on a dusty rose shag rug, surrounded by three windows that ushered in a warm breeze. Draped across the back of the couch was a quilt. Not your run-of-the-mill quilt, though. This was a vintage, hand stitched, diamond patch quilt made of various leftover pieces of fabric.

"My mother and I like sitting in here when it's raining or snowing or storming," Journey said.

Stepping back out into the foyer, Kizmic noticed another quilt. How she missed it when she first came in, she didn't know because it was enormous, reaching from the floor to the ceiling and stretching nearly as wide as the long

261

wall on which it hung like a painting. Sunlight from the tower room windows shined a spotlight on the quilt, animating the picture on it. The picture didn't come from a pencil, paintbrush, Polaroid, a 35mm, or even a Rolleiflex. It came from someone using a needle, thread, and cloth to depict mothers shopping with their children at a fruit and vegetable stall inside Lexington Market. Their skin was made of black, ginger, henna, chocolate, copper, and chestnut brown cotton and silk fabrics. The mothers and daughters' square, triangular, and rectangular dresses were made of Kool-Aid colored scraps of polyester. The sons' pants were pieces of dungaree. Raised, vibrant colored cotton apples, oranges, watermelons, bananas, tomatoes, string beans, potatoes, and corn looked real enough to pick off the canvas and eat.

"Who made these?" Kizmic asked.

"My mother." Tucking the football under her arm, Journey led Kizmic up the carpeted stairs.

At the landing in the middle of the staircase was a window through which the afternoon light pushed its way in and highlighted the quilt hanging to the right of the window. It depicted North Fulton Avenue and the corner of West Lafayette Street basking in a glorious sun, under a peaceful blue sky that had fluffy cotton white clouds. The remarkable thing about this quilt was Journey's mother had sewn together thousands upon thousands of tiny pieces of red, cloth bricks to construct the seventeen three-story rowhouses that lined the block.

Kizmic ran a finger along the stitched mortar between the bricks. This must have taken forever.

There were three bedrooms on the second floor in addition to the tower room. Journey put a finger to her lips, signaling for Kizmic to be quiet. With the thick carpet muffling her footsteps, she padded to the center room. Kizmic could see a woman lying in bed.

Journey closed the door without making a sound. "My mother's taking a nap," she whispered.

They went up to the third level, passing two more quilts on the staircase. To the left of the stairs was the bathroom, directly in front was a bedroom (the door to which was closed), and to the right was the last tower room. Sunlight coming in the three windows, bouncing off the baby blue walls, made the small, round room airy and bright.

Journey handed Kizmic her football and walked over to a Steepleton Stackable record player that was on a stand beside the first window. Hair styled in a foxy Afro, a shirtless Minnie Riperton wearing denim overalls and holding a brown sugar cone topped with vanilla ice cream melting all over her hand smiled from her "Perfect Angel" album cover propped against the stand. Her other four albums were laying on the floor.

"She's my favorite singer." Journey took the *Minnie* album off the record player and slid it inside its cover. Next, she set the needle down on the title track of the *Adventures in Paradise* album.

As Minnie Riperton sang, Kizmic played with the football, turning it over and tossing it from one hand to the other as she looked around. A five-shelf mahogany bookcase crammed with comic books, books on drawing, and books on drawing comic strips took up the left wall. Newspaper comic strips of *Andy Capp, Beetle Bailey, Charlie Brown, Moose Miller, Wee Pals,* and *Friday Foster* lined the walls to the right of the door and between the windows.

Meatball, Fatboy, and Peanut would love it in here, Kizmic thought.

There were also drawings of Bumblebee, Redeye, Mickey Mouse, Dick Tracy, and Spider Man.

"You drew these?" she asked.

"Every one," Journey said proudly.

There was a three-foot, light oak, tilting drawing table in the middle of the room. It had a white, swing arm lamp clamped to it and was tilted toward the windows so that the sunlight illuminated it as well. In front of the table was a stool. Three-drawer storage carts on either side of the table had jars, cans, and cups of pens, markers, pencils, crayons, erasers, rulers, and paintbrushes sitting on top of them.

"I want to be a cartoonist like Morrie Turner and Charles Schulz," Journey said, grabbing a few drawing tablets out of a cobalt footlocker that was behind the drawing table.

Kizmic took a seat on the stool. Journey flipped open the first tablet and on its pages were these amazing comic strip drawings of Man 'n 'Em! Kizmic looked up at Journey in total surprise.

"The first time I saw you, you were chasing behind them on your bike and they were trying like crazy to get away from you," Journey laughed. "Every day I watched you run past my house after them and I wondered, what does that girl want with those boys?"

She turned the page and Kizmic dropped the football at the sight of a comic strip that featured her! Journey put on paper all the things that made Kizmic Kizmic, only in a more exaggerated form. Her head was twice its size, her body, arms, legs were shorter, her feet were smaller than usual, but it was unmistakably, hilariously her. The figure had her long braids, her pug nose, plump lips, navy blue, high top Chuck Taylors, jeans, and green Underdog t-shirt.

Kizmic read the comic strip the way she had read so many others, but those didn't have her running upright, full tilt, face straining, left arm up and in front, right arm up and in back, knees bent, feet off the ground, speed lines flying off her body to show she was bookin'. Kizmic's eyes jumped to the second frame. Man was riding his Sting-Ray, his big eyes large as golf balls. Head as big and round as a pumpkin, Meatball was on his 3-speed truck. Redtop, wearing a cast on his left arm, stood on his Huffy with one foot on the seat and the other on the handlebars. Babyfrog was flying on his Schwinn, wearing a football jersey and his Elmer Fudd hat. Peanut was riding his Slingshot, his short legs barely touching the pedals, his widow's peak as pronounced as Eddie Munster's. Green eyes glowing, Onion sat against the sissybar on his bike. With ears as pointy as Spock's on *Star Trek*, Steebo was riding his Huffy, his orange flag flapping in the wind. Reading a comic book, Fatboy pedaled his orange and yellow Schwinn. All their mouths were wide open with contagious laughter as they left Kizmic eating their dust, literally. Journey had drawn a cloud of dust trailing from the wheels of their bikes as they zoomed away from her.

"One day I snuck out of the house and followed you up to the school," Journey said and turned the page to a comic strip about the first baseball game Kizmic played with Man 'n 'Em.

Steebo was on the mound winding up with a sneaky, devilish grin marring his face. His arm was moving so fast that it was blurred. In the second frame, he hummed the baseball, which in the third frame turned into a rock, and in the fourth frame bounced off Kizmic's left thigh. In the fifth frame, Kizmic's cartoon-self grabbed her mouth to keep from crying while Man 'n 'Em stood with thought bubbles over their heads filled with their wish for her to "Cry and go home, girl!" The last frame in the strip showed Steebo at the plate shaking like a leaf. Kizmic was standing on the pitcher's mound with a thought bubble over head that showed her imagining Steebo shaking so much that he turned into a mound of leaves that she jumped into.

Kizmic laughed out loud at the comic book version of her story. She had never found any humor in the stuff Man 'n 'Em put her through.

"When he hit you with that ball, man, I thought you were going to quit, but you got up. The next day, you were right back with them and I snuck out of the house again and saw you playing football. And I was like, man, this girl is crazy."

Journey had a comic strip of that day, too. It showed Redtop tackling Kizmic, but in the drawing Redtop turned into a Mack Truck just before he ran her over. Her cartoon-self was lying on the ground as flat as a pancake with large, black tire marks up and down her body.

"I knew for sure you were going to run home crying, but you didn't. You got back in the huddle and I thought, Man, this girl is cool."

Cool? Kizmic chuckled to herself. She and no one else had ever referred to her as being "cool." A good first baseman? Sometimes. A great receiver? On her good days. A fantastic skully player? Twenty-four seven. But cool? Alright!

In the last frame, Journey had drawn Kizmic burning Redtop as she scored a touchdown. Redtop's face and body were scorched and smoke was coming from his burnt hair.

"The next day, I looked out and you were riding with them instead of behind them. And I thought, Wow! She did it. You had the biggest smile on your face."

"How come I never saw you watchin' us?"

"I guess because you weren't looking for me," Journey shrugged. "Last September I went away and when I came back, you were delivering our newspaper."

"Where'd you go?"

"The hospital."

If Journey were to draw Kizmic right then, she would have a thought cloud above her head asking, *What'd you go to the hospital for? And why'd you haveta stay so long?*

Journey turned to another comic strip. In the first scene, Kizmic was happily playing football with Man 'n 'Em. Diamond, Poochie 'n 'Em came by and distracted the boys in the second scene. There was a word cloud over the girls' heads that was filled with "Blah, Blah, Blah, Whine, Whine, Whine." The third scene had a thought cloud over Kizmic's head that showed her thinking, "I wish they would go away." In the fourth, Kizmic crossed her arms like Jeannie in *I Dream of Jeannie*, and Diamond, Poochie, 'n 'Em were engulfed in a big white cloud with the word "Poof!" written on it. In the final frame, the girls had vanished, and Kizmic, Man 'n 'Em were playing football again.

Journey opened a different tablet and turned to a drawing of Kizmic riding on the back of Onion's bike.

"I drew this one because I was trying to figure out what that little black box was you were holding," Journey said.

"A camera," Kizmic answered, staring at the drawing, remembering the smell of Onion's shirt, and thinking, Tide. It has to be Tide.

"That's what I figured after I found your pictures on the ground."

Annoyed that she was once again thinking about Onion in that way, Kizmic asked, "What does all this haveta do with the way I saw you in the window?"

She didn't mean to be rude, but Journey knew way too much about her, and Kizmic knew next to nothing about Journey.

Journey let Kizmic's questions hang in the air for a moment. Minnie Riperton sang "The Simple Things" in the lull.

"It's a wig," she confessed.

A wig? What do you mean a wig? What happened to your hair? Did you cut it off? Did somebody give you a bad perm? Is it gonna grow back?!

While staring at the bushy-head Journey in front of her and remembering the bald-headed Journey in the window, Kizmic saw it. Saw what was missing in her eyes. Or rather over them. Eyebrows.

She ain't got no eyebrows. Kizmic was perplexed.

Something else was missing on Journey's face, too.

Eyelashes. She ain't got no eyelashes.

Making all of this more pronounced and mind boggling was that Kizmic could see the veins under Journey's eyelids. Only they didn't look like veins; they looked like thin, green strikes of lightning.

"I have leukemia," Journey said, as if she were telling Kizmic she had chicken pox.

Kizmic didn't really know anything about the disease, except that it was some form of cancer. "Like Minnie Riperton?" she thought out loud, looking at the album covers on the floor.

Journey nodded. "Yeah. Only hers is in her breasts."

"Where's yours?"

"All over."

All over? What does that mean?

"Kizmic," Journey called softly. "I need you to help me do something."

"What?"

"Give my mother a Christmas present. Those pictures that you took of your friend—"

"You mean Onion?"

"That's his name?" she smiled.

"That's what we call him. His real name is Eric."

"Well, what you did for Onion, I want you to do the same thing for me. Only I want the pictures to be of me playing baseball, basketball, football."

Whoah! Wait a minute. Baseball? Basketball? Kizmic's head was swirling. Football? She wants to play football?

Playing catch with Journey today was the closest she'd ever come to playing football with a girl.

This ain't happenin'. I gotta be dreamin'.

"Everything you do I'm going to do and I need you to take pictures of me doing it."

She went inside a drawer then handed Kizmic a hundred dollars in five worn twenty-dollar bills. "Is this enough to buy film and get it developed?"

"Where did you get this?"

"My grandfather. Is it enough?"

"Yeah," Kizmic said, already thinking about how she was going to explain having a hundred dollars in her possession. Even with the paper route, she couldn't walk up in her house with that amount of cash without somebody raising an eyebrow.

"So, will you do it?"

Kizmic had to think. For one thing, she was a girl, but Journey was no ordinary girl. Ordinary girls didn't draw the way she drew. Ordinary girls didn't touch a football, let alone throw it the way she threw it. And ordinary girls most definitely didn't catch the way she caught that football. The second thing was, Journey had leukemia. *All over*, she said. Kizmic still didn't know what that meant. *All over*. But she did know that Journey was sick. "How you gonna do all that with leukemia?"

Journey picked up the football. "Hey, I wasn't the one who had to make up ground when we were playing catch," she reminded Kizmic.

"Yeah, but I wasn't the one who started sweatin' and losin' my breath."

"Look, if it makes you feel better, we can start off doing something easy." Journey's lightning struck eyes brightened as she asked, "Do you know how to play marbles?"

CHAPTER

30

MARBLES.

Come on! No way! I ain't never met no girl that played marbles. Somebody must be playin' a trick on me.

"Well, do you?" Journey's forehead rose where her eyebrows should have been.

"Do I what?" Kizmic asked to be clear that she and this girl were talking about the same game. Marbles. Get-down-on-your-hands-and-knees marbles. Lie-down-on-your-belly-in-the-dirt marbles. Hadn't-played-since-they-moved marbles.

"Do you know how to play marbles?"

Was this girl for real? "Better than anybody 'round here," Kizmic boasted. "Since nobody 'round here plays marbles."

"I'm around here," Journey shot back with a scrappy smile.

"Yeah, but can you play?"

Her lightning eyes flashed again. She walked out into the hall, opened the door to the other room, and waved her hand for Kizmic to follow. It was a peaceful, misty blue and white. A twin bed with cherry pine wood headboard and footboard occupied the middle of the floor and was decorated with a cozy, multi-colored patchwork quilt. On the nightstand beside the bed was an 8x10 picture of Journey and Minnie Riperton together, smiling, with Afros crowning their heads.

"She visited a hospital I was in. I was so glad I had gotten sick," Journey laughed. "I would have missed her otherwise."

To the right was a long, wooden table that had at least twenty prescription medicine bottles on it, along with bottles of rubbing alcohol, boxes of gauze,

268

needles, cotton balls, and tissues. There was a brown mini fridge on that side of the room. On the wall above it hung a small, rustic wood frame chalkboard, which had long medical terms written on it. Some words had been erased. Two white Styrofoam mannequin heads sat on the dresser. One had a curly wig on it. The other was bald. Probably because it was the head for the Afro wig Journey had on her head.

This was no ordinary girl's room. This was a sick girl's room. So, once again, Kizmic questioned how was this girl, who had leukemia *all over*, going to play any of those rough games, including marbles?

Then Journey walked to the left side of her bedroom. The wall, from one end to the other, had shelves, from the floor to the ceiling, that displayed a marble collection CJ and Sleepy-eyed Ted wouldn't believe! Kizmic's eyes stretched wide and her mouth dropped open. There were big jars, little jars, tall bottles, short bottles, fat jars, square jars, round bottles, mason jars, jelly jars, just jars and bottles, bottles and jars of marbles. Lemonades, Whities, Blackies, Snakes, Blue Ladies, Rainbows, Jelly Fish, Alley Swirls, Yellow Jackets, Tiger's Eyes, Helmets, Corkscrews, Ruby Dees, Turkey Swirls, Peacocks, Popeyes, Egg Yokes, Wasps, Dragonflies. Journey had marbles galore!

Kizmic hadn't seen that many in a kid's room since going in Sleepy-eyed Ted's bedroom. If he still collected marbles, his room would look like this.

"I'm sure I don't play as well as you," Journey said. "I collect them more than I play with them because they look like candy, and my mother won't let me have candy. But, yeah, I can play. All I need is a way out of the house."

Picking up a tall jar of Watermelons, Kizmic asked, "What do you mean?"

"My mother is . . . very protective of me. You ever see that movie *The Boy in the Plastic Bubble*?"

"Yeah."

"If my mother could put me in one of those things, she would. But since she can't, she keeps me in the house. She won't let me out if she thinks I'm going to be doing something that might . . . aggravate my condition."

"Why don't you just keep sneakin' out the house like you been doin'?" Kizmic couldn't believe she was suggesting this, considering the fit she had about Kalaya sneaking out of their house.

"My mother doesn't nap every day, and even if she did, I wouldn't have enough time. But I think I've found a way to get her to let me go outside."

"What is it?"

"Your route."

Kizmic put the jar back on the shelf. "Huh?"

"I'm going to talk my mother into letting me help you with it. We deliver the papers as quickly as we can. We play. I come home, and all my mother thinks I did was stroll around the neighborhood a bit," she grinned.

And I get to play marbles, Kizmic grinned, holding a mason jar full of Grasshoppers.

Journey snuck Kizmic out of the house as soundlessly as she snuck her in. She and her mother would be at Kizmic's house around six. In the meantime, Kizmic went to get her marbles. She, of course, had a ton of them in her bedroom, but some of her coolest marbles were in a Crown Royal pouch in a box inside the clubhouse.

Kizmic threw the football in her back yard as she rode up the alley. She leaned her bike against Steebo's fence. Onion's bike was there, too. The Jackson Five's "Dancing Machine" was coming out of the clubhouse window.

PJ greeted Kizmic at the gate. While petting her, Kizmic watched the clubhouse shake and thought, Onion must be in there gettin' off.

She opened the door. Onion was clapping and shuffling his feet, but he wasn't the one gettin' off. Poochie was. Wiggling and slinging every part of her scrawny body, she was dancing not like she was on *Soul Train's* main stage; Poochie was boogieing like she was alone in her bedroom *imagining* she was on *Soul Train's* main stage.

Kizmic was furious. No other girl had ever set foot inside the clubhouse, not even their mothers.

And he got Poochie up in here!

Kizmic likened Poochie being in their clubhouse to Goldie Locks breaking into the Three Bears' home, stealing their food, and vandalizing their property.

Man, I oughta —

Onion jumped next to Poochie and they started doing the bump. She was cheesin' like a Cheshire cat as they bumped their hips together to the drums and bongos all the way to the floor and back up again. PJ barked.

Onion looked up, and seeing Kizmic in the doorway, froze in mid-bump. Poochie, who hadn't noticed Kizmic, turned around to bump her narrow behind against Onion's hip and lost her balance as her backside hit the air. She fell against him, then quickly straightened up and started brushing one of the two long braids on either side of her head with her hands, trying to act as if she didn't almost bust her butt. Oh, what Kizmic wouldn't have given to see that.

"Hey, Kizmic!" Onion said, talking all loud. "I thought you was Man 'n 'Em."

Kizmic didn't say a word.

"Me and Poochie was just dancin'," he explained.

I don't care what y'all was doin', Kizmic glared. You know girlie-girls ain't allowed in the clubhouse.

Onion was sweating bullets, and it wasn't because of the heat. Kizmic rolled her eyes and stomped in. Two lemon-lime frozen cups were sitting on the table, melting back into Kool-Aid.

He don't even like lemon-lime.

At least he didn't use to. Then again, he didn't use to bring girls in the clubhouse. If he brought Poochie in there, did he take her in his bedroom and share his secret dream with her? Kizmic wondered, feeling the snapshots of that dream in her back pocket.

She went over to the shelf that held Babyfrog's bug collection. Inside a jelly jar, one of the black, white, and yellow caterpillars had wrapped itself up inside a green cocoon hanging on a twig. Kizmic kneeled in front of the box beneath the shelf and grabbed her sack of marbles.

"What you gettin' those for?" Onion asked.

Poochie, with her signifyin' self, asked, "What's in that bag?"

"Marbles," he told her, like Kizmic wanted her to know.

"Marbles?" Poochie squawked. "Don't nobody around here play marbles."

Oh, God! I can't stand her!

"See you at four," Onion said.

Kizmic slammed the door.

She didn't want to see him at four. Or at six forty-five tomorrow morning. In fact, she didn't want to see him at all.

I'm tryna have a good summer and him and Poochie keep gettin' on my nerves.

The only reason she didn't go back and tell Onion not to come was because if her mother didn't see him at four, her paper route days were done. Kizmic was hoping like she didn't know what that this thing with Journey worked out.

Mama said somebody had to be with me while I did the route. She didn't say it *had* to be Onion.

AFTER FINISHING THE ROUTE with Onion, during which she didn't speak to him the whole time, Kizmic hung her empty sack on the hallway banister and went into the kitchen. Magdalene was at the counter flouring some pork chops. Aunt Beana sat at the table reading aloud a passage from Stephen King's *The Shining*. The window above the sink and the back door were open and a small breeze circled in and out through them. Kizmic spoke and plopped in the chair across from Aunt Beana. Being mad at Onion was exhausting.

"Something's wrong with that man," Magdalene said, placing a pork chop in the pan of hot grease on the stove.

Aunt Beana looked up from her book. "Why do you say that?"

"He's always killing off children."

"No he doesn't," Aunt Beana said.

Magdalene waited for the grease to stop popping before placing another chop in the pan. "Look at *Salem's Lot*. He killed a bunch of kids in that book.

What kind of childhood did he have that makes him write about kids dying all over the place?"

"It happens. He's just writing about life," Aunt Beana argued.

"A lot of things happen in life. That doesn't mean I want to read about them every time I open a book. Why can't he write something happy?"

Aunt Beana lit a cigarette. After taking a couple of puffs, she said, "Well, you'll be happy to know that Danny's not dead."

"Not yet. Give him a few more chapters. Everybody in that book will be dead, including the dog."

Aunt Beana blew smoke out the side of her mouth. "They don't have a dog."

"That's because he bumped him off in the first draft," Magdalene laughed.

Chuckling and shaking her head, Aunt Beana took another drag off her cigarette.

The doorbell rang. Kizmic glanced at her watch. It was six o'clock on the dot.

Time to get rid of Onion and play some marbles. "I got it, Mama," she said, jumping up from the table.

Journey's mother had her back to the door, but Kizmic could see that the woman who made those fantastic mural quilts had velvety ebony skin and a short, silky soft natural. She was slender and toned, dressed in a purple, elbow sleeve, wrap shirt and bell-bottom jeans. With a pair of tan Kork Ease sandals on her feet, she stood a tad taller than average height.

Journey was on her knees rubbing Phyllis from the top of her head to the tip of her wagging tail. Kizmic scowled at Phyllis, who, taking great pleasure in Journey's strokes, rolled over on her back, closed her eyes, and purred. Journey, who was also taking great pleasure in her strokes, rubbed Phyllis' stomach, looked up at her mother and smiled. That's when she saw Kizmic standing at the door.

"Kizmic, this is my mother, Miss Sarah. Mama, this is our papergirl."

Miss Sarah regarded Kizmic with gentle, curious, brown eyes. She had a Nubian nose, triangular in shape with broad nostrils. Her mouth was small, but her lips were thick and luscious with a thin smile. Kizmic found her to be as splendid as her quilts, but not quite as vibrant or free. There was a rigidness in her stance, a reluctance on her smooth, oval face.

"It's nice to finally meet you," Miss Sarah said. "We should have met the day you got into that awful fight. I was resting when Journey yelled for me. By the time I came to the door a woman was walking you down the street."

"Miss Josephine," Kizmic said.

"That's her name?" There was a *Wow!* in Journey's voice that noted she had been wondering about more than just Miss Josephine's name.

"Well, I'm sorry I couldn't get to you before . . ." she gestured toward Kizmic's eye.

"That's okay," Kizmic said.

"What's your cat's name?" Journey asked.

"Phyllis. But she ain't mine."

Seeing the *ugh* on Kizmic's face and noticing that she had not stepped outside, Journey asked, "You don't like cats?"

"Uh-uh," she grimaced.

Journey gave Phyllis one last long stroke then carried her down the steps and gently shooed her on her way. Kizmic then opened the door.

Magdalene had another floured pork chop between her fingers about to ease it into the hot grease when Kizmic trotted into the kitchen.

"Mama, Aunt Beana, this is my friend, Journey, and her mother, Miss Sarah."

Kizmic made this announcement in an excited but routine manner, as if she had been playing with girls her whole life and this one was just another to add to her never-ending parade of girlfriends.

Knowing that couldn't have been farther from the truth, Magdalene held the pork chop over the frying pan. *This is your what?!* the shocked expression on her face asked.

Aunt Beana, who hadn't choked on the smoke from a cigarette since her first puff on one umpteen years ago, started coughing from the smoke she'd just inhaled.

Kizmic expected her mother and aunt to express some level of surprise upon seeing Journey, but in her honest opinion, they were going a bit overboard with their shock. Okay, so she hadn't played with a girl . . . ever. Still, it didn't call for them to carry on as if Kizmic hadn't known what a girl was until today.

"I'm sorry. You're in the middle of cooking dinner," Miss Sarah said. "We can come back later."

"No, no, no. It's all right. Have a seat." Magdalene turned to Aunt Beana to make sure she wasn't in the *Twilight Zone*.

Still coughing, Aunt Beana crushed out her cigarette and looked back at Magdalene to make sure *she* wasn't in the *Twilight Zone*.

See, all of that was uncalled for as far as Kizmic was concerned.

Miss Sarah sat across from Aunt Beana. "Are you sure?"

"Yes." Magdalene put the pork chop in the pan. "You have to forgive us. Kizmic has never . . . I mean . . . all her friends have been . . ."

"Boys," Aunt Beana coughed, patting her chest.

"Ahh. She's a tomboy."

"Since birth," laughed Magdalene. "But maybe she's beginning to grow out of it," she added, smiling gratefully at Journey.

Ha! That's what you think, Kizmic thought.

She wasn't growing out of tomboyhood; she was being evicted. But thanks to Journey, who was just as much of a tomboy as she was, Kizmic was going to be able to stay a little while longer.

"So, when did this unlikely pair become friends?" Aunt Beana asked after her lungs had cleared.

"That's actually why I'm here." Miss Sarah explained that while she was napping, the girls decided Journey would help Kizmic with her route.

"I thought Onion was helping you," Magdalene said.

"He is, but Journey wants to help now, too."

"It looks like fun," Journey said.

Miss Sarah said, "I wanted to clear it with you before I agreed to this."

For Magdalene, there really wasn't anything to clear except why her daughter, who hadn't played with a girl her entire life, was suddenly bosom buddies with *this* girl? Magdalene picked up a fork and turned the pork chops over in the pan. Something was fishy.

Magdalene irked the heck out of Kizmic. She had been bugging her to death about playing with a girl.

Now I'ma 'bout to play with one and she actin' like I'm up to no good. When all I wanna do is help the girl out.

And help herself out in the process. I scratch your back, you scratch mine. It ain't like I'm usin' her or nothin', Kizmic reasoned.

They had a deal. Although Journey didn't know that there was anything in this deal for Kizmic other than a few bucks. She didn't know that for Kizmic, being able to play marbles again was worth more than whatever money would be left over from the hundred dollars she'd given her.

I'ma tell her that one day, Kizmic thought.

Waiting for *one* day for Kizmic to be square with her about this new friendship wasn't something her mother was willing to do. She was determined to uncover the truth this day. So she focused on Journey.

Why couldn't her mother just be satisfied that she was playing with a girl? Why did she have to know *why* she was playing with a girl?

'Cause she nosey, that's why, Kizmic concluded.

Magdalene studied Journey for only a few moments before turning back to the stove. The suspicion that furrowed her brow was gone. Some thought scrunched her eyebrows together and twisted her lips as she took the pork chops out of the frying pan and placed them on a plate. She switched off the burner, and after putting the pieces of that thought together, Magdalene said, "You know, Sarah, I can't tell you how many times I've been in the kitchen cooking and daydreaming about Kizmic skipping in the house with some pretty little girl asking if she and her friend can have a glass of Kool-Aid or go up in her room and play. And today I got my wish. But I wouldn't be much of a woman and even less of a mother if I wasn't straight with you."

Straight with her? What's she got to be straight with Miss Sarah about? Kizmic wondered.

Miss Sarah sat up in the chair and gave Magdalene her full attention.

"Kizmic has to get up at six, seven days a week," Magdalene told her.

"I'm always up by then," Journey cheerfully said.

Miss Sarah nodded an okay to Magdalene.

"The route is a good twelve . . . thirteen blocks, going and coming."

"That's not too far," Journey insisted.

Her mother wasn't telling Miss Sarah anything about the route that warranted the serious tone in which she was describing it. That perplexed Kizmic.

"It takes about an hour in the morning and an hour and a half in the afternoon because there are more customers. And that's *with* them riding their bikes."

"That's not long at all," Journey said.

Miss Sarah began stroking her neck with her thumb and index finger. "Journey doesn't have a bike and I wouldn't feel comfortable with her on one."

"We'll walk then. Right, Kizmic?"

"Yeah."

Miss Sarah's eyes wandered to the floor as she began to have second, third, fourth thoughts about letting Journey do the route.

Was that what her mother was trying to do? Discourage Miss Sarah so she wouldn't let Journey do the route?

"Walk. Thirteen blocks. Even when it's raining," Magdalene said so Miss Sarah was clear.

Why would her mother not want Journey to help her? Was there something about her that she didn't like or trust? Her mother was always looking at somebody and saying, "There's something about that one I don't like." Or "That one's trouble." Did her mother see something in Journey that said she was trouble?

"Or hot," Magdalene said lastly.

Miss Sarah put her elbows on top of the table. Interlocking her fingers, she bowed her head. In that position, she appeared to be saying grace or praying. Since dinner wasn't ready, Kizmic assumed she had to be praying. That's when she realized what had happened.

Magdalene had been so caught up in her wish for Kizmic to have a *girl* friend finally coming true that she hadn't looked closely at Journey. When she fixed her prying eyes on Journey, her years of caring for the chronically ill revealed what her enthusiasm overlooked—the wig, the bald face, the frail body. She didn't see the Leukemia *all over* Journey. Her mother only saw a kernel of some sort of sickness. And that's what urged her to have that mother-to-mother talk with Miss Sarah.

Magdalene sought out Aunt Beana, who, with a nod, assured her that she had done the right thing in warning Miss Sarah that this job was challenging for a healthy twelve-year-old, let alone a sick one.

Tears welled up in Journey's eyes, just like they did in Kizmic's when Magdalene tried to stop her from doing the paper route. But Journey's tears were not working on her mother. Miss Sarah was there not of her own free will but of her caving into Journey's, and whatever she promised Journey because of that, she no longer had it in her to do. It wasn't hard for Kizmic to see that in her mind, Miss Sarah had already said no. It was just a matter of her saying the word out loud.

Kizmic was okay with not being able to play marbles, baseball, football, basketball or get rid of Onion. She had survived three years without touching a marble and the last few months barely playing any of those games. And if she had to, she could make it through the summer being around Onion. But the crushed look on Journey's face told Kizmic that if Miss Sarah said the "No" that was on the tip of her tongue, Journey wouldn't make it through another day sitting up in that wooden bubble drawing cartoons.

I gotta help her, Kizmic thought. But she didn't know how at first. Then she remembered how Onion came to her rescue and made it possible for her to do the route.

Kizmic stepped over to the table. "Excuse me, Miss Sarah."

Lifting her head, Miss Sarah cast worrisome eyes on Kizmic.

Speaking as sincerely and respectfully as she could, Kizmic said, "Please let Journey do the route. It will be three of us, so she won't be out there that long. We'll walk really slow. If she gets tired, I promise we'll bring her home right away. And if she gets sick, I'll stay with her and Onion'll come get you."

Kizmic astonished Magdalene. Her little girl sounded so brave, strong, and grownup.

Deeply touched by Kizmic's petition, Aunt Beana closed her eyes, placed her hand over her heart, and said, "Mmm Mmm *Mmm.*"

Journey looked appreciatively at Kizmic for the remarkable way she went to bat for her.

Miss Sarah gazed at Kizmic with the same worried eyes, leaving everyone unable to tell if her heartfelt plea had changed her mind or not. When Miss Sarah parted her lips to let them know one way or the other, James Brown screamed.

The crisp chick of hi-hat cymbals, the strum of a bass, the pluck of a guitar, shouts, whistles, hand claps, and the blast of horns filled the house.

"Soul Brotha Number One's home," Aunt Beana said.

Miss Sarah gave her a questioning frown.

"My husband," Magdalene sighed.

The Godfather of Soul started singing "Get Up Offa That Thing" and Turk, in his dried concrete-caked, brown work boots, did the Camel Walk out of the living room into the hallway. In one quick, stiff but smooth motion, Turk straightened his left leg, bent his right knee, popped up on the toes of his right foot, and skipped forward then straightened his right leg, bent his left knee, popped up on the toes of his left foot, and skipped forward then straightened out his left leg once again, popped up on the toes of his right foot, and skipped forward.

"Turk, we have company!" Magdalene shouted over the music.

"We do?" he shouted back. "Can they dance?"

Doing the James Brown Mash Potatoes, legs wriggling in his filthy jeans like he had no bones and feet squirming, Turk skated on the hardwood floor toward the kitchen in a zigzag path, stopping in front of Miss Sarah.

When Magdalene introduced them, he asked, "You know how to do the Boogaloo, Sarah?"

Putting his own spin on it, Turk threw up his arms, shook his hips and shoulders, and bobbed his head.

"Yes, I do, but I haven't done it in a long time and . . . not like that," Miss Sarah chuckled.

"Girl, you know I'm super fine and blowin' your mind." He boogalooed over to Journey.

"That's Sarah's daughter," Magdalene told him. "She's *Kizmic's* friend."

"*Kizmic's?*" Turk looked at Magdalene, looked at Journey, then looked at Kizmic. "Since when you start playin' with girls?"

"Daddy . . ."

He bent down and shoved his face in front of Journey's. "Kizmic ain't never played with no girl. What's wrong with ya?"

"Turk!" Magdalene yelled.

Standing upright again, he beamed down at Journey. "I mean, you must be somethin' special. And I think I see what it is. Look like you got some boogaloo in ya."

"No," Journey blushed.

"Bet you do. Com'on. Lemme show ya. It's kinda like the Jerk, only with a little more funk. You know how to do the Jerk, don't ya?"

Journey shook her head.

Turk whipped around to Miss Sarah. "You ain't teach this girl how to do the Jerk? What kinda mother are you?"

Laughing, she said, "Apparently not a very good one."

"Don't pay no attention to him," Magdalene said.

"Com'ere." Giving Miss Sarah a playful scolding look, Turk pulled Journey into the hallway, saving the girl from her mother's bad parenting.

Before he could start his dance lesson, Kalaya and Plum pranced in, exuding everything it meant to be a sixteen-year-old girl—beauty, vitality, independence, style, insecurity, sexuality, curiosity, immortality, and the future.

Kalaya and Plum mesmerized Journey and Journey stunned Kalaya and Plum.

"Kizmic's friend?" Kalaya asked with baffled amusement.

Plum raised her eyebrows and turned down the corners of her mouth, as if to say, *Stranger things have happened.*

"They're beautiful," Miss Sarah said of Kalaya and Plum.

"Don't tell them that," Aunt Beana said. "They already think they're hot stuff."

"Where have you been all day?" Magdalene asked.

"Nowhere." Kalaya patted the bangs of her mushroom hairdo then brushed something off her Jordache jeans. "Just hanging around the neighborhood."

A few months ago, that question would have led to a knock-down-drag-out between Magdalene and Kalaya, but ever since her breakup with Clive, Kalaya hadn't been so moody or defiant. She and Magdalene were having actual conversations that were often punctuated by laughter. Magdalene was even coaching Kalaya more on how to run the hurdles. (It still amazed Kizmic how much her mother knew about track.) Kizmic viewed Clive's cheating on Kalaya as a blessing in disguise, for it calmed Kalaya down, which made Magdalene calm, which made their household calm.

Plum walked over to her mother. Her hair was done up in a curly puffball, circled by three rows of braids, and she was sporting a pair of Sasson jeans and a yellow t-shirt with *Black Is Beautiful* over a black fist printed on it. She wasn't as shy as she used to be, but she still expressed her feelings more in her writing than she did talking.

"What's this?" Aunt Beana asked when Plum handed her a *Right On* magazine opened to page sixty-two.

"They printed one of my poems," Plum said softly.

Aunt Beana followed Plum's finger down to the page. "My baby got published!" she screamed and turned the magazine around so everybody could see Plum's name.

"It's just a short poem," Plum remarked.

"'Just' nothin'. Girl, you know how many people want their poem in that magazine?" Turk asked.

"Read it," Magdalene said.

Aunt Beana cleared her throat. "'Today is the day I accept me for me. Look out, World. Tomorrow I'll be free.'"

Cheers and claps erupted in the house.

"Hot stuff," Journey said.

"That's my baby! I can't wait until your daddy gets home!"

Turk pulled three dollars out of his wallet and handed them to Plum. "Buy two more copies."

"Two?" Magdalene questioned.

"Yeah. I want my own so she can sign it to Uncle Turk. I'm takin' it to work tomorrow and show everybody. Matter fact, Kizmic, go get your camera."

In the living room, they all gathered around Plum as she held up the magazine.

"This way, when you get famous, you can't act like you don't know none of us," Turk joked.

Kizmic set her Ciro-flex on the new tripod she'd bought, pressed the shutter release cable attached to the timer, then jumped in the shot next to Journey and her mother.

"I love your family," Journey whispered in Kizmic's ear.

Afterward, Turk put on the Lark's record "The Jerk." By the end of it, Journey was doing the Jerk like she'd been doing it all her life, and by the time Bobby Day's "Rockin' Robin" went off, she was mimicking Turk's unorthodox moves and doing the Boogaloo.

"Didn't I tell ya you had some boogaloo in ya?" Turk said.

Standing on the staircase landing, Kizmic secretly snapped pictures of Journey, and got one special shot of her dancing so happily and free that she put a hand on top of her giant Afro and tossed her head back.

That's gonna be the first picture in the album, Kizmic smiled.

Wholly enjoying the good time Journey was having was Miss Sarah. She put Kizmic in mind of some of the women in her enchanting quilts, staring out at the beauty in the world that was staring at the beauty in them. While Journey was dancing with Turk, Kalaya, and Plum to Tyrone Davis' "Can I Change My Mind," Miss Sarah and Magdalene went into the kitchen. When they returned, Miss Sarah agreed to let Journey go along with Kizmic on her route.

CHAPTER

31

"LEUKEMIA?" Turk asked.

It was eleven o'clock and the announcer on the television in the living room asked parents if they knew where their children were. As far as Turk and Magdalene knew, their children were in bed. However, that was true for only one of them. Kizmic was at the top of the stairs, where she had been lingering on and off since "going to bed" at ten o'clock, waiting for her parents to have this conversation. She wanted to know exactly what Miss Sarah and her mother discussed.

Turk turned off the TV. "Well, why'd you let me ask what's wrong with her?"

"I didn't know you were going to say that," Magdalene said. "And nobody took it *that* way."

"How bad is it?"

All over, Kizmic remembered Journey saying. How bad is that?

"Bad enough for Sarah to worry about Journey overexerting herself walking a few blocks," Magdalene said.

That still didn't tell Kizmic how bad Journey's leukemia was. It did, however, tell her that they definitely needed to sneak and ride their bikes instead of walking, especially since she swore it wouldn't take long. In the morning, they had to finish by seven-thirty, at least up on Garrison and Linden Heights, and in the afternoon be finished by five-thirty. That way Journey would have a good half hour to play each time. That wasn't going to happen if they walked.

Journey can hold the sack of papers while I ride her on the back of my bike, Kizmic thought. That way she won't get tired and we can get done faster. We'll do her block after we finish playin'. But we can't take too long 'cause then

280

people'll start complainin' to Mr. Bollinger 'bout their newspapers bein' late.

Magdalene switched off the kitchen light and Turk put the chain on the front door.

Standing at the bottom of the stairs, Magdalene confessed, "I wasn't too particular about Kizmic being out there with Journey even with Onion. I kept thinking she won't be able to handle it if Journey gets sick."

"Kizmic's tougher than you think she is."

"I know. You should have heard her, Turk. She made me feel like she'd be okay. She made Sarah feel that way, too. That's one of the things she brought up when we went into the kitchen. She's worried about what affect Journey's illness will have on Kizmic. But we both agreed that our baby girls were going to be all right."

If all we gotta worry about is Journey's Leukemia makin' her a little tired, yeah, we'll be good, Kizmic thought.

AT FIVE O'CLOCK, Kizmic opened her diary and scratched out everything she had planned for her and Man 'n 'Em to do on Thursday, June 7. Beneath it she wrote *Journey and I will play marbles!*

She knew where they would play, too. Man's back yard, on their basketball court, which was a big patch of dirt.

Six twenty-five, Journey jumped out of her mother's burgundy, Dodge Aspen Station Wagon, ran in Kizmic's house, and fell to her knees in front of the stack of newspapers Kizmic had waiting for her.

"Paper, roll, rubberband, toss," Kizmic said, showing her the technique.

Journey watched Kizmic's hands and followed her instructions. "Paper, roll . . . rubberband, toss."

"You got it," Kizmic said.

Miss Sarah came in with an ill at ease look on her face, like she had dropped Journey off at a military installation that was sending recruits to war in Iran. Staring at Journey's inky-black hands as if they were covered in blood, she said, "I can drive you all so you won't have to walk."

Neither Kizmic nor Journey had the heart to say, *We don't wanna ride around with you.*

Turk came out of the kitchen. "Or you can go home and run around naked while you got the house to yourself."

Magdalene pushed Turk aside. "What my husband means is, you can go home, Sarah, and take some time for yourself."

"Ain't that what I said?" Turk asked.

Miss Sarah laughed. "You're right. Thank you."

Admiring Magdalene's pink headwrap, Journey said, "That looks really pretty on you."

"You think so?" Magdalene said, fussing with the bow she had tied the scarf into above her forehead. "I was thinking about wearing it on the side today." She twisted the scarf until the bow tie was on the side of her head. "What do you think?"

Journey inspected the bow's new position. "Side," she said.

"All right."

"Hold up, it's a little crooked." Turk reached for the bow and Magdalene slapped his hand away.

"Don't you touch my scarf. I'll have to do it all over again," Magdalene said.

"She actin' like I don't know how to tie a bow in a scarf," he said to Miss Sarah.

"That's because you don't," she said.

"I got bow ties," he argued.

"They're clip-ons and *I* clip them on you," Magdalene pointed out.

"Not all the time," Turk countered.

He kissed Magdalene goodbye and smiled at Kizmic and Journey. "Y'all be safe and have fun."

"We will," they said.

"Don't forget to close them curtains, Sarah," Turk said, going out the door. "Don't want none of your neighbors callin' the cops on ya."

"No, I don't," Miss Sarah said.

Aunt Beana and Onion arrived as Turk walked down the steps. He gave Aunt Beana a hug.

"Gimme five," he said to Onion. When he slapped his palm, Turk flipped his hand over. "On the black hand side."

Onion slapped the back of Turk's hand then rushed up the steps in search of what his mother told him would be there. A girl friend of Kizmic's. Magdalene called his mother and explained the situation to her. She had no objections to him helping. Said he was a big boy.

Onion said it wasn't possible. Everybody knew Kizmic didn't play with girls. So, when he walked in and saw Journey, he gawked at her like she was a two-headed martian that Kizmic had found on the playground after he, Man 'n 'Em left with Diamond, Poochie 'n 'Em. Then Onion cocked his head to the side, squished his eyebrows together, and his facial expression asked, *Who's the girl with the 'fro, what you doin' hangin' with her, and what she doin' in my spot?*

Kizmic didn't expect the last question. Did he actually call himself being jealous?

Good, Kizmic thought. Now he knows how I feel.

Journey was starstruck. She had been watching Onion, drawing cartoons of him, and looking at pictures of him. Now she was up close and personal with him.

"I didn't know his eyes were green until I found your pictures," Journey whispered to Kizmic. "I pulled out all my drawings of him and colored them green."

"So I'll see you around eight," Miss Sarah said, hovering over Journey.

"Mama, it might take a little longer."

"You have to—"

"I know. By nine o'clock."

"Eight fifteen then," Miss Sarah said.

Journey got up and kissed her mother on the cheek. "Eight-fifteen."

"Come on, Sarah," Aunt Beana said. "We have to go to work and so do they."

After all the grownups left, Onion asked, "Alright. What's really goin' on with y'all?"

Kizmic wasn't going to tell him anything. She wanted Onion to stew over Journey being in his spot the way she stewed over Poochie being in hers. But she got to thinking. She and Journey could play marbles by themselves, but all the other things Journey wanted Kizmic to take pictures of her doing were much more fun with more people. She needed Man 'n 'Em. To trick them into playing with Journey like Miss Josephine did with her would take days too long, and she figured they were too old to fall for something like that a second time. Kizmic also figured that she shouldn't have to trick them. If girls were good enough for Man 'n 'Em to go with, eat frozen cups with, have in the clubhouse, then girls were good enough to play whatever game they wanted to play with Man 'n 'Em. But she couldn't have them running off in the middle of a shoot every time Diamond, Poochie, 'n 'Em showed up. So, she thought it best to tell them the truth.

"See, I told you there was a black princess locked up in there," Onion said, jumping on board with their plan.

Journey's brown face flushed rosy red.

ONION LENT KIZMIC his bike. He never let anybody hold his bike. He'd ride people on it, like he did Kizmic the day of his photo shoot. But to hand it over . . .

Naturally, Kizmic asked, "Why?"

He said, "It'll be easier to ride her on it 'cause she can lean back on the sissybar."

Journey grabbed the handlebars, ran her hand over the banana seat then up and down the sissybar. Eyes glistening with excitement, she said, "I've never been on a bike before."

"Never?" Kizmic and Onion found that hard to believe.

"I had a tricycle when I was really little, but . . . I've been sick for a long time so . . . I haven't been able to . . ."

With his newspaper bag slung over his shoulder, Onion mounted Kizmic's bike. "Let's go."

Kizmic straddled Onion's bike. Journey stuck her left arm through the shoulder strap of the newspaper sack. Ducking her head, she carefully pulled it over her Afro and hung it on her right shoulder. She then climbed onto the back of the bike.

"You ready?" Kizmic asked.

"Uh-huh."

"Hang on."

Journey leaned back against the sissybar and put her hands on Kizmic's waist. She lifted her feet once Kizmic started pedaling. They cut down through the alley in back of the houses on Spaulding and turned left on Litchfield. As she pedaled toward Garrison, Kizmic felt a twinge of guilt for riding their bikes instead of walking like they told Miss Sarah they would do. To ease her guilt and keep one promise she made to Miss Sarah, Kizmic rode slowly. But then Journey complained.

"Why are y'all riding so slow?"

"It ain't me," Onion said. "It's Kizmic."

"You can go faster, Kizmic. I won't fall off," Journey joked.

"Yeah, com'on." Onion popped a wheelie. When his front tire hit the street again, he raced off.

With guilt riding on her shoulders, Kizmic increased her speed. Onion turned the corner at Garrison fast and sharply, sticking his right leg out to keep his balance. Kizmic turned shortly after him.

"Last one to the end is a rotten egg," Journey yelled.

"What?! I can't beat him with you on the back," Kizmic said.

"Sure you can."

"That's easy for you to say. You ain't the one pedalin'."

"I'll give you a head start," Onion said.

He hit the brakes. Kizmic kept going, pedaling faster and faster.

Looking over her shoulder, Journey said, "Here he comes."

Onion was on the other side of the solid yellow line in no time flat.

"I told you this wasn't fair," Kizmic said.

Riding with no hands, Onion said, "I gave you a thirty-second lead. Face it. You startin' to ride like a girl."

Kizmic shot him a hard look. "I got your girl."

"Oh, yeah?" he asked.

Kizmic dug in, leaned forward, and started giggin'.

"Go, go, go!" Journey pushed.

Reisterstown Road was coming up. Onion was ahead, although not by much. His bike rocked side to side as they battled it out. The muscles in

Kizmic's legs burned. As they soared down the center of that two-way street, Journey spread out her arms like they were wings and hollered, "Woooooo!" She sounded like Kizmic when she flew down concrete hill on CJ's skateboard. If it weren't for CJ and Sleepy-eyed Ted, she would have never experienced that unforgettable, incredible thrill. And if they had walked, Journey would not have experienced the unforgettable, incredible thrill of being on a bike. Kizmic's guilt slipped away. Every kid should have a concrete hill. Garrison Avenue was Journey's.

Kizmic pedaled with all her might, but with Journey's arms catching the wind, Onion took the lead. A car came up the street.

"*WHOAH!*" the three of them hollered.

Onion stomped on his breaks, Kizmic swerved over into his lane, then they rode onto the sidewalk.

"I won," she declared, leaning on the handlebars and breathing so hard her lungs now joined her legs in burning.

"Uh-uh," Onion panted. "The car came."

"So?"

"So, if I didn't stop, you and Journey woulda got hit."

"You stopped. I won," Kizmic said.

"You startin' to cheat like a girl too," Onion said.

They turned around. Onion went on the left side of the street and Kizmic and Journey took the right.

"Oh my God! This is so much fun," Journey said, tossing a newspaper on a porch.

"Again that's 'cause you ain't the one pedalin'."

"Maybe one day I will be," Journey mused.

By seven-thirty, they were done on that side except for D. Tinkle's house. He was lurking on his porch. *I can get you under the porch, set you on fire like a torch. I can get you in my house, make you squeal like a mouse.* That was the thought cloud Kizmic saw over D. Tinkle's Afro as he leered at Journey.

"Hello," he said to Journey.

"Don't say nothin' to him." Onion stepped in front of Journey and threw D. Tinkle his paper.

He caught it with one hand then laughed. Kizmic imagined another thought bubble above his giant bush: *But they can run, run, run as fast as they can. They can't catch me. I'm the boogeyman.*

"Wow! He *is* creepy," Journey said.

"You feelin' alright?" Kizmic asked, changing the subject.

"Yeah. Why?" Journey seemed annoyed by the question.

"Just wanna make sure you ready for your butt whuppin'."

They went into Man's back yard. It was seven thirty-five.

"Don't drop it!" Kizmic told Onion.

"I won't." He took off his baseball cap, lowered his head, and Kizmic put the camera strap around his neck.

"You haveta press—"

"The lever right here," Onion said. "I've seen you do it a million times. Go on. Play your stupid game."

"It's not stupid," she said.

"It's marbles. It's stupid."

Journey picked up a stick and after surveying the ground, she used it to draw a large ring in the dirt. Kizmic inspected it, kicking little rocks out and picking up twigs. She then smoothed the dirt by brushing it with the bottom of her tennis shoes.

Standing across from each other inside the ring, Journey held a black, netted bag full of Girl Scouts and Ruby Dees and Kizmic held her sack of Jelly Fish and Bumble Bees.

"Don't move." Onion grabbed the bill of his cap and turned it around backward. He looked down into the viewfinder then clicked the shutter.

Journey arranged thirteen of their marbles in a "t" shape in the center of the ring. Kizmic hadn't seen that in so long. She could have cried, she was so happy.

"Are we playing for keepsies?" Journey asked.

"Oh yeah," Kizmic answered.

The moment she kneeled on the edge of the ring and knuckled down with her Dragonfly shooter, Kizmic was in another world. One where she played marbles in *Man's* back yard. And as if that wasn't hard enough to believe, she was playing marbles in Man's back yard against a *girl*. A girl who had a wall of marbles. Granted, she didn't win them, but she *had* them. Putting a cherry marble on top of everything, the girl had some skills. With her Wasp shooter Journey made some impressive shots and won a few marbles, but she was no match for Kizmic. The years she spent playing marbles coupled with the years she spent pining away for the game were too much for a girl who mainly put marbles in jars and bottles because they looked like candy.

Clack! Clack! Clack!

Oooh! It felt so good to be playing again.

Clack-Click! Clack-Click-Click-Click!

Kizmic stretched out on her belly in the dirt, which felt as comfortable and familiar as lying in her bed.

Clack! Clack-Click! Clack-Click-Click-Click! Clack! Clack! Clack!

Game one done and won.

Clack! Clack! Clack! Clack! Clack-Click-Click!

Kizmic was knocking marbles out of the ring like she'd never stopped playing against CJ and Sleepy-eyed Ted under their tree in the park.

Clack-Click-Click! Clack! Clack! Clack! Clack! Clack!

Game two done and won.

Clack! Clack-Click-Click-Click! Clack-Click-Click-Click-Click! Clack!

Journey wasn't upset about losing nair-one of her marbles. She was just happy to be playing.

Clack-Clickety-Clickety-Clickety! Clack! Clack! Clack!

Game three done, and Kizmic was twenty-one marbles richer.

"Wow!" Journey said. "You really love playing marbles."

Onion came over to them. "Now I know why you're so good at skully."

"Did you get some good shots?" Kizmic asked him.

"Yeah," he said. "I think you'll like 'em."

"What y'all doin'?" Man stuck his head out an upstairs window.

Onion gave Kizmic her camera. "Man, they playin' marbles!"

"Marbles?! In my yard?" he asked, as if it were the most offensive thing that could have taken place there.

"Uh-huh! I told them not to come in here," Onion claimed. "But Kizmic said forget you."

Kizmic said what?! Kizmic thought, head flinching back slightly.

"Said she can play marbles wherever she wanna play marbles."

"What?!" Man bellowed.

Onion turned around, laughing so hard he could barely talk.

"Who's that girl?" Man shouted.

Collecting himself, Onion said, "I'on't know." He cupped his hands around his mouth and shouted, "But she said skully was STUPID!"

"*STUPID?!*" Man snatched himself out of the window.

Onion ran and grabbed his sack. "Com'on," he laughed.

Kizmic and Journey scooped up the marbles and the three of them booked out of Man's yard, down the alley, and across Belvedere. They didn't stop running until they reached the bend on Beaufort.

Kizmic punched Onion on the arm. "You better tell Man we ain't say none of that stuff."

"Maybe I will, maybe I won't."

Kizmic had Journey hold her Ciro-flex then put Onion in a headlock. "Tell him," she demanded.

"Alright," he chuckled.

"What's skully?" Journey asked.

Kizmic and Onion looked at each other and fell out laughing. As they came out of the bend, they spotted Miss Sarah on the porch. Journey slipped Kizmic's Ciroflex in the newspaper bag.

"Here you go, papergirl." Onion handed Journey her newspaper. "I'll deliver the rest."

"Thanks," Kizmic smiled.

"For what?" he smiled back.

For being so nice, Kizmic said to herself. At the end of the summer, she would say it to him.

"Hey, Miss Sarah," Onion waved.

Miss Sarah waved back. She was sitting on the glider bench. Her feet were planted on the porch and she was pushing the bench back and forth, back and forth at a steady, nervous pace. It hadn't had a workout like that in years, Kizmic bet.

"You're supposed to be naked," Journey said to her mother.

The wrinkles covering Miss Sarah's brow and the way she repeatedly stroked her neck said she had spent the last hour and a half worrying herself almost to death about Journey. Kizmic stood tall and proud because not only did she bring Miss Sarah her daughter back safe and sound, she brought her back cracking jokes.

"So, how was it?" Miss Sarah asked.

"Awesome," Journey said.

"That's good. The walking wasn't too much?"

"Nope. I didn't get tired at all."

Miss Sarah looked at Kizmic. "What about sick?"

"No, ma'am," Kizmic said. "She didn't get sick."

She almost got hit by a car, Kizmic laughed to herself. But she didn't get sick.

"So you're feeling okay?"

"I feel great, Mama."

Miss Sarah breathed a heavy sigh of relief. "Okay. You have to get something on your stomach. Kizmic, have you eaten breakfast yet?"

"No."

"Well, you're welcome to have breakfast with us, but Journey has to follow a special diet, and it's pretty bland."

Bland didn't sound like the bowl of sweet Captain Crunch Kizmic had her lips all set for, but Journey wanted her to stay, and to tell the truth, she wanted to go back inside and look at Miss Sarah's quilts.

Breakfast consisted of dry toast, a small bowl of oatmeal, half a grapefruit, a glass of milk, and a glass of orange juice. After they'd eaten, Kizmic walked around admiring the quilts. It was like being in a museum.

"You can touch it if you want to," Miss Sarah said, reading Kizmic's mind.

There was movement in the fabric canvas Kizmic discovered as she put her hand on the shoulder of one of the women strolling through Lexington Market. On a wall in the living room she felt a thunderous movement on a quilt that pictured five black jockeys racing in the 1902 Kentucky Derby. The detail was such that Kizmic could see the dirt the horses' hooves kicked up as they galloped head-to-head into the stretch. In the dining room and in the hallway, quilts adorned the walls with serene scenes of life-sized dogs lying in a grassy field, dazzling flowers as tall as Kizmic leaning in the wind, summer, winter, spring, and fall sunsets boldly coloring a blue sky. Some were tall, some were wide, some were big, some were small as patches over a hole in a pair of jeans. All were phenomenal to Kizmic.

"How did you make these?" Kizmic's face wrinkled with marvel.

"Can I show her, Mama?" Journey said.

Miss Sarah nodded. "Sure."

Up the short hallway on the second floor, Journey opened the door to a second bedroom.

This room was more somber than the others as light struggled to penetrate the heavy curtains covering its two windows. Taped all over the right wall were quilt designs sketched on graph paper using colored pencils. The wall to the left had three thread racks that held mixed colors of spool and cone thread. Following those was a ruler rack with yardsticks, tape measures, and quilting rulers of several shapes and sizes. Against the far wall was a bookcase jammed packed with sewing, quilting, embroidery, and knitting books and magazines. Shelves piled with colored wool, cotton, silk, polyester, denim, leather, cordurory, African print, and mudcloth fabrics took up the rest of the wall. Near the closet was an ironing board. A big, white cutting table with a swing arm lamp attached to it was across from the windows. Occupying the center of the room was a large wooden table with a swing arm lamp and two Singer sewing machines on it.

One machine was off to the side. The other had a quilt held together with safety pins sitting under its presser foot. Miss Sarah was in the middle of sewing it together when something interrupted her.

Journey took Kizmic to the tower room on that floor, where Miss Sarah's museum illustrations hung on rows of quilt ladders.

"My grandmother owns a store up in Philly," Journey said. "It's called Matilda's Fabrics. She named it after my great-grandmother because she was the one who taught them how to sew. She made that quilt on the loveseat in the sunroom. It's almost eighty years old. People come from all over to buy my mother's quilts. We usually drive up twice a month to deliver them but . . . we've been kind of busy the last few months."

"These should be in a museum," Kizmic said.

Miss Sarah walked into the room. "My grandmother would disagree with you. She made quilts to keep her family warm, not hang on the walls. That's what she would say if she were still with us."

Kizmic would have been content to spend the rest of the morning looking at those quilts, but Miss Sarah wanted Journey to get some rest before the afternoon delivery and Kizmic had some things she had to take care of.

First, she went to Rite Aid and bought four rolls of film and put in the roll she'd taken of Journey to be developed. At one o'clock Kizmic went to talk to Man 'n 'Em about Journey. Fatboy was in his yard cleaning his pigeon coop by himself.

Kizmic scooped up a handful of seeds from the feed bucket. She held out her palm and a few pigeons flocked around her and started eating. "Where everybody at?"

"Man went to Lucille Park to play basketball," he said, using a paint scraper to remove feathers and dried poop from the floor of the coop. "Peanut's up at C.C. Jackson doin' karate."

"Karate? When he start doin' that?" Kizmic asked.

"He signed up last week." Fatboy scraped the poop and feathers into a bucket. "Redtop's up the alley. I don't know where everybody else is."

This was so weird. They all usually helped to take care of the pigeons, but everybody was off doing their own thing, and Fatboy was enjoying his time alone with his birds. Kizmic felt lost. Things between them were changing . . . fast.

She grabbed some more seeds and while the pigeons feasted, she told Fatboy about her plan.

"Is she cute?" he asked, replacing the wooden grate over the coop's floor.

"What's that got to do with anything?"

He hunched his shoulders but still waited for an answer.

Kizmic flung her head back in exasperation and looked up at the sky. "Yeah, she's cute."

"Okay then."

Kizmic went home to get her bike. She couldn't believe she had to actually track down Man 'n 'Em. Things between them weren't changing. They *had* changed.

Steebo wasn't hard to find. He was in the Fish Store. Mr Charlie had squeezed a Space Invaders arcade game inside and Steebo was obsessed with saving the world from aliens. He spent hours hogging the game, dropping every quarter he begged his mother and sisters for into the machine.

When Kizmic came in, he had fourteen of the fifty-five aliens left to destroy, almost none of the four barriers to shield his laser cannon from the aliens' missiles, and one extra ship. He never once took his squinty eyes off the video screen as Kizmic told him about Journey.

Rapidly hitting the fire button, Steebo muttered, "Yeah. Okay," to get Kizmic out of his ear so he could focus on shooting the red mystery point alien spaceship that suddenly started flying across the top of the screen.

She found Babyfrog in his back yard practicing football drills with his older brother, who was on break from Bowie State University, where he played running back for the Bulldogs.

"Can she play football?" he asked. "Like you, I mean."

"A little bit."

He threw the football to his brother. "Well, you can count me in."

Around the corner, Meatball was sitting on his front steps secretly listening to *Wanted: Richard Pryor Live In Concert* on his Lucky Radio Cassette Recorder.

Taking off the headphones, Meatball asked, "Is she cute?"

"Very cute," Kizmic assured him.

"Alright." He put his headphones back over his ears, rewound the tape, and started rolling about whatever joke Richard Pryor told.

Kizmic rode up the alley by Onion's house. It came to a dead end at a bank of old garages that boys used as a giant ramp. Several boys were there doing tricks on their bikes.

"Here he comes," one of them said.

Redtop rode his Huffy fast across the flat, tar rooftops. When he got to the last one, he made a sharp right turn and flew off the edge like one of Fatboy's pigeons. His wheels spun as he turned the bike completely around in mid-air before crash landing on the ground to the cheers and applause of the other guys.

Ignoring the rip in the left leg of his jeans and bleeding cut on his knee, Redtop checked his front wheel to make sure it wasn't bent. "Long as she cute," he said after Kizmic told him about Journey.

Inside C.C. Jackson, Kizmic stood in the doorway of the small martial arts room. The instructor, a lanky but fit black man, dressed in a white karate jacket and trousers with a black belt around his waist, stood in the middle of the room surrounded by eight teenaged, black boys wearing white karate jackets, trousers, and white belts. He walked barefoot inside the circle, emitting these powerful yells. The boys repeated the instructor's yells as they threw punches in synch. Peanut was in a corner fighting with his belt, which he was having a difficult time tying.

"What girl?" Peanut gritted his teeth in frustration as the belt once again unraveled and fell on top of his bare feet.

Kizmic picked up the belt and tied it correctly around his waist as she told him about Journey.

He stared at the belt. "How'd you—never mind. Okay, yeah. I'll play with her," he said, then joined the rest of the class.

Just as Fatboy had said, Man was playing basketball at Lucille Park. He was the tallest guy on the court in his back yard. Here, he was short. But he showed them that he wasn't a scrub by scoring even when the older, bigger boys played dirty.

Kizmic whistled to get his attention. As his team hustled down court, he ran over to the fence.

"That girl who was talkin' junk about skully?" he puffed.

"Onion was jokin' about her sayin' that stuff," Kizmic swore.

"Alright. She looked kinda cute, anyway," he said and ran back into the game.

MISS SARAH DROPPED JOURNEY off at Kizmic's house at ten minutes to four and said she expected her home by six. Kizmic, Onion, and Journey completed the route with lightning speed. By five fifteen, they headed up the alley to Steebo's yard.

Man was dribbling his basketball while listening to Meatball, who was leaning against the clubhouse telling corny jokes from a book entitled *100 Pet Jokes*. Redtop was on the clubhouse roof practicing a new dance called Popping that looked something like the robot, only its smooth, mechanical movements ticked fast like the second hand of a clock. Fatboy sat in the clubhouse's doorway engrossed in a *Friday Foster* comic book and snacking on a pack of Butter Crunch cookies. Inside, Babyfrog was sticking leaves in a mason jar full of lightning bugs, Steebo was sitting on the floor, squinty eyes glued to the small screen of his hand-held, electronic football game, thumbs rapidly pressing the arrow keys as he tried to maneuver the tiny, red blip into the end zone. And Peanut was at the table drawing Storm from an X-Men comic book.

With everyone's legs, arms, and feet growing, all of them couldn't fit in the clubhouse as comfortably as they used to. Man had gotten so tall that he had to keep his head bowed in order to stand in there. When they were all packed inside, it was difficult to move about without bumping into one another, and since Man 'n 'Em didn't want to get punched in the face by Kizmic for accidentally (for real this time) brushing up against her, some of them hung outside to cut down on any confusion.

Hanging out with Man 'n 'Em was a dream come true for Journey, especially when Man, Redtop, Meatball, and Fatboy started giving her googly eyes because they saw that Kizmic hadn't lied about Journey being cute. But playing marbles with Man 'n 'Em was a dream come true for Kizmic. It was like the last piece of a 2000 piece jigsaw puzzle that formed the perfect picture of their friendship.

When Man 'n 'Em agreed to play marbles, they did so believing that they would play a few minutes then introduce Journey to a real game, like skully. They never thought marbles was something they had to learn *and* certainly never imagined they'd be interested in actually knowing how to play. They never thought they would care which marbles they played with until Man became captivated by the flaming yellow, black, and orange bands of the Tiger's Eyes, Steebo by the beautiful green and black swirls of the Green Hornets, Babyfrog by the crisp blue, yellow, and white ribbons of the Popeyes, Onion by the layers of vibrant red, blue, yellow, and white swirls of the Onion Skins, Redtop by the dazzling red bands of the Superman Corkscrews, Meatball by the creepy splatter of red over green on the Zombies, Fatboy by the brilliant red and aqua blue swooshes of the Seahorses, and Peanut by the bright yellow and black ribbons of the Bumblebees. Not to mention the sheer coolness of Kizmic having a shooter made especially for her and *named* after her.

Man 'n 'Em never thought they'd be intensely eyeballing every shot; laughing at Meatball for missing Fatboy's marble, which was sitting right in front of his thumb; teasing Fatboy for losing his turn when his marble slipped from his thumb and forefinger; cheering when Journey missed Steebo's marble by a mile; arguing about whether Redtop's marble was on the line or not; crying out "OOOOOOH!" when Kizmic hit two of Babyfrog's marbles *and* his shooter out of the ring; jumping up in premature victory when Onion hit Kizmic's marble out; spinning around in frustration when Peanut missed his shot; throwing up their arms in defeat when Kizmic knocked Man's marble out for the win; then realizing that marbles was the reason Kizmic played skully so well.

At quarter to six, Kizmic—with the help of Onion, who took pictures when it was her turn to play—had captured nine great shots that retold the story her great-grandfather told with the black-and-white photo he'd taken of those boys playing marbles, only Kizmic's version included two girls. Funny thing was, Journey started out as the center of the story, but she ended up not being the focus. By the fifth shot, Kizmic was telling the story of *that* day when *that* group of kids kneeled and squatted in the dirt to play marbles. *That* was the story Kizmic set out to tell Miss Sarah every time she aimed her Ciroflex at Journey. That was a story she was sure Miss Sarah would hold and look at over and over again. It was a story Kizmic was sure she would hold and look at over and over again herself.

CHAPTER

32

HEAVEN WAS PLAYING MARBLES with your friends. It had to be, because that's how Kizmic felt the past few days—like she was in *puredee heaven*.

Friday and Saturday morning, she, Onion, and Journey rolled through the route in no time, then played marbles in Man's back yard. After the four o'clock delivery, Kizmic played marbles with Journey and Man 'n 'Em. In between, she enjoyed breakfast with Journey and Miss Sarah, who talked to her about quilting. She never knew that love and history could be woven out of pieces of fabric. Miss Sarah also let Kizmic stay a whole half hour after breakfast, during which she and Journey hung out in her room playing with her magnificent marble collection.

Shoot! Her summer was turning out to be way better than it started. But come Sunday morning, Kizmic and Onion couldn't play marbles, nor could she stay for breakfast.

"Why not?" Journey asked.

They were rolling up newspapers in the hallway and in the eye of the frenzied church-going ritual that took place in Kizmic's house every Sunday morning. Magdalene hated being late for church more than she hated missing church.

"Ya get to work on time, don't ya?" Reverend Douglas I. Miles was apt to ask from the pulpit. "Ya get to the bar on time, don't ya? Ya get to the Colts game on time, don't ya? Ya get to the disco on time, don't ya?" He'd do a little jig when he said that one.

Anybody that was two minutes late for service got the side-eye from Reverend Miles and everyone else in the congregation, if only in their guilt-ridden imaginations.

"You get anywhere ya wanna go a hour before you 'posed to be there. But ya wanna operate on CP time when it comes to gettin' to the Lord's House. Come stragglin' in like you doin' God a favor by showin' up. You ain't doin' God no favor. Remember, He *died* for *you*! You ain't die for Him. And as late as some of y'all roll up in here, He be done died of natural causes by the time you got around to dyin' for Him."

"AMEN, REVEREND!" and "PREACH! PREACH!" the congregation shouted.

Magdalene had never been and was never going to be the focus of that sermon. So, at the ungodly hour of five-thirty, the alarm clock on the nightstand in Turk and Magdalene's room sounded, waking Magdalene, who ran around like the Tasmanian Devil—showering, waking Kizmic up at six, (before Kizmic had the route, she would pull the covers over her head and pray her mother wouldn't make her go to church) whizzing down to the kitchen to cook breakfast, listening to gospel music on WWIN-AM, whirling back upstairs to wake Turk at six-thirty and six-forty and six-fifty.

"Church," Journey said, like she didn't know people still went. "That's why your hair is always pressed on Sundays."

Yep. It was one of the excuses her mother came up with to try to stop her from doing the route. "You're going to sweat your hair out," she claimed.

"Not if you put it in a puff ball," Kizmic countered. "You can't sweat out a puff ball. It's already puffy."

Magdalene burled back down to the kitchen to fry bacon and told Kizmic not to take all day when she, Onion, and Journey headed out the door.

From the seat of Onion's bike, Journey tossed a newspaper onto a porch. "Can I come?"

"To church?" The bike wobbled as Kizmic snapped a look back at Journey that asked if she was crazy. She didn't know any kid that *wanted* to go to church. Especially not in the summer, because they still had to go to Sunday school, which Kizmic didn't think was fair. Regular school was out, so why wasn't Sunday School? And every Sunday school teacher she ever had always made them stand up and read those long passages from the Bible with long names that nobody, not even the teacher sometimes, could pronounce. And Journey was volunteering to go to church?

"We haven't been in a long time," she said. "I think it will be good for my mother."

"I guess you can come, if you really want to," Kizmic said, pedaling.

Kizmic didn't have a chance to say anything about Journey and Miss Sarah coming to church, because when she came in at eight-fifteen, she was immediately swept back up in the tornado that was her mother, who yelled "Girl, get in here and eat," then hurried everyone upstairs at eight-thirty to put on the church clothes that had been ironed and laid out the night before, do her makeup, comb her hair, touch up Kizmic's hair, told Kalaya, "I suggest—and it's only a suggestion, you can do what you want—but I suggest you get a move on," sprayed on perfume, took the chicken out to thaw for dinner, checked Turk's wallet to make sure they had money for the Missions Offering and their tithes, reminded Kizmic to grab the church bag that had their Bibles, rushed everyone out of the house, answered the phone that rang just as she was closing the door, hopped in the car and said, "Sarah and Journey are going to meet us at church this morning."

THE SUN WAS GLORIOUS in a blue, cloudless sky and at ten forty-five the day was only twelve degrees shy of its ninety-seven-degree high. Faithful members of Brown's were arriving from all over the city, taking up every available parking space along Fulton and Walbrook avenues. A flowing crowd of blues, pinks, blacks, grays, whites, they whisked down the sunbaked sidewalk in their Sunday bests. The men were looking and feeling dignified and handsome in their two and three-piece suits, razor-sharp creases up and down the front and back of their slacks, spit-shined dress shoes, charming neckties and bow ties around their starched shirt collars, silk handkerchiefs tucked in the pockets of their jackets, beards and mustaches trimmed, Fedora hats on their fresh haircuts, gold and silver rings, tie clips, and cufflinks sparkling. The women were looking and feeling fine and sanctified in their one and two-piece dress and skirt suits, sheer pantyhose on their brown legs, high heels on their feet, tall, pillbox, and wide-brimmed hats with ornate mesh, bows, flowers, and feathers decorating their pressed, permed, and natural hairdos, makeup above reproach, fingernail polish flawless, gold and silver rings, earrings, necklaces, brooches, and bracelets shining to the heavens. Little girls skipped about in darling dresses with bows, lace, ruffles, and ribbons, tights, bobbysocks, and Mary Jane shoes. Little boys scampered around in miniature versions of the men's suits. And teenaged boys and girls strolled along wearing scaled down but stylish versions of their parents' outfits.

They came in numbers too many, it seemed, for Brown's stone walls to hold. However, the walls had no trouble accommodating the worshippers. What they couldn't contain, or rather, what they weren't designed to contain was the call-to-worship music that piped out of the church as Henry Patrick, the church musician, played "May The Lord God Bless You Real Good" on the organ. Flocking inside through two glass doors, the parishioners were welcomed by the ushers, who were handing out church bulletins and Hurtt Funeral Home fans.

On the second row of pews in the center of the sanctuary sat Kizmic, wearing a modest, lavender, knee-length dress, black stockings, and flat, black shoes. Now that she was older, Magdalene no longer made her sit with Miss Mildred or some other adult that wouldn't let her have any fun during service. She got to sit near Kalaya and Plum, who always sat on the back row with the other teenagers. She didn't have much fun with them, though, because all they did was pass notes and exchange goofy looks with the boys. But Magdalene wanted Miss Sarah and Journey to have a good seat, so she made Kizmic sit as close to the pulpit as possible and hold a place for them. Pop Evans was sitting on the other end, holding his ebony wood walking cane that had a hand clutching the round handle. He was a tall, thin, dark-skinned man in his sixties, who always wore double breasted pinstriped suits, two-tone, wingtip shoes, and a top-hat. Kizmic liked Pop Evans, but she couldn't help laughing at him, because whenever he got happy, he shouted "Jesus," but it sounded like he said "Chees-its!"

At ten fifty-five, Aunt Beana escorted Miss Sarah and Journey up the aisle. Journey was looking angelic in a pretty, yellow dress, white stockings, black Buster Brown shoes, and, of course, her Afro wig.

"I didn't know you wore dresses," Journey smiled.

"I don't, but I can't wear jeans to church."

"You look so pretty. Not that you don't look pretty all the time, but . . . I didn't even know that was you."

Kizmic blushed and laughed at the same time.

Precisely at eleven o'clock, the choir, adorned in their magnificent blue and white robes, marched valiantly up the two aisles in time with the organ, clapping, striking tambourines, and singing "I'm On The Battlefield For My Lord." Those young, middle aged, and old, black men and women sang from their hearts and souls with a jubilant, fiery belief that they could whup the devil with their voices alone.

Fearlessly leading the choir into battle were ushers Aunt Beana and Sista Dorothy. Heads held high with white hats bobby-pinned to their hair, shiny gold usher's badges pinned to the jackets of their long-sleeved dress suits, white gloves on their hands, white, nylon pantyhose on their legs, and white polished shoes on their feet, Aunt Beana and Sista Dorothy didn't tramp or stomp; they marched, not only in sync with the jingles of the tambourines, the chords of the organ, the steps of the choir, but also in sync with each other. Eyes straight ahead, left hands in fists against the small of their backs, right arms swinging at their sides, the two women stepped. They were on a mission from God to get His warriors to the choir loft so they could minister to the congregation, and they were going to march over anybody that got in their way.

Journey was enthralled by it all, the procession of the choir, the invocation, opening hymn, which was "Pass Me Not, O Gentle Savior," scripture lesson, which was the third chapter of "Acts," verses one through ten, and the general prayer and chant. She had taken particular interest in Reverend Miles, who was sitting attentively in his tall, red oak chair, cloaked in his long, red and black robe that looked more like a beautiful cloth suit of armor. Clean-shaven, save the neatly groomed mustache above his full lips, Reverend Miles was a good-looking man, medium build, brown-skinned with a small bush and eyeglasses. Journey wanted to know everything about him from his family (Kizmic pointed out his teenage son sitting in the back with Kalaya and Plum, his younger son sitting a row ahead of them between his grandmothers, and his lovely wife, who was in the choir loft sitting behind her sister-in-law and beside her sister) to how well he delivered a sermon.

"Can he preach?" Journey asked.

Again, Kizmic gave Journey a strange look. What kind of question was that for a kid to ask? Most kids didn't care if a preacher could preach. They only cared about how long he preached, and Reverend Miles preached *forever*. Even so, ask any kid in Brown's what Reverend Miles preached about, and they would be hard press to answer one word, other than Jesus, of course. And that was because every preacher's sermon was about Jesus dying for everyone's sins.

When Kizmic was seven, she asked her mother, "If Jesus died for our sins, why do we have to be good?"

"Why wouldn't you want to be good?" Magdalene asked.

"I do, but just in case I lie or somethin'."

"Why would you lie or somethin'?"

Awww, forget it, Kizmic thought.

Kizmic didn't pay any attention to Reverend Miles' sermon until he got way up on the mountain top, as the grownups liked to say. That's when he would shout, "They took Him out to a hill called Calvary. They hung Him high and they stretched Him wide. He died for you and he died for me. But early on a Sunday morning, He got up with all power in his hands." And then Reverend Miles would do this sing-songy thing that Kizmic loved but couldn't describe.

She told Journey, "You'll see."

Journey sat back in her seat, waiting with anticipation and keeping a close watch over her mother.

Miss Sarah's silver, slingback heels were planted solidly on the carpeted floor, like she was trying to push the pew back and forth the way she did the glider bench on her front porch when she was full of nerves waiting for Journey to come home. She tugged on the hem of her silver skirt as if the old women of the church were giving her the eye because it was too short. And she seemed to be unreasonably hot. It was warm in the church, but Miss Sarah fanned herself like it was a hundred degrees in there. She had whipped the poor little fan back and forth so hard and fast that the thin piece of cardboard went limp.

Kizmic had never seen anybody so uncomfortable in church before. She thought Miss Sarah was going to run out of there any second. Journey whispered something in her mother's ear that made Miss Sarah close her eyes, inhale deeply, then exhale, "I know."

Journey gently took the fan from Miss Sarah, kissed her on the cheek, then put her mother's hand in both of hers. As she comforted her mother, the choir rose to sing a selection. Recognizing the song from the first few organ chords, the congregation began to shout and Miss Sarah opened her eyes.

It was a slow, old-timey spiritual that they didn't sing often (Kizmic could recall only hearing it three other times in her life), but when they did, the honor of singing the lead was always given to one of the old folks, reason being they had been around long enough to have gone through some things and therefore could sing the song with the credibility, power, and faith that could only come from those who had witnessed God's grace and mercy for themselves.

That Sunday, the honor was bestowed upon Mother Abigail Humphrey. Standing no more than four feet, Mother Abigail was a round, top-heavy woman with white hair that she styled using a straightening comb and curling iron. Her almond colored skin was thin, soft, and wrinkly. The wrinkles on her face were long and deep, like the rings etched in the trunk of a tree that told how old it was. Mother Abigail's wrinkles said she had to be ninety-five if she was a day. Her brown eyes were warm, watery, and alert, despite the heavy bags sagging under them. Looking divine in her raspberry and off-white top and skirt and low, matching pumps, Mother Abigail slowly got up from the first pew, and with shaky hands, took the microphone Sista Dorothy handed to her. Raspberry hat on her head tilted slightly to the right, she faced the congregation, and then in a low tone, Mother Abigail sang "Come On In My Room."

Mother Abigail had an old voice. Not just in terms of age, but also in generations. When she sang, you had the sense that you were hearing her mother's voice, her grandmother's voice, her great-grandmother's voice, her great-great-grandmother's voice, and her great-great-great-grandmother's voice embodied in her voice. It was like a family tree of voices and made Kizmic think of the family tree inside her grandfather's Bible. With all those voices helping her out, Kizmic thought Mother Abigail would sing a little better than she did. To be honest, she sounded like an old rickety rocking chair.

Miss Sarah, however, was captivated by Mother Abigail's creaking testimony. It relaxed the tension in her legs and she began tapping her foot. Journey squeezed her mother's hand.

Miss Sarah turned to her and said, "My grandmother sang this song to me when I was your age. She was really sick. Couldn't get out of bed. My mother had just finished giving her a sponge bath, and I was hanging outside her bedroom door. When she saw me, she said, 'Com'ere, li'l gal.' I wouldn't at first. I was scared. My grandmother pushed herself up in bed. The quilt that's on the back of the loveseat in the sunroom was draped on her shoulders. She smiled, stretched out her arms, and started singing this song. Her voice was weak from her illness. I thought she was moaning and humming at the same time. Then she sang, "Sa-ah-ruh," so sweetly that I couldn't *not* go in her room. My grandmother pulled me close to her bosom, rocked me like I was an infant, and sang in my ear. At times she struggled to fill her lungs with enough air to push out the lyrics, so she had me fill in when her voice gave out."

Miss Sarah wrapped her left arm around her waist. "My grandmother left us the next day and every time I tried to cry, I heard her singing that song and her voice wiped away my tears."

She looked back up at Mother Abigail and tapped both feet as the old woman sang to the glory of God.

"Sing it for me, Mama," Journey said.

Miss Sarah stared lovingly at her daughter. "I don't think I can do that, baby."

Staring just as lovingly into her mother's weary eyes, Journey said, "Please."

Miss Sarah shook her head and smiled with only the left side of her mouth. She then closed her eyes. The internal struggle was on her face. It twitched, like she had a nervous tic, and her eyes flittered under their lids as if she were having a bad dream. After a few moments, Miss Sarah timidly began to sing. Not a whole verse, though. Mother Abigail's voice filled in where her voice gave out.

Having made it through the first chorus, Miss Sarah opened her eyes and sang the lyrics behind Mother Abigail, like a child following her mother's footsteps. She had a melodic voice that more than likely had traces of her mother and grandmother's voices.

Journey smiled and nodded her head to the rhythm of her mother and Mother Abigail's voices. Tenderly, Miss Sarah patted Journey's hand, then rose to her feet. Journey stood with her. The two of them were so absorbed in the song that neither noticed when Kizmic grabbed the church bag and slipped away.

She had smuggled her Ciro-flex out of the house inside the bag. She wasn't sure what she would take pictures of Journey doing, but some of her best photographs were taken when she didn't think there was anything to take pictures of. So, she'd rather have her camera and end up not taking a shot because nothing noteworthy happened than to end up missing the shot of a lifetime because she didn't bother to bring it.

Kizmic quickly made her way to the back of the church and up the far right aisle. She waited several moments before pulling out her camera, because she didn't want anybody to see her taking pictures, especially not Miss Sarah. The grownups clapped and sang with Mother Abigail about going in a room where Jesus healed all their ailments, and the young kids and teenagers preoccupied themselves with one another. Reverend Miles was standing and rocking side-to-side as he pumped his fists, striking the emotional chords Mother Abigail was hitting and Mr. Patrick was playing. No one seemed to see Kizmic. It was as if she were invisible.

Taking full advantage of her invisibility, Kizmic pulled her camera out of the bag, snapped open the viewing hood, and turned the focus knob until Journey and Miss Sarah were sharply in frame. They were both wrapped in each other's arms with the most heavenly smiles on their faces as they sang.

Kizmic took a couple pictures of them from that angle, focusing on Miss Sarah. Then she hustled up the far left aisle and took two more pictures of them, focusing on Journey. Kizmic had the shots she wanted, but she couldn't stop shooting. An overwhelming feeling welled up inside her, like for the first time in her life, she had gotten caught up in the Holy Spirit herself, but instead of having the impulse to dance, shout, or run around the church, she wanted to photograph everything.

She snapped pictures of Kalaya and Plum with their heads together reading a note from one of the boys sitting next to them, and of the little kids playing Hangman and Tic-Tac-Toe. Kizmic panned her camera and photographed her father, mother, Uncle Monty, and Aunt Beana, capturing that certain serious stance they had when they were in church, that certain reverence on their faces when they were praising the Lord.

Kizmic looked in the viewfinder to take a wide shot, and as she stared at the reverse image on the screen of everyone gettin' happy, she came to understand that it didn't matter that Mother Abigail couldn't carry a tune. What mattered was how she made people feel. And Mother Abigail sang those simple lyrics in a way that testified to the goodness of the Lord and how he brought her through all her heartaches and pains, letdowns and struggles, and thus made people feel He could do the same for them if they trusted in Him.

Mother Abigail gave the mic back to Sista Dorothy and returned to her seat.

Reverend Miles stepped up to the podium. "How many of y'all know Him to be a doctor in the sickroom?"

He had a deep voice with a cadence that made him sound a little like Dr. Martin Luther King. That's what Kizmic thought, anyway.

Roars of "YES!" and "AMEN!" erupted.

"How many of you have laid upon a bed of affliction?"

"LISTEN!" someone shouted.

"Have had doctors walk out on you, shaking their heads in despair over your condition?"

"SAY SO, PASTOR!"

"But when *they* walked out,"

"WELL!"

"*God* walked in."

"YES, HE DID!" Mrs. Miles shouted.

"And He raised you up."

"YES!"

"Turned you around!"

"HALLELUJAH!"

"Put runnin' in your feet!"

"PREACH!"

"And clappin' in your hands!"

"MAKE IT PLAIN, PASTOR! MAKE IT PLAIN!"

Fans were waving, hands were shaking like tambourines, heads were nodding and turning left to right, like no one would ever understand how good the Lord had been to them. Accompanying the shoutin' hallelujah, good time was the one-man orchestra, Mr. Patrick. It was fascinating to Kizmic that he could not only play one keyboard but two simultaneously. She photographed his long, square fingers punching the organ keys and producing notes that sounded like he was beating the drums, crashing cymbals, strumming a base, and blowing a flute. Before she knew it, Kizmic had shot all twelve exposures and had to hurry to reload her camera.

Reverend Miles started to do that sing-songy thing that Kizmic hadn't heard any other preacher be able to do in the dynamic, spiritual, and inspirational way Reverend Miles did.

"*In your dark-est hour. . .*" Reverend Miles sang.

"WHAT YOU SAY, PASTOR?!"

Gripping the sacred desk with both hands, he repeated, "*I said in your dark-est hour.*"

"UH-HUH!"

"*Jesus will stop by!*"

"YES HE WILL!"

"*Jesus!*"

"CHEES-ITS!"

"*Mary's baby!*"

Using whole notes, half notes, and major triads, Mr. Patrick mimicked Reverend Miles' words.

"GO 'HEAD!"

He turned sideways and leaned on his left elbow. "*Jesus!*"

"LORD HAVE MERCY!" shouted Mrs. Miles.

"*The lily of the valleys!*"

"YES SIR!"

He turned and leaned on his right elbow. "*Jesus!*"

"YEAH!"

"The Bright Morn-in' Star!"

"GO ON 'N PREACH!"

"Can I get a witness?!"

"YEAH!"

The grownups clapped and stomped. Mr. Patrick's fingers rolled up and down the keys and his cinnamon brown Stacy Adams loafers danced on the pedals. He'd testified once that he was a country boy with city ways and loved playing jazz music on the piano. At twenty, he left the little place in Virginia called Amelia, where he grew up and went to the big city to play jazz. Twenty-three years later, Mr. Patrick said he found the Lord inside a club in Chicago. Halfway through his set, he gave up jazz to use his talent to glorify God. Feeling the Holy Spirit in the choir loft, Mr. Patrick was making the joy bells ring in a way that country boy with city ways never could playing jazz.

Reverend Miles stood straight up. "Is He alright?"

"YEAH!"

He took off his glasses and opened his arms. "Is He alright?!"

"YEAH!"

The heavy sleeves of his robe were flapping. The rhythmical fervor in Reverend Miles' voice and Mr. Patrick's musical fingers backing up every word he spoke didn't permit anyone inside that place to keep still or keep quiet. If they couldn't do anything but rock, they rocked. Kizmic took pictures.

"Is The Lord Alright?!"

"YEAH!"

"Say Yeah!"

"YEAH!"

"Say YEAH!"

"YEAH!"

"Say YEAH!"

"YEAH!"

"Say *YEEEEEAAAAAAAA-AHH!*"

"YEAH!"

"AMEN!"

"THANK YA JESUS!"

"THANK YA!"

"HALLELUJAH!"

"CHEES-ITS!"

Filled with the Holy Ghost, people fell out in the pews while a few men and women did the Happy Dance in the aisles. Kizmic often marveled at how those women, no matter how heavy they were, could jump up and down in those pumps and not fall or break a heel. Hugging her mother, Journey smiled euphorically at Reverend Miles. That's what Kizmic couldn't describe for Journey. She had to see it, hear it, and feel it for herself. As for Kizmic, she was able to use the last exposure on the second roll of film to capture Reverend Miles doing that sing-songy thing.

"THAT'S ALRIGHT!"

"Whatever you're goin' through," Reverend Miles said calmly, bringing everyone down from the mountain top, "if you wait on God, if you just keep still, if you put your hands in God's hands, then after while, by and by, the spirit of the Lord will move, and you'll see that He's a doctor that has never loss a patient."

Mr. Patrick began playing "We'll Understand It Better By and By."

Reverend Miles looked out at the congregation. "Don't you worry. Just walk yourself in my room and the Lord will give you joy and peace like you've never known it before. Ain't that right, Mother Abigail?"

Mother Abigail simply raised her hand as a witness.

"I feel like I ain't even gotta preach," Reverend Miles said. "Mother Abigail done told us everything we need to know. We can go on home. Come on, Sista Joyce Gibbs and welcome our visitors."

Reverend Miles took his seat and Kizmic packed up her camera. Not because she believed for one second they were about to get out of there. She didn't know why he wasted his breath saying things like "I'm only going to be before you for a few minutes," "I ain't gonna keep ya long," "My message today is short," "I ain't gonna take up much of your time." No matter what Reverend Miles said, they never got out of church before one o'clock.

Walking to their cars at one-fifteen, Journey asked her mother if they could go to Brown's every Sunday.

Miss Sarah gave Journey a little nudge of a smile and said, "I can't imagine another place I'd rather the two of us be."

CHAPTER

33

Tuesday, June 12, Journey wanted out the house. Not just for a couple of hours in the morning and a couple of hours in the afternoon. She wanted out the house, period.

The route did its job in serving as the perfect front for her escapades, but she could hardly call the two measly games of marbles she played with Kizmic and Man 'n 'Em escapades. In a lot of ways it was worse than her not being able to come outside at all, because she could see all the fun going on in that neighborhood but she couldn't put her hands on it, couldn't stick her feet in it, couldn't bury her nose in it, couldn't put her lips on it, couldn't put her ear against it. Kizmic likened Journey's situation to Kalaya and Plum's. Their parents let them go to parties, but they always had to leave "just when things started gettin' good," Kalaya and Plum often complained. Journey was tired of leaving just when things started gettin' good.

"Mama, I know what you're going to say, but I'll be fine," Journey insisted, holding their copy of the newspaper in her hand.

Miss Sarah sat on the glider bench pushing it back and forth, back and forth, regarding Journey with keen eyes that said she had been waiting for this argument and had her rebuttal sitting on her tongue. "No, Journey."

"Why not?"

"You know perfectly well why not."

Kizmic leaned against the banister near the tower. She wanted nothing to do with their argument, but if Miss Sarah were to ask her who was to blame for it, she would come straight out and tell her that it was Diamond, Poochie, 'n 'Em's fault.

"We ain't playin' no more marbles," Peanut announced when Kizmic, Onion, and Journey met Man 'n 'Em in Man's back yard after the route.

"Yeah. We playin' skully," Steebo huffed.

Kizmic knew they were going to do that. Not to toot her own horn, but she was killing them in marbles. Nevertheless, they could of at least had the decency to wait until they actually played a game before they quit. That was common I'm-quittin'-'cause-you-kickin'-my-butt courtesy. Having to give up her treasured game so soon after getting back into it was bull, but Kizmic let it go because Journey wanted to know what was up with this skully game they kept mentioning and she was eager to show her.

Once they got to the skully board, Kizmic looked down at the viewing screen of her Ciro-flex irked to no end. She had planned to teach Journey everything Miss Josephine had taught her about skully, what seemed like ages ago. But Man 'n 'Em were not only arguing about whose top Journey should use (Kizmic was going to show Journey how to make her own top), they were shoving one another aside, trying to be the one to tell her how to play.

They wouldn't even tell me the name of the daggone game when I met them, Kizmic thought.

Now, there they were talking over one another, spilling all the beans about skully to Journey. Yeah, Kizmic asked them to play with her, but she wasn't stupid. That's not why they were doing it. Steebo, Babyfrog, Onion, and Peanut were trying to redeem themselves after losing so horribly at marbles in front of Journey, and Man, Fatboy, Meatball, and Redtop were doing it because Journey was cute.

Kizmic turned the focusing knob. Man, they a trip.

Surrounded by Man 'n 'Em, soaking in the attention like she soaked in the warmth from the sun, Journey stood in the number one square, holding Man's green skully top and listening to Babyfrog and Peanut give her pointers on how to shoot. Kizmic, positioned outside the number two square, cocked the shutter, wishing she had a picture of her first game with them.

Journey missed the shot, but did Man 'n 'Em rag on her about it? No. They told her she did good.

Let that've been me, Kizmic scoffed.

Of course, it wasn't long before Diamond, Poochie, 'n 'Em got wind of Man 'n 'Em playing skully with a girl other than Kizmic and came to tell Journey that they didn't know who she thought she was, but she better go on somewhere. Faces tore up, Diamond, Poochie, 'n 'Em stood on the sidewalk, looking Journey up and down, talking about her shoes, her hair, her clothes, and "whispering" loud enough for Journey to hear, "Where she come from anyway?"

"Don't pay no attention to them," Kizmic told her.

"Why not?" Journey asked, eating up their unfriendly whispers, snickers, and side-eyes, like candy from a Pez dispenser.

Diamond, Poochie, 'n 'Em were doing everything she had seen them do from her window and had drawn in her comic strips. So oddly enough, all that they did to make Journey feel like an outsider made her feel more like an insider, because she expected them to react to her that way. Journey, on the other hand, wasn't reacting to them the way they expected.

Diamond pooted her hand at Journey. "Something's wrong with that girl." She then pushed Man, called him Leslie, and ran around the corner. He ran after her.

That was Poochie's cue to push Onion and run around the corner, too. Onion chased her. Soon the hormonal bunch of them had run off.

"Where are they going?" Journey asked.

Closing the hood of the Ciro-flex, Kizmic said, "I don't care."

Rather than start another game, Journey asked to go to the Fish Store.

"You live in the castle house," Miss Josephine said when Kizmic introduced them.

"How did you know that?" Journey asked with her lightning struck eyes twinkling as she admired the exquisite scar on Miss Josephine's knee.

"Well, I've seen you, Shugga."

"When?"

"Lots of times. Up in the window." Miss Josephine gave her a sly look. "Up at Arlington."

Journey smiled, totally diggin' that she was on Miss Josephine's radar.

"Langston Hughes wrote a poem called 'Winter Sweetness,'" Miss Josephine said. "Whenever I see you in the window, I think of it."

Miss Josephine handed Kizmic and Journey a Sugar Daddy. Kizmic immediately unwrapped hers and popped it into her mouth. Journey put the candy to her nose, breathed in the rich smell of caramel, then stuck the pop in her pocket.

"'Winter Sweetness'?" Journey repeated, wanting to hear more.

"It's about a maple-skinned girl peeking out a window. The first time I read it, I got the feeling that the little girl was really pretty." Miss Josephine smiled at Journey. "I was right."

Now that Kizmic was looking back on everything that led up to Miss Sarah and Journey's argument, she couldn't lay the blame solely at Diamond, Poochie, 'n 'Em's feet. She had to spread it around, starting with Man'n 'Em fighting over who was going to teach Journey to play skully, Diamond, Poochie, 'n 'Em pushing Journey out and in with their jealousy, and Miss Josephine saying Journey was as pretty as a girl in a Langston Hughes poem. Who could blame Journey for wanting out the house after all that?

"Mama, Dr. Bell and Dr. Freemen said I could do anything I want," Journey said.

"Within reason," Miss Sarah replied sharply, pushing the bench back and forth, back and forth.

"This is within reason."

"I don't call running around in the hot sun all day within reason." Miss Sarah pushed the bench so hard that it glided back and hit the wall.

Kizmic wished her father would come driving up the street blasting one of his oldies but goodies, get out the car and make Miss Sarah dance. That's how Journey got out the house in the first place.

Miss Sarah stomped inside.

Journey followed her. "Mama."

She stopped in the hall but kept her back to Journey.

"Since I've been sick, I've done things your way, Dr. Hubbard's way, Dr. Yearling's way, Dr. Dearborn's way, Dr. Stinchcomb's way, Dr. Bell's way, Dr. Freeman's way, and anybody else who had a way. I need to do this one *my* way, Mama."

Miss Sarah dropped her head. Kizmic was sure she was going to cave in. How could she not? Kizmic asked herself that after Miss Sarah said flatly, without even looking at Journey, "No. And I don't want to talk about it anymore."

Miss Sarah and Journey didn't talk about it for two days. Kizmic, Journey, and Onion continued tossing the world's news on their customers' steps and porches, squeezing in a game of marbles here, a game of skully there, then coming home like she was told. Miss Sarah was sitting on the glider bench waiting for her every day. The Friday following their argument, Kizmic and Journey returned from the morning delivery and found the bench empty and became alarmed. Miss Sarah had been quiet and sad since she and Journey argued. Journey blamed herself.

"If I had just stuck to the plan, my mother wouldn't be feeling bad."

To ease her mother's mind, Journey came home earlier than she had to, but that made her mother even more withdrawn.

"Mama!" Journey shouted, when they ran in the house and didn't see her in the sunroom, living room, dining room, kitchen, or her bedroom.

"I'm up here," her mother called back.

Miss Sarah was in Journey's studio sitting at her drawing desk. The bag of Sugar Daddy pops, Now and Laters, bubble gum, Squirrel Nuts, and Mary Jane candy she had stashed away in her footlocker was on the desk.

Kizmic gave Journey that *Oooooh. You in trouble* look.

"You left it open," Miss Sarah said.

"I didn't mean to. I was rushing and—"

"You're not supposed to eat candy, Journey."

"I know. That's why I—"

"Hid it from me. Like you hid these." She held up several of the comic strips Journey had drawn of Kizmic.

Kizmic gave Journey the *Oooooh. You* really *in trouble* look.

"You've been watching Kizmic," Miss Sarah said with a catch in her voice. "Drawing her all these years, wishing that you could go out and pla . . . play like a regular kid."

Journey walked slowly into the room and stood beside her mother. Kizmic stayed in the doorway.

"Mama—"

"And I've kept you in this house, in this room, like a prisoner."

"No, Mama. Not like a prisoner," Journey said. "Like a mother trying to keep her only daughter safe."

Through quivering lips, she said, "That's all I wanted."

"I know."

"And where has it gotten you?"

Journey said, "Still here with the best mother I could have had."

Miss Sarah's tears fell on the drawing of Kizmic chasing after Man 'n 'Em on her bike. Journey turned her mother around and the two of them embraced.

After some time, Miss Sarah wiped her tears then handed Journey a Mary Jane. "This was my favorite when I was a kid." She unwrapped one for herself. "It's good, isn't it?"

"Um-hum," Journey answered, cherishing the molasses and peanut flavored candy sticking to her teeth.

Miss Sarah gave her another. "I was thinking that we should do this your way."

"Huh?"

"Kizmic, would you mind getting your bike for me?"

Kizmic ran all the way home. She didn't know what Miss Sarah wanted with her bike, but if getting it was going to make her happy somehow, then it was hers.

Miss Sarah and Journey had eaten all the Mary Jane and Squirrel Nut candy by the time Kizmic returned.

"What are you doing, Mama?" Journey asked.

"You haven't ridden on a bike before," she said, sitting on the bike.

If Miss Sarah were looking at Kizmic and Journey's faces instead of inspecting the handlebars and chain, she would have seen that that wasn't exactly true.

"I'm going to teach you how to ride. I just have to remember how to ride myself."

Miss Sarah had a wobbly start but soon proved true the saying "Once you learn how to ride a bike, you never forget." She rode up to Arlington, then came back down the street, flying past Kizmic and Journey.

"Wooooo!" she hollered, leaning into the bend.

"I think your mother had too much sugar," Kizmic joked.

"You're supposed to be teaching me how to ride," Journey said when her mother finally hit the breaks.

Panting, Miss Sarah said, "I forgot . . . how much fun this is. All right. Your turn."

Journey jumped on the bike. Miss Sarah held the left handlebar and the back of the seat.

"All you have to do is pedal. I won't let you fall."

Miss Sarah steadied Journey on the bike and off they went. Up and down the street, Journey pedaled while her mother held her up and guided the bike. Kizmic stood on the side encouraging Journey and, when Miss Sarah wasn't looking, snapping pictures of them.

"That's it," Miss Sarah said. "Keep pedaling. There you go."

"You got it, Journey," Kizmic said.

The third time they went down the block, Miss Sarah let go of the bike and Journey held it steady on her own.

"I'm doing it, Mama! I'm doing it!"

"Yes, you are, baby," Miss Sarah smiled with pride.

CHAPTER

34

THE NEXT DAY, MISS SARAH planned to take Journey to the store to buy her a bike, but Journey wanted to get it from Christmas. That Sunday, after they came home from church, Christmas staggered to Journey's house croaking Three Dog Nights' "Joy To The World" and gave her a violet Schwinn Stardust. It had a violet and silver striped banana seat. A white basket was clamped to a chrome rack attached to the front of the handlebars.

"I can put the newspapers in here," Journey said, reaching into the basket and pulling out imaginary papers to throw as she rode along.

Miss Sarah then bought a camouflage fanny pack for Journey's medicine.

"You're going to be running and riding around enough as it is. I don't want you having to rush home to take your medicine," she said.

She also wanted to buy Journey a digital wristwatch. Journey asked Kizmic if she could borrow her Teeter Totter watch instead.

"But it doesn't have an alarm," Miss Sarah said.

"I'll keep track of the time," she promised.

So, armed with her fanny pack full of medicine around her waist and Kizmic's Teeter Totter watch on her wrist, Journey went outside after breakfast. For fifteen minutes, she sat on her bike on the island in the middle of Belvedere not knowing what to do.

"It's like being in an amusement park trying to decide which ride to get on first," she said.

In the end, Journey chose jacks.

"*Jacks?!*" Kizmic couldn't believe it. With all there was to do, after all that arguing she did with her mother, she wanted to play *jacks!* Come on! She can't be serious.

Face broke down, Kizmic pedaled behind a very serious Journey over to Litchfield. Kneeling on a brick porch playing jacks by herself was an eight-year-old girl with a bundle of braids on top of her head.

Journey walked up the steps. "Hi."

The chocolatey brown girl regarded Journey and Kizmic with curious, half moon shaped eyes. "Hi."

"My name is Journey, and that's my friend, Kizmic. What's your name?" she asked, kneeling across from her.

Staring at Journey's bush, she answered softly, "Rachel."

"That's a pretty name," Journey smiled.

Rachel's eyes fell to Journey's wrist. "I like your watch."

"I do, too. Kizmic let me hold it. Hey, Rachel, would you mind if I played jacks with you?"

Rachel's round mouth stretched into a gap-tooth smile. "Uh-uh."

As she photographed them playing, Kizmic couldn't help but feel that she had been bamboozled. Journey said she wanted to play the games Kizmic played.

She ain't never see me play no daggone jacks.

But that feeling of having been tricked went away as the happiness on Journey and Rachel's faces triggered memories for Kizmic of when Kalaya played with her when she was that age. Oh, the fun she used to have with her big sister.

After about twenty minutes, Journey told Rachel she had to go.

"Already?" Rachel asked, disappointed.

"Yeah. Kizmic and I are getting ready to go play football."

"You gonna come back?"

"I sure am."

"When?"

Journey laughed. "Tomorrow."

When it came to playing, Journey was all over the place. There was no rhyme, no reason, no nothing. One minute she was playing basketball with Kizmic, Man 'n 'Em, the next she was playing A Sailor Went to Sea and Miss Mary Mack hand games with Rachel and some other little girls, who claimed her as their play big sister. One day all she wanted to do was play football. The next day she was playing hopscotch with her play little sisters. The day after that she was all into baseball. The day after the day after, she was double dutching, feeding Fatboy's pigeons, playing Red Light Green Light, drawing cartoons with Peanut, playing fetch with PJ and Butch, playing four square, making yuk faces as Babyfrog showed her his prized bug collection, cuddling Phyllis, playing Space Invaders against Steebo, and playing bat 'n ball.

Kizmic loved that about Journey, which really tripped her out because she never imagined that she would love anything about being friends with a girl. Especially once she learned Journey couldn't play none of the games Kizmic loved. She couldn't block nobody, couldn't stick nobody, couldn't shoot a basketball, couldn't hit a baseball, could barely catch a football even when she was wide open. The only games Journey was remotely good at were marbles and skully.

That should have been a deal-breaker, but part of the reason Journey wasn't able to play as well as Kizmic expected was because she couldn't tackle or juke anybody or run really fast without getting winded and she had to keep one hand on top of that wig to keep it from flying off her head. The other thing that kept their deal intact was that Journey was so comical with her fumbles, bricks, and strikes. She celebrated her misses as much as she celebrated her lucky shots. And she never got mad and wanted to quit when Man 'n 'Em eventually began to rag on her about how badly she played.

"I thought you said she could play football like you," Babyfrog said.

Redtop laughed, "She might be cute, but she can't play worth jack."

To Kizmic, Journey was like that hula hoop her mother had bought her—full of unexpected fun. One of the most fun things Kizmic got to do with Journey was go roller skating, thanks to Kalaya, of all people.

During the Girls Scholastic Association Track and Field Championships, Kalaya was able to exact revenge on Gladys Stackhouse for messing around with Clive by not just beating her but demolishing her in the 100 meter hurdles, destroying her in the 300 meter hurdles, and blowing her out in the Mile Relay. In doing so, she attracted the attention of several college scouts and a boy named London Jay Johnson.

London ran the 110 meter and the 300 meter hurdles for Poly High School. He was lean, tall, and well-built with creamy, cocoa brown skin, a mass of lustrous, curly black hair, heavy eyebrows over dreamy brown eyes, a splendid, broad nose, and thick, moist lips. Aside from being the finest boy Kalaya had ever gone with, London was also the most different. He didn't have her scaling the upstairs back porch and sneaking out the house in the middle of the night. He picked Kalaya up at the front door at a decent hour and had her back by her ten o'clock curfew. He didn't only come around when Turk and Magdalene were at work. London came to see Kalaya early in the evening when Magdalene was in the kitchen cooking dinner and Turk was in the living room listening and dancing to music. He didn't stay past ten and he didn't call past eleven. Turk and Magdalene liked London a lot. However, there was one major difference about him that gave them pause. London had a car. A 1974, gleaming, cameo white Pontiac Firebird.

"A seventeen-year-old boy with a muscle car?" Magdalene said. "You know where that's leading."

"Uh-huh," Turk said.

Magdalene had a talk with Kalaya that began with the threat, "I better not catch you in that car parked on the side of the road somewhere."

Kizmic could see her mother and father patrolling the streets, slamming on the brakes every time they saw a white car.

Oddly enough, Kalaya didn't put up a fuss. "Okay, Mama," she said in the sweetest voice.

"I mean it!" Magdalene said, furiously shaking a finger at Kalaya.

"I know," Kalaya said calmly. Then she hugged her mother.

"Shocked the sugar, honey, ice, tea out of me," Magdalene later told Turk.

What's wrong with her? Why ain't she carryin' on? Kizmic wondered.

That was the biggest difference between London and Kalaya's other boyfriends. Her entire demeanor changed once she started going with him. Kizmic didn't know what London did to Kalaya, what he said to her, but every ounce of negative attitude she had was gone. Instead of griping, she was singing in the shower, in her room, walking down the hall, coming down the stairs, going out the door. She was singing Amii Stewart's "Knock on Wood" when she knocked on Kizmic's bedroom door and asked if she and Journey wanted to go roller skating.

"Shocked the sugar, honey, ice, tea out of me," Kizmic told Journey.

That Thursday night, Kalaya sat in the passenger side seat of that Firebird. Her hair was in two long, French braids on either side of her head and she was wearing a peach tank top and peach and light blue shorts. Sitting in the back with Journey and Plum, Kizmic couldn't recall a time when her sister looked prettier. But the beauty she was exuding didn't come from her hair and clothes. It came from the happiness inside her that was making her sing.

London drove to Painters Mills Roller Rink. Drac tearing up the guitar solo on Slave's "Slide" could be heard from inside the building out in the parking lot. Wall to wall, girls were dressed to kill in low cut and off the shoulder blouses, skin-tight jeans, short skirts, and short shorts; guys were dressed to impress in jeans, shorts, t-shirts, and sweat pants. A bunch were wearing some fashionably outrageous getups. All had skates on their feet—black skates, white skates, orange skates, brown skates, red skates. Skates with yellow or green pom-poms and bells, skates with pink or blue fuzzy dice. Flashing, colorful disco lights reflecting off mirror disco balls hanging from the ceiling whirled around the shiny maple wood skating rink floor with the people dancing on their skates.

"It's like *Soul Train* on wheels," Journey said.

She had never had her feet in a pair of skates, let alone been in a skating rink. On the carpeted floor they taught Journey how to stand, balance, roll, and stop.

"How do you skate so fast without falling or bumping into people?" Journey asked.

"By not being afraid to fall and bump into people," London replied.

"Here comes your boyfriend," Kalaya said.

"Where?" Plum asked excitedly, resisting the urge to look.

"Behind you," Kalaya said.

Plum quickly and subtly spruced up her bush ball and checked to see if the white blouse and purple shorts she decided to wear looked as fabulous on her now as they did when she checked herself out in her bedroom mirror.

Almost as if Alonzo Ellis paid the DJ to switch to his theme song when he gave the signal, "Brick" by Dazz played. Wearing a white t-shirt and white jeans, he rolled in their direction on black skates with white laces and no toe stops. He was average height, willowy but kind of on the muscular side. His skin was deep brown and his hair was closely cropped and wavy. He had thick eyebrows, squinty, frisky, brown eyes, peach fuzz above his wide, irresistible lips, and a dimple in the center of his chin.

Plum moved her shoulders to his beat as she watched him with sparkling eyes that said she thought he was the cutest thing on eight wheels.

London and Alonzo greeted each other with a long-winded dap that included five slaps of their palms, tapping the backs of their hands together three times, some finger wiggling, a couple chest bumps, and four finger snaps.

"What's up Black Lightnin'?" Alonzo said to Kalaya.

"Nothing. How you doing, Alonzo?" she asked.

"I'd be doin' a lot better if your girl here stop treatin' me bad," he said.

"What are you talking about, Alonzo?" Plum asked, amused.

"I'm talkin' 'bout you makin' me wait a whole hour for you. Girl, you know how many fine sistas I had to fight off 'fore you got here. I was doin' the rope-a-dope tryin' to save myself for you." Clutching a white towel, Alonzo shielded his face with his arms while walking in place on his skates. "You gonna lose me if you don't start actin' like you know."

"If all it takes to lose you is for me to be an hour late, then bye," Plum said, waving him away.

"Girl, you know I was jokin'! I don't know why you keep playin' so hard to get."

"I'm not playing hard to get. Maybe you're not working hard enough to get me."

"Ooouuu!" Kalaya and London said.

"Awright, y'all. It's Couples Skate," the DJ announced. "Get your baby and let's get this party rollin'."

Alonzo tucked his towel in the front pocket of his jeans, then took Plum by the hand. "I'ma show you how hard I work."

They dipped onto the floor through a brief gap in the crowd of skaters.

"Y'all keep practicing," Kalaya said to Kizmic and Journey.

She and London followed Plum and Alonzo.

The DJ was playing Stephanie Mills' "What Cha Gonna Do With My Lovin'." Standing at the railing, Kizmic and Journey watched Kalaya and London hand dance on their black wheels. London twirled Kalaya, all the while doing scissors skating backward. Kalaya came out of the twirl and she and London skated side by side, kicking out their feet—left bounce, right bounce, left bounce, right bounce. As others whooshed by, they held hands, talked, and smiled like they were taking a lovely stroll in the park. London then got behind Kalaya and pulled her close to his body. He wasn't groping her. He was cuddling her. On his face, Kizmic saw the same happiness that was on Kalaya's when she was singing. Kalaya cozied up in his tender arms and they smoothly rolled and rocked and bounced.

The DJ kept the slow jams going with the Ohio Player's "Sweet Sticky Thing." Plum and Alonzo were swaying side-to-side and gliding, doing the two-step backward in synch effortlessly. With the swell of the horns, Alonzo skated in front of Plum. Rolling backward, he squatted and while alternately pushing his skates back and forth on his front wheels, he opened and closed his slim legs, making them wiggle as loose as cooked spaghetti. He looked up and said something to Plum. She bit her bottom lip and shook her head. Alonzo smiled, rose, and turned his back to her. Spreading his legs, he bent over and reached between them. Plum grabbed his hands and sat on her heels. Alonzo quickly pulled her through his legs. Briefly, the momentum flung Plum back. Her body was inches off the floor as she rolled under him. Once through, Alonzo pulled her upright again in front of him.

"Wow! Did you see that?!" Journey asked.

Bug-eyed, Kizmic said, "Yeah."

Plum spun around, grabbed the towel out of Alonzo's pocket, and wiped the sweat from his forehead.

"Looks like he's working pretty hard to me. Can you skate like that?"

"Uh-uh!" Kizmic said, flabbergasted by their moves.

"All Ladies Skate," the DJ announced.

The guys cleared the floor.

"Show the fellas what you workin' with, ladies," he said and put Chaka Khan's "I'm Every Woman" on the turntable.

A sweet-smelling wind whipped across the guys' faces as the girls strutted on their skates around the rink. Grooving to the music, Kalaya and Plum pivoted on their front wheels and skated backward, then pivoted on their back wheels and skated forward again. Kizmic, Journey, London, and Alonzo were completely entranced by them.

"All Skate, Ya'll! All Skate!" the DJ shouted and started bumping Vaughn Mason's "Bounce, Rock, Skate, Roll."

"Come on, Journey," London said. "You can't be a wallflower on the roller skating anthem."

They formed a train with London in front, followed by Journey, Kalaya, Kizmic, Plum, and Alonzo.

"Hold on tight," London said.

Journey put her hands solidly on his waist.

In the midst of skaters performing elaborate synchronized routines that involved flips, twirls, jumps, and splits, London led them out onto the floor. A wobbly Journey closed her eyes and squealed.

"I got you," Kalaya assured her.

When Journey opened her eyes, they were soaring around the rink. On London's cue, everyone except Journey shuffled, crossed over, rocked, and kicked to the rhythm of the music. Kizmic felt like she was floating. Intermittently, Alonzo and Plum let go, spun, dipped, then hooked back up to the train. As they zig-zagged through the throng of skaters, the wind blew through their hair, which made Journey nervous about her wig. Fearing it would slip off, she reached for it, and their train came off the rails. Everybody hit the floor, cracking up.

"Now see that's how you skate fast without falling," London said.

"But we fell," Journey pointed out.

"And you're going to fall again. Get used to it," he said. "Let's get it."

Yeah. London was different.

He's so cool, Kizmic thought. And that Firebird is sweet.

CHAPTER
35

SURROUNDED BY RACHEL and her other play little sisters, Journey sang the lyrics to the mimicking game "Donna Died." While she was shaking her thing, Journey glanced at the boy and girl on the teeter totter and saw that it was one-thirty.

With Kizmic holding her Ciro-flex and Journey pressing her hand on top of her wig, they raced to the Fish Store. Journey grabbed two bottles of grape soda from the freezer. Kizmic got a package of Twinkies for herself and a Butterscotch Krimpet for Journey.

"I don't think your mama had Krimpets in mind when she said you have to have something on your stomach when you take your medicine," Miss Josephine said.

Journey grinned and gobbled up the three sponge cakes. She zipped open her fanny pack, pulled out two bottles of pills, popped one of each in her mouth, then chased them down with swigs of soda.

"Is that thing hot, sweetie?" Miss Josephine asked.

Journey crossed off the names of the medicine written on an index card. "What thing?"

Miss Josephine nodded to Journey's wig.

"Sometimes," she said, putting the card and pencil back inside her fanny pack.

"Why do you wear it?"

"Because it makes people uncomfortable when I don't," Journey said.

"I'm sure it does." Miss Josephine tilted her head and stared curiously at the wig. She then called to Mr Charlie. "Baby, we're gonna go see Sweets."

Watching Miss Josephine kiss Mr Charlie, Journey asked Kizmic, "Who's Sweets?"

Sweets was a hairdresser. Her shop was on Belvedere, across from the race track. Kizmic wasn't too thrilled about going to see Sweets. Magdalene, Aunt Beana, Kalaya, and Plum went to "see Sweets" every other week, and they didn't come back for hours. Granted, their hair looked fantastic, but not fantastic enough to be sitting up in the hairdresser all day.

Nude pumps click-clacking and the handkerchief hem of her peach floral dress sashaying above her scarred knee, Miss Josephine walked them across Park Heights, past Bealie's Drug Store, Pimlico Carry-Out, and Westside Market, stopping at Sweet Dos Hair Salon. A shiny brass shopkeeper's bell jingled when Miss Josephine pushed open the glass door. Along the left wall inside, three women and a young girl sat with their feet up, so to speak, in four of the five salon chairs as their beauticians pressed, permed, trimmed, and curled their hair. Straight ahead, two women were laid back at the shampoo bowls as their hairdressers washed and conditioned their hair. Two women and a little girl sat under the hair dryers against the right wall. The first woman was napping, the other was smoking a cigarette and reading Jerome Dyson Wright's novel *Poor Black and in Real Trouble*, and the little girl was on a booster seat coloring pictures in a Woody Woodpecker coloring book. Directly to the right of the door, two more women relaxed on the couch in the waiting area, one reading the *Afro-American Newspaper*, the other flipping through the July edition of *Ebony Magazine*. The smell of hairspray, chemical relaxers, shampoo, cigarette smoke, and hot combs and curling irons scorching kinky locks permeated the air. Howls, giggles, and "Girl, let me tell ya," "That ain't what I heard," "Chile, stop playin'," "You lyin'," "What you say now?" "Ain't that the truth" rose up over the white noise of the dryers and Donna Summer singing "Hot Stuff" on the radio.

"Josie?" Sweets called, walking her customer to the dryer.

Sweets was tall and slender with skin the color of perfectly baked bread-pudding just out of the oven. Everything about her was long—face, neck, arms, legs, feet, fingers, which appeared even longer because her orange nails were two inches long. A thick halo braid crowned her head and large hoop earrings dangled from her earlobes. She was wearing an orange plaid blazer, white t-shirt, a long, orange skirt, and white Chuck Taylors.

"How you doin', Sweets?" Miss Josephine asked.

Lowering the dome on the field of rollers on her customer's head, she answered, "Can't complain."

After setting the timer, Sweets came over to Miss Josephine. "I just did you the other day," she said, teasing Miss Josephine's loose curls with her long fingers. "What, you done let that husband of yours sweat your hair out already?"

"Now, Sweets, you know I don't let no man make me sweat," Miss Josephine replied.

"I know that's right," Sweets laughed. "Then what you doin' back here so soon?"

"Came to ask a favor." She turned to Kizmic and Journey. "You two have a seat," she said, pointing to the waiting area.

Miss Josephine locked arms with Sweets and before they walked away, Sweets said, "You next, baby," to the woman reading *Ebony.*

She tossed the magazine on the coffee table as she stood, then followed them to Sweets' booth. Journey picked it up. On the cover, Grace Jones held a microphone, wearing black gloves, a crazy-looking black dress, and a disk-shaped thing attached somehow to her nearly bald head.

"Look how short she cut her hair," Journey marveled.

"Yeah," Kizmic muttered, not looking at Grace Jones but scowling at Poochie.

She was the girl Kizmic noticed sitting in the second salon chair when they first walked in. Her head was down because the beautician was wrapping her hair around the curling iron, so Kizmic didn't see her face until now.

"Oh, Miss Connie!" Poochie exclaimed, staring at her reflection in the large, octagon, beveled mirror on the wall, admiring the curls all over her head.

Taking a drag off her cigarette, Miss Connie slowly turned the chair to the left and right so Poochie could see the sides of her hair.

"Everybody's going to think you gave me a perm," Poochie said.

Miss Connie handed her a round mirror, then spun the chair around so she could look at the back.

It was pretty, Kizmic admitted, touching her week old, frizzy braids.

She looked at the Afro Sheen, Ultra Sheen, and Clairol posters on the walls that featured black women with fluffy curls and sleek, straight hair.

"Mama said I can get a perm when I turn sixteen. I can't wait!" Poochie lowered the mirror and saw Kizmic envying her curly hair. A smirk raised the corner of her mouth that taunted, *Don't you wish your hair was as pretty as mine?*

Kizmic cut her eyes to the window and looked at the hot sun. I hope every last one of her curls falls by the time she gets home.

Miss Josephine took the magazine out of Journey's hands. "Come with me, Shugga."

The woman sitting in Sweets' chair got up and smiled, "You next, baby."

Next for what? Kizmic wondered.

She sat on the edge of the couch as Journey hopped enthusiastically in Sweets' chair. The glow on Journey's face made her look like she was six years old. Kizmic snapped a picture of her.

Sweets draped a black apron on Journey, placed her Converse on the metal foot pedal, and pumped up the chair. She then turned Journey around to face the mirror. "Look at those cheekbones! Josie, you seen this girl's cheekbones?"

"They were the first things I noticed when I met her."

"If I were a hundred pounds lighter, I'd have cheekbones like that," Miss Connie said, spraying Poochie's curls with Ultra Sheen hairspray.

"And those eyes!" Sweets smiled. "They're beautiful."

Journey dropped her head as she blushed.

"How long you had this?" Sweets asked, picking at Journey's wig.

"Almost a year," Journey answered.

Poochie was stunned. She didn't know Journey's hair was a wig.

"She's a beauty, but I think it's time to trade her in. I got some nice ones in the display case."

"But I don't have any money," Journey said.

"I don't recall anybody asking you for any," Miss Josephine said. "Poochie, go get two wigs and bring them over here."

"Yes ma'am." She glanced shamefacedly at Kizmic as she walked by.

That's what you get for always talkin' 'bout somebody, Kizmic thought.

Carrying two Styrofoam heads with Afro wigs on them, Poochie slunk by Kizmic, eyes begging, *Please don't tell Miss Josephine on me.*

"These are smaller," Sweets said of the two wigs Poochie presented to Journey. "People are starting to get away from wearing those big bushes. Which one do you like?"

Journey thought for a moment. "This one might stay on better," she said, pointing to the shorter of the two.

"You want to try it on out here or in the back?" Sweets asked.

"What she gotta go in the back for?" Miss Connie asked.

"Yeah?" the beautician in the next booth chimed in.

"She ain't got nothin' to be ashamed of," said another woman.

"She sure don't," Sweets' customer said. "Take that thing off right here."

In the face of Journey's reluctance, the women got up from the chairs, washbasins, from under the hairdryers, and encircled her.

Miss Josephine said, "Somebody's always trying to make you feel bad, whether you have hair or not." She held up the *Ebony Magazine.* "That's why Grace does what the hell she wants with hers."

Journey stared at Grace Jones, looked at the women surrounding her, then pulled her wig off.

"Awright!"

"That's what I'm talkin' 'bout!"

"Lord, have mercy! This child is gorgeous!"

"Didn't I tell you?" Miss Josephine said. "Didn't I tell you?!"

Their response was something out of this world to Journey. She was sitting in a beauty shop with her bald head on display for all to see, surrounded by women with hair to spare, yet she was feeling like she could be on one of those Ultra Sheen or Clairol posters.

Sweets took Journey over to the wash bowl.

Another beautician said, "Hey, use this." She unlocked a small cabinet and pulled out a bottle of shampoo and a bottle of conditioner. "I save these for my big tippers," she said with a wink of her eye.

Sweets rinsed warm water over Journey's brown head, then gently washed it with the expensive, sweet-smelling shampoo and conditioner. Afterward, Sweets massaged cinnamon scented oil on her scalp. When she was done, Journey rose from the chair and moved closer to the mirror. Poochie stood beside her holding the wig she had chosen.

Journey looked at the wig, then at Poochie's curly hair with longing. A hush fell over the shop. On the radio, Stevie Wonder was killing the lyrics to "Isn't She Lovely" with his harmonica. Journey turned to the mirror again.

"I *am* pretty," she said, bringing happy tears to everyone's eyes.

Sweets put the wig back in the display case and then Kizmic and Journey ate ribs, fried chicken, collard greens, string beans, potato salad, macaroni and cheese, and sweet potato pie that the women had ordered from Leon's Pig Pen and the Yellow Bowl on Park Heights. They danced and sang and helped the women negotiate with the hustle man who had come into the shop selling soap, lotion, jewelry, socks, and cassette tapes. It was like being in a grown woman's clubhouse. No wonder it took all day for her mother, Aunt Beana, Kalaya, and Plum to get their hair done.

Kizmic captured every fantastic moment on film. The last picture was of Journey sitting in Sweets' chair with everyone, including the hustle man, gathered around her.

As they were leaving, Miss Josephine said, "Thanks, Sweets."

Sweets shook her head. "No, Josie. Thank *you*."

Miss Sarah wasn't on the porch when they got home from the route. The day she let Journey out the house, she dusted off her sewing machine.

"It was like riding a bike," Miss Sarah said of her picking up where she'd left off on the quilt she was working on two years ago.

Journey, of course, was thrilled that her mother was quilting again. She could truly enjoy herself now that she knew her mother wasn't spending her days worrying.

The house was filled with the sound of the sewing machine running and Miss Sarah and Aretha Franklin singing "Rock Steady." Journey shushed Kizmic and they tiptoed up the stairs.

When Journey first showed Kizmic Miss Sarah's sewing room, the curtains were drawn, and it was dark and lifeless. Now they were wide open and sunlight came through the windows, shining its vitality on everything, in particular Miss Sarah.

Sitting at the sewing table, Miss Sarah was lost in the colorful, peaceful world she was stitching together. Kizmic couldn't wait to see what that world looked like beyond the orange, blue, purple, and green bundle of cloth under Miss Sarah's ebony hands.

Miss Sarah bobbed her head and watched the needle plunge in and out of the fabric. When she paused to remove a safety pin, she glanced up and saw Journey standing in the doorway. Miss Sarah stopped grooving. Frowning, she slowly pushed her chair back, got up, and walked over to Journey. First she put her left hand on Journey's bald head, then her right hand. Bringing her hands together under Journey's chin, she lifted her face and smiled. Then she sat down again and went back to rockin'. No worries. Just her fabric, her sewing machine, and Aretha.

CHAPTER

36

WITH THE WIG AND MISS SARAH'S FEARS gone, Journey was free to do whatever her heart's desire.

"Swimming," she told Kizmic her heart desired.

Remembering the disastrous time she had when she went swimming at the beginning of summer, Kizmic's heart desired to do anything but. She was so self-conscious about her body that day. Now, however, she understood that her self-consciousness wasn't all about Man 'n 'Em seeing how her body had filled out. It was fearing that Onion would see that her body hadn't filled out like Poochie's.

That admission was supposed to wait until the end of summer, but more and more, Kizmic was comparing herself to Poochie. Her dark skin to Poochie's light skin. Her medium length braids and bush balls to Poochie's long, curly hair. Her small breasts to Poochie's smaller but darling breasts. Her round behind to Poochie's skinny behind. Her slim legs to Poochie's lean legs. Her smile to Poochie's dogtooth but knockout smile. No way was Kizmic ready to chance being humiliated when Onion compared how she looked in her swimsuit to how Poochie looked in hers. Still, there she trotted up to C. C. Jackson with Journey, Man 'n 'Em, and Diamond, Poochie and 'Em.

Ugh! Kizmic thought.

It was ten-fifty and already a blazing ninety degrees. They had to get to the pool by eleven o'clock if they wanted to go swimming at twelve. Any later, they would have to wait until the one-thirty session, because the line would be wrapped around the fence, all the way up to Park Heights.

The line of kids waiting to beat the heat was just starting to form when they arrived, so they were among the first to rush in when the lifeguards opened the

324

gate. Kizmic watched Man 'n 'Em grin and stare at Diamond, Poochie 'n 'Em as they stripped down to their boldly patterned bathing suits and tucked their hair under colorful swim caps. Kizmic avoided getting undressed, thus Man 'n 'Em's stares, by hiding behind her Ciro-flex.

Never, ever having been in a swimming pool, Journey wanted photographs of her wading in the water for the Christmas album. Kizmic brought her camera, but she couldn't very well go swimming and leave it on the bench. Somebody might break it, or worse, steal it.

"We'll take turns watching it," Journey said, taking away Kizmic's perfect escape plan. "You should be in some pictures swimming with your friends, too."

"Okay, but you go first."

Kizmic looked through the viewfinder and snapped a picture of Journey in her t-shirt, shorts, and head scarf Magdalene had given her.

Ditching the wig not only gave Journey the freedom to do what she wanted but to also wear what she wanted to protect her head from sunburn. Sometimes she wore a baseball cap, but mostly she wore one of the head scarves Magdalene had given her. She'd long admired Magdalene's collection, which she said was as vibrant as her marble collection. To match her solid lavender swimsuit, Journey wrapped her head in a purple scarf that had swipes and swirls of white, blue, green, black, and of course, purple.

"It has all the colors of a Purple Haze marble," Journey pointed out.

The next few shots were of a bald-headed Journey running with Meatball, Redtop, and Fatboy toward the pool and jumping in.

"Oh my god! This feels awesome!" Journey shouted, bobbing up and down.

She couldn't swim a lick. Kizmic photographed Man, Meatball, Redtop, and Fatboy teaching Journey how to hold her nose, then her breath underwater, float, tread water, and dog-paddle. She stood next to Redtop on the edge of the pool and after he back flipped into the water, Journey let herself fall in backward. She cannonballed, cartwheeled, and flipped one-handed and two-handed into the water. Journey was having so much fun, Kizmic thought she would bust. She came out when Man 'n 'Em and Diamond, Poochie and 'Em started playing Marco Polo.

"Your turn," Journey said. She dried off and put the Ciro-flex around her neck.

Poochie was swimming like a mermaid near Onion, who was floundering about with his eyes closed trying to tag someone.

Kizmic took off her shirt then her shorts. She'd never felt so naked. She reached for her towel to cover up, but Journey placed Kizmic's blue swim cap in her hand. Kizmic looked at Journey. The sun was shining on her bald head.

"Polo!" Poochie shouted so loud her voice echoed in the hot air.

Unable to tag anyone, Onion cheated and peeked, but instead of tagging Poochie, who was right in front of him, he trod water with his green eyes fixed on Kizmic.

"Polo!" Poochie screeched again.

Man 'n 'Em and Diamond 'n 'Em looked to see what made Onion stop chasing them and *they* too started treading water as each of them stared at Kizmic with open-mouthed, googly-eyed gazes.

Onion had compared how Kizmic looked in her admiral blue, one-piece swimsuit to how Poochie looked in her brand new blue, green, and white two-piece swimsuit, and his eyes, as well as Man 'n 'Em and Diamond 'n 'Em's eyes said that she looked as cute as Poochie. The thing was, Kizmic didn't feel as cute as Poochie. She *knew* she was cute, like Kalaya and Plum knew they were pretty when they were skating around the rink, and Journey knew she was pretty when she took off her wig in Sweets' chair.

With her newfound cuteness strutting inside her, Kizmic smiled. Onion, thinking she was smiling at him, smiled back.

"ONION!" Poochie squalled and hit the water with her hands, splashing it in his face. "PO!" *SPLASH!* "LO!" *SPLASH!*

Onion squeezed his chlorine-filled eyes closed and pinched his nostrils. "Girl! What's wrong with you?!"

Poochie went off. "Ain't *NOTHIN'* wrong with me! What's *wrong* with YOU?! You 'pose to be *TAAAAAAGGIN'* ME!"

Onion got the most irritated look on his face then . . . "Here!" He poked Poochie on her arm. "I *TAAAAAAGED YA!*"

Man 'n 'Em burst out haha-ing and hehe-ing.

"Shut up!" Diamond said and splashed water in Man's face.

Man slammed his big hands on top of the water and splashed her back. Water flew up Diamond's nose, and she started coughing and gurgling like she was sure 'nough drowning.

"Don't be splashing water on her!" Poochie yelled.

"Tell her don't be splashin' no water on him then," Peanut said.

Princess smacked the water with both of her hands, but Peanut ducked the splash by sinking to the bottom of the pool.

Returning to the surface, he said, "Ha-ha! You mi—"

SPLISH! Precious got him from the side.

"Girl!" Peanut yelled and whacked the water with his hands, splashing Precious and Ebony.

Soon, Man 'n 'Em and Diamond, Poochie 'n 'Em were at war, laughing, shrieking, and eeking as they wailed on the water, sending it whooshing, splish-splashing in one another's faces. Kizmic plunged in and Onion swam over to her.

"I like your swimsuit," he said.

"Thank you," Kizmic said.

"You look really good."

Kizmic opened her mouth to say thank you again, because she didn't know what else to say. That's when Steebo and Babyfrog snuck up behind her, walloped her with water, and swam away.

Spitting out the water, Kizmic threatened, "Ooooo! I'ma get y'all!" She turned to Onion. "I'ma get you, too, 'cause you saw them."

Onion sloshed away laughing. Kizmic teamed up with Diamond, Poochie 'n 'Em for the first time since the skully game she played against Man way back when. And just like the skully game back then, Diamond, Poochie, 'n 'Em abandoned her.

"Y'all play too much!" they cried, climbing out of the pool at every end.

Left alone, Man 'n 'Em menacingly closed in on Kizmic. Diamond, Poochie 'n 'Em must have rubbed off on her, because she had to reign in this impulse to whine in the girliest, girlie-girl voice, *Stop! Y'all play too much!*

When Man 'n 'Em were just a few inches away, they beat the water like bongos to the theme music for *Jaws*.

As Journey took pictures of them lighting her up, Kizmic thought, This feels awesome!

Kizmic and Journey left fifteen minutes before the swim session was over, because Journey had to take her medicine by one-thirty. Poochie couldn't have been happier to see Kizmic put her clothes back on and walk out that gate. No matter. Journey said they should go swimming every day and Kizmic agreed. So Poochie may as well get used to seeing her in a bathing suit.

When they got to Kizmic's house, London's Firebird was parked out front. He and Kalaya were running summer track for Ed Waters Track and Field Club, where Kalaya and Gladys Stackhouse continued their rivalry, even though they were now teammates. They had to be at Carver High School for practice by two. London usually came at one-twenty and hung out in the living room listening to Turk's records, because Kalaya was never ready.

Kizmic and Journey could hear Minnie Riperton's "Inside My Love" playing, but it wasn't coming from the living room. The music was coming from upstairs.

He's not up there! Kizmic said with her eyes stretched, not wanting to believe in the slightest that Kalaya would have London in her bedroom.

The lightning veins striking under Journey's eyelids said, *Oooh, yes he is!*

While Kizmic didn't want to believe that London was up in Kalaya's room, she wasn't surprised. If her mother and father walked through the door right now, they'd be pissed as hell, but not surprised. With a guy like London, how could they be? He was a teenage girl's dream and her parents' nightmare all rolled into one fine dude.

Kizmic and Journey tip-toed to the bottom of the stairs. They couldn't hear anything above the smooth, intimate sounds of the guitar, piano, drums, cymbals, and Minnie Riperton's rapturous voice.

Fascination covered Journey's bald face. "You think they're . . . ?" she whispered then put a hand over her open mouth.

Kizmic didn't know what to think. As far as she knew, Kalaya had never had a boy in her room before. And what she'd unintentionally gathered from the snippets of Kalaya and Plum's conversations, neither of them had done *it* before. They were waiting for that special guy, that special feeling, that special moment, that special place.

Pulled by her own wonderment, Kizmic crept to the top of the stairs and down the hall. Journey followed. Standing outside Kalaya's bedroom door, Kizmic's heart raced as she tried to detect sounds that told her Kalaya and London were doing *it*. All she heard was Minnie Riperton sweetly hitting that long, whistle-high, heavenly note, which made Kizmic's mind flash back to the birds that flew out of the trees when Bootsy and Twin cried out while they were doing *it*.

Journey, not detecting any doing *it* sounds either, pointed to the keyhole. Kizmic got down on her knees and peeked through the tiny slot. She saw Kalaya's dresser. Back on her feet, she dropped her eyes to the gold doorknob. If she really wanted to know what was going on in that room, she was going to have to open the door.

She grabbed the doorknob. Journey shook her head.

"Just a crack," Kizmic mouthed.

Journey fixed her eyes on the doorjamb. Kizmic slowly turned the knob. The music covered up the small, intruding sounds of the latch disengaging.

Easy, Kizmic said to herself and pushed the door.

The hinges creaked. Then, in the sunlight breaking through the long slit of an opening, Kizmic saw her nine-year-old-self opening Plum's diary and Plum slamming it closed, chiding, "That's private!"

The memory was so fresh and vivid that Kizmic shot a look down the hall, expecting to see Plum rushing out of that time to this time to shut the door. Rattled, she took Journey by the hand and led her away, leaving the door ajar for fear Kalaya might hear her attempt to close it.

Still haunted by Plum, Kizmic glanced at the front door when they got downstairs.

Journey asked, "What'd you see?"

"Nothing."

Kizmic may not have been surprised that Kalaya had London in her bedroom, but she was certainly surprised that she wasn't upset with Kalaya behind it. If that had been Angelo or Clive, Kizmic would have been hot as a firecracker. But she liked London. In fact, she would go so far as to say that she had a jive crush on him. Not like her crush on Onion, of course, but that innocent crush younger sisters had on their older sisters' boyfriends, which was more connected to the adoration they had for their older sisters, who were the epitome of what it was to be beautiful, smart, and cool. Kizmic's crush on London was also deeply connected to Kalaya singing a whole new different tune since she started going with him, and as a result, her relationship with their parents had never been better. That could all change if her mother came home and caught London in Kalaya's bedroom, whether they were doing *it* or not.

Kizmic went into the kitchen and made Journey a peanut butter and jelly sandwich. Journey gobbled it up then downed her medicine with a glass of water. Afterward, Kizmic sent her to Miss Irene's to get frozen cups—Journey's first ever. Sitting on the chair closest to the front door, Journey turned her chunk of frozen orange Kool Aid upside down and began devouring it from the bottom, where much of the sugar had settled. Kizmic peeled off the Styrofoam brim and licked her icy, cherry treat as she stood on the far end of the porch like a day watchman and kept a nervous eye out for her mother. If Kizmic spotted her, she would signal for Journey to run upstairs and make enough noise to alert Kalaya.

To Kizmic's relief, London came down at two o'clock. She could breathe now. "Act natural," she cautioned.

Journey nodded and sat up straight in the chair. Cool. Just chillin'. Eating her first frozen cup on this hot summer day. Kizmic leaned against the railing. Cool. Just chillin'. Eating her frozen cup on this hot summer day. Yeah. That's all they were doing. Chillin'. Not spying on him and Kalaya trying to see if they were doing *it*.

London opened the screen door and Kizmic and Journey's cool fell off their faces. They gaped at him, unable to mask their curiosity. Luckily, he attributed the inquisitiveness in their eyes to their infatuation with him.

He bopped out. He had such a nice bop. Not too hard, not too showy, not too slick. So they didn't uncover any evidence there. If he were Angelo or Clive, Kizmic would have been able to tell right away, because they would have strutted around with their chests stuck out.

"Hey pretty girl," London said to Journey and kissed the top of her bald head. His soft lips tickled her skin and she dissolved into giggles.

"Hey Kizmic," he smiled.

"Hey Kizmic," she repeated.

Kizmic would have been embarrassed, but the part of her brain that let her know when she had said or done something idiotic was on the fritz, because she had dedicated all her mind powers to finding out if he and Kalaya had done *it*.

London raised his broad eyebrows. "Your frozen cup is melting."

Cherry Kool-Aid was dripping all over Kizmic's fingers and down the back of her hand. London went inside, returned with a wet paper towel, and began cleaning her up. As he wiped her hand, Kizmic and Journey examined him closely. London chuckled at the attention.

Kalaya dashed out. Kizmic and Journey turned their scrutinizing eyes to her. Kalaya's hair was in a neat bun and she was wearing red shorts, a red t-shirt, white socks, and red and white Nikes, none of which revealed if she and London had done *it*.

"Let me carry that for you," London said, taking Kalaya's blue canvas gym bag off her shoulder.

Kalaya bounced down the steps. She didn't move like she had done *it*. Poochie said that her sister said that her cousin said it hurt the first time. Kalaya didn't look to be in pain. So maybe they didn't do *it. Or* . . . That wasn't her first time!

Maybe they did *it* in the Firebird on the side of the road like Mama and Daddy said they would.

"Kizmic, we're going to track practice, okay?" Kalaya said.

"Uh-huh."

"Bye, girls," London waved, holding the car door open for Kalaya.

"Bye," they said.

"Heaven Must Be Like This" by the Ohio Players blared from the car stereo as London drove off.

"You think they did *it*?" Journey asked.

Kizmic hunched her shoulders. "Do you?"

Journey hunched her shoulders.

At six o'clock, Kizmic skateboarded home for dinner. Kalaya was in her room blasting the Staple Singers' "Let's Do It Again." It was one of Turk's all-time favorite tunes. He was in the living room, but he wasn't singing or dancing. He wasn't even nodding his head or patting his feet. He sat on the couch with his head back, eyes closed.

"Hey, Daddy," Kizmic said.

"Hey, baby girl," he said.

Seeing that he wasn't his normal energetic self, Kizmic asked, "What's wrong? You got a headache?"

"No. I'm alright."

He didn't look all right, Kizmic thought.

Magdalene was stomping from the kitchen to the dining room, slamming plates down on the table.

Okay. They must be mad at each other, Kizmic concluded.

From Kalaya's stereo came the long version of Donna Summer's "I Love To Love You Baby."

"Kizmic!" Magdalene snapped.

"Yes, ma'am."

"Go up there and tell your sister to turn off that music and get down here and eat." She slammed a glass on the table.

Kizmic experienced a bit of déjà vu standing at Kalaya's door. "Dinner, Kalaya," she hollered and knocked.

Kalaya opened the door, singing, dancing, and plucking her fingers. Kizmic tried to get her to tone it down.

"Mama and Daddy are in a bad mood about something," she warned her.

Kalaya continued singing, then she grabbed Kizmic's hands and made her dance with her.

"Come on before Mama starts fussing," Kizmic said.

Kalaya shook her head to the music. Kizmic felt like Miss Shelly had to feel when she was trying to coax Christmas home after he'd been drinking. She snatched away from Kalaya and turned off the stereo. As they walked down the stairs, Kalaya sang "Love To Love You Baby."

"Stop singing that song!" Turk yelled then got up from the couch.

Kalaya smiled, *Okay*. Then she started humming the song.

Magdalene tramped in. "Didn't your father tell you to stop singing that song?"

Kalaya stopped humming and sat there with a silly smile on her face as she ate. No one was talking about anything. Not work, a neighbor, the news, which was strange. Lately, Turk, Magdalene, and the rest of the world were concerned about the energy crisis. Just the other day he came home complaining about the five-dollar minimum gas purchase law that Governor Hughes put into effect. All week, photographs of cars lined up for miles dominated the front page of *The News American*.

"I burned up over five dollars worth of gas sittin' in that long line at the Crown for two hours," Turk said.

Some truckers held a demonstration to protest the high cost of diesel fuel in Levittown, Pennsylvania. Uncle Monty was planning to go, but Aunt Beana talked him out of it.

"Good thing," he laughed when it was reported that a riot had broken out. "They would have thrown my black behind in jail."

"Or killed you," Aunt Beana said without a laugh.

Turk and Magdalene talked about none of this while they were eating.

"Hey, Daddy," Kalaya called. "What's that song Betty Wright recorded that her mother didn't want her to sing?"

Turk looked across the table at Kalaya with *Are you serious?* wrinkling his forehead. "I don't know, Kalaya," he said.

She turned to Magdalene. "Do you know it, Mama?"

"No."

Kizmic knew the name of the song, but dang if she was going to say it.

"Mmmm, Mama!" Kalaya exclaimed. "This is some good fried chicken."

Turk dropped his head and rubbed his temples like the headache he said he didn't have was getting worse. Magdalene threw her head back and closed her eyes for the same reason.

"What'd you do to it?" Kalaya asked.

Kizmic took a bite of her chicken leg. What's she talkin' about? It don't taste no different.

"It's the same fried chicken I make every week, Kalaya," Magdalene said.

"Really? Well, it sure tastes different." Kalaya munched on the tip of her chicken wing and started humming Diana Ross' "Love Hangover."

"Will you stop humming!" Magdalene demanded.

For a few minutes, Kalaya said nothing, sang nothing, and hummed nothing. Then, "'Tonight Is The Night.'"

"What?" Magdalene asked.

"That's the name of that Betty Wright song."

Kalaya took her plate into the kitchen, and while getting another piece of chicken, she happily and quietly sang the song to herself. Turk and Magdalene looked at each other in the same scared, weary way they'd looked at each other the day Kalaya bled on the marble step back on Proctor Street. And Kizmic figured out what her parents had figured out, even though they were not home to witness it. Kalaya had done *it* for the first time!

Oooouuu! Wait 'til I tell Journey!

Kizmic never had anybody she wanted to tell this kind of stuff to. Her mother and Aunt Beana had each other. Kalaya and Plum had each other. Now she had Journey.

"Well, she didn't do *it* in the car," Journey said.

Kizmic and Journey were riding beside each other on their bikes, delivering the morning paper. Onion was pedaling his bike on the other side of Garrison, knocking out his half of the customers.

"You ever think about what your first time will be like?" Journey asked.

"No," Kizmic said.

"Why?" Journey asked.

She tossed the rubber-banded newspaper onto a porch. "Because I didn't think I'd grow up."

Journey backpedaled, hitting the brakes. "What do you mean?"

"I knew I'd get older," Kizmic said, braking, "but I thought I could stop certain things from happening."

"What things?" Journey plucked a newspaper out of her basket and threw it on the next porch.

"Getting my period," Kizmic confessed.

"You thought you could stop your period from coming? Why?"

"Misunderstanding something I heard my mother say when I was nine."

Journey rode four houses up, flung the newspaper on the porch, and rode back. "What else?"

With a dwindling sense of embarrassment, Kizmic lowered her eyes to her breasts.

"You thought you could stop them from growing?" she asked, perplexed.

Journey got a good laugh out of the story Kizmic told her about the morning she woke up and discovered she had breasts. It was fun making light of the things that used to terrify her.

"What else? Wait. I bet I know." Journey delivered a paper three doors up. When she rode back, she said, "Liking Onion."

Kizmic fessed up to that as well. It felt good to have somebody to tell that to.

"Kizmic and Onion sittin' in a tree k-i-s-s—"

Kizmic cringed. "Shhhh! He might hear you."

"What? He don't know that he likes you?" Journey snickered. "Or that you like him?"

Kizmic shook her head in amusement.

"Why's he going with Poochie?"

"She grew up faster than me." Kizmic retrieved another paper from her bag and pedaled to the next house. "Do you think about what your first time will be like?"

"I didn't until we were standing at Kalaya's bedroom door the other day."

"Why not before?"

"I learned what you learned," Journey said, grabbing a paper. "You can't stop certain things from happening." She chucked the newspaper and watched it land on the porch. "So what's the use of thinking about them?"

CHAPTER

37

THE HIP SHAKIN', RUMP WRIGGLIN' strike of the cowbell in Anita Ward's chart climbing single "Ring My Bell" could be heard blocks away from the earthquake speakers it was pumping out of. It was five o'clock and the Pimlico Neighborhood Association's First Annual 4th of July Cookout and Block Party was underway. And even with the vice grip of sweltering ninety-five-degree temperatures Baltimore's typical summer heatwave had the city locked in for the past three days, folks were looking forward to the good time the fliers advertising the event promised.

Kizmic could hear the bass booming all the way up on Garrison. Her heart boom just as hard with excitement.

"We missin' it!" Peanut fretted.

"How we missin' it and it just started?" Redtop asked.

Man 'n 'Em volunteered to help Kizmic, Onion, and Journey with the route so they could finish before the festivities began. Peanut and Redtop went with Kizmic, Journey had Man, Meatball, and Fatboy, and Steebo and Babyfrog had gone with Onion. Together, the friends fanned out across the route on their bikes and planned to meet at the block party when they were done.

"Come on, y'all. We only got four more houses," Kizmic said. "Hurry up."

Peanut and Redtop each took a house and Kizmic, knowing the addresses like the back of her hand, took the last two.

"Alright! We done. Let's go!" Kizmic said, speeding back up the block.

Following the funky electric guitar riff of Chic's "Good Times" as if the Pied Guitarist Nile Rodgers himself were playing it live, people rushed on foot, bicycles, skateboards, rollerskates and flooded over and around the two white, wooden saw horse barriers that blocked Beaufort off to car traffic at the corner of Spaulding going toward Belvedere. Kizmic spotted Journey's purple, green, and red headwrap at the Duck Pond game. She and Rachel were trying to fish some yellow rubber ducks out of a blue kiddie pool with orange plastic fishing rods. Babyfrog and Fatboy were at the Quarterback Toss booth, throwing a football through some numbered holes in a wooden board. Man was at the Basketball booth shooting free throws. Steebo and Onion were at the Milk Pyramid booth, attempting to knock over three aluminum milk bottles with rubber baseballs.

Eating an egg custard snowball, Meatball walked up to Kizmic, Peanut, and Redtop. "Man, y'all slower than a mug!"

"We had more houses than y'all did," Peanut said.

"Hey! They got a trampoline!" Redtop said and made a beeline to it.

"Com'on, Kizmic," Peanut said.

"I'ma get my camera," she told him.

Everyone except Lawyer Balil and D. Tinkle had fired up grills in their back yards. The smoky, tantalizing aroma of hotdogs, hamburgers, barbecued ribs and chicken scented the air, along with the delicious smell of steamed crabs and grilled fish, for Mr Charlie was selling bushels of crabs and cooking lake trout on a grill he made out of a black oil drum. Long folding tables with red and white checkered tablecloths were piled with plates of deviled eggs, bowls of potato salad, macaroni salad, coleslaw, fruit salad, ears of corn, trifle, banana pudding, cake, apple pie, pitchers of iced tea and half 'n half. Large coolers were packed with soda and beer buried in ice. Grownups leaned on fences and strolled in and out of cookouts, taking a bite of this, a taste of that, a sip of something else as they told stories, threw in their two cents, tossed up thigh-slapping laughter, and sang, and did old dances whenever DJ Smooth As . . . played a song they liked.

DJ Smooth As . . . BKA Plum's boyfriend, Alonso, was on the black, wooden stage erected in the middle of the street, surrounded by throngs of dancing, shouting teenagers. On stage with him was Plum, exhibiting none of that jive she was talking at the skating rink about Alonso not working hard enough to win her affections. Smiling broadly, she watched with fascination and adoration as he expertly worked the two turntables and mixer. From what Kizmic could tell, there was no doubt Alonso had earned Plum's affections.

Using his bassy voice like an instrument, Alonso said into the microphone, "Yo! This is DJ Smooth As..."

"Crisco!" Kalaya and London shouted with the crowd.

"That's right. Y'all know I am," he said. "Now let's turn this sucka out!"

Alonso adjusted the headphones over his blue Colts baseball cap and ears. Plum handed him a twelve-inch from one of the seven crates of albums beside her. He placed it on the left turntable, set the needle on the groove, then put his fingertips on the wax. Rocking, bopping, and bouncing to the beat of "Good Times," Alonso spun the record counterclockwise a few times before stopping. Then he simultaneously lifted his fingers and shoved the crossfader on the mixer all the way to the left, and "Get Off" by Foxxy started playing seamlessly, like it was part of "Good Times." Plum handed him another twelve-inch, which Alonso put on the right turntable and rotated counterclockwise as well. He threw the fader to the right and the intro to "Get Off" looped again. He did that three times without making it sound like the record was scratched. The crowd jumped up and down and waved their hands in the air as Alonso artistically played records on those turntables like he was playing a fine-tuned instrument.

Walking in time with the music, Kizmic pushed her bike to the house. Turk and Magdalene had set up their cookout in the side yard so they could be closer to the block party.

"See, he's doin' it again!" Turk said in a disapproving tone.

"Doing what again?" Magdalene asked, then took a bite of her hotdog.

"Puttin' his hands all over the records," Turk said, appalled. Not surprising for a man who used a velvet brush to clean dust off his records before he played them. "And he keeps playin' the same part over and over."

Magdalene moved her shoulders to the groove. "That's how they're doing it these days."

"He's scratchin' those records up, that's what he's doin' these days," Turk said.

Whether her father liked it or not, Alonso had his fingertips on the beat of the record and on the pulse of the crowd, which included his wife.

Chewing a mouth full of macaroni salad, Aunt Beana watched Plum wipe sweat off Alonso's face with a towel. "I'm looking at Plum standing up there like a groupie."

"*I'm* looking at the van the boy rode up in," Uncle Monty said and sipped his beer.

Alonso had a black Chevy van that he treasured as much as his turntables and albums.

Miss Sarah said, "With all that equipment, you're lucky he's not driving a tractor trailer."

Kizmic got her camera and stood on the porch. The block was packed. She had to take three wide shots because the breathtaking crowd couldn't fit in one. DJ Smooth As... — "Lotion!" people shouted—transitioned to Sister Sledge's "We Are Family." Kizmic took pictures of White Betty drinking and swaying in her window, Christmas and Miss Shelly boogieing on their porch, Lawyer Balil and Phoebe standing in the alley, Magdalene and Turk hand dancing, and Uncle Monty doing the bump with Aunt Beana on his left hip and

Miss Sarah on his right.

Kizmic moved through the crowd with the shutter of her Ciro-flex *clicking, clicking, clicking* as she captured Redtop double and triple flipping on the trampoline, Journey, Man 'n 'Em, and Diamond, Poochie, 'n 'Em competing in the Balloon Dart game, Bean Bag Toss, and Ball In Basket Toss. Seeing Miss Josephine standing in line at the Funnel Cake booth, Kizmic centered her in the viewfinder. DJ Smooth As... — "Peter Pan Peanut Butter!" his fans yelled—began mixing "I Like The Girls" by the Fatback Band. Miss Josephine smiled and posed for the shot. Then, as cool as anything, she shot up two short, piercing whistles. Kizmic had heard other adults whistle like that before and each time, D. Tinkle was lurking nearby. He was eating cotton candy and ogling some little girls at the Ring Toss game.

Wearing a yellow dress that was as radiant as the sun, Miss Josephine strutted over to D. Tinkle in her yellow heels and stood in front of him, an action that both blocked his view of the girls and made it easy for the adults to spot him. Their shotgun eyes held him in their angry sights. D. Tinkle smirked at them until Mr Dale came and looked at him like he was the most disgusting thing on the planet. The crooked smile on D. Tinkle's face turned sweaty and twitchy. Not a full thirty seconds passed before D. Tinkle headed up the alley and went into his back yard. The way all of that went down let Kizmic know that the adults were planning more than cookouts and block parties at the neighborhood association meetings.

DJ Smooth As . . . — "Silk!" the dancing teens screamed—played Chic's "Le Freak" and the teenagers started doing The Freak, which freaked the adults out.

"These kids done lost their minds," Magdalene said, frowning at Kalaya and London dancing face-to-face and pelvis-to-pelvis.

Kizmic had seen Kalaya freak before, but never like she was freakin' with London.

Uncle Monty's dead eye widened. "What's in them snowballs?"

"Oh, I know how to stop this," Turk said.

Kizmic, Kalaya, and Plum watched with embarrassment as Turk stormed on stage. Alonso took off his headphones. After listening respectfully to Turk, he nodded his head and started digging in his crates. He pulled out two records, handed one to Turk, and placed the other on the right turntable.

"Yo! We 'bout to take it back!" Alonso said into the microphone. "Y'all wid me?"

"Yeah!" the crowd yelled.

"I said, Are Y'all Wid Me?!"

"We wid you, Smooth!"

Putting back on his headphones, Alonso spun the record counterclockwise three times. "Stay wid me now," he said, then hit the fader and let the record spin.

"The Way You Do The Things You Do" by the Temptations came out of the gigantic speakers. The adults hollered, "Awwww Shucks Now!" and started plucking their fingers and clapping their hands.

Turk was using his shirt to wipe the fingerprints off the record he was holding when Alonso took it from him and placed it on the left turntable. He rotated it backward and against Turk's visible objections, he forced Turk to put his fingers on the record and hold it still. Alonso put his fingers on the fader and pointed at Turk, who lifted his fingers, releasing the intro again.

"OOOOOH!" the crowd went wild.

"That's my father, y'all!" Kalaya screamed.

Plum danced and pointed proudly at her godfather to the beat.

"Yo! Your daddy's mixin'," Meatball said to Kizmic in surprise.

Prouder than she'd ever been of her father, Kizmic ran on her porch so she could get a better shot of him scratching up records to the delight of himself and everyone else.

"Yo! This is DJ Smooth As . . ."

"Icin'!"

"That's right. And I'm rockin' with DJ . . ." He shoved the mic in Turk's face.

Turk's eyes rolled around nervously as he thought of a name. "Way Back! Yo!"

"YEEAAAAH!"

Alonso took out two more records and handed one to Turk. After placing the other on the turntable, he said, "One! Two! One, Two, Three—"

Turk hit the fader and The Temptation's "Ain't Too Proud To Beg" brought young and old onto the dance floor. It was incredible.

At nine o'clock, twinkling stars and a round, shining moon replaced the blazing sun in the sky and lowered the temperature a whopping five degrees. People were still out eating, playing games, socializing, and dancing to Mass Production's "Firecracker" that was being mixed by DJ Smooth As . . .

"Sh—"

"Yo! Don't say it," Alonso laughed.

"Satin!" the crowd yelled instead.

Kizmic used up three rolls of film and went in the house to get a fourth. When she came back downstairs, Onion was waiting for her in the hallway.

"I been meaning to ask you about the pictures from my photo shoot," he said. "You never showed them to me."

That's right. She hadn't. After she'd caught him and Poochie dancing in the clubhouse, she threw the pictures in a box.

"Can I see them?" he asked.

"Now?"

He nodded, "Yeah."

"I guess so." Kizmic hurried to her room.

"You made me look like a movie star," Onion said, going through the photos. "There it is."

"There what is?"

Onion held up the photograph of them goofing around. "That smile I was tellin' you about. You smiled like that at the pool the other day."

"Yeah?"

"Uh-huh. I really meant it when I said you looked pretty."

"I know," Kizmic said.

With that out in the open, he asked nervously, "Do you know that I . . . I wanna . . . kiss you?"

Of course she knew he wanted to kiss her, because she wanted to kiss him, too. And not at the end of summer like she planned. Kizmic wanted to kiss Onion now. But . . .

"Don't you think you should break up with Poochie first?"

"I don't have to break up with Poochie."

"Why not?"

"'Cause I never went with her."

"Does she know that?"

"Yeah."

"You ever kiss her?"

"No. I've never kissed a girl before."

"Why?"

"'Cause I never liked one the way . . . I like you."

Staring into his handsome, green gaze, Kizmic's heart started pounding in her chest the way the bass was pounding in Alonso's speakers. Onion moved his face closer to hers. She took a deep breath to calm herself and got a nose full of whatever detergent his mother used to wash his clothes.

Onion closed his eyes as his mouth neared hers. Then Kizmic put her forefinger to his lips.

Popping open his eyes, he mumbled around the pressure, "What's a matter?"

"What kind of detergent does your mother use to wash your clothes?"

Onion furrowed his brow. "Huh?"

Removing her finger, she asked, "Tide? Cheer?"

"Cheer, I think?" Onion answered, shaking his head in confusion.

"You think or you know?"

"It's in a blue box. Cheer. Why?"

"Just something I wanted to know."

"Okay," Onion said, and licked his lips.

Oooh, they looked so moist and tender.

Then Onion kissed Kizmic, and she kissed him back. And guess what! Nothing slipped away. Not her love for marbles or skully or her skateboard, basketball, football, baseball! All the things she loved stayed right there, including Onion. With that kiss, Kizmic realized her life wasn't ending. It was at the start of the beginning. Just like Miss Josephine said.

Kizmic let herself indulge in the kiss. It was so soft and warm and sweet and electrifying. It raised the tiny hairs on her arms. It was also arresting. Everything stopped, her heart, her breathing, the music.

BOOM!

Wow! she thought as the kiss rocked her body. It was like fireworks going off inside her.

BOOM!

This feeling had to be why Kalaya risked her life climbing down the upstairs back porch.

Kizmic heard a roaring "OOOOOHHH!" in her ears as another *BOOM!* shook her. She opened her eyes and saw bursts of yellow lights exploding in the sky.

"Fireworks!" she said.

"Was it that good?" Onion smiled.

Kizmic laughed. "Boy. Outside. They're settin' off fireworks."

She took him by the hand and they ran out the door. Everyone was applauding and oohing and aahing as Turk, Uncle Monty, and Mr Charlie set off the fiery lights.

Journey was standing on the porch steps. "I've spent almost every holiday in the hospital. They had clowns, magicians, and Santa come to cheer us up. But they never did anything like this."

Journey found her mother and Kizmic took a beautiful shot of the two of them looking up at the colorful lightning storm. When the fireworks ended, Journey's lightning struck eyes were still cast upward, sparkling. Kizmic was still sparkling, too, inside.

She whispered in Onion's ear, "It *was* that good."

CHAPTER

38

"Kizmic and Onion sittin' in a tree—"

"We were standin' in the hallway," Kizmic clarified.

"I know, but that doesn't rhyme," Journey said. "K-I-S-S-I-N-G."

She pedaled her bike up Belvedere, delivered three morning papers, and rode back.

"What did it feel like?" Journey asked.

"Fireworks," Kizmic said, grinning at Onion, who was delivering papers on the other side of the street, grinning at her.

Later, when they all went to C.C. Jackson, Kizmic and Onion did more grinning at each other than swimming.

"Forget him," Diamond told Poochie.

"I ain't like him anyway," Poochie snorted.

Kizmic noticed that Journey wasn't doing a whole lot of swimming, either. She spent most of the time sitting on the side of the pool with her feet in the water, content to watch the splashing fun around her.

On the way home, Journey strolled several steps behind Kizmic and Onion. Occasionally, she glanced back and found Journey smiling adorningly at them or letting her eyes linger on the trees, birds flying in the sky, people walking by or sitting on their porches.

"What do we do now that we go together?" Kizmic asked.

"My brother talks on the phone with his girlfriends," Onion said.

"Yeah. Kalaya and London stay on the phone."

"And we go to the movies."

"We already do that."

"Well, we can do whatever you wanna do."

"I wanna do whatever you wanna do."

"I wanna hold your hand," Onion said.

Kizmic held out her hand and they intertwined their fingers. When they got to Onion's house, he wanted Kizmic to come inside so they could kiss for the second time, but Journey needed to eat something so she could take her medicine.

"I'ma go with Journey to the Fish Store then I'll come back," she told him.

They grinned at each other until Kizmic turned the corner.

"I'm glad you stopped waiting for the end of summer to like him," Journey said.

"Me, too," Kizmic said.

At the Fish Store, Journey sat on the steps. Sweat was dripping down her face and her breathing was labored.

"You okay?" Kizmic asked.

"I think I'm overheated," Journey answered, dabbing at the sweat with her towel.

Yeah. That was probably it. The heatwave still had a sweltering grip around the city's neck.

Miss Josephine brought Journey a grape soda and two Butterscotch Krimpets.

"Thank you, Miss Josephine, but can I have some water?"

Miss Josephine eyed Journey. It wasn't like her to turn down grape soda.

"Sure, Shugga." Miss Josephine went inside and was back in seconds. "I'll be right in here if you need anything."

Journey ate one Krimpet, then took her medicine with the water. She grimaced each time she swallowed.

Christmas' cart rattled as he pushed it across Beaufort and up the alley. The sun reflected off the precious metals he hauled.

"I like that 'Joy To The World' song Christmas sings on Sundays," Journey said. "Do you think they'll let someone sing it in your church?"

"It's not a church song," Kizmic said.

"I know, but it would be nice if they sung it during service." She raised the glass of water to her mouth.

"Yeah, Mother Abigail can sing it," Kizmic joked.

Journey choked. "Chees-its," she then said in her best Pop Evans voice.

Kizmic and Journey laughed all over each other on the steps.

"We have to hurry up and finish the album," Journey said once their near hysterical laughter turned to small snickers.

"Christmas is five months away. We still got the Labor Day cookout and Halloween, and then there's Thanksgiving. The leaves are so pretty around that time. We can go to Cylburn and you can lie in a pile. If we're lucky, we might get some snow in December."

"It would be wonderful to have pictures of all that in there, but do you think we could have it done before the end of August?"

Kizmic scratched her braided head. "I guess so. I already put the pictures from the block party in to be developed. We just need to buy an album."

"Let's buy it tomorrow."

"Okay."

She bumped Kizmic with her thin thigh. "Now go kiss your boyfriend," she whispered.

"What?" Kizmic looked guiltily over her shoulder for Miss Josephine. She was in the back of the store.

"Go ahead." Journey took off the orange headscarf.

"What are you gonna do?"

"Sit here, eat this other Krimpet, and enjoy the sun on my bald head."

THAT NIGHT, KIZMIC LISTENED out for Kalaya. She came in fifteen minutes before her scheduled curfew. Kalaya was so different from the argumentative, rebellious girl who went out of her way to pluck their mother's nerves. Aside from sneaking London in the house when their parents were at work, Kalaya now went out of her way to stay on their mother's good side.

Kizmic went to her room and asked, "Do you think London would mind driving me and Journey to the mall tomorrow? She wants to buy something for Miss Sarah."

Kicking off her tennis shoes, Kalaya said, "He's going to call me when he gets home. I'll ask him then. I'm sure he won't mind."

"Okay. Thanks." Kizmic opened the door to leave, but Kalaya called her back.

Sitting down on her bed, Kalaya regarded Kizmic with nurturing, soft-hearted, big sister eyes. For a moment, she appeared as if she didn't know how to say what she wanted to say. Amused by her hesitancy, she went ahead and spit it out. "So, you and Onion are a thing."

Kizmic gawked at Kalaya, shocked as all get-out. "How'd you hear that?"

"The same way I'd hear whenever you played marbles with Leon back on Proctor Street."

"That's not tellin' me how," Kizmic said.

"You want me to tell you my source? I won't be able to keep tabs on you if I do that," she grinned. "But I can tell you that if you need to talk about the feelings you have for Onion, I'm here."

Kizmic didn't know what to say. Thank you sounded hollow compared to the bond between them that was getting stronger each day. The only words big enough and sincere enough to convey Kizmic's feelings for her big sister were, "I love you, Kalaya."

Kalaya smiled, "I love you, too."

Kizmic turned to leave, then spun back around. "Does this mean I'm old enough to eat cornbread without gettin' choked?"

Kalaya's eyes got big, and she vehemently shook her head as she laughed, "Noooo! Don't be eatin' no cornbread."

Next time I'll ask her what the heck that even means, Kizmic thought.

Friday evening, instead of London pulling up in front of their house in his Firebird, Alonso drove up in his van with Plum in the passenger side captain seat.

London pushed open the barn doors and hopped out. "What's happenin', ladies?" He got between Kizmic and Journey and put an arm around each of their shoulders.

"You are such a ham," Kalaya said.

"Don't get jealous. I can't help it if I'm a babe magnet."

London helped Kizmic and Journey climb in and they sat in the other two captain seats. Taking Kalaya's hand, he helped her in, and they snuggled up on the bench seat in the back. The air-conditioning was a welcome relief to the scorching ninety-plus-degree heat that wouldn't let up.

"Be Ever Wonderful" by Earth, Wind & Fire came on the radio as Alonso cruised onto the parking lot at Security Square Mall. He cranked up the volume, and the music boomed from the speakers, subwoofers, and amplifier. Wiggling her fingers, Kizmic mimed playing the sax. Journey beat the drums with imaginary sticks. London simulated the horn. Singing lead, Alonso pulled into a space near the front entrance while Kalaya and Plum sang backup. When the song reached its climax, the van rocked as Kizmic, Journey, and London put down their instruments, Kalaya and Plum stepped from the background, and they all joined Alonso and Maurice White in singing that vital verse to one another.

"All right, this is the plan," London said. "You two go get whatever you came for, then meet us back here by eight because we're gonna go see 'Alien.' My homeboy works in the ticket booth so we can sneak y'all in."

Kizmic and Journey looked at each other. *Sneak us in? Alright!*

"Com'on with DJ Smooth As..."

"Ice Cream," Journey said.

"Shoot! That makes me cool, too," Alonso said.

"No, that just makes you corny," Plum said.

Kizmic and Journey went to JCPenny, Hecht's, Kodax store, Waldenbooks, and B. Dalton Bookseller, but there was nothing unique about the albums on their shelves. Journey got more tired than discouraged. At seven-forty, they sat down to rest at a table in the food court. There was a novelty retail gift cart called Impressions across from them. A small, plain, black box on the bottom shelf called to Journey. Kneeling on the floor, she opened it. Enclosed in bubble wrap was a 5-1/2 x 7, dark Cherry wood cover photo album. Its spine was crafted from black velvet. It had black pages under clear plastic sleeves that could hold one hundred photos. But what set this album apart from any other were the silver, heavenly angel wings open in flight that had been sculpted out of cast iron and affixed to the front cover.

Journey repeatedly ran her fingers over the fluffy, metallic feathers. "It's perfect."

Noticing the "Personalize Your Gift Have It Engraved" sign, Journey told the saleswoman to carve *I* on the left wing and on the right wing, *Lived!*

Kizmic and Journey spent the next few days deciding which pictures to put in the album. They started out by spreading the hundred and eighty-odd photographs on the floor in Kizmic's bedroom, but the fan kept blowing them around.

"I know what we can do," Journey said. "Can I?" She pointed to the wall that had posters of "Charlie's Angels," "What's Happening," and Todd Bridges taped to it.

She and Journey took down the posters, taped the photographs to the wall, then pulled off the ones they wanted to put in the album.

Journey laid across the bed. "All your friendships are on these walls," she said drowsily.

Kizmic looked at the medley of photographs, including the ones of her and Man 'n 'Em on the wall above her bed, and she thought with a smile, I lived, too.

CHAPTER

39

Six o'clock Tuesday morning Journey called to say she couldn't help with the route.

"I forgot that I have a doctor's appointment at eight o'clock," she said.

"Oh." Kizmic was bummed out that Journey wasn't coming that morning, but she'd be there that afternoon, right?

"I won't be home by then. I have to do this test and . . . it takes a long time."

"How long?"

"A week."

A glum feeling settled inside Kizmic. She and Journey had spent every day together since they met. Not only had she gotten used to being with Journey, she loved being with her. What was an entire week going to be like without her?

"What hospital are you at? Can I come visit you?"

Journey paused so long that Kizmic thought they had gotten disconnected. "Journey?"

"I'm at Johns Hopkins."

"Can I come see you?"

Another long pause. "Yeah, but call first because I might not be in my room."

As Kizmic jotted down the phone number, she got a sinking feeling in her stomach as she remembered the baseball on her nightstand with CJ and Sleepy-eyed Ted's numbers on it and how they were never home when she called, and never called her back even though she'd left her phone number with their mothers a hundred times.

"I gotta go, Kizmic. I'll call you tonight."

"What time?"

"Seven."

"Okay."

Hearing the sadness in Kizmic's voice, Journey said, "I just thought of something. With me gone, you and Onion can spend the whole week smoochin'," she offered as consolation, then made kissing sounds over the phone.

Kizmic giggled.

"DON'T GET ME WRONG," Onion said, hanging his sack of newspapers on his shoulder. "Journey's cool and all, but I'm glad I get to be alone with my girlfriend."

They took their time delivering the front-page news about the Skylab plummeting back to earth. They rode side by side talking, ducked behind big trees and smooched, then got back on their bikes, grinning. After the route, they snuck inside the clubhouse to smooch some more. They sat cross-legged on the floor facing each other.

"When did you start likin' me, Onion?" Kizmic asked. "I mean *likin'* me *likin'* me."

"I always liked you liked you."

"No, you didn't."

"I swear," Onion said, putting his forefinger to his chest and crossing his heart.

"Really?"

"Since the first day I saw you."

"Why?"

"I never saw a girl dribble a basketball like that. Or look so cute."

Kizmic tried to hide her bashfulness by asking, "Well, why were you so mean to me?"

"'Cause Man 'n 'Em would've ragged on me if they knew I liked you. And I didn't want you to know."

"Why not?"

"'Cause I was afraid that you didn't like me the way that I like you."

"I didn't."

"What?!"

Kizmic chuckled.

"When did you start *likin'* me *likin'* me?"

"Last September."

"What took you so long?"

"I was afraid, too."

"Of what?"

Kizmic sighed and glanced around the clubhouse. "Losing all this and one of my best friends."

"I ain't goin' nowhere," Onion said.

They leaned forward and kissed. Fireworks exploded inside Kizmic again. Then the feeling fizzled out when Steebo's mother opened the screen door and walked down the steps, carrying a big basket of laundry. Kizmic and Onion froze as Miss Jackson hung clothes on the line. They had been alone in the clubhouse neither knew how many times, playing cards or something, but never kissing. With the *uh-oh* on their faces, if Miss Jackson caught them in there, she would know instantly that they hadn't been playing Tonk.

The sun was high and hot, and it was boiling inside the clubhouse. Kizmic and Onion were drenched in sweat. Luckily, Steebo called his mother. The second her flip-flops hit the kitchen floor, Kizmic and Onion bolted out the door and ran to her house, laughing and gulping fresh air.

When they went swimming that afternoon, Steebo swam over to Kizmic and Onion and started splashing water all over them.

"Man, what you doin'?!" Onion yelled, using his body to shield Kizmic from the attack.

"Just helpin' y'all cool off." Steebo gave them a wicked grin. "I saw you lovebirds sneak in the clubhouse this mornin'."

Kizmic and Onion tried not to look guilty.

"Yep. Then my mama came out, and I was like, Ooouuu! If she catch them in there, they gonna get it."

"Nuh-uh, 'cause we wasn't doin' nothin'," Onion claimed.

"*Pssshh!* Yeah, right," Steebo scoffed. "I was gonna call my mama sooner, but I was dyin' laughin' 'cause I knew y'all was in that mug roastin' tryin' not to get busted."

Steebo cackled then backstroked away, kicking his feet hard, splattering water on them again.

Seven o'clock, Kizmic was sitting at the kitchen table waiting for the phone to ring and holding the baseball CJ and Sleepy-eyed Ted had given her. The numbers had faded, but she could still make them out. She thought of calling them, but didn't want the line to be busy when Journey called. If she called.

She's gonna call, Kizmic assured herself.

Ten after seven, the phone rang. Kizmic snatched up the receiver and was relieved to hear Journey on the other end.

"You called," Kizmic said.

"I told you I would," Journey said.

Kizmic planned to tell Journey all about kissing Onion and getting stuck in the clubhouse, but she sounded half asleep.

"Are you okay?"

"Tired."

Kizmic waited for Journey to say something else, but she didn't. "Um . . . Alright. How about I call you in the morning after the route?"

"Yeah."

"Kizmic," Miss Sarah said.

"Hey Miss Sarah."

"Hi, sweetie. I'm sorry, but Journey had a long day, and the doctors gave her something to help her sleep."

"O . . . Okay."

"She'll call you tomorrow."

"Okay."

"Have a good night, Kizmic."

"You, too."

After Miss Sarah hung up, Kizmic went to her room and traced over CJ and Sleepy-eyed Ted's numbers with a blue ink pen.

THURSDAY, JULY 12, Minnie Riperton passed away. It was on the front page of the *Afro*. V-103 played her records on the radio all day. Knowing that Journey would take her hero's death as hard as a close family member's, Kizmic had to go see her.

Kizmic, Man 'n 'Em were on the front porch rolling up the newspapers when Magdalene and Aunt Beana came home from work. Kizmic rushed to the car.

"I need to go see Journey." She was almost in tears.

Seeing how distraught Kizmic was, Magdalene asked with controlled panic in her voice, "Baby, what's wrong?"

"Minnie Riperton died," Kizmic said. "Journey loves her. I need to make sure she's all right."

Magdalene said, "Okay. Let me change my clothes and I'll take you."

"I'm going, too," Aunt Beana said.

THE ONCOLOGY WING of Johns Hopkins was busy with nurses, doctors, aides, and janitors moving constantly. Walking down the white hallway, Kizmic held her head low, trying not to intrude on anyone's privacy. But most of the doors were open and her eyes wandered into the rooms. They were filled with children—black, white, Asian, Hispanic, young, teenagers. Some with hair, some without, some in wheelchairs, some using canes, some asleep, some awake, some hooked up to tubes and machines, some laughing, some talking, some crying, some watching television, some staring out the window, some looked gravely ill, some looked like they were there for something as routine as having their tonsils removed.

Seeing those kids made Kizmic remember Journey saying as if it were no big deal that her cancer was something like Minnie Riperton's. "Only hers is in her breasts," Journey explained.

"Where's yours?" Kizmic asked that day standing in the castle room.

"All over," Journey had said.

'All over'? Kizmic wondered, but didn't ask.

Seeing those kids gave Kizmic an uneasy feeling that said Journey just being there was a big deal.

Her room was at the end of the hall. Nearing it, they heard Journey quietly singing. Magdalene, Aunt Beana, and Kizmic stopped at the door.

In a blue gown covered with black snowflakes, Journey was sitting up in bed. She wasn't connected to a bunch of tubes or machines, but she did have an IV in her arm. Miss Sarah was napping in the chair beside the bed.

Journey's bald head was down. She was drawing in her sketchbook and singing "Come On In My Room." All her concentration was on the quick, sharp, and wispy strokes of her yellow pencil on the paper and the song.

"Well, listen to you," Magdalene said.

Journey raised her head, closed her sketchbook, and smiled big and bright. "Miss Magdalene! Miss Beana! Kizmic!" She hugged each of them twice.

"You're lucky Reverend Miles didn't hear you," Aunt Beana said. "He'd make you join the children's choir."

Journey laughed, then called her mother, who didn't stir despite the noise.

"Let her sleep," Magdalene said.

"I'm awake," Miss Sarah said groggily. She yawned and stretched. Her eyes were red and tense.

"How are you?" Aunt Beana asked Journey.

"I'm good."

Magdalene asked, "You need anything?"

"Just Kizmic."

"Journey, we're going to step out into the hall for a bit," Miss Sarah said.

When they left, Kizmic asked, "Did you hear about Minnie Riperton?"

"Yeah. My mother told me. The world's not as bright without her in it." She sighed, and opened her sketchbook to the drawing she was working on.

It was a one-frame comic strip of Kizmic and Onion kissing with fireworks exploding around them.

"Is this right?" Journey asked.

"Yes," Kizmic said.

"I tried to get it the way you described it, with fireworks all over."

"'All over.'"

"Uh-huh."

"What does that mean? 'All over'?" Kizmic wasn't talking about the fireworks. She was talking about Journey's cancer.

Journey closed her sketchbook and stared Kizmic in the eye. "It means . . . I'm going to die, Kizmic."

CHAPTER

40

"THE END OF AUGUST . . . maybe."

Sitting on the living room sofa with Turk and Kalaya, Magdalene told them what they all had been thinking but was afraid to say out loud, for to say it out loud was to claim it.

"Sarah said she's had leukemia since she was five."

Turk and Kalaya were silent. Kizmic sat at the top of the stairs, listening.

"Journey got a nose bleed one day and a week later, the doctors told Sarah that Journey had leukemia. She's been in and out of hospitals ever since. Last year, they gave her this experimental drug and it seemed to work. It looked like she was going into remission, but . . ." Magdalene sighed heavily. "In May, it came back, aggressively. They don't know why. All they know is, by the end of the summer . . ."

Kizmic stomped to her room. She didn't believe it. Why should she? She didn't know not one kid who died. Not one! Kids didn't die. Old people died. But that wasn't true, was it? The news articles in her great-grandfather's trunk proved that people old and young died all the time.

But they didn't just die. They were killed. That's different. They didn't get sick and die.

Journey didn't even look sick. She looked like she *could* be in the hospital to get her tonsils taken out.

"She doesn't look sick, so how is she gonna die?!"

Kizmic went to the wall and with tears stinging her eyes, she examined each photograph she had taken of Journey. And she saw what she'd been refusing to see. Journey was a lot thinner than when they first met. Her face was narrower. In the earlier pictures, Journey was standing up or riding something, but in the later pictures, she was sitting down. Sure, she was drawing, petting Phyllis, holding a pigeon, playing cards, but she was always sitting, always catching her breath. Getting sicker.

Kizmic's head hurt so badly. She rubbed her temples and her left eye burned and twitched. The same eye Tori had blackened. The same eye that let her see Journey in the window after all those years of looking past her. Now, even though Journey wasn't anywhere near her, Kizmic saw her for the very first time it seemed. Saw why those veins in her eyelids were so visible. Saw why her breasts and behind were so flat. She hadn't been to Netherland. There was no Netherland. Journey's body was stuck in time because it was wrapped in leukemia.

"All over." Kizmic held her pounding head and closed her eyes. "All over all over all over all over."

Her head was throbbing so hard that she didn't know that her mother had come into her room until Magdalene put her arms around her.

"Mama, is she really gonna die?" Kizmic asked into her mother's breasts.

Magdalene squeezed her tighter. "I'm afraid so, baby. I wish I could tell you differently."

Kizmic wished the same as she cried, cried, cried.

Magdalene and Aunt Beana called parents and explained what was happening with Journey so they could break the sad news to their children. Everyone was as unbelieving as Kizmic. And everyone cried.

Journey came home the following Thursday. She wasn't well enough to go outside, of course, but that didn't stop the outside from coming in to her.

Miss Josephine and Mr Charlie came by with boxes of Butterscotch Krimpets and two cases of Fanta Grape soda. Sweets dropped by and washed Journey's bald head, then lit some sandalwood candles and gave Journey a therapeutic full body massage. Miss Connie delivered barbecued spare ribs, collard greens, potato salad, cornbread, and a whole sweet potato pie from the Yellow Bowl. Man 'n 'Em brought candy, jokes, pigeons, comic books, cards, electronic football and baseball games, PJ and Butch. While Journey sat up in her hospital bed, Man 'n 'Em played marbles on Journey's bedroom floor and watched television with her. Diamond, Poochie 'n 'Em came in to say hi. Lawyer Balil didn't come in, but he had Onion bring Phyllis over to visit. Rachel and Journey's other play little sisters came over and played jacks and hand-clap games. Kalaya, London, Plum, and Alonso brought poetry, music, and dancing. Turk and Uncle Monty brought their hands, wit, beer, and raw oysters. Magdalene and Aunt Beana came by every day to help clean, cook, and take care of Journey so Miss Sarah could run errands, talk with the doctors, and rest, and they planned to continue doing all of that even after Miss Sarah's parents arrived from Philly.

That house was so alive that it was hard to believe someone was dying inside.

ONE AFTERNOON, Kizmic arrived and Journey was sitting at her drawing desk in her pajamas listening to Minnie Riperton's "Memory Lane," tears flowing too fast for her to bother trying to wipe them away. As the song neared its peak, Minnie Riperton pleaded over and over to be saved from where she was going. Journey pleaded with her and they sounded so helpless that for a few beats in the middle of the song the lyrics transitioned to a prayer. When Minnie Riperton went back to singing, Journey turned and saw Kizmic in the doorway holding an orange frozen cup.

"Miss Irene told me to give this to you," Kizmic said, handing it to her.

Journey smiled through her tears. Kizmic sat on the floor between the windows and stared at her tennis shoes.

"Last year, I got really, really sick. Sicker than I had ever been," Journey said. "Again, the doctors told my mother that I wasn't going to make it, and I started thinking like you in a way, telling myself that I didn't want to grow up, go to school, have a period, a boyfriend. I told myself that none of that stuff mattered. And for a longtime I didn't care about dying. I thought it would be better if I did die. I was unhappy, my mother was unhappy. I thought the best thing I could do for both of us was get this over with and die already. So when they told me in May that I only had a few months left, I thought, Well, it's about time. Then I met you, and I played marbles and skully and football and basketball. I took off my wig. I ate stuff I hadn't eaten before. I danced, went swimming, learned to ride a bike, saw fireworks. I got to be friends with some really awesome people. I had four boys have a little crush on me. I watched your sister fall in love." She lowered her voice. "Lose her virginity. I watched you have your first crush. I watched my mother laugh, sew, sing, dance, eat oysters. Ride a bike!" She sighed and took several licks of the frozen cup. With her tongue now orange, Journey said, "And now . . . I don't want to die, Kizmic. What am I going to do?"

She threw the frozen cup in the trash then shuffled to her bedroom. Kizmic sat on the floor for a long time not knowing what to tell Journey. Then she saw it clear as the day coming through the windows. Kizmic wasn't sure if she had the right to say it; she just knew she had to. She got to her feet and marched into the bedroom. Journey was curled up in bed, facing her jars of marbles.

Standing beside her bed, Kizmic said, "Fight."

Journey rolled over. Defeat and depression dulled her once bright eyes. "I've been fighting since I was five. I'm tired. I can't win. No matter what I do, no matter what the doctors do, no matter what my mother does, it always comes down to the same thing."

"Last year, my teacher made us read this poem. 'Do Not Go Gentle Into That Good Night.' It's about this guy wantin' his father to fight death. He said you shouldn't just sit there and die. I say we don't sit here. I say we get up and fight."

"Fight how, Kizmic?"

"The same way you've been doing all summer. You live. You live like there is no tomorrow."

"I don't think I can," Journey said.

"Sure you can." She held out her hands. Journey took them and Kizmic pulled her up. "Tell me somethin'. What's your biggest wish?"

"My biggest wish?"

"Suppose today was your birthday." Kizmic went over to the medicine table and lit two vanilla candles Sweets burned when she was giving Journey a massage. "You have a big cake sittin' in front of you with candles waitin' for you to make a wish and blow them out." Kizmic held the candles in front of Journey. "What would you wish for?"

Watching the flames dance in the small glass jars, Journey breathed in the uplifting scent of vanilla. When her wish came to her, she said, "I'll tell you my wish if you promise to do something."

"Anything."

"When your time comes, I want you to dance."

"My time?"

"Yeah. When your time comes, dance. Like we danced with your father the first time I came to your house. Dance."

"Okay," Kizmic said. "I promise."

Journey closed her eyes. "I wish I could spend one more Christmas with my mother." She took a deep breath and softly blew out the candles.

The smoke from Journey's wish wafted up Kizmic's nose and an idea of how to make it come true billowed in her mind.

CHAPTER

41

THE FIRST PERSON Kizmic told her idea to was Onion.

"You think we can do it?"

"Shoot, yeah!" Onion said, humming a newspaper onto a porch.

Riding side by side on the sidewalk, they stopped behind their favorite big tree for a smooch.

"Remember when you asked me why I like you?" Onion said.

Kizmic nodded.

"What you're talkin' about doin' for Journey is why I like you."

They kissed, grinned at each other, then finished the deliveries on Garrison.

While coasting down Beaufort, Onion said, "Steebo's mother came out before I could ask why you like me like me." Onion said.

"You make me laugh. You didn't feel me up. You told me your dreams. You like my pictures."

"Everybody likes your pictures."

"No, not the way you do. You make me think I can take the kind of beautiful and important pictures my great-grandfather took."

"That's 'cause you do. Why else do you like me?"

"You're cute and . . ."

"And what?"

Bashfully, she said, "You kiss good."

"Oh, shucks. We're gonna haveta find a smoochin' tree around here," he laughed.

356

"Hey, Mama. Hey Daddy," Kizmic called, coming in the house.

Turk got up from the living room couch and followed her into the kitchen. Magdalene turned off the eye under the pot of spaghetti.

"Journey wants to live until Christmas and I wanna help her," she announced.

Turk and Magdalene gave each other concerned looks. Kizmic was obviously suffering from denial.

Magdalene took her daughter by the hand. "Baby, Christmas is a long way off, and . . ." She didn't have the heart to speak it.

"And we haveta make it happened," Kizmic said.

"How, baby?" Magdalene asked.

"The way we did the fourth of July."

LATER THAT NIGHT, Kalaya came in fifteen minutes after her ten o'clock curfew. Magdalene called Kizmic down from her room. On the floor beside the coffee table was a barrel steamer trunk, like the one in the basement that belonged to her great-great-grandfather. It was smaller and not as old and beat up.

Soon as Kalaya hit the door with London standing there to back her up, she started explaining. "Mama, we got here at quarter to ten and were sitting out front talking and lost track of time. I swear."

Magdalene dismissed her explanation. "With everything going on with Journey, we . . . your father and I . . . need to talk to you and Kizmic."

"Okay," she said, detecting the sense of worry in her mother's voice.

Kalaya walked London out to his car. Afterward, Magdalene and Turk sat on the couch. Kizmic and Kalaya sat on the loveseat.

"We didn't tell you this before because we didn't want you to think that you ruined anybody's life," Magdalene said. "When I was in high school, I was a straight-A student and the captain of the girls track team. I was number one in the state for the 100-meter hurdles, the 100-meter dash, and third in the long jump."

Kalaya and Kizmic peered at their mother, amazed and confused.

"Twenty colleges offered me full athletic scholarships." Magdalene pushed out a laugh and shook her head. "People were calling me the next Wilma Rudolph."

"Wilma Rudolph?" Kalaya was astonished. "You were that good."

"Damn straight, she was," Turk said.

"One day, I met this tall, handsome guy. He was the captain of the basketball team."

"*Daddy?*" Kalaya said.

"*Daddy?*" Kizmic echoed.

"Why y'all sound so surprised?" Turk asked. "Yeah. Daddy. I was a baller."

"I wish you could have seen your daddy play. It was like watching Wilt Chamberlain," Magdalene boasted.

"No it wasn't. It was like watchin' Turk Waters! Wilt ain't have nothin' on me."

Magdalene rolled her eyes. "He was being recruited by it seemed like every college in the world. He had scholarship offers—"

"Up the ying-yang. That's right, your *Daddy*."

Magdalene smiled. "And girls."

"What can I say? I was a playa. Couldn't keep the women off me."

Magdalene sighed. "One day, he saw me practicing. When I left to go home, he followed me, talking about, 'What's your name, girl?' I kept walking and said, 'Don't you think you better worry about the names of your girl-friends.' He said—"

"I ain't got no girlfriends," Turk remembered. "Told you, I was a playa. I ain't have no time for no girlfriends."

"The next morning, he's standing outside my yard waiting to walk me to school. I didn't let him know it, but I was happy to see him."

"You ain't haveta let me know it."

"He was the finest thing in school."

"*Daddy?*" Kizmic and Kalaya said again.

"Why y'all keep sayin' '*Daddy*'?"

"He could have had any girl he wanted, but he was running behind me."

"Naw. Your Mama coulda had any dude she wanted. I was runnin' behind her, tryna catch her before some sucka did. Talk about seein' somebody. I wish y'all coulda seen your *Mama* run. She was so pretty. Look."

Turk pulled pictures from the trunk and spread them out on the table. A young, well built Magdalene jumping over hurdles, soaring through the air over a sand pit, and running with all her might was in every photograph. Kizmic and Kalaya pored over the pictures, completely stunned. Their father was right. Their mother was beautiful. The trunk was also filled with first and second place medals. Their mother was a track star.

"Why didn't you tell me?" Kalaya asked.

"Back then, when a girl got pregnant, it was like it was the end of her life. Families didn't want anybody to know that their good, southern Christian girls, black and white, had gotten themselves knocked up. They wouldn't even say that's what happened. Parents would go around saying that their daugh-ters 'broke their legs' and then sent them to 'visit' relatives up north. I didn't know that I'd broken my leg until I came home and tripped over my suitcases in the front hall. That's when it hit me. I hadn't had my period. My mother had this calendar in her bedroom, and she kept track of our periods the way a farmer keeps track of the weather. When our periods came, we went to Mama, and she handed out the sanitary napkins. I was so in love with your daddy that I didn't realize that I hadn't gone to her to get any sanitary napkins."

"She had arranged for me to leave the next day. That night, I snuck out of the house to tell Turk, and he said, 'I'm comin' with you.'"

Kalaya was crying now.

Magdalene held Kalaya's face in her hands. "Not once did your father or I think that having you ruined our lives. But that doesn't mean that we want you to follow in our footsteps. You need to go to school and be all that you can be before you start having children. Do everything you can think of doing, because once the babies come, it can't be all about you anymore. It has to be all about them so that you don't ruin their lives. You understand what I'm saying?"

"Yes," Kalaya cried.

"Where's all your trophies and stuff, Daddy?" Kizmic asked.

"At Grandma and Granddad's house in the basement somewhere. I don't know. Once your Mama told me I was gonna be a father, I left that life behind, never looked back. No regrets. And married her quick, too, 'fore Granddad could get up here with his shotgun."

"Shotgun?!" Kizmic and Kalaya looked at Turk like he was crazy.

"Yeah. We ain't never tell y'all about that? He drove up here and banged on our front door four o'clock in the mornin' with the shotgun, talkin' 'bout, 'Boy, get your ass up and com'on go marry that gal.'"

Kalaya turned to Magdalene. "For real, Mama?"

"For real," Magdalene laughed.

"But see, we was one step ahead of my crazy daddy. We got married four days 'fore he came. So I was like, 'Dad, we already married.' Magdalene showed him the ring, then he lowered the shotgun and said, 'I'm hungry. What y'all got to eat around here?'"

Their laughter could be heard up and down Beaufort.

CHAPTER
42

Magdalene called an emergency meeting for the Pimlico Neighborhood Association. Two days later, she had a permit that allowed them to block Belvedere off in both directions from the corner of Denmore down to Litchfield for two hours, Sunday, August 5, starting at nine P.M.

As early as eight o'clock Saturday morning, folks were standing on ladders, railings, and chairs, inflating, staking, nailing, looping, stringing, taping, and hanging things on their porches, roofs, windows, fences, and the islands in the middle of the street. Merriment jingled in the hot air as shouts of "Move it to the left!" "A little more to the right!" "That's it!" "Perfect!" rang out.

Passengers riding on buses and people driving in cars up and down Belvedere were rubbernecking and pressing their faces against the windows with their eyebrows knitted together in confusion.

D. Tinkle may as well have been one of those people riding through, because he knew no more about the peculiar goings-on in his neighborhood than they did. Standing on the outside looking in from his doorway, D. Tinkle came across the lens of Kizmic's Ciro-flex all morning long while she photographed the joyfulness people felt at being able to do something more than wring their hands and shake their heads. Then he was gone. His front door was still open. Kizmic could see straight into his house. Figuring he was in a room out of view, Kizmic panned her camera left. D. Tinkle showed up on her lens again, standing on the sidewalk two houses down from Ace of Spade.

A group of about seven little girls were in their yard trimming a broad, dark green Holly. When they finished, they locked hands around it and began playing Ring Around the Rosie. Whatever it was living and breathing inside D. Tinkle that made him notice little girls fixated on them. Whispering the nursery rhyme off key, D. Tinkle unconsciously moved his head in a circle as his gaze followed the girls skipping around the beautifully dressed bush. His eyelids opened and closed like the shutter of a camera on a fast speed, catching sharp images of them in their pretty sundresses and sandals and storing them in his mind. When the girls threw themselves down on the grass and their dresses landed above their skinny and chubby knees, D. Tinkle's jack-o-lantern smile trembled.

Mr Dale came over and stood next to D. Tinkle. The ugly smile on D. Tinkle's face melted away, as if Ebenezer Scrooge had come along and ruined his good cheer. Giggling, the girls got to their feet and ran into the house. Mr Dale watched them until they were all inside. Then he did something he hadn't done in three years. Mr Dale spoke to D. Tinkle.

"They four and five years old, man. Babies. And you lookin' at 'em, foamin' at the mouth like they grown women." Usually, he stood beside D. Tinkle, but he never said a word to him. Usually. But today. Today Mr Dale asked, "What the fuck is wrong with you?"

D. Tinkle focused on the Holly the whole time Mr Dale was talking. In response to Mr Dale's question, he stepped left. Usually, Mr Dale followed D. Tinkle from one corner to the next, one tree to the next, one fence to the next, until D. Tinkle got so irritated and uncomfortable that he retreated to his pink house. Usually. But today. Today Mr Dale stepped left, too. D. Tinkle stepped right. So did Mr Dale. He stepped left again. So did Mr Dale. If it were Mr Dale and any other person, onlookers would assume the men were engaged in some very awkward dance. But everyone witnessing Mr Dale and D. Tinkle's interaction saw it for the confrontation the grownups had been waiting for since D. Tinkle climbed the upstairs back porch of Mr Dale's house and tried to molest Diamond.

Stepping right, D. Tinkle tried once more to get by Mr Dale. Mr Dale stepped into his path and kept stepping, stepping, stepping and bumping, bumping, bumping D. Tinkle back, back, back, back, ba—

"Get outta my way, nigga!" Usually, D. Tinkle was composed. Usually, nothing got under that high yellow skin of his. Usually. But not today. Today D. Tinkle screamed, "And leave me the fuck alone!"

"Oh, shit!" somebody said in place of the whistle that usually sounded the alarm when D. Tinkle was lurking about.

Mr Dale stared viciously into D. Tinkle's eyes. "What you gonna do if I don't get out your way?" He put his face an inch away from D. Tinkle's. "What you gonna do if I don't leave you the fuck alone?" He cocked his head to the side. "*Nigga.*"

Keeping his piercing, death stare on Mr Dale, D. Tinkle took a step back. When Mr Dale didn't follow, he took another.

"Yeah, I didn't think so. Take your sick ass on in the house," Mr Dale spat.

He moved out of D. Tinkle's way, but in walking by, D. Tinkle slightly brushed against Mr Dale's arm.

"You just bump into me, muthafucka!"

D. Tinkle kept moving toward the safety of his pink house.

Mr Dale headed him off and planted his palm in the middle of D. Tinkle's chest. "Touch me again."

D. Tinkle looked at Mr Dale's hand on his chest then snapped up his Afro head and punched Mr Dale in the mouth, splitting his bottom lip.

Why would he do that? Kizmic wondered. Why didn't he stay in his house?

Mr Dale put his tongue on the split in his lip then grinned. Blood coated his teeth. "I'ma whup your ass," he said with delight.

D. Tinkle turned down the corners of his mouth and with a well-com'on-then flair spread opened his arms, welcoming Mr Dale.

Mr Dale punched D. Tinkle and punched D. Tinkle and punched D. Tinkle. When his arms got tired, Mr Dale kicked D. Tinkle and kicked D. Tinkle and kicked D. Tinkle. When his legs got tired, Mr Dale punched D. Tinkle and punched D. Tinkle and punched D. Tinkle. And with each punch or kick, Mr. Dale grunted, "MMMM!" D. Tinkle yelped, "AHHHH!" the adults screamed, "HIT HIM AGAIN!" and the children cried, "MAKE HIM STOP!"

D. Tinkle lay limp as a Raggedy Ann doll on the sidewalk. Mr Dale, exhausted from all the punching and kicking, teetered over him. In one last burst of anger, he grabbed D. Tinkle by his bloody shirt collar, pulled back his fist and —

BANG!

The sound of a gun stopped Mr Dale's fist, D. Tinkle's yelping, the adults' screaming, and the children's crying. Lawyer Balil and Phoebe were standing on the island directly across from them. He was holding Phoebe's leash in his left hand and a black gun in his right.

Nonchalantly, Lawyer Balil waited for the traffic to let up then walked across the street.

The bloodthirsty mob, including Mr Dale, backed away from D. Tinkle, who slumped to the ground.

"Sit," Lawyer Balil said to Phoebe and she obeyed. He dropped her leash and picked D. Tinkle up, not by his arm or hand, but by a fistful of his bushy Afro. He put the gun to his blood-streaked temple. "Y'all want this brotha dead?" he asked the mob.

He's just a bomb without a lit fuse. That's what Daddy said, Kizmic thought. *Give him some time . . . Somethin's gonna light it.*

The adults had lit Lawyer Balil's fuse and now they hoped their silence would extinguish it.

"I said, do y'all want this brotha dead?" His voice was calm and as scary as the quiet on the block. "If y'all want 'im dead, just say the word. I'll put a bullet in his head. Ya'll know it don't make me no never mind."

And they all knew he was telling the truth. It didn't make him no never mind. Lawyer Balil was crazy enough to pull the trigger, go home, and eat a bowl of Corn Flakes while he waited for the cops to arrest him. But it made Turk and Magdalene some never mind. It made Uncle Monty and Aunt Beana some never mind. It made Miss Josephine and Mr Charlie some never mind. It made Christmas and Miss Shelly some nevermind. It made everybody in the neighborhood some never mind. It even made Miss Belinda and Mr Dale, who wanted nothing more than to see D. Tinkle in his grave for what he tried to do to their little girl, some nevermind.

"Seein' as how ain't nobody sayin' nothin', I assume y'all done playin' like you a bunch of killers."

Lawyer Balil opened his fingers and D. Tinkle slumped back to the ground. He wrapped Phoebe's leash around his hand. "Come on, girl," he said. And the two of them strolled up the street.

It was Magdalene who kneeled at D. Tinkle's side to see how badly he had been beaten. Kizmic would forever remember the horror in her mother's eyes when she saw both of D. Tinkle's eyes swollen shut, his nose lopsided, and his mouth puffy and bloody. Kizmic would forever remember the heavy shame that brought tears to her mother's eyes as she saw the trauma in the children's eyes because of what they had done.

Someone called 911. As the paramedics strapped D. Tinkle on the stretcher, one asked, "Sir, do you know who did this to you?"

Through his puffy, bloody lips, D. Tinkle said softly, "No."

CHAPTER

43

Kizmic sat in the passenger seat of Uncle Monty's semi and watched the last speck of sunlight belonging to this day, that took all night to come and all day to leave, disappear behind the Old Folks' Home.

Leaning on the steering wheel, Uncle Monty looked at Kizmic with his dead-alive eye. "You ready?"

"Since five o'clock this mornin'," Kizmic replied, draping the strap of her Ciro-flex around her neck.

"Let's hit it." He straightened his floppy, green fisherman's hat then fired up his Peterbilt.

The engine sounded like hundreds of Harley-Davidson motorcycles idling at the same time as he pulled off. Uncle Monty loved that sound. Said it was like music to his ears. To most other people, it was just loud.

Crossing Belvedere, Uncle Monty grabbed one of the twin stick gear shifters, both of which extended from the floor up to the middle of the dashboard and had what looked to Kizmic to be oversized, yellow acrylic clackers for knobs. Giant puffs of black smoke sputtered out of the two chrome stacks mounted on either side of the cab. Every time he shifted the truck took a deep breath then blew it out of the stacks. At the bend in Beaufort, Uncle Monty handled that long nose Pete as if it were a Pinto, never coming close to hitting the cars parked on the right.

The brakes hissed and whistled as he stopped in front of Miss Sarah and Journey's house.

"Uncle Monty, what if she's too sick to come out?"

Spiritually and mentally, Journey was putting up a good fight, but she was getting weak. She still loved her Krimpets and grape soda, but she couldn't keep it or anything else on her stomach. The only thing her body allowed her to keep was the medicine for her pain.

"Naw. She's comin' out," Uncle Monty said.

"How do you know?"

"'Cause God gave this gift to you to give to her. He's already made it so she can get it. You think you two became friends by accident?" He laughed. "That was God workin' back then so you could do this here thing tonight."

Hearing the loud rumbling of the truck's engine, Miss Sarah came to the door.

Uncle Monty handed Kizmic the mic for the CB. "Let base know we on our way."

"What should I say?"

"Breaker, Breaker one nine. This is . . . what's your handle?"

"Uh . . . Dragon Fly."

"Dragon Fly?"

"It's the name of my favorite marble."

"Okay, *Dragon Fly*. Tell 'em we pickin' up the package and to hang tight."

Kizmic held the mic and watched anxiously as Uncle Monty spoke with Miss Sarah. The engine made it impossible for her to hear what story he was spinning, but after a few hand gestures and head nods, Uncle Monty winked his dead eye at Kizmic then went inside with Miss Sarah. Kizmic pressed the talk switch on the CB mic and relayed the message to Plum. Not long after, Uncle Monty came out carrying a smiling Journey in his big arms.

"You alright to sit up front?" he asked her.

She was wrapped in her great-grandmother's quilt, even though the temperature was in the eighties. "Yeah. But what if I have to throw up?"

He shrugged his shoulders. "Throw up then. It ain't gonna hurt nothin'."

Kizmic moved to the sleeper cab. After making sure Journey was comfortable, Uncle Monty opened the door to the sleeper for Miss Sarah. "Don't worry. Beana changed the sheets," he told her.

Uncle Monty revved the engine. "Everybody ready?"

"Yeah!"

He put the truck in gear. It was a bumpy ride up Hayward and down Park Heights. Journey enjoyed every bounce. When they got to Belvedere, the truck started jerking harder than normal.

"Ah, shoot!" Uncle Monty grumbled.

"What's wrong?" Journey asked.

"Her gears are stickin'."

He pushed one shifter down, then pushed the other up. The truck lurched forward then hissed as it stopped in the middle of the street in front of the Little Tavern.

"Dang it!" Uncle Monty got out and slammed the door. He walked to the back of the truck. "Hey, Journey," he called. "Can you get in my seat and yank that strap hanging from the ceiling?"

"I'll do it," Miss Sarah said.

"No. I got it, Mama." Journey discarded the quilt. With Miss Sarah's help, she got behind the wheel. "This black one?"

"Yeah. Give it a tug," Uncle Monty instructed.

Journey pulled the strap and the blaring sound of the train horn mounted on top of the truck reverberated out and down the block, vibrating windows. Miss Sarah covered her ears.

Journey hooted. "That was cool!"

"Oh, yeah?" Uncle Monty asked. "Pull it again."

Miss Sarah put her hands to her ears again. Journey blew the horn, but this time when its sharp, high-pitch sound faded, the big broadway sound of horns, strings, and possibly a flute rose in the nighttime air.

"What's that?" Journey squinted her eyes as she looked down the street.

Then came the musical ooooh's and the magical sound of the xylophone and jingle bells. Diana Ross began singing "My Favorite Things" in her gleaming voice and Belvedere lit up like the night sky during the 4th of July.

"Oh!" Journey and Miss Sarah gasped.

Uncle Monty opened the driver's side door. Turk, Magdalene, and Aunt Beana were waiting with a wheelchair. Uncle Monty lifted Journey out of the cab and placed her in the wheelchair and covered her with the quilt. Magdalene and Aunt Beana hooked arms with Miss Sarah and Uncle Monty did the same with Kizmic. They followed as Turk pushed Journey down the middle of the street, through a fantastical Winter Wonderland in the height of summer. Diana Ross was singing about her favorite things while Journey was gazing in amazement at her favorite things:

Miss Josephine and Mr Charlie smiling and waving at her from the island as they stood beside a red and green neon sign that wished everyone "Merry Christmas."

Christmas dressed like Santa Claus waving and "Ho-Ho-Hoing!" from an inflatable reindeer drawn sleigh further down the island. Because, of course, drunk and all, who else would be Santa but the Iron Man they called Christmas?

Rachel and Journey's other play little sisters filled with laughter greeting her alongside six wooden, life-size Nutcrackers standing at attention.

Miss Irene and an eight feet inflatable Frosty the Snowman stood in a fluffy blanket of white, cotton snow, waving Season's Greeting from the North Pole.

Mr Dale and Miss Belinda spreading Christmas cheer from a field of tall candy canes decorated with large red ribbons.

Diamond, Poochie 'n 'Em chasing Man 'n 'Em in front of Ace of Spade as an airblown Grinch stole presents from under a tree decorated with gold, silver, and white ornaments and a beautiful black angel on top.

Kalaya and London hanging out at Santa's Workshop in front of the Basement Store, where elves were hard at work making toys.

Reverend and Mrs. Miles smiling and reminding everyone of the true spirit of Christmas from the bright and colorful Nativity Scene in front of D. Tinkle's dark, undecorated house.

Sweets, Miss Connie, and the women from Sweet Dos wishing her peace from beside a Christmas tree decorated with nothing but Charlie Brown ornaments.

Alonso and Plum behind his turntables in front of the Fish Store, donning Santa hats and spreading the joyful sounds of the season through his gigantic speakers.

Blinking Lights, goodwill, Phyllis, green garland, tidings, red ribbons, tinsel icicles, wreaths, candles, bells, PJ, presents, bows, Butch, lanterns, toy soldiers, snowflakes, wise men, stockings, kinaras, Lawyer Balil and Phoebe, gingerbread houses, Christmas carols, love, family, friends, joy, Baby Jesus.

It was something out of a dream for everyone, but especially for Kizmic. Who would imagine that when she spotted that bald head in the window of the castle house that she would have organized something as important as this? All she wanted at the start of this summer was to live the end of her childhood like she'd never lived before. And because of Journey, she was not only able to do it, but she was able to go out swingin'.

Donny Hathaway's "This Christmas" played and Onion came up to Kizmic, singing it to her. Taking her hands, they danced and sang together.

"There's that smile again," Onion said.

Kizmic looked at Journey. "She's happy."

"'Cause of you."

"Uh-uh. 'Cause of us."

Kizmic and Onion ran to her house. White Betty was leaning out her window filled with holiday cheer and Budweiser. Kizmic snapped her picture.

"Happy New Year!" she shouted to them.

"Happy New Year, Miss Betty!" they said.

Kizmic got the photo album, which was wrapped in plain brown paper and tied with green and red ribbons.

"Is that it?" Onion asked.

"Yeah. What's that?" she asked, noticing something in his hand.

"Mistletoe." Onion smiled and dangled it above her head.

When he put his soft lips on hers, Kizmic thought, Yeah. I went out swingin' like a mug!

After Eartha Kitt finished singing "Santa Baby," the piano and strings of Nat King Cole's "The Christmas Song" filled the air. Kizmic and Onion got back to Belvedere and searched the crowd for Journey.

"There she is," Onion pointed.

Journey was in the wheelchair beside the Christmas tree topped with the black angel, surrounded by Man 'n 'Em and Diamond, Poochie 'n 'Em, who were cutting up. Rachel came skipping by and Kizmic saw she was wearing her Teeter Totter watch.

"I know it's yours," Rachel said. "Journey said I could hold it if I promised not to break it."

Kizmic stared at her watch. "It's okay. You can have it."

"I can *have* it?!"

"Yeah, but you gotta do somethin' for me."

When Rachel delivered the package, Journey knew immediately what it was and called for her mother. Shaking, Miss Sarah touched the angel wings, then opened the album and cried happy, happy tears. The adults gathered around her oohing and aahing as Miss Sarah showed off her present as if it were the coveted toy every adult wanted for Christmas.

Turk bragged, "Our baby took them pictures!"

Journey got Meatball to push her over to Kizmic. "Thank you. This is the best Christmas I've ever had."

"Me, too."

"I'm okay now, Kizmic."

Okay? How could she be okay? Kizmic certainly wasn't okay, and it wasn't happening to her. So how in the world could Journey be okay? How can anybody be okay with dying? she cried inside.

Suddenly, Christmas belted out the name Jeremiah. Standing in the street in his red and white Santa outfit, Christmas started singing "Joy To The World." But that wasn't the kicker. Brown's choir was with him! Kizmic didn't know who was more ecstatic—Journey at hearing the choir sing that song or Christmas at having a choir sing background for him. Watching Christmas sing joyfully to the screaming crowd and Journey joyfully clap and rock in her wheelchair, Kizmic called it a tie.

Christmas got so intoxicated by the applause that Miss Shelley had to pull the ham off stage. The choir then lifted their beautiful voices and sang "Silent Night."

Kizmic looked at Journey and her lightning struck eyes were as bright and alive as when she first met her. How?

Seeing Miss Sarah holding the photo album close to her heart, Kizmic thought, Because she lived.

"Merry Christmas, Kizmic," Journey smiled.
"Merry Christmas, Journey."

CHAPTER 44

"You must be Kizmic."

Miss Sarah had planned to have the Home Going Service in Philly. But that plan was made before Journey met Kizmic.

"Where's Kizmic?"

And since most of her family had come down to spend time with Journey and never left, it made sense to have the service in Baltimore.

"Kizmic is where?"

Her uncles, aunts, grandparents, cousins, and friends were everywhere—on the porch, in the sunroom, living room, dining room, hallway, sewing room, kitchen, back porch, Journey's bedroom, and drawing room. Again, the house was so alive that it was hard to believe someone—Journey—had . . .

"This is Kizmic."

They didn't know about her from the photo album. They didn't see it until they got there, and, "Oh my god! Those pictures!" was their collective response.

"Journey told me so much about you."

"She said you were the coolest person she'd ever met."

"She said you meant a lot to her."

"She said you were so nice."

"She said you made her laugh."

"She said you were tough."

"She said you were so pretty."

"She said you helped her a lot."

"She said you were so smart."

"She said you were a lot of fun."

"She said you were the best marble player in the world."

"She said you were her best friend."

On and on, over and over, they told Kizmic how much Journey "loved herself some Kizmic." She wanted to tell them how much she loved herself some Journey. But every time she tried, she looked for Journey to come down the stairs, sit at her drawing table, come out onto the porch, come into the kitchen, sit on the living room couch, sit on the loveseat in the sunroom, come into her bedroom. Kizmic waited five, ten, fifteen, twenty, twenty-five, thirty, thirty-five, forty, forty-five, fifty, fifty-five, sixty, sixty-five, seventy, seventy-five, eighty, eighty-five, ninety, ninety-five, one hundred. Ready or not! Journey didn't come. Her family and friends put their arms around Kizmic and said, "That's all right. We know how you feel. You don't have to say anything."

And Kizmic didn't say anything. Not during the wake, which lasted longer than the half hour noted on the obituary, because of the quilt Miss Sarah had made. The 10-foot by 12-foot canvas was displayed in the lobby of Brown's Memorial and featured Journey, her round head outlined in dark brown, cotton yawn, her forehead sewn out of vibrant, purple silk, her smiling eyes stitched out of warm, brown velvet, her broad nose and laughing lips quilted from electric, cobalt blue cotton. Body in a flowing, white gown, white angel wings spread wide across the light blue sky, Journey soared above the people, rowhouses, the Fish Store, Basement Store, Ace of Spade, Paint Store, The Bar, The Old Folks Home, quilted out of dark brown, crimson red, orange, yellow, green, purple, and blue cotton and linen. It was what Miss Sarah had busied herself with while Journey was outside playing. It was the only quilt of Miss Sarah's that Kizmic didn't admire, because Journey should have been one of those vibrant pieces of fabric strolling down Belvedere instead of flying above it. But all the other mourners had a difficult time pulling themselves away from the bold, colorful life embodied in the quilt.

Between Miss Sarah's family, the church congregation, and everybody from the Pimlico neighborhood, including Lawyer Balil, Brown's was packed to capacity and more. Man 'n 'Em and Diamond, Poochie 'n 'Em sat with their parents, crying. Kizmic sat in the family section. "If you're not family, I don't know what family is," Miss Sarah said.

Kizmic's head was on her mother's lap, because she couldn't bear to see Journey again laying in the shiny silver casket at the front of the sanctuary, even though she was beautiful. Miss Josephine had dressed Journey in a stunning, bright yellow dress that Miss Sarah had picked out. Sweets had washed, patted dry, and oiled Journey's bald head.

Kizmic didn't open her mouth or lift her head when the choir rose in their grand blue and white robes and sang the opening hymn, "One Day At A Time." Magdalene stroked her back as she sang and rocked side to side. Kizmic didn't utter a single verse from Psalm 23 or Romans Chapter Five, verses one through five. She didn't sing one line when the choir sang "Two Wings." And she said nothing during the part of the service where people got up to give their two-minute remarks. She felt bad not telling the world what Journey meant to her, but she couldn't move. She sat in the pew with her head in her mother's lap, sobbing and listening to what other people had to say.

Man said, "Journey showed me that you don't always have to win to have fun."

"Journey was one of the bravest little girls I've ever had the privilege of caring for," Dr. Freeman said. "She never complained. She never felt sorry for herself and refused to let you feel sorry for her."

Except that one time, Kizmic thought. But she blew it away with her wish.

Alonso said, "I know Journey is dancin' up in Heaven because she sure danced down here."

"One of the blessings of having someone as darling as Journey in your life is that you never have to let her go, "Miss Josephine said. "She stays in your heart forever."

Meatball mumbled, "I'm gonna miss her."

"Journey didn't know it, but she helped me be a better big sister," said Kalaya.

Sweets said, "She was brave, and she taught me—taught *us*—to be brave."

Plum read a poem she'd written. "*Pretty brown-skinned girl, what a joy to the world. We're going to miss your smiling, sunshiny bliss. To be sad that you're gone is just what we have to go through. It's all part of that heaven-bound journey that brought you to us and us to you.*"

Turk said, "Journey wasn't only our kids' friend; she was our daughter."

"Journey was my princess," London smiled.

"When I was little," Onion began, "I used to get mad at my mother and father for makin' us go to church all the time." He looked at his parents, then dropped his head to the podium.

"Take your time, son," his father told him.

After wiping away the tears he'd cried, Onion took a deep breath, then filled the sanctuary with the first four words of a song that anyone who had been to church for any length of time in their life recognized. "Goin' Up Yonder." It was an almost sacred gospel song that had the power to turn pain into praise like no other song Kizmic had ever heard. And while everyone in that church knew it lyric by lyric, they didn't utter a sound. Henry Patrick, who knew it note by note, didn't put his fingers on the keys of the organ. As much as Onion needed to sing it, they all needed to hear it without anything getting in the way of the words, in the way of their pain. And once the message was clear and they felt it in their hearts and souls, the choir rose to praise God with

Onion. Henry Patrick accompanied them on the organ, and everyone clapped, stomped their feet, and shouted, "Awright!" "Sing your song," "Com'on," "Yes, Lord," and Pop Evan screamed out, "Chees-its!"

Kizmic raised her head. *His voice does do the same thing that Mama's voice does to people.*

Testifying to that, Kizmic lifted her voice and sang with the sorrow, joy, hope, glory, and comfort in knowing that Journey was in a better place, she was no longer in pain, she wasn't always tired, she didn't have to fight anymore, and most of all, she went out swingin' like a mug.

CHAPTER

45

Tuesday, September 4, Kizmic awoke to Journey's smiling, brown face. Not from the collage of pictures on her wall, but from the quilt Miss Sarah had given her before moving back to Philly. It was hanging between the window and the door to the back porch.

Smiling back at Journey, Kizmic got up and walked out onto the porch. The morning was a little cool, but not bad for the first day of seventh grade. She would be going to Pimlico Junior High School.

Kizmic looked down into Fatboy's yard at the pigeon coop. She couldn't see them through the trees, but she visualized the basketball hoop in Man's back yard and the clubhouse in Steebo's yard, and she remembered the first time she saw Man 'n 'Em come riding through the alley on their bikes.

She felt something warm. Warm and wet. With a slight cramping in the lower part of her stomach. Kizmic went back into her room and closed the back porch door. She felt the warm wetness again. She stretched her pajama pants and underwear away from her body, looked down, then ran to Kalaya's room.

"Kizmic?" Kalaya asked, groggily. "What's going on?"

"Remember you said I can talk to you about stuff?"

"Yeah."

"I think . . . uh . . . well, my . . . my *friend* is here."

"Your friend?" she asked, not getting it at first. Then, "You mean your *friend friend*?"

Kizmic nodded.

Kalaya jumped out of bed. "Okay, um. Don't be scared. It's no big deal."

She sure wasn't acting like it wasn't a big deal.

"You tell Mama?"

Kizmic shook her head.

"All right. Stay right here."

"Kalaya, does *this* mean I'm old enough to eat cornbread without gettin' choked?"

"Definitely not."

"What does it mean, and when will I be old enough?"

"I'll tell you when I come back." Smiling, she hurried out the room.

Kizmic stood there not knowing what to do. She was just thankful it didn't happen in class. In thinking that, she heard Journey say, "When your time comes, dance. Like we danced with your father the first time I came to your house."

She went over to Kalaya's stereo. Chuck Brown and the Soul Searchers' "Bustin' Loose" was on the turntable. She put the needle down on the record, turned up the volume, and at the sound of the drums and congas, Kizmic danced like she promised.

THE END

ABOUT THE AUTHOR

ODESSA ROSE received her B.A. in English from Coppin State University and her M.A. in Literature from the University of Maryland at College Park. Her first novel, *Water In A Broken Glass*, captured the #6 spot on the On-Demand Best Seller list, received the Just About Books Annual Book Award, is ranked #17 on Accredited Online Colleges' 20 Essential Novels For African-American Women list, was recorded for the Maryland School for the Blind, is included in *The Greenwood Encyclopedia of Multiethnic American Literature, Ethnic American Literature: An Encyclopedia for Students*, and *Black Like Us: A Century of Lesbian, Gay, and Bisexual African American Fiction*. *Water In A Broken Glass* was also adapted into an award-winning feature film of the same title. Rose's second novel, In the Mirror received the African American Expo Award for Fiction. Rose is a member of the Black Writers Guild of Maryland. She and her husband are the creators of the television magazine, *This Is Baltimore, Too*. Rose resides in her hometown of Baltimore with her husband and their three children.

9 781736 717387